C000083763

FIRST IMPRESSIONS

AUCKLAND MED. 1

JAY HOGAN

SOUTHERN LIGHTS PUBLISHING

Published by Southern Lights Publishing

Copyright © 2019 by Jay Hogan

This is a work of fiction. Names, characters, places, and incidents are either the product of the author imagination or are used fictitiously, and any resemblance to actual persons, living or dead, business establishments, events, or locales is entirely coincidental.

All rights reserved.

This book is licensed to the original purchaser only. Duplication or distribution by any means is illegal and a violation of international copyright law, subject to criminal prosecution and upon conviction, fines and/or imprisonment. No part of this book may be reproduced in any form or by any electronic or mechanical means, including photocopying, recording, or by any information storage and retrieval systems, without written permission from the author, except for the use of brief quotations in a book review. Any ebook format cannot be legally loaned or given to others.

To request permission and all other enquiries contact the author through the website

https://www.jayhoganauthor.com

Trade Paperback ISBN:978-0-9951324-2-9

Digital ISBN: 978-0-9951324-1-2

Digital Edition published December 2019

Trade Paperback Published December 2019

Third Edition

First Edition published by Blackout Books, 2018

Second Edition published by Dreamspinner Press, 2019

Cover Art Copyright © 2019 Kanaxa

Cover content is for illustrative purposes only and any person depicted on the cover is a model.

Proofread by Lissa Given Proofing

Printed in the United States of America and Australia

For my family who read everything I write and keep on saying they love it all, blushes included.

ACKNOWLEDGMENTS

FIRST IMPRESSIONS, the first of the Auckland Med Series, was my first published book and will always hold a special place in my heart. I hope this reedited edition with only some minor editing changes finds the same wonderful welcome that the first edition did.

As always, I thank my husband for his patience and for keeping the dog walked and out of my hair when I needed to work, and my daughter for her incredible support.

Getting a book finessed for release is a huge challenge that includes the help of beta readers, editing, proofing, cover artists and a tireless PA . It's a team effort, and includes all those author support networks and reader fans who rally around when you're ready to pull your hair out and throw away every first draft. Thanks to all of you.

UNTITLED

FIRST IMPRESSIONS

Auckland Med One

By Jay Hogan

FIRST IMPRESSIONS

By Jay Hogan
Auckland Med Book One

BLURB:

Michael:

Two years ago I made a mistake—a big one. Then I added a couple more just for good measure. I screwed up my life, but I survived. Now I have the opportunity for a fresh start. Two years in NZ. Away from the LA gossip, a chance to breathe, to rebuild my life. But I'm taking my new set of rules with me.

I don't do relationships.

I don't do commitment.

I don't do white picket fences.

And I especially don't do arrogant, holier-than-thou, smoking-hot K9 officers who walk into my ER and rock my world.

Josh:

One thing's for certain: Dr Michael Oliver is an arrogant,

untrustworthy player, and I barely survived the last one of those. He might be gorgeous, but my daughter takes number-one priority. I won't risk her being hurt again. I'm a solo dad, a K9 cop, and a son to pain-in-the-arse parents.

I don't have time for games.

I don't have time for taking chances.

I don't have time for more complications in my life.

And I sure as hell don't have time for the infuriating Dr Michael Oliver, however damn sexy he is.

AUTHOR'S NOTE

FIRST IMPRESSIONS, the first of the Auckland Med Series, was my first book accepted for publication and will always hold a special place in my heart. I hope this reedited and rereleased edition finds the same wonderful welcome that the first edition did.

In this edition, I have made some minor changes, corrections and a couple of slightly altered plot points, but nothing that changes the essence or major plot structure of that first release. It was an opportunity to change some things that had bugged me after the first publication.

CHAPTER ONE

THE YOUNG MAN MOVED TO THE SULTRY BEAT LIKE WARM caramel, fluid and sinuous beneath the unrelenting furnace of the club lighting. Acres of luminous olive skin with nary a wrinkle in sight slid seductively over lithe muscle slick with sweat, all rolling with the slow thumping bass and catching the hungry attention of more than a few men lined against the bar.

No more than twenty, the man's rangy body still bore the soft angles of youth, though now tempered by the mouthwatering promise of hard-muscled maturity yet to come. Dark curls lapped the nape of his neck, more than enough to offer a solid grip, and a criminally tight ass poured into a pair of painted-on black jeans that had Michael's own denims straining in appreciation.

But that young? Hell, Michael had dental work older than that. He shouldn't even be looking. Still, the hunger in that steamy gaze was anything but virginal, and damn, if he couldn't pry his eyes away, glued to every undulating swell of flesh like it provided the answer to all things that ailed him. And maybe it did, for tonight at least.

His body fairly thrummed with arousal, and he became increasingly convinced the young man knew exactly what he was doing—

checking out his admirers—all that freshly scrubbed youth just screaming compliance. This was a performance designed to seduce interest, and Michael was on board one hundred percent. He only hoped the young man had the wherewithal to follow through on the promise his body was so damn busy throwing around.

They'd locked eyes once or twice already, including right then as the young man drilled Michael with a heated stare while running his hands across his chest and down the succulent ridges of a nicely developing set of abs. Promising for sure, and although Michael wasn't usually one for browsing the "baby gay" section when he cruised, he thought he could make an exception in this case because, damn, this boy was all kinds of yum.

Still, first picks didn't always pan out, and this particular fish had a partner in tow, an older man whose possessive hand never left the young dancer's hip. Sensing the boy's distraction, the man followed his gaze and levelled Michael with a cool stare. He slid his hand to the small of the young man's back and pulled him tight in an unmistakable display of possession.

Well, shit. Michael blew out a sigh. He wasn't in the habit of poaching. There was more than enough flesh to go around without complicating a simple hookup with unnecessary grief. But the young dancer's response to the territorial claim stayed Michael's eye a moment. It was long enough to catch the annoyed expression the dancer barrelled the older man's way, and his accompanying two steps back. Two steps that created distance between the two of them and opportunity in Michael's mind. And when that eager gaze locked back on Michael... *well, hell yeah, game on.*

Abandoning his soda, Michael threw the barman a wink and received a flirty one in return. He checked the guy's name tag, James, and squirrelled that away for future reference. The man was built like a linebacker and clearly interested, but tonight, Michael had other fish to fry.

He ripped off his shirt, tucked it into the back of his jeans, and headed for the steaming dance floor, catching a few looks of his own.

He knew he was no slouch in the looks department; he ate well and worked out regularly, aiming for buff rather than ridiculous. Gym bunnies didn't do it for him. A pair of sleek black barbells threaded his nipples and large tribal tattoos wrapped around his back and biceps. After six months in New Zealand, he'd added a stylised kiwi above his heart.

The temporary upheaval in countries had reaped benefits he was more than grateful for. He felt lighter, more comfortable in his own skin than he had in years. Yes, the gay scene was somewhat quieter in Auckland than Los Angeles, light years quieter, but he'd adjusted quickly, appreciating the laid-back approach to life that Kiwis enjoyed as some recompense for the limited club scene.

Acceptance as a gay man hadn't been difficult, and although no country was free of bigoted assholes, New Zealand was overall a liberal gem with more legislated LGBT protection than many other countries. True, there wasn't a lot of gay PDA on display, but then Kiwis weren't much into PDA, period.

The change of scenery was, in a word, spectacular, and the anonymity was a godsend, providing the space he'd needed to get his career and personal life back on track. With another eighteen months left on his contract as an ER doctor at Auckland Med, he'd made it his personal mission to fuck his way through as much of the hot, eligible male population as humanly possible before that time was up.

And lucky for him, tonight Downtown G was packed to the rafters with possibilities, its dance floor tight and slick. It had become his favourite spot to cruise but had been closed for two weeks undergoing renovation. Gone were the dark booths, wooden bar, and tired décor; the club now sported an upmarket, polished-steel and leather interior, cool New York loft–style furnishings and mood lighting while retaining just enough dark corners to satisfy the carnal agenda of many of its clientele, including Michael. After a shitty week at work, a night of dancing and a satisfying fuck was exactly what the doctor ordered to get his head back in happy land again.

The thumping bass sparked his buoyant mood as he threaded

through the sea of heaving bodies, angling for the young dancer who'd caught his eye—and that of about a hundred others, he mused. The intoxicating tang of cologne, male sweat, and arousal hung like a palpable haze over the crush of people, and Michael breathed it deep. Hands slid over his chest, his ass, and a few ghosted his semi-hard dick. *Fuck, yeah.*

He worked his way across the floor, stopping to dance just behind, and therefore out of view of, his target's older partner. The young man had shamelessly tracked Michael's approach over the man's shoulder, sending an encouraging smirk, and when Michael arrived, they locked eyes. Bingo. Michael's cock filled with the heavy dose of lust that spilled his way in that one sizzling glance, and his eyes drifted south to those full pouty lips that promised so much.

While Michael was still appreciating the view, someone closed in against his back, cupped his ass, and rocked an ample hard cock against him. *Mmm.* Keeping his gaze fixed ahead, he lifted his arms and allowed his new faceless partner to slip his hands around and over his chest. Sliding his tongue slowly across his lower lip, Michael enjoyed the responsive burst of fire in the young dancer's gaze. And when he pushed his ass back against the anonymous guy's dick and tilted his head to expose his neck, he swore he heard the young man groan. *Yep.* His partner spun and threw Michael a filthy look.

Michael grinned at the older guy, tossed the young man a wink, and made his way to the far edge of the dance floor. He didn't bother checking to see if the dancer followed—that heated look had meant only one thing. Close to the wall, he found some space and swayed in time to the music as he waited, eyes closed. Sure enough, a few seconds later, a warm body slid up against his chest, and Michael opened his eyes with a smile.

"Not your boyfriend, then?" he asked, flicking his gaze in the direction of the older man. The young eyes boring into him were a pool of forest green edged in brown. Not a single crease marred their corners or apparently any other facial surface, further underscoring his youth. Michael ignored the curl of disquiet that rolled through his gut. He was looking for a fuck, not a fiancé, and the guy was legal. He didn't need more than that.

The dancer ran his hands over Michael's chest, pausing to tease the barbells in his nipples. "I'm here, aren't I?" he answered, leaning in to nip Michael's earlobe.

Michael wrapped an arm around the lean waist and drew the dancer close, brushing their groins together. A soft moan escaped the young man's lips, and Michael's body heat rocketed. "Excellent," he replied. "Because I'd hate to break up a good thing and all." He gripped the dancer's ass and pulled him flush, rocking the two of them into a slow grind.

The young guy snorted. "Hardly." He draped his arms over Michael's shoulders and gave his body over to Michael's direction. "He's pretty cute for an old guy but not really my type."

The dancer's scent was a heady mix of spicy mint, youth, and sweat, and as Michael ran a hand up the lean frame of his back, enjoying the muscles bunch and tense beneath his caress, he had only one thought. *Lordy. This one is just built for fun.* His dick strained hard against his zipper. *Fucking hell.* If he wasn't careful, he'd blow in his damn jeans before they even got started.

He cleared his throat roughly. "So, what is your type, then?"

Dancer boy smirked and leaned close. "Thought I'd made that pretty clear," he whispered against Michael's ear, then teased his tongue along the crease of Michael's lips. But when he pressed for entry, Michael turned his head. "Sorry, sweetheart, no kissing."

The man frowned, then shrugged. "Whatever. I can work with that. Plenty of other places to stick my tongue." He licked a path from Michael's shoulder to his ear.

Michael groaned. "Good news. Now, let's dance." He rocked them together and let his hands explore the hard young body pressed against him. They entwined in and around each other for several more songs, the heat ramping up between them, hands brushing cocks, cradling balls, teasing, probing, grinding. Twenty minutes later, when the DJ swapped in a new playlist, the young man's dick pressed like granite against Michael's hip.

"How about we take a walk?" he hummed against the dancer's neck. A flirty smile and a brief nod were the young man's only reply. Michael grabbed a hand and pulled the guy into the hallway leading to the bathrooms, the emergency exit, and a handful of semiprivate mood-lit alcoves. There was a bit of a queue for one of those prime spots, leaving time for a little making out in the hall—not that they were alone in that agenda, blending into a sea of groping hands and grinding hips.

Michael had never understood why the whole back room thing was considered such a sordid deal among his straight friends. It beat the hell out of a cramped car. Sex was sex, and back rooms of any description were just anonymous geography. He guessed women were probably pickier in that regard, but that was just another plus for being gay. He wasn't planning sleepovers, boyfriends, or brunch the next day with the guys he fucked. He didn't need a bed unless the guy was worth a few hours. Hell, he didn't need a name. This was getting off, pure and simple. Catch and release.

And the young man currently plastered to his front certainly seemed to have no issue with the concept. The kid knew enough to not even offer his name, and Michael appreciated that. Backed against the wall with Michael pushed hard up against him, the dancer was a handful of eager enthusiasm, so much so, that Michael considered taking the action elsewhere for a more prolonged encounter, but first things first. Clearly not shy, within seconds the guy had Michael's belt unbuckled, jeans unzipped, and a hand down the front of his underwear, gripping Michael's erection and stroking with some serious finesse.

Michael's eyes drifted closed as he shut off his brain and allowed himself to simply feel. The week's stress drifted away as his body focused and responded to the familiar sensations. A second hand slipped down the back of his jeans and into his crease, teasing his opening, but not too boldly. He spread his legs slightly in approval, allowing easier access, and flirted with the idea of returning the favour, but whatever, the kid was way eager enough. Michael didn't kiss, suck, or bottom his fucks, topping without exception. He was happy to jerk his partner off after a quick encounter, and he was a generous top in any extended playtime, ensuring his bottom got off, but that's as far as he went. If they didn't like it, they could leave, but he'd yet to get any complaints.

Facing the wall and lost in the mounting rhythm of the young man's efforts, Michael was only vaguely aware of urgent voices and hurried movement behind him in the hall. That was until the music stopped, and the hand on his dick stilled, all about the same time he felt a not too gentle tap on his shoulder. His eyes flicked open, noting the young man's were blown to the size of saucers and fixed on something over Michael's right shoulder.

Huh.

"You need to leave the club... sir." The rich voice slid over his shoulder, a hefty dose of scorn attached to the "sir."

What the fuck? It was a struggle to turn with the young dancer's hands still buried deep in Michael's jeans, but when he finally did... *Holy shit.* Immune to the rush of patrons scattering for the front door, Michael couldn't move a muscle, anchored in place by the sexy-as-sin man facing him.

Six four at least, in full police gear including stab vest with an inordinate amount of equipment attached, the guy wore an expression that radiated a whole lot of barely restrained pissy attitude, and an antsy German shepherd glued tight to his left side. The dog's demeanour was quiet but intently focused, on Michael apparently. Aware of the dancer's hands sliding free of his jeans, Michael turned to watch the boy's epic ass disappear into the bar and groaned. *Fuck.*

Turning back to the handler, Michael noted the officer's critical gaze had also tracked the dancer's retreat, lingering a little longer than was strictly necessary. Once it fixed back on Michael, the man's expression could have been mistaken for polite impatience if it weren't for the withering dismissal evident in those pretty brown eyes. Chocolate, melt-me-in-a-puddle-on-the-floor-and-fuck-me-while-I'm-there eyes. That Michael found the guy scorching hot was the understatement of the century.

The dog handler flicked him a thin smile that finished light years from those gorgeous eyes. "Sorry to interrupt, sir."

Yeah, I just bet you are. Ignoring the sarcasm, Michael refused to squirm, although he did glance down to check if his dick was still hanging semiexposed and, *yeah, not awkward, much.*

He slid his gaze over the officer, top to toe, as if he had all the time in the world, while casually tucking himself in and zipping his fly, leaving the top button undone in an unspoken "fuck you" to the man standing before him. It was a statement that might have carried more weight if Michael had actually managed to keep his eyes from roaming. *God, he was delicious.*

The officer smirked. "Perhaps you should run after your... date?" he deadpanned, his gaze dipping to Michael's mouth, then lower.

Had he just been checked out? Michael didn't know whether to preen or bristle, taking closer inventory of the snarky beauty before him. Tall and leanly muscled, he guessed the officer to be in his midthirties. A few smile lines creased the corners of an eminently kissable mouth, proving against current evidence that he did in fact laugh on occasion. There was the barest hint of a receding hairline in the otherwise short, blond hair that sprang roughly spiked from his scalp. It wasn't styled so much as the end result of fingers being dragged through it on a regular basis.

He had an athletic build, a swimmer's body. Wide shoulders and narrow hips, not heavily muscled but tight and fit. A beautiful man, drop-dead, eye-on-the-prize, read-'em-and-weep gorgeous, and yes, Michael was man enough to admit he was even a touch intimidated. The guy belonged on a cover wearing Andrew Christian briefs, not on a police team in overalls. And regardless of the man's sneering sarcasm, Michael's gaydar was pinging at full volume. He gathered his wits and made a valiant attempt at indifference.

"I don't run after anyone, sunshine," he replied evenly, his gaze raking over the dog handler. "Although I could possibly make an exception for you." *Ugh. Could he sound any more like a cheap romance novel?*

The handler's nostrils flared in either annoyance or attraction—pretty damned hard to tell in that otherwise irritatingly bland expression—and then just for a second, Michael thought the man might even smile. Then the officer's shoulders tensed, his feet moved slightly apart, and his fists balled. *Well, shit.*

The shepherd's ears pricked in nervous anticipation, a low growl rumbling in its throat. *Double shit.* Michael briefly wondered what Kiwi police cells were like, kicking himself that he hadn't hightailed it minutes ago. Why he hadn't didn't bear scrutiny as the reasons started and ended with his dick.

"That's assuming I would make one for you, which I wouldn't, by the way," the handler responded flatly.

Michael blinked. "Huh?"

"An exception, sir. I wouldn't make an exception for you. Now, I need you off the premises, and I won't be asking again." The dog moved into the space between them, and Michael's confused dick didn't know whether to deflate at the pointed rejection or rise to the bossy tone, the latter option a surprise to all concerned.

The radio on the handler's vest crackled. "Five minutes," it spewed a disembodied warning. The handler acknowledged the call, keeping his eyes fixed on Michael.

A second, younger officer joined them from the bar, eyeing Michael curiously. "Problem, Josh?" he asked.

Josh. His cop had a name. His cop? Michael really needed to get his head in the game. Something serious was going down in the bar, and he was doing what, dicking around with a hot cop? What the fuck was wrong with him?

The handler raised a brow. "Is there a problem, sir?"

Michael finally freed himself of his stupor and raised both hands, palms out. "No problem whatsoever... Josh."

The handler narrowed his gaze.

His colleague's eyes flicked between the two of them. "You know this guy?"

"No." Unmistakable irritation laced Josh's tone. "You go enjoy your evening, sir. Perhaps you can find your young... friend. And we'll need his name, just in case."

The handler's expression remained polite, but Michael wasn't fooled. He obviously knew there was a good chance Michael couldn't give a name, so Michael simply rolled his eyes, not about to give the jerk the pleasure of seeing just how royally he was pissing him off. "I don't have that information." He stared the other man down. "But if I do find him, I'll make sure to get his number for you. It would appear you need it way more than I do."

The handler's—Josh's lips twitched, and no way that wasn't almost a fucking smile. Michael held his gaze a second longer than necessary, and then with a nervous glance at the German shepherd who was only inches from his thigh and other related appendages, he turned and headed into the bar, sensing the heat of Josh's gaze on him every step of the way.

In the bar, Michael finally released the breath he'd been holding and blew out a sigh. The bar itself was damn near empty, the last of its patrons being herded through the door by a third officer. Michael caught the barman's eye and raised his brows. The man shrugged. "Fucked if I know. Boss just said to do what they say."

Michael veered to grab his coat.

"Hey, you," the officer manning the front door called to him. "Sir, you need—"

A deafening crash thundered from the rear of the club. Michael instinctively ducked and spun into the bar front, cracking his head. *Goddammit.*

Risking a quick look, he couldn't see Josh, only his dog. Frantic shouting and what sounded like a gunshot only added to the pandemonium and the shepherd went nuts, barking and pulling at his leash until Josh finally stepped into view, shouting into his radio.

More yelling and something slamming into the emergency exit

door made Michael instinctively slide farther round the end of the bar and into a booth by the corner wall. Ducking down behind the table, he could still see the hallway but hoped he was better hidden. He should get out of there, but he wasn't sure how to do that safely, and he couldn't rip his eyes from Josh, and his dog. *Yeah,* call him stupid.

"Callum?" Josh shouted. "Secure that fucking back door."

The third officer spun on his heels and headed into the kitchen. Josh waved the remaining officer to a covering position at his rear, his dog going crazy, front legs off the ground, every muscle bunched and straining for release. Resting a palm on the dog's head, he murmured something too quiet for Michael to hear, and the dog immediately calmed. And for some bizarre reason, Michael's dick found that sexy as fuck.

Glass shattered amid a loud tangle of shouts from the club's rear parking lot. The dog went off again, and Josh's radio crackled to life. He leaned over the animal as he listened, coveralls tight on his ass, his hand poised on the shepherd's collar. The dog flicked up his gaze, awaiting instruction. Something unspoken passed between the two, and Michael's chest tightened. It was bizarrely intimate.

Josh signalled the officer at his rear, and the man moved ahead toward the exit door, disappearing out of sight for a couple of seconds before scrambling back into position. Josh tapped the animal's nose twice, and the shepherd's body tensed.

Seconds later, all hell broke loose. A door slam echoed down the corridor, and a dark figure burst into view, smashing Josh head first into the wall. He grunted and slid to the floor as the intruder stumbled into the bar.

Michael sucked in a sharp breath. *Shit.* The newcomer now blocked Michael's exit. He'd been such a fucking idiot not getting out of there sooner. He dipped his body deeper into the shadows and aimed for inconspicuous.

Two seconds later, freed from his lead, the shepherd lunged, teeth snapping right up in the intruder's face. The guy froze, eyes wide, arms flailing at the attack. Something glinted in his right hand. A knife. *Goddammit.* Michael's breath caught in his throat as the young officer covering Josh stepped behind the shepherd to block the man's exit through the bar.

"Drop it," the officer shouted, while behind him Josh stumbled to regain his feet.

The intruder ignored the warning and sliced the knife sharply through the air. The dog immediately launched itself, latching on to the man's wrist and dragging him down. Finally on his feet, Josh was hot on the animal's heels, cuffs at the ready, but before he could restrain the guy, a second man burst through the door and straight into the tangle on the floor, forcing the dog back into Josh's chest and sending him once again crashing sideways.

The shepherd turned and locked on to this second intruder just as another officer rushed in from the car park to grapple him to the ground. But going after the second man had meant the dog could do nothing to stop the first as he scrambled to his feet and sliced the defensive arm of Josh's young partner from wrist to shoulder, throwing the poor guy back against the wall with a sickening crack. He slid to the floor, a spray of bright red blood arcing up against the cream paint.

Arterial. Shit. Michael instinctively surged from under the table toward the injured young man but stopped short when he realised his movement had drawn the knifeman's attention. They locked eyes, staring at each other for no more than a few seconds before the guy lurched toward him. Michael stumbled back against the wall just as the shepherd erupted from the corridor to his right and hurled himself at the knife once again. The guy's arm spun in a wide arc toward the airborne animal, sending it careening into the bar, granting him just enough time to make it out the front door before the dog scrambled to its feet in pursuit.

"Paris!" Josh shouted as he got to his knees, but the dog was long gone. Then he caught sight of his colleague sprawled in a pool of blood on the floor. "Fuck." He spoke urgently into his radio as he fell to his knees alongside the young officer. A commotion from the other side of the emergency exit broke in waves through the bar, but Josh ignored it, focused solely on his injured colleague and putting pressure on the pumping wound as he shook the officer's shoulder. "Jackson!"

In seconds, Michael was alongside Josh, dimly aware of his heat as their thighs pressed together. The wound was pumping big time. "Move," he ordered, realising his mistake too late.

Josh spun, latched his free hand on to Michael's arm, and threw him sideways, pinning him to the floor. "What the fuck are you doing?"

Ouch. Goddammit. Michael at least had the common sense to freeze until recognition dawned in Josh's scowl and the vicelike grip eased.

"Get the fuck away from him," he said in a low growl, shoving Michael away. "And get out of here, now."

The third officer appeared from the kitchen at a run, his expression turning to shock at the sight of the three men on the floor. "What the hell happened?" His gaze landed on Michael. "And what the fuck are *you* still doing here?"

"Get the paramedics and let the team in the back," Josh barked. "Paris is after the little bastard who did this, and arsehole number two is being arrested back through there." He gestured behind. "What a fucking cock-up." He glared at Michael. "And get this dickhead out of here before I fucking arrest him."

"No," Michael protested. "I can help."

"Shut the fuck up." Josh eyeballed him. "You're nothing but—"

"A doctor. I'm a fucking doctor, all right?" Michael snarled, their faces barely centimetres apart. The handler smelled of adrenaline, testosterone, and something maddeningly elusive. "A *trauma* doctor, to be precise. So how about *you* get the fuck out of here and go do whatever you need to and leave me to look after him?"

Josh's gaze slid over Michael's shirtless frame in disbelief. "A doctor? You're fucking kidding me."

Two more officers entered through the front door, the first leading with his gun drawn. Both froze in place when they spotted Jackson on the floor. "What the fuck happened?"

Josh held up a hand. "In a sec." He glared at Michael.

But Michael was having none of it. "He's pumping blood. You really want to do this shit now?"

"You sober?"

"Stone cold."

Josh's gaze flicked to Jackson, then back up, and Michael saw the moment he caved.

"Fuck it," he snapped. "He's all yours." He released Jackson's arm, allowing Michael to take over. "One of you watch this guy like a hawk, and for fuck's sake don't let him leave. The other, go help Callum get that cuffed piece of shit outta here." He threw Michael one last scowl before disappearing through the front doors, leaving him painfully aware of his fully invested dick trapped in his jeans. *Christ almighty*, it had a mind of its own.

Turning his attention to the injured man on the floor, he went to work, conscious of the remaining officer's eyes on him and the rumbling voices in the hallway behind.

"I'm gonna need you down here," he spoke without looking up.

The constable, a skinny guy, twentyish, about five foot seven with skittish eyes and dull brown hair held in tight curls, knelt beside him. "Right, shit, okay. What do you want me to do?"

Jackson was pale but breathing steady and beginning to rouse. His skull had taken enough of a whack on the wall to account for the brief time out. The blade had sliced a clean line up Jackson's right arm, and although not too deep, it had nicked the radial artery on entry, hence the pumping blood.

"Put your fingers here and press hard." He indicated a spot a few centimetres up from the wrist. The officer did as instructed while Michael probed the wound itself to try and stem the flow from the damaged vessel. He was dimly aware of police moving around the bar area with one or two stopping to check what was happening. A slower set of boots came to stop alongside just within sight and this time his helper offered a polite, "Sir," by way of greeting.

"Who's this, constable?" The owner of the boots had a deep, fluid voice laced with a comfortable authority.

"A doctor, sir," the cop answered without taking his eyes from his fingers clamped down on the offending artery. "He was here, when it happened." The answer was met with silence.

"Boots" remained another few seconds before leaving Michael to his work, and Michael appreciated both the space and the implied trust. The last thing he needed right then was a slew of questions.

More footsteps approached. "Hey, Michael. Fancy meeting you here."

He glanced up, recognising the two paramedics heading his way. "Ah, the gruesome twosome."

"Thought you were off this weekend, Doc?"

He snorted. "I am, can't you tell? Hey, Peter." He spoke to the other man. "Got any suture packs in that magic bag of yours, or is it full of all that scrapbooking shit you so love?"

"Hey, don't knock my mad creative skills, man. And it happens to be graphic prints, not scrapbooking, dickhead," the paramedic tossed back. "Besides, there are more than a few hot ladies that attend those damn classes. It's the new Tinder, I tell you."

Michael chuckled as the two medics knelt and began to set up their gear alongside.

Peter opened a suture kit and held it out. "Looks like you've got a spot of darning on your hands there."

Peter's partner, Rob, took over from the cop, allowing Peter to assist Michael to glove up and get the bleeder under control. He nodded approvingly. "Nice job. We'll haul him back to the ER to finish up. He's a bit groggy, yeah?"

Michael nodded. "Unconscious for a bit. Nothing major. Cracked his head on the way down."

"Cool." Peter set about repacking his kit while his partner put an IV in place and recorded vital signs. "Sorry it took a bit to get here.

There's another cop round back, two stab wounds to the belly. Carol's on that one. Looks nasty. Same offender, probably. Then the other ambulance got caught at the viaduct in some damn traffic pileup it ran smack into."

A second cop? Michael's stomach coiled on itself remembering Josh heading out after his dog. "A dog handler?"

"Nah, regular, I think."

An odd relief coursed through Michael for the well-being of a man he'd barely met and certainly didn't like. Lust, maybe, but not like. Then, as he stood and watched Jackson being rolled onto a stretcher and prepped to leave, the skin on his neck prickled unexpectedly, and without even turning, he knew Josh was somewhere in the bar.

Seconds later, the man in question walked Michael's way apparently uninjured, although the shepherd at his side sported a gauze bandage wrapped over his neck and shoulder. The dog was hyped, nervous energy rolling off him in waves, but he stayed close and attentive to his handler. Josh stopped alongside Michael, and it was all Michael could do not to lean into all that delicious body heat and simmering adrenaline, but the guy had eyes solely for his injured colleague.

"Your dog's hurt?"

Josh turned those simmering eyes Michael's way betraying a hint of surprise. "Just a nick. He'll be fine."

"Good." Michael held his gaze for a moment before they both turned away. *Fuck.* The guy was beautiful.

"Is Jackson gonna be okay?" The worry was evident in Josh's voice.

Michael opened his mouth to answer before realising Josh had, in fact, addressed the question to Peter and not him. It was hard not to take offence, and so he did.

"He should be," the paramedic answered. "Your colleague outside is a different story, though. He's stable with Carol in the ambulance now, but he's not out of the woods. Doc here did a bang-up job on this one. You're damn lucky he was here. Kid lost a lot of blood."

Michael made a mental note to send the paramedic a Christmas card.

Rob took a few steps back to take a call on his radio, then turned to catch his colleague's eye. "Second ambulance is heading back to Auckland Med with three major traumas on board from that crash. We need to take both these guys in our rig and deal when we get there. The bad guy from the hall has some nasty bite wounds and a foul temper but not much else—he can cool his heels and wait until the next ride."

Michael winced. Three patients at least from the bar, maybe more, and three traumas from the crash. "ER's gonna be swamped," he stated. "Mind if I tag along, if you've got the room? Not like I had better plans, right?" He slid a glance Josh's way and thought he almost caught the hint of a grin, almost.

Peter grabbed his bag. "The more the merrier. Could do with another pair of eyes in back anyway."

An older man approached, no uniform but carrying an air of authority. Boots, if he had to guess.

The guy stuck out his hand. "Detective Inspector Hanover."

Michael accepted. "Doctor Michael Oliver."

"Apparently you saw our knifeman, that right?"

Michael nodded. "Briefly. It happened pretty fast. Can't tell you much."

"I heard. Still, we'll need a full statement at some point. If you're heading for the hospital, we can catch you there for a brief chat tonight to start things rolling, but you'll need to come in and make a formal one tomorrow."

"No problem." Michael stole a glance at Josh. "You catch him?"

Josh flushed, his lips pressed together in a thin line. "Still looking."

Hanover clapped Michael on the shoulder. "Thanks for your

help, Doc. Just as well you were here by the looks." He pulled Josh aside, but not out of hearing distance.

"Follow up at the hospital and see what you can get from our injured guys and this one." He indicated Michael. Then he dropped a hand to rub the shepherd's head. "A right royal fuck-up, eh, Paris?"

Josh sighed loudly. "Sorry, sir." His ears flushed pink, his mouth set in a grim line.

The older man laid a hand on his shoulder. "You did good work tonight, Rawlins, you and Paris. We'll catch the guy. I heard you got roughed up a bit. You okay?"

Michael frowned and ran an eye over Josh again, but he looked okay.

"I'm fine." Josh brushed his boss's concern aside. "Nothing serious. I just didn't get a damn look at him."

Hanover shrugged. "It is what it is. Don't sweat it."

Josh didn't seem reassured, and Michael almost felt sorry for the jerk. Almost.

He gathered up Paris's lead, then slid those mahogany eyes over Michael's chest, lingering on his piercings. The heat emanating from Josh's stare could have set Michael's chest hair on fire, even though his outward expression suggested he'd swallowed something nasty instead, but Michael wasn't fooled. *Yep. Gay, bi, curious... or just a fucking closet case? Yeah, that would make all kinds of sense.*

Pondering the options, he was caught off guard when Josh leaned in and lowered his voice, his lips inches from Michael's ear. "You might wanna put a shirt on and button your jeans before you leave, *doctor*. Just saying."

Instinctively, Michael glanced down and... *shit.* Sure enough, his jeans were still unbuttoned, and with the fly partway down, he was lucky his junk wasn't waving in the breeze. He lifted his eyes and cocked his head. "I'm touched you noticed. I'd offer you the honours since it appears you're so interested, but it's a bit crowded in here, don't you think? I suppose a date is out of the question?" He added a wink for pure piss-off value.

Josh's cool demeanour faltered just for a second before sliding back into casual distaste, which surprisingly stung.

"You'd be right about that," he answered flatly, turning for the door. But he didn't leave. Instead, his shoulders dropped with a sigh and he turned back, a softer expression on his face. "Still, thanks."

Michael raised a questioning brow.

"For Jackson," Josh qualified. "He's a good kid."

And then the arrogant fucker threw Michael a goddamn smile: a fucking sun-shining, riveting glimpse of genuine warmth, humour, and soft appreciation that shocked the hell out of Michael. *Goddammit.* He'd just got comfortable hating the guy and now everything he thought he knew changed in that one split second. *Well, shit.*

Josh stroked his dog's head once and left without even a backward glance, leaving Michael struggling to regain his equilibrium. He blinked slowly and took a few deep breaths.

To say it had been an interesting evening didn't even begin to cover it, but two things were certain. The handler was crazy hot, and Michael was pretty sure Josh didn't swing straight. Still, even if Michael *had* glimpsed a very different person behind the prickly front, the bastard was clearly a complicated bag of shit, and most definitely not worth Michael's interest. *Yeah, right.* His traitorous cock was rock-hard, at full mast and waving a white flag in dispute. With a quick check to make sure no one was looking, Michael rearranged his dick, buttoned his fly, and grabbed his shirt from the floor. *Nope. Not even remotely interested.*

CHAPTER TWO

JOSH FUMED. THE LAST THING HE NEEDED WAS TO BE BOGGED down in rambling witness statements and hospital red tape, not to mention that damn doctor up in his face again. Michael Oliver was trouble—mouthwatering, sizzling, blue-eyed trouble. Exactly the trouble Josh went out of his way to avoid. Rocking that athletic body, stunning tats, and fucking nipple piercings, it was all Josh could do not to drool on the fucker's shoes, but Michael was a player, and Josh didn't need another one of those in his life ever again.

Discovering the arsehole was a doctor had been a bit of a surprise, sure, but it didn't change the facts. Shitheads came in all walks of life, something Josh was well aware of. The whole night had been a balls-up crap-fest from start to finish. Called in as backup to the drug sweep, they'd been sent inside the club to evacuate and control the crowd and to secure the rear exit. A police dog pretty much guaranteed the immediate attention of all concerned and offered better odds of snappy crowd compliance.

He knew the club, had even been a few times, but it wasn't really his scene. He'd heard the owner ran a tight ship, and Josh didn't think the guy was knowingly involved in drugs, but people surprised you.

The tip they'd received the week before had been accurate but incomplete. Not just a couple of guys in a car out back selling, but six, and not in one car but three, a regular shopping mall. And what's more, they'd arrived to find the dealers tipped off and scrambling to pack their shit and get outta Dodge, frantic and armed. It went downhill from there. Out of six guys, they'd hauled arse on only two, and at the cost of two of their own injured. The remaining four had fled into the night, including the guy who'd knifed Jackson.

Josh pulled into the hospital car park and glanced at his watch. Just on midnight. He opened his phone and hit Call, taking a deep breath as the other end picked up. "Hey, pumpkin," he said.

"Daddy!"

His daughter's delight sent a surge of warmth through his chest. "What are you doing up at this hour, young lady?" He'd tried for stern, failing miserably. "I expected you to be asleep."

"Then why did you call?"

"Why did you answer?" he shot back, grinning widely. The familiar teasing banter helped sweep the night's ugly aside.

"Because you called." She giggled. "Like, duh."

He pictured the pout. His eleven-year-old had her mother's sass for sure. He'd bought her a cheap cell phone, so he could call her direct, never knowing what hours he'd end up working. She kept it with her always. "I called to say goodnight."

"Good thing I'm awake, then, isn't it?" came her reply. "Be a shame to miss your call if I was, you know, asleep."

He chuckled. "That it would, sunshine. I'm just letting you know I'll be late tonight. Won't see you until breakfast."

"That's okay. Aunt Katie and I watched *Frozen* again. It was cool. Jamie Collins chucked his drink over my work at school today, so Miss Stevens sent him to the principal's office, and he has to write me an apology. You should've seen his sucked-in lemon face."

Josh grinned. "Well, you remind Jamie Collins that your dad's a police officer with a big dog, and he's planning to visit your school again soon."

"Oh, Daddy, get a grip," she scolded.

Josh drew a breath. At nearly twelve, his daughter was growing up. He should be happy, right? Yeah, not so much.

Sasha continued, "Jamie's not so bad." She chatted on, "I think he likes me."

A wave of panic flared in Josh's stomach. He was so not ready for this. He breathed out and opted for the default position shared by all parents faced with the horror of approaching teenage years: rock-solid denial.

"Okay, honey, I just rang to say goodnight." He made kissing noises into the phone, and Sasha sent a loud smooch back.

"Love you, Dad."

"And you, pumpkin." He hung up and caught a pair of eyes watching him from the back of the car. "Sorry, mate," he apologised to Paris. "There's nothing for you to do here. You may as well sit tight." The dog whined softly and curled up on the floor of his cage. Josh sighed. "Yeah, you and me both, partner. You and me both."

The ER waiting room was humming. Josh headed to reception, pleased to find one of his favourite nurses behind the desk. He sent Janice a wink as she buzzed him through.

"I should have your butt for that winking shit," she growled. "Unless I've grown a dick I don't know about recently."

He blew her a kiss. "You love me, Janice."

"Yeah, yeah," she flipped him off. "Talk to someone who gives one. Hard enough finding a decent straight guy in this town without your gay arse clouding up my search criteria."

Josh leaned in. "A question."

"Shoot."

"You got an American doctor on staff?"

"Michael Oliver?"

Josh nodded. "Any good?"

The nurse's mouth turned up at the corners. "A reason for asking?"

He rolled his eyes. "Just ran into him tonight."

"Ah." She grinned. "So, you're the 'arrogant, jackass dog handler' who needs 'taking down a peg or two.'" Her fingers worked the silent speech marks. "Should've guessed."

"He said that?" *Fucker.*

"Close. That was the 'family fit' version." Janice cocked her head. "You know he bats for your team, right?"

Josh ignored the question. "Bye, Janice."

She put a hand on his arm. "He's a damn good doctor, for the record." She regarded him over her glasses. "He's here on some exchange thing, two years, I think. Gorgeous waste of all those genes for us girls, but that works in your favour, I'm thinking."

He put a finger to her lips. "I'm not interested in the guy. He worked on Jackson, is all. See you later."

Measured chaos reigned in the trauma room, not an unusual state of affairs for a Friday night. Trolleys loaded with monitors, intravenous equipment, suture material, and all manner of medical paraphernalia littered the corridors. The shouting of orders, ringing of phones, and relatives' demands for attention provided white noise as staff moved to and fro in an intense dance of attendance and observation. Doctors milled around the central desk, writing notes, talking on phones, or grouped in urgent discussion around X-rays, cardiographs, and lab results, but no American doctor in sight. Not that Josh was looking, much.

He nailed down a staff member and discovered the whereabouts of his two colleagues and the drug dealer. The officer with the stomach wounds was off limits, being prepped for emergency surgery. That didn't sound good.

The offender, sporting a number of righteous dog bites to his arm, was heavily sedated and being treated with a constable keeping an eye. Josh saw no point in giving the guy more than a cursory check, and he reminded himself to feed Paris an extra biscuit for sinking his teeth through the bastard.

That left Jackson. Josh found his colleague conscious and resting in one of the treatment rooms. The young officer looked pale and a bit out of it with his right arm heavily bandaged from hand to shoulder. His eyelids fluttered open, and a thin smile creased his face when Josh entered.

"Hey, man." Jackson sounded weak and tired.

"Hey, kiddo. How you doing? Need anything?"

"A slug of tequila or six."

Josh laughed. "Good luck getting that past this lot, kid."

"Not a kid. Plus, getting knifed must've earned me a fuckload of respect points, right?"

Josh snorted. "Maybe one or two. Probably not gonna make up for that pile of baby fluff you've been trying to grow on those cheeks, though." He scuffed the young man's hair.

Jackson jerked away. "Hey, careful with the do, man. That styling cost a bomb. Not all of us can roll out of bed looking like a *GQ* model."

Josh grinned. "I'd see about getting my money back if I were you. Besides, I'm an old man with a near-teenage daughter. Nothing *GQ* about me."

Jackson snorted. "Tell Tomas down in Evidence that. The guy's been hounding me about you. Told the fucker I'm no gay whisperer and he can do his own damn dirty work."

Josh laughed. "I owe you."

"Damn right."

"So, you get a look at our guy?"

Jackson shook his head. "Nothing decent. European, fast on his feet, and quick with a blade is about all I had time for. Someone must have clocked him, though."

"Yeah, well, I was otherwise occupied trying to stop my head from ringing after he shoved me into that damn wall. Which means you'll be in the witness stand for this one, so be prepared. By the way, thanks for having my back there, kid."

Jackson's cheeks pinked. "No problem. How about outside? Anyone get a look?"

"Too dark. He ran when he saw us coming, made it behind a

parked car by the club's fire exit, and they couldn't get to him. That's why we got you to pop the door open, give him an out. Would've worked too if it hadn't been for the second bastard following him in. Came out of nowhere."

Jackson licked his lips. "I'm so fucking thirsty. Why won't they give me something to drink?"

The curtain cracked open. "Because we haven't decided if we need to amputate."

Jackson laughed.

The frown on Josh's forehead deepened. Michael fucking Oliver. Still, it saved him the job of tracking the guy down for his statement.

Michael continued, "Your arm's all good, and yes, you can have some water. We just needed to be sure. It was a joke. Maybe not a good one."

"Smart-arse." The young man huffed. "So, when can I go home?"

"We'll need you for twenty-four hours in case that artery gives us any more trouble, but after that you can go. Maybe hold off on the tequila, though, concussion and all that."

Jackson grinned. "I can do that."

Josh's radio crackled to life, informing him his relief had arrived. Finally, something to smile about.

"So..." Michael Oliver took a step toward Josh. "Anything else I can help you with, officer?"

Jackson snorted, and Josh scowled at the young man, who simply shrugged.

He narrowed his gaze at Michael. "I need ten minutes of your time. See you tomorrow, kid."

"Not a fucking kid." Jackson flipped Josh off.

They left the young man to doze on his pain-relief meds, Josh following Michael to a quieter corner of the ER.

"All yours," the doctor declared, leaning against the wall, arms folded. "Though ten minutes seems a little on the pessimistic side. I have a feeling we could do a lot better than that."

Josh refused to bite. "We need a description of the man with the knife, the one in the bar. And can we just stop whatever this is going on here?" He waved a hand between them. "We obviously don't like each other, so let's just get this done, and then we can be out of each other's hair and just maybe we can catch the guy who knifed two of my colleagues, okay?"

Michael flushed and dropped his hands to his sides. "Yeah, of course. Though, to be honest, I didn't get more than a three-to-four-second glimpse of the guy. He ran out of the corridor, saw me, looked like he was going to have a go, and then your dog went all Cujo on him, so he took off instead."

The change in the doctor's manner was so dramatic that Josh struggled to reconcile the two impressions. "Even so, it appears you're our best option." He dug his notebook from the pocket of his trousers.

Michael seemed surprised. "Really? Well, then: European, about six foot maybe. Dark, wavy hair, shoulder-length, early twenties at a guess, didn't look drunk or high." He caught Josh's raised brows and shrugged. "Everyday triage. I'm trained to pick up on that shit pretty fast. Can't be a hundred percent sure, but let's just say, he didn't ring my bells in that regard."

Josh nodded. "Anything else?"

"Dark sweatshirt, dark trousers, and a silver chain on his right wrist. I noticed because it was the hand with the knife. A tattoo on his neck, right side again, a bird maybe, not sure."

"Facial features?" Josh pushed.

"Nothing that really stood out. Maybe a scar in his left brow. I only say that because it didn't match the arc of the other." He shrugged at Josh's raised brows. "It's a doctor thing."

It was a lot more detail than Josh had expected. "Thanks."

Michael cocked an eyebrow. "You're welcome, and I hope your guys do okay."

Josh nodded and slid the notebook back to his pocket. Michael tracked the movement, his gaze resting on Josh's groin a second or two longer than was comfortable. The guy just couldn't help himself.

Josh let it go. He was too damn tired. "We'll need a formal statement tomorrow at the main city station, and they'll want you to look through our books, but someone will call to set that up for Monday, I would guess. For now, that's it. Have a good one." He turned and headed toward reception.

"Hey," Michael called from behind.

What now? Josh turned to face the doctor.

"You are, without doubt, fucking gorgeous, you do know that, right?" Michael held his gaze unflinchingly.

Ugh. The doctor was infuriating. Josh spun on his heels and left without answering.

MICHAEL ADMIRED Josh Rawlins's ass for as long as possible until the ER doors swung shut. Josh might be a jerk, but he made a damn fine exit.

A set of soft fingers alighted on his forearm. "I'll need to mop the floor if you don't haul that tongue of yours back in your mouth."

"Fuck off, Cam," Michael snapped at the ER's dynamo of a charge nurse. Cameron Wano was a stunning man with flawless cinnamon skin, thanks to a mixed Polynesian heritage, a wide bright smile, and canny, dancing golden eyes. He turned heads for all sorts of reasons before you even got to the makeup. Tonight, his lush black hair was stacked into short spikes gelled to within an inch of their life, and Michael swore he wore two colours of eyeliner, both flecked with glitter. It shouldn't have worked, but the guy looked like a fucking rock star, albeit with a decided swing to his hips.

"Just saying." Cameron grinned. "The man has a mighty fine arse." He elbowed Michael in the ribs.

Michael scowled. Cam was annoying as hell, and the closest thing to a friend he'd made in New Zealand so far. Gay as the day was long, Cam was thirty years old, and five feet eleven of highly capable ER nurse wrapped up in a witty, sarcastic personality that was tempered by a huge heart.

He'd saved Michael's bacon, along with most of the attending medical staff, more than once through skilled assessment and careful practice, not to mention his ballsy take-no-crap attitude toward the hierarchy. He didn't care whether you were a cleaner, consultant, or freaking hospital administrator, you'd better have your shit together before you messed with Cameron or his ER and its staff. He protected his nurses like a lioness.

To his surprise, Michael had become an immediate fanboy. He'd never been into flamboyant guys particularly, but there was something about Cameron that had him flirting shamelessly. He'd even pushed his luck with the nurse once, to test the waters, see if Cam might be interested, only to find his balls perilously close to mincemeat in the nurse's hands. Since then the two had developed a mutual respect and friendship that Michael wouldn't trade.

The nurse leaned against the wall, studying him.

"What?"

Cameron smirked. "You like him."

"Who?"

"Him." Cameron flicked his head toward the ER exit doors.

"He's an asshole."

"You two should get along just fine, then."

"Fucker."

Cameron grinned and pushed off the wall, running a finger down the side of Michael's face. "Aw, poor baby."

Michael glared. "How is it you can touch me whenever you want, and I get my balls crunched if I even think of returning the favour?"

"Because, my darling man—" Cam patted Michael's cheek. "—I have no desire to fuck you in a million years. The same, however, cannot be said for you, and I'm obliged to protect my virtue."

Michael rolled his eyes. "You're a damn tease."

Cameron chuckled. "But you love me. Now go home and get some sleep." He patted Michael on the arm and sashayed toward the depths of the ER.

. . .

BACK IN his vehicle, Josh called in Michael's description of the knifeman to Mark Knight, his best friend and lead detective on the case. Then he transferred his notes to his on-board laptop and turned to Paris. "Home time, mate." The shepherd regarded him with sleepy eyes before collapsing on his side, causing Josh to yawn in sympathy. His partner had only suffered a minor nick and the paramedics had cleaned it and pronounced it fine at the scene, but Josh would still get Paris to the police vet tomorrow, just to be sure.

Driving by the entrance to the ER, he saw Michael Oliver waiting at the taxi rank. *Fuck.* Michael's car was probably still back at the club. He did his best to ignore the niggle of guilt as he drove past, but an image of Michael on his knees beside a bleeding Jackson ramped it up. *Shit.* He hung a U-turn and pulled in alongside the irritating man.

To say Michael seemed surprised, put it mildly.

He dropped the passenger window and leaned across. "Where are you heading?"

Michael hesitated a second before answering. "Eastern Bays."

Josh nodded. "It's on my way. Get in."

Michael hesitated. "Get in? *You're* offering *me* a ride?" he clarified. "Did I miss a blue moon or something?"

Josh bit back a smile and shrugged. "Consider it thanks for Jackson, nothing more."

"Well, okay. Great. Thank you." He slid into the passenger seat and shut the door, filling the car with that seductive smell of oranges and spice, albeit with a slight antiseptic tinge. "Have to say I'm surprised." He looked amused. "Wouldn't have thought helping me out would've been high on your to-do list."

Josh kept his attention ahead. "Just being polite."

Michael snorted. "Right."

Paris repositioned himself inside his cage, and Michael turned at the sound. "Hey there, fella," he spoke softly to the shepherd. "You get a good workout tonight?"

Paris replied with a soft whine. *Traitor.* The dog was a sucker for a compliment. "So where to?" Josh asked.

"Boulder Drive, 15D. You can drop me at the corner with Huntingdon if you like."

"Suits me."

They rode in silence the rest of the way, something Josh was thankful for. He dropped the doctor right outside his apartment building and not at the end of the street as Michael had suggested.

Michael made no comment. Instead, he turned to Josh with something approaching a friendly expression. "Look, I know we got off to a bad start, but I don't suppose you'd be interested—"

"Nope." Josh's expression cooled.

Michael frowned. "You don't like me much, do you?"

Josh shrugged. "Don't have any feelings about you."

"Right. You didn't like me from the minute you met me, yet you know nothing about me."

Josh's gaze slid away. "I know enough."

Michael snorted. "Really? I'm impressed. How the rest of us mere mortals cope with having to actually get to know someone before shitting on them is a damn miracle, then."

Michael had a point. Josh was being a dick. "You done?"

Michael sighed. "Whatever. Thanks for the lift, I guess." He pushed open the passenger door.

"Look," Josh blurted. "It's nothing personal. You're just not my type."

Michael's eyes dipped to Josh's lap, then back up. "Uh-huh. Right," he quipped with a smirk. "Not interested. Got it."

Michael left the car and headed up his drive, and Josh thumped his fist on the steering wheel in self-disgust. Nope. Absolutely not interested, absolutely not watching the Michael's arse as he left, with his own dick absolutely not fucking rigid in his pants.

Paris whined.

"And I don't need your damn opinion either," Josh grumbled. *Fuck.*

. . .

"Daddy!"

Josh rolled to his side and hauled the sheet over his morning wood just seconds before his daughter hit the bed, closely followed by Paris. The two were never far apart. The shepherd took one look at Josh's scowl and slid to the foot of the bed, curling into an instant ball.

"I can still see you, you know," Josh growled. The shepherd's ears drooped, and he dug his nose under the blanket.

"Let him stay, Daddy, please?" No one threw a pout quite like his daughter. Paris opened a hopeful eye, then immediately closed it when he saw Josh still staring his way.

Josh sighed and glanced at the clock. 7:00 a.m. *Damn*, he was tired. "Okay, he can stay for a bit." He cupped Sasha's face. "Hey, you. What have I said about knocking first?"

She frowned. "But Jase isn't here anymore, and it's just you, so no sex, right?"

Holy shit. Josh had always been open with Sasha about being gay, but she rarely made such direct comments. He'd been out since she was six months old, so basically she'd never known any different. There'd been no big sit-down explanation—he'd simply added in conversations and information as he felt she was old enough to understand. His few gay friends such as Mark had always been a part of her life, and Josh had schooled them on what was appropriate for his daughter to see and hear along the way.

"That's true," he answered, keeping his tone as even as he could. "But it's not just about sex. I need privacy, just like you."

Sasha considered that for a minute before answering. "Okay." She dragged Paris's head onto her lap. "Is it bad?" she asked, fingering the bandage on the dog's shoulder. "Did he do good?"

Josh scratched the animal's chin. "He always does good, honey. But last night the bad guy got away. It's a small knife cut, nothing serious."

Sasha pursed her lips. "Damn it."

"Language," Josh warned with a smile. "That's twenty cents in the swear jar before netball."

She sighed and patted his hand indulgently. "Okay. But I'm not promising I don't swear at school. I won't be a Goody Two-shoes. It's not a good look."

He bit back a laugh. "I get that."

Sasha shuffled off the bed. "Just so you know." She disappeared to her room, and two seconds later, Paris and his bushy tail swished out the door to join her.

JOSH'S SISTER, Katie, eyed his postshower appearance with alarm as she put a mound of scrambled eggs and toast in front of him. The smell elicited a loud rumble from his stomach.

"Hate to think what you looked like before. What time did you finally roll in?"

Josh rubbed the stubble on his chin, debating whether his decision to forgo a shave that morning had been a good one. "Gone two, I think. Did I wake you?"

"Not on your life." She flicked her long blond hair off her face and patted his hand. "It takes more than that to wake this piece of gorgeousness."

A willowy blond firecracker of a woman, at thirty-two Katie was four years younger than Josh. Full of sass and grit, Josh couldn't understand why she hadn't been snapped up years ago. *Because she spends all her spare time looking after you, idiot.*

It was true. Katie had rented a house less than six houses away from the small weatherboard bungalow Josh owned. It had been a deliberate decision on his sister's part, so she could help cover Josh's work shifts without either of them needing to drive a long distance. She was crucial to the smooth running of his household, a fact that worried him no end. They needed to be more self-reliant, but it was too easy when Katie was right there. The debt Josh owed his sister was immeasurable, and he wasn't sure he could ever repay it.

"I have to swing by the vet on the way to netball, so if you can take Sasha with you, I'll see you there," he said, chewing on a piece of toast.

"No problem."

"And thanks again for staying over," he added. "I know it was short notice. Hope I didn't screw up any plans."

"Nah. My hot date cancelled."

His eyes popped. "Really?"

She shook her head at him in disbelief. "No, idiot. God, you are so easy." She shovelled a forkful of eggs into her mouth.

Sasha appeared at the table, shepherd in tow, and eyed her plate of pancakes with obvious delight. "Yum."

"How come she gets pancakes and I just get eggs?" he grumbled.

"Because she isn't getting podgy round the middle."

He patted his stomach. "I'll have you know this is all muscle."

Katie snorted. "Right."

They ate in silence for a time. Sasha finished and went to get ready for netball. Josh tried to remember the last day off he'd been able to have an actual sleep-in. Nothing came to mind.

"Busy night, I take it?" Katie asked, finishing the last of her eggs.

Josh nodded, mouth full. "Drug raid on a bar."

"Which one?"

"Downtown G."

"The gay bar?" Katie sounded surprised.

Josh nodded.

"See anyone you know?"

"Nah."

Katie was quiet for a bit. The type of quiet that let you know she was building up to something. "You should go there one night. You haven't been out in ages. Be good for you."

And there it was. "Katie—"

"Just hear me out, okay?" She leaned her back against the bench and eyeballed him.

He sighed. "Get on with it, then."

"I worry about you. There, I've said it. You've been like a monk since Jase."

"I have a kid—"

"And? Look, I just want you to have some fun. You're a great dad, the best, but you deserve some playtime, a bit of loving or even just some mind-blowing sex, shit, any sex for that matter. You're as cranky as hell and don't think she doesn't notice." Katie flicked her head toward Sasha's room.

Josh sighed. "I know. I'll do better, okay? I just... I just can't go there at the moment. And I'm not discussing my sex life with my sister. Or lack of it as it happens. As if I don't feel enough of a sad fuck already."

Katie walked over and pulled him into a hug. He let her hold him for a while, the warmth of the physical contact too damn nice to give up. *Fuck.* He really did need to get laid. And with that, Michael Oliver popped into his head.

It wasn't rocket science. He knew why Michael pushed his buttons. He was gorgeous, but he was also just another Jase, another arrogant manwhore who wouldn't know commitment if it bitch-slapped him in the face and didn't care who he hurt in the process of getting his dick off as often as possible. Josh wasn't about to be hurt like that again.

They'd met at a party. At six foot two with shoulder-length black hair and physically muscled from his job as a builder, Jason was a striking-looking man. He was laid-back, fun, flirtatious, addicted to Snickers bars and glam rock, and, as it later turned out, allergic to monogamy. In many ways they'd been complete opposites, but they seemed to work, at least Josh had thought so. And Sasha and Jason had hit it off from day one. He was just another big kid in lots of ways. That should have been a warning in itself.

Then, after two years living together, Josh discovered Jason cheating on him. And when confronted, the fucker owned up to multiple hookups throughout their relationship. Josh had been devastated. Within hours, Jason had packed up and left and Sasha had been distraught. First her mother had abandoned her and then Jason.

Jason had agreed to keep in contact with Sasha as she adjusted to the split, and even after two years, he still made an effort, though she needed it less. Josh had remained polite but tried to keep out of Jason's way, except for that one time, but he wasn't going there again.

MICHAEL'S MORNING didn't go exactly as he hoped. It began with morning wood dancing single-mindedly to the image of one supremely irritating dog handler. *Goddammit.* Josh was a class-A jerk and Michael had decided before even hitting the sack that he wasn't going to waste any more headspace on the prick. Josh Rawlins had a stick up his ass for no better reason than Michael picking up a little fun in a club. *Well, fuck that.* He was gay. It went with the territory. He wasn't looking for a relationship. *Been there. Done that. Fucking disaster.*

The two years he'd spent with Simon had ended as a complete fuck-up. He'd learned his lesson and he now kept his "relationships" to the hit-it-and-quit-it variety or at the most, an occasional more regular fuck buddy. Which only served to remind Michael that he'd left the club last night as frustrated as he'd entered. Another thing to be pissed about.

Simon. *Shit.* He thought he'd put that one to bed already. But he'd been coming up more frequently in Michael's thoughts lately, accompanied by an unexpected twinge of unwelcome guilt. Did he miss Simon? Yeah, he could accept that. Or at least he missed the easy company they'd shared. They worked at the same hospital, Simon as a gastroenterologist. So, his ex had known about the NZ contract and had been surprisingly supportive of Michael's decision.

Simon was one of the good ones, too good for Michael as it turned out. He'd genuinely loved Michael, made that abundantly clear, but for whatever reason, Michael had never been able to return the words, and Simon had never pressed. They'd gotten on well and fitted easily into each other's lives, understanding the long hours and stress of their respective jobs. The sex had been fine if not earth-shattering, and if it hadn't been for Michael's giant cock-up eighteen months before, well, who knew what might have happened.

But when the shit hit the fan, Simon's persistent, ever-so-patient understanding and attempts to get Michael to talk about it eventually drove Michael to shut him out completely. Then he'd driven the point home with a very indiscreet fuck in a club that Simon had walked in on. They'd split, no surprise there, and Michael had got his shit together while Simon had gone on to find someone else. He seemed happy, and Michael was genuinely pleased for him.

Michael was lucky, and he knew it. He didn't have to work too hard to hook up with practically anyone he wanted, and he certainly didn't need to be obsessing about some hot fucking dog handler. So his pride had taken a dent, so what? Kick it to the kerb and move on. Forget the sexy cop and enjoy the first day off he'd had in two weeks. First, he needed to collect his car and get that damn statement out of the way.

Not so easy as it turned out. According to the man at the station, Michael's car was firmly locked behind crime scene tape for at least another day. Now his weekend was fucked. Still, it could have been worse. Truth was Michael was more rattled than he wanted to admit about the previous night. Stitching a knife wound was vastly different from witnessing the actual attack, and reading about a drug bust was preferable to being in the middle of one. Neither things Michael wanted to revisit.

At least he'd finished his statement. It took two hours, but he was out of the cold, which was no small thing. November aside, the chill of the brisk southwest winds direct from Antarctica had sent spring temperatures in Auckland plummeting to midwinter levels so inside was good. The modern central station with its large glass windows had a stunning harbour view, and the detective taking his statement was certainly no slouch in the looks department either. He counted that a win.

Michael signed his statement, then dropped his pen on the table. "I told the other guy all this last night." He ran his gaze over the eye candy that was Detective Mark Knight.

Mark grinned. "Officer Rawlins, you mean?"

"If that's the dog guy." Michael failed to keep the sneer from his voice.

Mark's grin widened. "That would be him. I take it you two didn't hit it off?"

His gaze dipped to Michael's lips for a brief second, and Michael looked at him sideways. The detective had a charming smile and solid, handsome features even if neither quite matched up to the handler. The handler, who'd apparently been telling tales out of school. *Fucker.*

"Wasn't looking to make friends," he answered glibly.

Mark snorted. "Just as well. Josh isn't much into clubbing, as you probably guessed. Been a while since I've got him out to the G. Anyway, we're done here for now. We'll need you to come back in to look at some photos, see if you can firm up an ID on the guy in the bar. I'll let you know a time."

Michael nodded and turned to leave, almost running into an older, balding guy blocking the doorway. They locked eyes.

"You're the doctor from the bar last night, right?" the man asked.

"Yes." Michael glanced at Mark, who nodded briefly at the newcomer before introducing them. John Stables was apparently the area commander.

Stables ran his gaze over Michael. "I saw you were in and wanted to thank you personally for helping our young guy out last night."

Michael nodded. "Just doing my job."

"Maybe so. But we might have lost two if you hadn't been there." Distress stole into Stable's expression.

"The other officer didn't make it?" Michael wasn't really surprised. The guy hadn't looked too good.

"Unfortunately, no." Stables cleared his throat. "Lots of overtime getting done on this one. He was well liked."

"I'm sorry," Michael sympathised.

"Thanks." Stables ran a hand over his face. "We don't lose many, and it always hits hard. You're American, right?"

Michael grinned. "So they tell me."

"Don't suppose you played ball back home?"

"Baseball," Michael admitted. "Second base."

Stables looked pleased. "Can you hit?"

Michael frowned. "I do okay. Is this going somewhere?"

"It is. We have a station team, with a few civilian ring-ins, part of a softball summer league starting in a few weeks. We're down two players. Interested?"

Michael was surprised just how much he was. It would be good to meet people away from the usual hospital crowd.

"I'm not familiar with the rules of softball," he warned. "I may screw it up."

The commander laughed. "You and every other mug on the team, including the umpires."

Michael grinned. "Just so long as you know."

"Excellent." The commander slapped Michael on the back, causing him to nearly swallow his tongue. "Leave your email contact with the desk sergeant, and we'll send you a copy of the schedule and team contacts. Next practice is tomorrow at ten. Mark, here, will pick you up, seeing as how we've left you without transport." He walked off leaving Michael with Mark.

Mark snorted. "Looks like I'll see you at nine thirty, then."

Michael pulled on his coat. "I'll be ready." He hesitated, wondering if he had the balls to ask. *Fuck it.* "I'm going to go out on a limb here," he said cautiously. "You mentioned clubbing at the G. Are you and pretty dog boy both—"

"Gay?" Mark grinned. "I am. Josh speaks for himself."

Michael pulled on his coat. "Yeah, he mentioned it. You both out?"

"Yeah. It's not always pretty but most of the guys are okay with it. If you want to know about Josh, you'll have to ask him."

"Yeah, no," Michael said. "Guy's an asshole."

Mark pursed his lips. "I think you two got off on the wrong foot. He's a good guy." He shrugged. "A bit intense, maybe."

Michael threw back his head and laughed. "Yeah, the guy's got that nailed as well."

TRUE TO his word, Mark was at Michael's gate on the dot of nine thirty, driving a beat-up, tacky yellow Prius.

He eyed Michael's hair. "Rough night?"

Fuck. Michael had slept through his alarm and hadn't checked the mirror, let alone grabbed a shower before flying out the door. "Something like that," he grumbled, slipping his seat belt on and running his fingers through the tangled nest on his head in an effort to create some style before finally giving up. He popped his can of V, hoping caffeine would help, and cast an eye around. "A Prius, man? Really? My testosterone plummeted just looking at it."

"Hey, don't dis my ride, which is actually your *only* ride today," Mark protested.

"Yeah, well, don't get me wrong, I'm grateful for the lift, but you may as well write Loser Gay in pink letters down the side, just saying."

"Now you're just being nasty." Mark laughed, pulling away from the kerb. "Besides it's reliable and efficient."

"Fuck me." Michael shook his head and laughed.

"Not today, sunshine."

Michael snorted. He missed this kind of banter, missed his friends back home. He'd spent the remainder of the previous day alone, again, lazing on his couch watching ESPN with his neighbour's tabby cat, Scout, perched on his chest. The damn cat spent more time at his place than his own. The animal had offered no opinion on the problem of the good dog handler, except to lift his leg midconversation and clean his balls. Michael reflected that maybe that was about as apt a statement as could be made.

He shot a glance Mark's way. He was looking good in a pair of loose grey sweats and a shirt that showed off finely tuned muscle. Mark elicited some interest on the part of Michael's dick, but, in reality, Michael saw potential friend more than fuck buddy. *Christ.* Cats and friends—he must be growing old.

He was introduced to the team, who seemed welcoming to someone they didn't know from Adam, although Michael guessed his assistance to their colleague was mostly responsible for that. He got his fair share of pats on the back and thank-yous. He couldn't deny it felt good.

He trialled at second base and was damn grateful he'd boned up on the rule differences, so he didn't look a complete fuckwit on the field. As much as Stables had downplayed the competitive nature of the league, Michael knew better. No police team chock-full of alpha-male testosterone was going to take losing well. It only took one glance around the field to know these guys were serious.

The end of the practice didn't come soon enough for Michael's aching muscles. He thought he'd at least held his own with only a few cock-ups. The worst had been a promising hit he'd made in the second game only to be caught out by none other than Josh fucking Rawlins. The man wore a shit-eating grin for the remainder of the practice. Yep, Mark had omitted that tidbit of information, and Michael hadn't checked the team list. Josh had arrived wearing a pair of snug training pants and a soft Nike sweatshirt, still managing to look like a damn magazine cover. Unlike Michael, who spent most of the game trying to pat his bed head in place. Josh had some good ball skills too, goddammit.

Still, Michael had hit some good balls as well, scored a couple of runs, and caught three runners out. Not too shabby for a first time, and the captain was pleased enough to offer him the permanent spot. Even Josh had shaken his hand, briefly.

Mark was the last to congratulate him, giving Michael a friendly one-arm hug. "Not bad for a Yank."

Michael shoved him away playfully. "As opposed to a pretty gay boy driving a nana car, yeah?"

Keeping with their apparent tradition, the team headed for Kendrick's after the practice, a pub conveniently situated within a short walking distance from the field. Michael went along, finding himself sitting opposite Josh, not his choice or Josh's, it would seem. Josh's expression turned to irritation every time it landed on Michael. *Well, fuck him.* Michael had really enjoyed the morning, dickheads aside, and he wasn't about to let one idiot fuck up his mood. Even if that guy happened to look fifty times this side of fuckably delicious with his damp blond hair slicked back and all that freshly showered aroma wafting across the table, playing havoc with Michael's traitorous dick.

JOSH WAS fuming, again. Fast-pitch was one of the few activities he got to enjoy on his own and now he had to put up with Michael fucking Oliver. Arriving at Kendrick's, he'd immediately collared Mark at the bar as the guy was buying a round.

"What the fuck, man? Whose idea was it to invite him?"

His friend plastered a huge grin on his face and held up his hands in surrender. "Nothing to do with me, mate. Boss man just asked me to deliver him."

"And you couldn't think of any reason that wouldn't be a good idea?"

"What was I going to say?" Mark studied his friend. "And honestly, he seems a good guy, and he plays a solid game."

"I don't give a flying fuck if he plays like Nathan Nukunuku, he's an arsehole."

"Funny, that's what he called you."

"Wait. He called *me* an arsehole?"

Mark snorted. "Lighten up, Josh. Anyone would think you actually liked Michael."

"Fuck off."

Mark whacked him on the back of his head.

"Ow," Josh protested.

"Suck it up. You deserved it. So, the guy was cruising you. So what? Oh. My. God. What a scandal. And he even got lucky with a gorgeous young man, well good for him. It's not a crime. And besides, he's hot. And he hit on you. I would think that was reassuring, that you haven't lost it. You're both obviously hot for each other."

"I'm a father of an eleven-year-old girl for Christ's sake."

"And that came with getting your dick cut off, did it?"

"You wouldn't understand." Josh dismissed the comment.

Mark glared. "Oh, right. Because I'm an ignorant, single gay guy who can't keep his cock in his pants, you mean? Not a holier-than-thou family man who's so sexually constipated that his jizz turned to concrete months ago. You must be jacking off bricks by now."

Mark had a point and Josh sighed. "You're right. It's me."

"Better."

"It's just..." Josh sighed.

Mark sighed. "Hey," he said gently. "Not every guy's like Jason."

Silence hung between them.

"I know that," Josh admitted softly. "But guys like Michael treat people like they're there solely for their own amusement, and I can't risk that. Sasha got attached to Jase, and then he screwed everything up. And the worst part, I didn't even see it. I'm a police officer, for Christ's sake, and I missed the fact he'd been fucking around on me for two years."

"What can I say?" Mark said. "People suck sometimes. Jase was a fucking idiot who didn't know when he was onto a good thing, a great thing. It's his loss. Doesn't mean you give up on the rest of us. Besides, I'm not saying marry the guy, just have a bit of fun, a confidence boost. You've already said he's not relationship material for you, so what's the problem? And he sure as hell looks like fun. You deserve a life outside of Sasha and that damn dog, you know."

"So everyone keeps saying," Josh grumbled. "Okay. I'll think about it. Happy?"

"Deliriously. Also, if you end up chickening out, let me know, so I can tap that?"

Josh couldn't summon more than a strangled grunt in reply.

Mark sent him a wicked smile. "Thought so. Come on, let's have a beer, you idiot." He grabbed the tray of beers from the barman and headed for the two tables the team had pushed together.

JOSH WAS forced to take the only seat left, directly opposite Michael Oliver. Of course it was. His gaze slid over Michael, an irritating reminder of just how fit the doctor was. In a pair of tight, acid-washed jeans, and a black button-down shirt he was hard to take your eyes off.

He watched as Mark made it his mission to educate the doctor on the finer points of rugby. The two were huddled over beer coasters and scraps of paper, laughing and heads bumping. He found the whole thing increasingly irritating for reasons he wasn't prepared to analyse. God, he really did need to get laid.

On one occasion, when he lifted his beer and glanced across, he found Michael's gaze locked on his mouth, and there was heat in his eyes, lots and lots of heat. Caught staring, the doctor never even flinched, just raised his water in salute, and Josh's cock twitched to life. *For crap's sake.* It didn't seem to matter how much he tried to ignore the man, Michael Oliver simply turned him on like a fucking switch. The guy was a menace to Josh's self-control.

So he swallowed hard and got to his feet to head home. It was either that or drag the good doctor out back and nail his arse against the wall. But of course it was never going to be that easy. Barely out of his chair, and his best friend suddenly decided he needed to visit his sister and could Josh drop Michael back at his apartment, seeing as it was on his way? All said with a shit-eating grin, the fucker.

So here they were again. Michael cracked the passenger door and got in smelling of musky body wash and some kind of citrus cologne that made Josh's mouth water. His jeans rode tight on his thighs, stretching sinfully as he settled into the leather and ran his fingers through his damp hair.

"So here we are again, officer."

Michael reached between them to fasten his seat belt, brushing hands with Josh, who was busy doing the same. The contact sent every one of Josh's nerve endings on high alert, and it was all he could do not to shut Michael's irritating mouth with his own. He sighed and started the car, pulling out into traffic. This stupidity had to stop.

"Look..."

Michael turned to face him with a curious look.

Josh continued. "You're a good ballplayer, and I get they want you on the team. So, seeing as we're gonna be spending time together, as teammates, can we just cut this crap between us and maybe... start again?"

Michael went quiet, then turned away to stare out the front windscreen. "Okay, done."

Josh rolled his eyes. "Just like that?"

Michael snorted but kept his eyes front. "This may come as a shock to you, Josh, but you're not as irresistible as you seem to think."

Well, okay, then. Josh kept his eyes on the road, and they rode in silence for the remainder of the journey. He pulled in at the same spot he had two nights before. "So, um, if you need a lift next weekend, you can call. My number's on the team list."

Michael regarded him flatly. "I'm sure I'll have my car back by then but thanks. See you around."

"Sure." Josh watched the doctor disappear up his drive. *You got what you wanted,* he told himself. *So that's good, right?*

CHAPTER THREE

Sunday and Monday could be as hellishly busy in the ER as any Saturday. People didn't want to screw up their Saturdays stuck in an ER waiting room, but when Sunday afternoon rolled in and work/school loomed, those waiting rooms filled like hourglasses.

Michael had at least managed to collect his car on Sunday, and with his Monday shift having less than two hours remaining, he looked forward to his couch, a cold soda, and taped coverage of the recent Lakers game. Desperate for a bit of quiet, he'd snagged a drink and found an empty treatment room and shut the door. He'd missed lunch, and his feet felt like they'd been through a metal crusher.

Cameron stuck his head through the door just as he was taking his first guzzle. "Hiding, are we?"

Michael groaned. "Failed epically, then, didn't I?"

"Hey, I gave you five before I tracked you down—consider yourself lucky." He patted Michael's thigh. "Come on, sexy. The girl in three is ready to go. Just need you to sign off on her."

"Get Max to do it. My feet are killing me, and Lucinda's been crawling up my butt with crampons all day." Lucinda, or Lucifer, as most of the staff called the X-ray technician behind her back, was a weightlifter in her spare time with a mouth straight out of a prison rec room. Interactions with Lucinda usually involved strategic delegation to junior house surgeons if at all possible or failing that, body armour. The woman worked mostly afternoon and night shifts, but she'd swapped that day to attend her daughter's school drama production. The thought of Lucinda as a parent was almost too frightening to contemplate.

Cameron chuckled. "That charm failing you, huh?"

Michael scowled. They were barely six inches apart, and from that distance, he noted the eyeliner of the day was not in fact purple as he'd first thought but a deep blue embedded with glitter that matched the small-gauge piercing in Cam's right ear. It was... hot.

He cleared his throat. "Firstly, the subject of said charm needs to be of the human variety, and secondly, they shouldn't possess a venomous overbite and more muscle than me. Neither of those applies to our Lucinda."

Cameron snorted. "I can always hold your hand if you need it."

"Shut up, you queer fuck."

"God, I love it when you talk dirty," Cameron deadpanned.

Michael laughed. "The offer's still there, you know."

"You couldn't handle it, Yankee." Cameron grabbed Michael's coat lapels and dragged him through the curtains into the hallway. "Now back to work, Cinders."

Over the next hour, Michael miraculously avoided being assigned a new patient, though he suspected that was down to Cameron feeling sorry for him. It did, however, mean that he got all his notes up-to-date so he wasn't held back at the end of shift. Not wanting to push his luck by poking his head into the nurses' station, he grabbed his duffel and headed for the door, only to be intercepted by Cameron swishing toward him from the waiting room.

"Been a guy at the front desk asking for you," he said. "Hot date, Doctor?"

Michael frowned. "Do I look like the dating kind? Let alone have his date turn up at his gossip-fuelled workplace?"

Cameron crossed his arms over his chest. "Didn't think so. Besides, he hardly looked your style, unless you're crushing ghetto lately." He leaned sideways as his attention was caught by something behind Michael. "Joanne. If that brand-new infusion pump is going anywhere other than back into Trauma One where you got it, I'll knit your fallopian tubes into booties. Now put it back." He straightened and turned back to Michael. "Fucking physicians. Anyway, I gotta go. I swear I'm gonna chain those damn machines to the wall. See you tomorrow."

They parted company, and Michael headed for the staff car park. He'd just made his way through the alley beside the ER when a guy bent over the hood of Michael's car brought him to a stop.

"Hey," he yelled.

The man spun and took off. Michael launched into a sprint and caught him halfway down the row of cars. "Not so fast," he puffed, latching on to the guy's forearm. But the man was no slouch. He spun in Michael's grip, rounded, and threw out his leg, sweeping Michael's feet from under him.

What the...? Michael slammed into the ground, landing on his shoulder and snapping his head sideways. His temple hit the rough surface with a sickening thud. Pretty lights danced for a moment behind his eyes, but he didn't pass out. It took some effort, but Michael managed to raise his head to get a look at his attacker, but the man was gone. The sound of spinning tyres ripping through the car park sealed the deal. With nothing else for it, he waited until the swimming mud in his head settled, then set about retrieving what appeared to be a note from his windshield and dragged his sorry ass back into the ER. Just what he needed.

"It's just a bang on the head, Cam," Michael snapped at the charge nurse, deflecting Cam's attempt to pry open the wound's edges. "Leave it."

Anger flared in the nurse's pretty eyes as he stepped into

Michael's space and jabbed a finger at his chest. "Is being a trauma doctor not enough of a fucking rush for you, you have to get mugged as well? And what about that guy who was out front looking for you earlier? Make sure you tell Mark about him. Christ, man. You've given me a mound of fucking paperwork to complete, not to mention Health and Safety crawling up my arse tomorrow. And stop dripping blood on my floor."

Michael stared at the charge nurse, open-mouthed. Cam *never* lost his shit. *Oops.* He reached for Cam's hand. "Sorry, I'm just being a dick."

Cameron sighed. "Whatever. I'm just pissed I'm not going to get off on time... again." But he made no attempt to pull free of Michael's grip.

They exchanged a silent look, and Cameron finally tugged his hand loose. "What have I said about touching me?"

Michael grinned. "Are my balls in mortal danger?"

The charge nurse patted his cheek. "They would be if I thought I could find them. Now, if you're done screwing up my day, I have work to do."

AN HOUR later and Michael had completed all the incident reports Cam had thrown his way. Mark Knight arrived at some point to walk him through his statement and collect security footage, though there was little hope of any useful evidence. Both in the car park and the ER reception the man had worn his hoodie up and kept his head low. The detective also took charge of the note Michael had retrieved from his windscreen, something he'd chosen not to share with Cam. The nurse was freaked enough as it was.

Keep your mouth shut about who you saw in the club if you don't want that pretty face of yours shredded.

. . .

Charming. So, not exactly a random mugging, then. Michael didn't know what to think about that other than being monumentally pissed off. He was supposed to go in and look at mug shots the next morning, but Mark said to give it a day. The knock on his head wasn't going to help a valid ID.

Michael bristled at the implication. He knew what he'd seen, and he wasn't about to be threatened into silence, but the detective made his concern clear. The cops were all out on this one, and they didn't want anything fucking up a murder conviction for one of their own.

Mark also drummed into Michael the need to be extra vigilant with his security at home and at work until they got to the bottom of it. He'd then left, promising to call the next day, and with that Michael headed home with a freaking headache the size of Africa.

It was 3:00 a.m. when he woke with a churning cesspool in his stomach, crawling skin, and his heart pounding out of his chest. White corridors and flashing lights slowly gave way to the soft green curtains of his bedroom—the iron-tanged stench of blood in his nose, and the heart-wrenching sound of a woman's cries the last things to fade.

He pushed himself off the floor and sucked a bucketload of air into his lungs. He focused on his breathing and reining in the fear mushrooming in his head. It was the first panic attack in months. He'd really thought that shit was over. *Think again, asshole.*

Familiar tremors rolled through his fingers as the craving hit, that desperation for something to settle the flight of terror in his gut. His tongue rolled over his lips, and the thought oozed in like a slick stain on his heart. A drink. Just to get his panic back under wraps and let him sleep. Michael mentally slapped himself. *Yeah, right, idiot. One drink and a fuckload of months clambering back on the wagon. Been there, got the T-shirt.*

Marcia. Just the name was enough to cue the damn tears, let alone the nightmare. *Goddammit. Why couldn't he just let it go?* Cute as hell at ten, she'd have been damn beautiful by womanhood. Latino skin with electric-blue eyes, cascading copper-blond hair, and great cheekbones. But he'd ripped that chance away. Dr Michael fucking Oliver, who hadn't been able to pull his head out of his ass long enough to figure out the kid's right renal artery had been sliced damn near through when the truck slammed into the rear of the small Toyota and threw her clear through the front windshield. Funnily enough, not having her seat belt fully secured had probably saved Marcia from immediate death. The impact had propelled the girl from the small Toyota before it was crushed flat as a paper plate, sending her mother, who was driving, to an early and undeserved grave.

Michael understood none of that was on him. Shit happens and life sucks sometimes. If you couldn't leave the guilt and grief in the room, you didn't survive as an ER doctor. He'd had no control over the accident, but the minute Marcia was rolled into his trauma room, that was his turf. He called the shots and took the hits. And that night, eighteen months ago, he'd taken the biggest hit of his career.

She'd come in spewing blood from a half-dozen major lacerations and a deep, sucking chest wound to her lower left lung from being impaled on a damn lawn sprinkler spike when she'd landed. It was chaos. The kid was blue, hungry for oxygen, and with a morbidly downward-tracking pulse and blood pressure. They got blood up and running, got her lungs plugged and vented, then found and tied off a nick to her femoral artery that had dumped nearly a litre of blood onto the trauma room floor in less than ten minutes.

With the obvious shit attended to, Michael had completed a more thorough top to toe, called for blood work and radiology, and allowed the girl's aunt to duck in for a two-minute visit. Then he'd stepped outside the room to consult with a neurologist. He'd been gone less than a minute when the code alert called him back. The girl was damn near flatlining. *What the fuck?*

Apparently, the minute they'd tried to move her for the X-ray, Marcia bottomed out. Best guess, a hidden bleeder. But where? There was no time to get her to surgery. It was either get her open where she lay or book her a toe tag. But where to open up? Michael would get only one shot. Everyone held his or her breath. Red wire or blue? He opened her left side, directly under the lung injury, betting on the proximity to suggest a logical connection. But what he found was a lake of blood, and in seconds the girl was dead. A postmortem would reveal the right renal artery had been partially severed, not by the sprinkler spike but a splinter from a fractured rib, a fracture that would've shown on the aborted set of X-rays.

No one blamed him. Michael had done everything expected of him and no one suggested otherwise. But Michael knew. Going over his scrawled handover notes, he saw a paramedic's mention of a crunching sensation in the lower right rib area, but it was nothing compared to the girl's obvious injuries, so Michael hadn't made the connection. But it was his fucking job to make the connections, to paint a fucking picture and save a life. It didn't matter that no one blamed him, Michael blamed himself. And with that, Michael's perfectly ordered little world blew apart.

Cue the indulgent self-recriminations, the nightmares, and the drinking. Not original but effective. Always sober during his rostered shifts, outside of those days Michael was a fucking disaster. Simon had been so patient, so understanding, so irritatingly supportive. He'd managed to hide his drinking for six months but then made the mistake of answering a call for an extra pair of hands in the ER on his day off. He'd felt fine, but his manager had smelled the alcohol from Michael's previous night's efforts and breathalysed him. He had blown well over the legal limit to even drive. To be truthful, he'd scared himself.

He was sent home on a month's leave to sort his shit out, lucky to keep his job. The fact he wasn't rostered that day but had been a last-minute ring-in, ultimately saved his bacon. He checked himself into rehab, got his life on track, forced Simon to cut and run so he wouldn't have to deal with or talk to anyone, and returned to work. Not long after, encouraged by his manager, he applied for a medical exchange in New Zealand, figuring a change of scenery couldn't hurt.

He was now about a year sober, but fuck he missed it. Especially on nights like this.

He held out his hand, relieved to find the shaking eased. A shower and some binge television would sort the rest. Maybe then he could grab another couple hours of sleep. He could only hope.

WITH A beer in hand, Josh took a long guzzle and crumpled onto the couch. Every muscle ached, every joint rubbed like sandpaper. "When the fuck did I get so old?" he grumbled, eyeing Paris, curled at his feet.

The two-day training exercise had been gruelling to say the least. Delta 4 Canine Section had been tasked to work alongside search-and-rescue southwest of Auckland in the Waitakere Ranges. Rainfall had meant the tracks were slick with mud, ensuring both dogs and handlers spent most of their time filthy wet. Paris had done well, with Josh's team responsible for the eventual capture of the "fugitive."

Josh had made the most of the opportunity to catch up with colleagues he hadn't seen for a while, but bad weather meant the exercise was overlong and exhausting. He had, however, taken the plunge and accepted an invitation to coffee from one of the search-and-rescue guys. It took a minute, but eventually it came to him. Brent.

The guy was short but cute, had a Harley and a nice full sleeve of tatts. He spent perhaps a little too much time talking about both, but he seemed nice enough. Much more his style than Michael Oliver. So look at him, then, going out on a date and all. That should shut the others up. It would be worth it just for that. Wouldn't it? *Fuck.*

Katie had stepped in, as usual, to look after Sasha while he'd been gone, depositing her home just minutes after Josh walked in the door. God, he loved that smile on his daughter's face, so fricking pleased to see him.

Katie had seemed a bit distracted, not her usual bubbly self, but Josh was too tired to delve into the whys of that. She refused the offer of a drink and left them to it. And after hearing an exhaustive account of her time from Sasha, Josh had deposited a yawning daughter into bed and finally relaxed.

He finished his beer and was thinking about a refill when heavy footsteps on the kitchen floor stayed his meagre effort to rise. With Paris sounding no alarm at the new arrival, Josh didn't have to think too hard about who it might be.

"Grab more beer on your way in, douchebag," he shouted.

"Already there," Mark answered, ambling in with two bottles in hand. Depositing them on the coffee table, he sank to his knees next to Paris, who dove in for a slobbery kiss before running a mad circle around the detective, whining softly.

"Hello there, gorgeous," Mark cooed softly, grabbing the shepherd's dark ruff and pulling him in forehead to forehead. "Missed me, huh?"

"Don't encourage him," Josh grumbled. Mark and Paris had a long-standing bromance to rival his own relationship with the shepherd, though it wasn't unrelated to the fact the detective spoiled him rotten at every opportunity.

"Aw, poor baby." Mark stood, his fingers tapping Paris's nose. "Daddy's got a stick up his butt, huh?"

"Fuck off." Josh flipped Mark off, then sent him a grin.

They'd known each other since their teenage years, and along with Katie, the two had been his main support when Anna, Sasha's mother, had left them to it and sought greener pastures when Sasha was barely six months old. Anna had become pregnant after a drunken one-nighter with Josh while he was still fucked-up and stupid enough to be tucked snugly into his closet. She'd handed over custody to Josh with barely a backward glance.

Josh "came out" pretty damn near the minute he'd thrown the remainder of Anna's clothes in the bin. Anna's parents helped with Sasha as best they could, but they were much older. Josh's own parents, true to homophobic form, had been, in their words, appalled and sickened by Josh's "gay" revelation, and not much had changed since. The unresolved issue wept like an open wound in the family, but Josh had learned to live with it. They adored their grandchild— the only reason he bothered keeping in touch. Sasha, though, was increasingly more reluctant to spend time with them, as they made little attempt to keep their bigoted views hidden from their grand-daughter. It was a conversation Josh knew he couldn't avoid much longer.

Josh had heard nothing from Anna until a phone call a year ago. Married to an architect, she had a child on the way, was living in suburban New York, and had decided it was time. Took her long enough. Josh was all kinds of wary, but for Sasha's sake he listened. Now, mother and daughter Skyped every month or so, and Josh prayed one day Anna might actually visit. Sasha still had a lot of healing yet to do.

Seated in the recliner, Mark raised his beer. "Here's to kids, dogs, and fucking piss-awful weather."

Josh snorted, returning the gesture.

"Two bucks in the jar, detective," Sasha yelled from her bedroom. "That's inappropriate language for a child my age to be exposed to."

Mark's grin widened. "Jesus, mate," he whispered. "She's like eleven going on seventeen. When did that happen? I'm gonna have to watch my mouth."

"I know, I know." Josh glanced toward the hall. "I'm seriously fucked for the foreseeable teenage future. Hang on." He carried his beer to the hall, closing the door to Sasha's room and then the lounge door as well, before taking up his spot on the couch once again.

"She's asked to go to a boy's party," Josh whispered. "Jamie some-one." The fact that Mark's eyes nearly bugged out of his face as much as Josh's had was of some relief.

"Fuck."

"Yeah," Josh sighed. "Fuck. I said no, of course. So then she told me she wasn't a baby anymore and that I was going all 'psycho parent' on her. That the boy was thirteen and just a friend. That they weren't going to be raiding the booze cupboard or making out in the bedroom or nothing."

Mark choked on his beer for the second time. "Holy shit. So what did you say?"

Josh slumped in his seat. "Fuck. I said I'd think about it. And I'd have to ring the parents."

Mark sniggered. "Well, that told her real good, huh? I take it she gave you the pathetic 'I love you so much, Daddy, and I'll be such a good girl' look, am I right?"

Josh hunkered down and took a long swig of beer. "Maybe." He made a mental note to stockpile some Prozac.

"You are so fucked," his friend whispered. "She's got you pegged from here to Sunday and back."

"Tell me something I don't know," Josh grumbled.

Mark shook his head. "I am never gonna have kids."

"Only because no one would have your sorry arse."

"And I'm damn proud of that fact. I can't deal with all that clingy shit."

Josh booted him with his foot. "Change of subject, please?"

"Fine." Mark stretched his long legs out in front of him. "So, I got a call from your good friend, Michael Oliver, on Monday, while you were busy playing games in the bush."

Josh's eyes widened. "And? On second thought, let me guess. He wants to apologise for being such an obnoxious prick."

Mark snorted, choking on his beer and sending it spattering down the front of his Pretenders T-shirt. "You have a real problem with him, don't you?" He flicked the droplets off.

Josh said nothing.

Mark shook his head. "Whatever. Anyway, he called because someone left a nasty note on the good doctor's car, at work. He caught them in the act, but the guy threw him to the ground and took off. The note pretty much warned him to stay away from the police and forget he saw anyone in the club that night or they'd 'shred his face.'"

"What?" Josh rocked forward on his chair.

"Yeah, exactly what I thought. Seems our knife guy isn't just some lackey. Someone like that would've just gone to ground and hoped for the best. This warning reeks of bigger fish at play."

"Is he okay? Michael?" Josh tried for casual, as if Michael hadn't been the subject of Josh's jack-off shower fantasies for the last four days.

Mark grinned, not fooled for a minute. "A nasty cut above the eye, nothing more. He's got some grit, though. Never even questioned ringing it in."

Josh felt a sudden urge to check on the doctor but what would he say? He didn't want to encourage Michael but—"You get a description?"

"Nada. Guy wore a hoodie, and Michael only caught a side view before he hit the deck."

"Wow." Josh sat back, thinking. "Kind of unexpected. You think it's serious? Is Michael in danger?"

Mark shrugged, rolling his beer bottle on the arm of the chair. "Who knows? Just thought you'd be interested, seeing as how you seem to have this weird connection with the guy."

Josh glared. "I don't have *any* connection with him." Other than the irritating fact that he couldn't get his mind off him, of course.

Mark rolled his eyes dramatically. "Of course you don't."

Josh ignored the comment. "Are you guys taking the threat seriously?"

Mark nodded. "Yeah, but there's not much we can do without any leads. At least Michael isn't backing down, and he's all for testifying. We need him, considering you saw zip of the offender, and Jackson really didn't see too much more. For what it's worth, I think you're wrong about Michael. He's okay."

"Yeah, he's a fucking riot."

Wednesday was a crappy day in the ER. The weather had thrown torrential rain and high winds into the usual chaos of school and rush-hour traffic. Toss a few idiots behind the wheel, and you had the perfect cocktail. The volatile mix resulted in five motor vehicle accidents before noon. None involved fatal or even major trauma injuries but that didn't stop them from eating up hours and hours of paperwork and filling the treatment rooms while people were stacked up in the waiting room like a parking lot. Not to mention Michael's head had throbbed like a bitch through the whole day.

Mark had called Michael as promised on Tuesday afternoon, only to inform him that the car park security footage had given them nothing more to work with, so there was little more they could do at that point. They still wanted him to look through their digitised mug shots, so he'd obliged by going in after work but hadn't been able to nail an ID as yet, although he'd only made it through about half the images so far. He was going back tomorrow. And shock horror, he'd even exchanged a few texts with Josh, who'd contacted Michael to ask if he was okay. What the fuck was he gonna say to that? No, and he'd really love it if the sexy man could find time to drop by and hold his hand, or something else, for a bit? Hardly. Still, the fact he'd checked on Michael at all had left a not-unpleasant warmth simmering in his chest. One that had remained hard to shift.

Home at last, Michael had crashed out on his couch, watching a rerun of a Bulls-Celtics game, glad he only had one shift left in the week. He was still debating whether to go to the young cop's funeral on Friday—not something he'd usually do, but he felt a strange urge to attend. Sunday was a late shift, so he'd be able to make softball practice. It surprised him how much he was looking forward to that, and he tried not to delve too deeply into the whys of that, like seeing Josh again. Josh had featured in one too many of Michael's jerk-off sessions as it was. Still, at least he'd come in useful for something.

Scout was curled in his lap having forsaken his family home yet again, busy kneading Michael's thigh, uncomfortably close to his groin.

"Unsheathe those claws and you're in big trouble," he warned the cat, covering his balls. The cat fixed him with a bored expression and continued his mission unabated.

"Enough." He carried the cat through the open sliding doors and deposited him on the flagstones outside. "Home, mister." He flicked Scout's tail and shooed him toward his neighbour's apartment. The animal promptly turned tail and headed off in the complete opposite direction.

Before sliding the door closed, Michael caught sight of another tenant hauling his trash to the bins in the car park. *Damn. Collection day.* He grabbed his own bags and followed his neighbour's example, then locked the glass slider behind him and collapsed back on the couch. The Celtics were ahead by six points. Things were looking up.

Seconds later, as the Celtics point man was wrapping up a three-pointer, Michael felt his neck prickle. He glanced up in time to catch a moving reflection in the glass sliders opposite. Someone behind him. *Shit.* He spun but failed to register a damn thing before his head exploded, and he was slammed to the floor, taking half the couch with him.

A rain of blows and kicks pummelled his stomach, kidneys, and thighs from several directions at once. More than one person—had to be. Agonising pain lanced through his body, sometimes from two directions at once. He couldn't breathe, let alone think, with no time to recover between the blows. A strangled cry spewed from his throat, all he could manage under the blitz of kicks. He dragged himself forward only to be booted to his side, rolling to his stomach to try and protect his face. *Fuck.* It needed to stop. *Goddammit.*

He wrapped his arms around his head to protect himself from the heaviest of the blows, but the force of the beating made its way through regardless. His ear split under one particularly vicious kick, and his skull rocked as another connected with his temple. His head reeled, and he was a whisper away from blacking out.

The half-empty soda bottle he'd held seconds ago lay in sight of his faltering gaze, its contents soaking the floor close to his head. If he could only get to it... Then it was gone, and the glass coffee table exploded above him. Shards rained down on him, more than a few finding their way into his skin with stinging accuracy. Then things went quiet.

Footsteps landed close to his head, glass crunching underfoot. "Should've listened, Doc," a muffled voice spoke close to his ear.

He vomited blood and bile onto the rug, too stunned to lift his face clear. The room dipped in and out of focus. He knew he had to remain conscious but... *fuck*, everything hurt. And nothing in his body goddamn worked. Then his head was jerked back, and a pair of Converse, blue with white laces, came into view along with a hand wrapped around the neck of a broken bottle.

"If you don't want that pretty face shredded..." The words came to Michael with startling clarity. *Shit.* He tried to shout only to choke instead as blood and saliva poured down his throat and he threw up again. *No...*

"No one to blame but yourself, Doc," the muffled voice continued, the jagged bottle twirling ominously before Michael's eyes. "All you had to do was pay attention. No cops, no statement, no ID. Simple."

Someone tilted his chin up and blood ran into his one remaining open eye. Half a face swam in and out of view, crimson, smiling, mouth covered and sunglasses in place.

"A shame to mess with such a pretty face. Not sure your patients will want you anywhere near them after we're done. Your cruising days are over. Best you'll hope for is a pity fuck. Or maybe I'll sell your arse to some gang as a fucking glory hole. Lots of options."

Michael hacked up another stream of fluid, and damn near choked on it. He tried again to shout but all that came out was a low groan.

"Hold his head," the voice directed, kicking the collapsed steel frame of the coffee table aside.

Oh God. This was it. Michael felt his body hauled off the floor and someone pulled his head back. Three or four men, Michael decided. The hand holding the bottle drew back, and Michael cowered in on himself, praying to anyone who might be listening.

"Michael!" A voice at the door.

The bottle froze in place. *Thank Christ.*

"Michael?" Same voice.

God, yes. Scout's owners. Michael tried to shout. Sobbed instead.

"Michael, what the hell's going on? Donna's called the police. Are you okay?"

"Fuck." The bottle disappeared. "Later, Doc. You best change your attitude and shut your fucking mouth, or we'll be back to finish this."

Michael heard nothing more as his head exploded and everything went black.

Voices swam in Michael's ears, distant murmurings. A hand on his arm, a weight on his leg. He tried to pry his eyes open, but his body refused to cooperate. He lifted his arm, but something pushed it back down again.

"You've an IV in there, dickhead," a familiar voice chided gently.

Cameron. Oh fuck. Fuck. Thank God.

"Welcome back." The charge nurse patted his arm. "Jesus Christ, you do have a flair for the dramatic. Hold still."

His eyes were wiped, his face cleaned. "Ow!"

"Baby," the charge nurse scolded, but Cam's voice was anything but steady. "Try your right eye, it's the better of the two. You took a fair whack above the eyebrow, same one you kissed the asphalt with, by the way, shiner's probably gonna be awesome. The leather boys will love you."

Michael groaned. "Don't make me laugh." He tried to shuffle upright in the bed, but everything hurt. It felt like he'd been hit by a freight train. "Fuck me."

Cam snorted. "Not the way you look, sunshine."

"Shut up." He finally got his right eye cranked open. "What the fuck happened? Scratch that, I remember. Jesus, someone got into my apartment. Must have been when I took the trash out."

Cam said nothing, continuing to clean his face as the washbowl water turned a fetching shade of deep red.

He winced. "Ow, ow, ow."

Cam apologised. "You took a fair few blows and a particularly good one in the head. Lucky for you it probably glanced off your thick skull. Jesus, Michael. Some arsehole's taken a real dislike to you."

The nurse set the cloth down and patted Michael's cheek affectionately. "At least now you look less like you've just finished five rounds in an MMA ring." He checked Michael's IV and added a syringe of something to the chamber. "I take it you think it's the same motherfucker from the car park?"

Michael frowned, and fuck, even that hurt. "You know about that?"

Cam simply arched a brow and eyeballed him.

"Sorry. It was stupid of me not to tell you."

"It was."

Michael glanced at the syringe. "What was that?"

"Antibiotics."

"Which one?"

"A good one. Now stop being a pain in the arse and let us do the medical shit for a change." He started tidying and cleaning the room.

Michael frowned. "You don't do this bedside stuff anymore, Mr Very Important Charge Nurse."

Cam's hesitation was brief, and Michael would've missed it if he hadn't been paying attention. Keeping his back to Michael, Cam bundled the bloody sheets into the linen trolley as he answered. "Let's just say I have a vested interest in getting your sorry arse back to work as soon as possible and leave it at that."

"Hey," Michael spoke softly. The charge nurse sighed and turned to face him, those expressive tawny eyes moist, their copper liner smudged. Now that was a first. Michael held out a hand.

Cam took it. "Okay, I admit it," he said quietly. "You scared me.

You were pretty messed up when they brought you in, bloodied face, clothes ripped, bruising from shoulder to hip, not to mention you'd been out for the count in your apartment. You were a fucking mess. So, yeah, I've been a bit... concerned."

Michael managed a smug, painful grin. "Aw, you really do like me."

"Fuck off." Cam prodded Michael's good shoulder. "I just can't afford to replace you at the moment."

"Right," Michael chuckled and then winced with the effort. "Now tell me what shape I'm in other than a slightly fat eye and... fuck, my ear hurts. What's with that?"

"Leave it alone." Cam brushed Michael's hand away from his dressed ear. "Basically, you got the shit beat out of you, but nothing life-threatening. You woke up pretty quick in your apartment but have been nodding on and off ever since, plus we gave you an analgesic after the scans and radiology were clear. Whoever it was didn't have much time with you, from what I gather. Your neighbour got to your door quick. Said his cat leapt a metre in the air from the sound of the glass exploding."

Michael made a mental note to get some fresh meat for Scout.

Cam continued, "Your right side took the brunt. Right forehead, split ear, but nothing you won't heal from, though the bruising is gonna be awesome. Some contusions on your shoulder, stomach, and right kidney, but you aren't pissing blood, so that's a bonus."

Michael scowled. "Yeah, fucking fantastic."

"You spit up some blood, both in the apartment and again in the ambulance but nothing for the last hour, and the scans and stomach washings don't show anything major, so we'll just keep an eye on it. Bloods are fine. The team wants you to stay overnight, but I figure without due cause that's got little to no chance of happening, right?"

Michael looked at Cam sideways. "None."

"Figured. So, once this antibiotic is through, we'll allow you to go, under a couple of provisos. One, you aren't on your own tonight.

Concussion, remember? And two, you get your butt back here in the morning for a check-over. Oh, and you're off for five days at least."

"Five days! But—"

"Shut it or I'll make it ten." Cam's eyes blazed. "Aside from the fact you couldn't run a cardiac arrest to save yourself, you need to get all this police shit sorted. I won't have my staff under threat because you're in some bad guy's sights."

Michael swallowed an angry retort. Cam was right. "Agreed." He swung his legs over the side of the bed and nearly blacked out.

"Whoa there." Cam steadied him. "My point exactly."

Christ almighty, his body felt like every nerve had been set on fire. "I'm okay. Just moved a bit quick, that's all." He held up the arm with the IV. "Can I get this thing out?"

Cam flicked the empty chamber and ran a little fluid through to chase the drug. "Yep. All done." He removed the cannula and put pressure on the site. "You want an elephant Band-Aid?"

Michael sent him a withering look.

"So, that's a no." The nurse taped some gauze in place and stood back. "The police want a chat before you leave."

Michael groaned. "Of course they do."

"And you're not setting one foot out that door without me knowing exactly who'll be with you tonight. I'd offer my couch, but I've got family staying."

"I get the message. I'll sort something." *God knows how.* Michael knew few people he could impose on like this. "Tell the cops to come in."

Cam smirked in a way that prickled Michael's neck. "Your clothes are in a bag under the bed. Had to cut them off, sorry. But you can borrow the scrubs, the colour's quite good on you."

He threw a pillow Cam's way, but the charge nurse dodged, and it was caught by Mark, poised in the doorway.

Cam waggled his eyebrows at the detective. "I expect a dance next time I see you at the G, Mark. You've been avoiding me."

Mark grinned. "You're on, gorgeous. And I would never avoid

you, you make me look good, I can't dance for shit."

Cam laughed. "Right. Gentlemen, if you'll excuse me, I need to fix my makeup."

Mark placed the pillow on the bench and took a seat. It was only then that Michael noticed the second man standing behind him. Josh. *Fuck.* He really, really didn't have the energy for this.

"Well, well, if it isn't Batman and Robin," he sighed. "I guess you want the story in triplicate, detective?" He spoke to Mark, ignoring Josh.

"That, and we thought we'd come to offer you our frequent flyer card." Mark smiled. "Every third assault gets you a free ride in the police vehicle of your choice and a gift box set of handcuffs. I'm sure you could find a suitable use for them."

Michael laughed in spite of himself. "I'm sure I could." He glanced at Josh. "What's he doing here?"

"He lives close to you. We used Paris to try and pick up a trail."

Oh. "And?"

"As far as the next road, where they must have had a car waiting."

Shit. "Surprise, surprise."

"However," the detective continued, "we did get a description of one of them from a guy parking his car outside the apartment block as they ran past. Parts of it gel with the one you gave us of the man at the club. European, six foot, dark hair, and a tattoo of some description on the right side of his neck, but nothing more. Yours is better, but at least they tie up."

"I guess that's something," Michael muttered. "There were more than two of them, I think."

"Go on," Mark encouraged.

He told his story while the two men listened without interruption. It was like he was almost disconnected from the whole thing, like he was talking about a movie he'd watched. That was until he spoke about the broken bottle. That's when his voice cracked, and he had to ask for a glass of water while he got himself under control. If the other men noticed, they said nothing, for which he was grateful.

Christ. How could he have forgotten that? How different things could have ended. He gripped his hands together to quell the shaking and managed to finish. Mark clarified a few details and they all sat in silence as the detective added to his notes.

Michael was acutely aware of Josh Rawlins's constant scrutiny. He flicked a glance Josh's direction, absurdly pleased to see him flush and look away. *Not interested, my ass.*

Mark tucked his notebook in his pocket and pinned Michael with a sober gaze. "I don't have to tell you that you were damn lucky tonight. This guy clearly means business and that implies someone higher up the gang hierarchy than we'd thought. High enough to garner support and muscle to shut you up. A low-flying gangbanger couldn't do it. He'd be hung out to dry by his bosses rather than risk further attention from the police. And then there's the vexing question of how they even knew you'd been in to view the ID photos."

Michael raised a hand. "Before you ask, no one I know, including Cameron, knew anything about that. I wasn't about to advertise after the note. I'm not stupid."

"Okay, so that's a potential problem." Mark nodded thoughtfully. "Unless they had eyes at the station. We may have a leak." Mark flicked his gaze to Josh, then back.

Mark got to his feet. "The doctors say you're okay to leave but you need company the next twenty-four hours. You also need to ramp up security on your apartment before you contemplate returning or find some temporary accommodation elsewhere. For the time being, your apartment is off limits anyway, until forensics is done. Is that going to be a problem?"

Michael cocked a brow. "You're not offering me protection?"

Mark snorted. "This is New Zealand, precious, not Hollywood. Budget won't stretch to that. Currently you're just a witness providing a description. If you can positively ID the guy, then the powers that be might be more forthcoming."

Michael's stomach sank. "Fuck. So what if he comes back to finish the job?"

Mark glanced Josh's way again. "That's why we suggest you stay somewhere else in the interim and get security to accompany you to and from your car here at work. Cam is organising extra security around the ER as we speak. I'm sorry, but it's all we can do at the moment."

Fuck. He should've just said no to the damn photo ID. *Yeah, never going to happen.*

"So, any thoughts on where you'll stay? We'll need an address," Mark asked.

Michael blew out a sigh. "To be honest, no. I haven't been here long enough to have people I can call on like that. I'll just do a motel."

"I gather you need someone with you, though, for tonight at least?"

Michael rubbed his hand over his face, wincing at the developing bruising. "Shit. I forgot about that," he snapped wearily. "And fucking Florence Cameron Nightingale won't let me leave without that being nailed down."

He caught a soft snort of laughter from Josh and glanced his way. With his guard down and a smile on his face, Josh had moved from stupid hot and sexy to just plain devastating. *Christ almighty.* He couldn't stop from returning his smile. "I know, right? Damn fairy scares the shit out of me."

"Get in line," Mark snickered.

Josh pushed himself off the wall and tapped Mark on the shoulder. "A word?" he asked.

The detective frowned and followed Josh out the door. While they were gone, Michael managed to haul up a pair of green scrubs without too much difficulty and was just finishing when the two men returned.

"Done with the secret squirrel routine, then?" he asked, rolling his eyes.

"Yeah, sorry about that." Mark stood at the end of the bed, hands resting on the footboard. "We have a possible solution for you, for tonight at least."

Michael's gaze flitted between the two men. "Why do I think I'm not going to like this?" he asked. "Don't tell me. It involves a room with bars, crappy food, and drunk neighbours."

The detective smirked. "Wish we'd thought of that. Plan B perhaps? Can only make plan A look a winner, right?"

"Go on, then, tell me plan A."

"Okay. So, Josh has a sister who lives just down the road from his place. He called, and she agreed to you spending the night there. She's a trained first aider and has no problem with keeping an eye on you. In the morning, Josh will give you a lift back to the hospital. That gives you twenty-four hours to sort other accommodation."

Michael opened his eyes wide. The idea was ludicrous on so many levels. One, he hated Josh—well, not entirely true, but there was no way he wanted to be beholden to the dick. Second, it was plain and simple a stupid suggestion. "No way. If those guys track me there, I'd be putting her at risk."

Josh answered, "Only we will know where you are. And the commander. No one else will be told."

"What if there *is* a police leak like you said?"

"I repeat," Josh reassured, "no one else will know. You're not under any official protection. This isn't official, it's a private arrange- ment, and she's a civilian. And Katie is fine about it. I offered to swap with her, but she wouldn't have it. And I'll leave Paris there for the night as well, just to be sure."

"You can do that?"

Josh nodded. "We're off duty until tomorrow afternoon, and I live only a few houses down. I'll drop you on my way home. She's waiting for us."

Michael's head spun. The offer felt too close, too... nice to accept, but really, he was past arguing anything tonight. He was tired and sore beyond ridiculous. He just wanted to get his body into bed and sleep. So he raised both hands in surrender. "Whatever gets me the hell out of here tonight," he agreed. "One of you gets to tell Florence, though."

CHAPTER FOUR

Josh spent a restless night with Katie and Michael Oliver mere houses away. He'd been worried sick about Michael, more than seemed entirely warranted if he was honest with himself, and leaving Paris there hadn't eased his concerns much either. He should've insisted Katie swap places with him, but she could be damned stubborn if she set her mind to it. That aside, she'd really come through for them, and he owed her big time, again.

As much as Michael Oliver was a pain in the arse, he needed their help. He'd had the crap beaten out of him and needed a safe place to stay. And Josh wouldn't sleep until he made sure that happened. For whatever reason, he felt protective of the man. Michael was a visitor to New Zealand, after all—no family, few friends. And if the reasons maybe went deeper than that, well that was no one's business but Josh's, right? With only six of them knowing his location, chances were slim anyone would find him.

Josh's own house had been off limits, of course—he didn't want Sasha involved in any way. Plus, a witness staying with a police officer might raise a few eyebrows, even if Josh wasn't directly involved in the investigation itself. Josh's boss had been clear on that. Katie's place was cutting it fine, but it had got the nod of approval from the prosecutor since Josh had already been dismissed as a potential witness, having not actually seen the assailant and there were others better placed to testify. Jackson was taking point on that. And the arresting officer of the second man would have his day in court for that side of things. So Josh was in the clear.

Katie called before she left for work. Michael was still asleep. She'd woken him twice in the night to find him lucid both times. Josh organised his daughter for school, showered, and threw a razor around his face before heading to his sister's place, a 1970s spacious brick townhouse. Over the years she'd shared it with various flatmates to reduce costs but was now earning enough from the dive shop she owned and operated to afford the luxury of living alone.

At the back door, he paused and took a deep breath, ignoring the flutter in his gut at being alone with the doctor for the first time other than in a car. He could hear Paris through the door, the shepherd's soft, welcoming whines a balm to his ridiculous nerves. Even just for a night, he'd missed the mutt. He'd known handlers suffer months of depression following the death of their dogs, the intense work and home relationship 24/7 providing the glue in each other's lives.

"Hey, boy," he whispered, opening the door and dropping to one knee. Paris ran his rough tongue over Josh's face, finding every crevice, ears included, whimpering nonstop.

Josh roughed his neck and pushed him away. "How's our charge?" He made his way to the guest room door and knocked. No answer. He quietly popped the door open to find Michael facing away, snoring softly, the bedclothes tangled around his legs. The waistband of a pair of black Calvin Klein briefs peeked just above the sheet.

So sue him if his gaze lingered just a little longer than necessary on Michael's smooth skin and thick biceps, and on the large tribal tattoo that ran the width of his back and disappeared into those briefs. But when his gaze landed on the mottled blue-green bruises blooming over Michael's ribs and loin, an unexpected surge of anger and concern fired through him.

Michael had taken more than just a couple of hefty kicks. He was hurting badly, and seeing the reminder in living colour had Josh seething all over again for those responsible. He'd spent most of the night figuratively sitting on his hands so he didn't bug Mark constantly for updates on whether they'd arrested the fuckers yet. His friend would let him know if they had, but still. Josh closed the door and left Michael sleeping as he battled his emotions. This was more than just physical attraction and Josh knew it. Not that it changed anything.

He smiled at Paris waiting patiently at his side. As always, the shepherd's presence calmed him. "Right, Tonto, coffee and lots of it." He slid the glass door open to let Paris come and go, emptied a couple of ibuprofen and an antibiotic onto the breakfast bar with a glass ready to go for Michael, and set about making breakfast. Michael was Josh's responsibility while he was here, and Katie would boil him in paint thinner if he wasn't a good host.

The bread was in the toaster when Michael himself appeared in the doorway, running his hands through his roughed-up hair. Josh's breath hitched. *Sweet Jesus.* Shirtless and fresh from bed, the sexy sight evaporated Josh's every rational thought. That damn kiwi tattoo instantly drew his attention, lying over Michael's heart amidst a soft flush of chocolate hair that arced down into a tempting treasure trail. And there was no hiding what looked like a hefty package behind those scrubs hanging low on Michael's hips, low enough for Josh to wonder what had happened to the briefs. The fastening was knotted altogether too loosely—wouldn't take much... *Oh for crap's sake.*

"Michael. You're awake," he said, his gaze hovering over those damn bruises. *Shit.* He was behaving like such an arsehole. Ogling the poor man's body when he'd been through the fucking wringer the night before. "Come here."

Michael's gaze narrowed, the bruising around one eye looking tender but not yet closing the lid.

Josh rolled his eyes. "I just want to check those injuries." *Of course he did.* Michael approached and Josh had him turn around, then take a few deep breaths, noting how Michael winced with each one of them. "How bad is the pain?"

"Better than it looks."

"And your head?" Josh leaned in and peered at Michael's eyes. "What day is it? Do you remember what happened—" He reached for the cut above the eye but Michael grabbed his wrist and the heat of his touch nearly seared Josh's arm.

"I'm perfectly fine... Mom."

Josh stepped back and narrowed his gaze. "Knowing you, I would've expected you'd be a great liar. Turns out, not so much."

Michael's eyes remained on Josh. "I usually am. Why, have you been worried about me?"

"Yes." Michael looked startled and Josh realised he'd actually said that out loud. *Shit.*

Michael grinned slyly. "Good to know."

Neither looked away as a heated silence rose awkwardly between them.

Michael broke it first. "Also, I think you've got our professions reversed," he commented dryly. "I'm sore, yes, but things appear to be functioning as they should under the rainbow patchwork. And just for the record, you know nothing about me, Josh. Not for the lack of trying on my part. Just saying."

Josh blinked slowly. Michael was right. He was being an arsehole... again. "Sure."

Michael grinned widely. "There, was that so damn hard?" He reached around and slipped his hand under the waistband of his scrubs to scratch his lower back, dragging the material even lower on his hips and Josh...

Shit. His mouth ran dry and his cock plumped as every scrap of blood plummeted south. The toaster popped beside him, and he jumped in his skin, the scent of burnt bread filling the kitchen. *Goddammit.* By the time he managed to drag his gaze up and knit a couple of intelligent thoughts together, he found nothing but amusement dancing in Michael's expression.

"See something you like?" Michael baited.

And the man was back. Josh ignored the question. He threw the cindered bread in the bin and tried again with a couple of fresh slices. "Coffee's ready. Your pills. Take them." He indicated the medication on the bar and turned to scrutinise the toaster, giving his dick a chance to settle down. One could only hope.

"It could've been my sister out here, arsehole," he grumbled. "Don't you think your scrub top would've been in order, at least?"

Michael appeared at his back, reaching around to fill the glass from the cold tap. Their shoulders brushed, the contact lasting barely seconds. Long enough for Josh to register the delicious heat radiating off Michael.

"Your sister knows I'm gay," Michael countered. "She's nice, by the way." He poured himself a coffee. "Besides, she told me she'd be gone by seven thirty."

Josh rolled his eyes. "So, then all this was for my benefit, I take it?"

Michael snorted. "Don't flatter yourself. I thought I had the house to myself. I hardly expected to find you out here making breakfast, as romantic as that is. You're lucky I didn't stumble out naked."

The image went straight to Josh's dick... again. *Fuck.* The toast popped, and why was that suddenly such an erotic thing?

"I'll take my coffee to the shower," Michael said. "Try and steam out some of the aches."

He left, and Josh threw his tea towel at the wall. Why did he let Michael Oliver get to him? Because he was fucking gorgeous, exactly his type, and Josh was horny as hell after a two-year dry spell, that's why. It wasn't rocket science. The universe was definitely fucking with him.

Singing rose above the shower, and Josh caught the opening lyrics of Rod Stewart's "Do Ya Think I'm Sexy." *Bastard.*

Thirty minutes later they sat across from each other, finishing breakfast. Michael had been unusually quiet since reappearing from the shower. He was still wearing the same scrubs, top and bottom this time, thank Christ. Paris had immediately curled into a ball at Michael's feet, studiously ignoring any jab from Josh to get him to move.

"Leave the poor animal alone," Michael said, finishing up his third cup of coffee. "It really bugs you that he likes me, huh?"

Yes. "Of course not. He's just not allowed to beg for food." Josh collected the plates and moved into the kitchen.

"He's not. He's asleep, for fuck's sake."

Josh let it go. "Feeling any better after your shower? Meds kicking in?"

Michael ran a hand lightly over his ribs and kidney area. "Still feels like someone's run a marathon on my freaking back. And don't get me started on my head, but yes, better than earlier. Thanks for asking."

Josh nodded. "At least nothing was broken, right? Or worse, even?"

"Thank Christ for that. Last thing I need is a stay in my own damn hospital." He stretched his arms over his head, wincing at the pull.

Josh studied him quietly from the kitchen.

"What?" Michael prompted.

"I was just thinking. It must have been bloody scary."

Michael froze and for a minute he said nothing. Then he sank into his chair and his gaze slid from Josh to his coffee. "It was. I just kind of switched off in the end. You know how you get that feeling something is inevitable, and the best you can do is stop fighting and ride it out?"

Josh nodded.

"It was just like that. I hunkered down and prayed, as much of a coward as that might make me appear. Up until I saw that damn broken bottle in front of my face. Then I just fucking panicked." His cheeks pinked as his gaze met Josh's again. "Stupid, huh? I was almost more horrified at living and being scarred for life, than dying there on the rug."

Josh held his gaze. "Not stupid at all. I'd have been just as terrified. You were fucking brave is what you were. You kept your head and did what you had to do. Who knows what might have happened if you'd tried to push things? And you lived because of it."

That same awkward silence built again as the truth of those words settled between them.

It was Michael who once again broke the silence, wriggling in his seat and throwing Josh a smirk. "Well, you should be happy anyway."

"Why's that?" Josh set the dishwasher going. "More coffee?"

"Nah. My kidneys have had enough punishment."

Josh took a seat back at the table. "Why would I be happy?"

Michael slid him a sly smile. "Because I'm not gonna be cruising for a bit looking like this, am I?"

He couldn't help but return the smile and would take the distraction for what it was—Michael closing the wall he'd just let down. "Guess not. Though there's no accounting for taste, right?"

Michael chuckled. "Is that humour, Officer Rawlins? You wanna be careful with that. People might find out you're not such an asshole."

Josh rolled his eyes. "Couldn't have that." He took a mouthful of coffee. "Anyway, it's not so bad, your eye. Wouldn't put many off."

Michael eyed him curiously.

"What?" Josh asked.

Michael looked away. "Nothing. So, what's the plan?"

"I drop you back at the hospital to be checked out. After that, you head for greener and safer pastures until we give you the all-clear."

"Can I get my locks changed and an alarm installed today or are your guys still there?"

"They'll be done by noon. Go ahead."

"They find anything?" Michael reached to stroke the shepherd's head, and Paris tilted it sideways to ensure his fingers reached just the right spot. "You're such a slut," he told the animal.

Josh grinned despite himself. "Nothing yet," he answered. "Have to wait on fingerprints and forensics unless an eyewitness comes forward. The broken bottle's our best bet. There was blood on the neck. As they didn't get the chance to use it, the blood was either splatter from you or it was theirs. Mark thinks they were wearing gloves, but you never know."

Michael sat tense and quiet, avoiding Josh's gaze. The reminder was clearly unnerving and it only convinced Josh that Michael had been way more affected by the whole incident than he'd let on.

After a moment Michael said, "Your sister wants me to stay here... for a bit, or as long as I need, anyway." He glanced sideways at Josh.

Coffee sloshed over the brim of Josh's cup, scalding his hand. "Shit!" He reached for a cloth. "She what?"

"Yeah." Michael caught his eye. "Didn't think she'd mentioned it to you. Don't worry, I can stay at the hospital if it's a problem, which clearly it is." He stood and made for the door.

Josh fumbled for a response. Katie had said nothing on the phone about Michael staying. Why she'd do something like that without checking, he didn't know. "Stop." He blurted out. "Just, um, just hang on a minute, will you? I, ah, just need to talk with her." He stepped outside for some privacy.

She answered on the third ring. "Wondered how long it would take you," she said, and he pictured the smug smile on her face.

"What the hell, sis? You said he could stay?"

"Yeah, I did. It makes sense. No one knows where he is, and he's right down the road for you to keep an eye on. I'll just stay with you till it's over and look after Sasha there. See? Easy."

"No, it makes no sense whatsoever, and it's not easy. What if someone does find him? Then he's right down the road bringing a whole lot of trouble right to your freaking door. Not to mention right in my face while he's there."

"Hold on there. What the hell, Josh? He seems like a nice guy, and did I mention, hot? Thought you'd be happy with him being gay.

Taking care of the tribe, and all that. Besides, it's the right thing to do."

"He's not my tribe, and I don't need you telling me what to do."

Silence.

Damn. "Sorry. But this is exactly what he does to me, screws with my head. He came on to me when I was working a scene, for Christ's sake."

"Oh, well, that changes everything," she mocked. "You're gay, and you were in a gay club, idiot. And I'm guessing he didn't know exactly who you were and what was really happening to start with, right? The guy must be a total douchebag. Obviously needs his head read, and a much better pair of glasses if he came on to you. Oh, and then he went and saved a mate's life. The cheek of the man. He clearly needs to be arrested."

Josh took a deep breath. "Okay, when you say it like that, it does sound stupid."

"Well, duh." Her voice dipped low. "You like him, don't you? You like him, and you can't stand that you do. Hey, I have an idea. How about you give the poor man a chance. Sheesh."

God, he loved her. "You've been talking to Mark," he huffed.

She ignored that. "I did as you asked, by the way, and never mentioned Sasha to him," she said.

"Thanks. I just don't want him up in my business any more than he has to be. And you can stop worrying about me. I did actually listen, and I'm actually meeting a guy for coffee on Saturday." He could almost hear his sister's jaw hit the floor.

"Really? What the hell, Josh? And when exactly were you going to tell me about this?"

"I'm telling you now, and it is just coffee. Now, can we get back to Michael? Are you sure you want to do this?"

Katie sighed. "It's not for long, right?"

"A few days, a week at the most. If he can positively ID someone, then we can probably get him something official. If he can't, then he ceases to be a threat to them, and they *should* leave him alone. In that case he can go back to his apartment."

"Fine. Then we're agreed?"

He groaned loudly. "Yes, okay. He stays here, and you stay with me. Happy?"

"As a clam. Are clams happy? Whatever. You're a good man, Charlie Brown."

"Bye, Katie."

"But—"

Josh hung up and rejoined Michael, who was busy on his phone organising a locksmith. When he was done, he leaned back against the wall and eyeballed Josh.

"Verdict?"

Josh sighed and suspected he pouted as well. Whatever. "You can stay, but Katie comes to my house. Safer that way."

"Really?" Michael was clearly surprised. "And you're okay with that?"

Josh frowned. *No. Yes. Maybe.* "Doesn't matter. It makes sense, and it's what Katie wants."

A flash of what looked like disappointment crossed Michael's face, sliding quickly into schooled indifference. "Right. Well, tell Katie I appreciate the offer, but I'll sort something out at the hospital." He pushed off the wall to leave.

"Don't be an arse," Josh snapped. "I said you could stay."

Michael pinned him with an angry glare. "Look, sunshine, I don't stay anywhere I make people uncomfortable, and I won't be responsible for creating an issue between you and your sister. She's been great. I'll be perfectly fine in one of the doctors' rooms at Auckland Med." He turned away.

"Stop." Josh crossed the floor before he even knew it, put a hand on Michael's shoulder, and spun him slowly. "Don't be stupid. You're safer here." Michael froze on the spot, his eyes cobalt pools of anger, and Josh wanted nothing more than to take a dive into them.

"Take your fucking hands off me," Michael spat.

Paris appeared from nowhere, drawn to the tension. He planted himself alongside Josh, gaze fixed on Michael.

"Sorry." Josh loosened his grip and stepped back. Jesus, what was he doing? "Paris, stay." He drew a couple of slow breaths. "Look, I'm being an arse. Just take the offer. Katie will kill me if you're not here when she gets back."

Michael cocked an eyebrow. "And that's my problem, how?"

Michael's pissy attitude was a potent mix, and yeah, fucking sexy. Josh threw his hands up in defeat. "Fuck if I know. And you're right. It's not your problem. Do whatever you want. I'm done."

Michael stared, the silence hanging thick between them.

"You sure do have a problem with me, don't you?" he said. "What is it? Did someone like me kiss and tell when you were a horny teen full of angst, so you've hated on my type ever since? 'Cause you know what? It was fun for a while, riling you up, but I'm done being the shit under your shoe. Last night scared the fuck out of me, and your little personal freak thing going on here—" He flicked his index finger back and forth between them. "—it just doesn't rate anymore."

Paris growled softly in his throat, tuned in to the threat present in Michael's anger. Michael gave the shepherd a nervous glance but held his ground. Josh quieted the shepherd again and sent him to his mat, unable to come up with a single response to Michael's diatribe. It was too damn close to the truth.

Michael snorted in disgust. "I thought so. Fuck. Someone must've screwed you over well and good. Don't worry, I'll get myself to the hospital. It's been a blast." He spun on his heels.

Without thinking, Josh closed the distance between them in a second, sliding around in front of Michael, whose eyes widened in surprise and then narrowed in irritation. "What the hell do you think you're—" But he never finished the sentence as though suddenly reading the intent in Josh's expression, an intent Josh wasn't sure even *he* understood.

Michael hesitated for just a second, his gaze dipping to Josh's lips, then back up to his eyes, reading the barely formed question there.

Then heat fired in his eyes and he stepped in and hissed, "Yes," crashing his mouth over Josh's and pulling him back until he'd sandwiched himself between Josh and the wall.

Josh had just enough time to wonder what the fuck he was doing before he was all in, remembering to keep his weight off the worst of Michael's injuries. It surged, that inexplicable need he'd carried since he'd first laid eyes on him, desperate to taste and feel what he'd been craving more than air for the last week.

Pinned against the wall, Michael gripped Josh's biceps, his fingers digging in hard, holding Josh in place, keeping the kiss going, but with his lips still closed, as if he'd not entirely made up his mind what he wanted. Josh tentatively ran his tongue along the seam of Michael's lips, licking, nibbling, questioning, and a few seconds later he felt the shift. Michael's shoulders relaxed, his lips gave way, and Josh was inside.

The taste of Michael Oliver exploded over Josh's tongue as their mouths tangled, the kiss bruising and raw. Josh sucked Michael's tongue into his mouth, probed and tasted every inch. Arms encircled his back, pulling him close, as Josh's tongue was stroked, nipped, and dragged back into Michael's mouth. Josh dropped his hands to the doctor's waist, crushing their hips together, encouraged by the rock-solid erection pressed against his own.

Trying to stay aware of Michael's injuries, Josh couldn't contain the urge to gently grind against him, creating a delicious friction, relying on Michael to shove him away if needed. There was apparently no chance of that as Michael responded with a gritty moan and arched into the pressure instead. Jesus, the man smelled and tasted as good as Josh had imagined. Woodsy orange from the shower gel mixed with coffee and something sweet on his tongue. Josh couldn't get enough. A nagging voice pounded away in his head, insisting this was a bad, bad idea, but there was no way Josh was stepping back now.

Hungry for each other, neither seemed willing to break the punishing kiss. Josh suspected it was based on fear that any space between them might end things. Instead there was a constant realignment of lips and hips and crushing demands. Nipping, biting, sucking, taking as much as they could from the other.

Josh snaked a hand between them, cupping Michael's erection through his scrubs, feeling its heft and adding a few rough strokes. *Fuck.* He moaned into Michael's mouth. The guy was commando. Michael immediately responded, pressing his dick hard into Josh's fist, then nipped Josh's lower lip to show his displeasure when Josh withdrew his hand.

Josh grinned against Michael's mouth. "Hang on, handsome. I'll get you there."

He slipped his hand inside Michael's waistband and gripped his erection, skin to skin. *Oh fuck.* He was uncut. *Yum.* Silky and thick, the feel wasn't nearly enough. Josh was desperate to look and taste, but he was too far gone. He ran his thumb over the broad head of Michael's erection, sliding the foreskin back and forth. Then he slicked his hand with precum and began a slow stroke up and down the length.

Michael hummed with pleasure against Josh's mouth and still neither broke contact. With one hand tangled in the back of Josh's hair and the other up under his tee, working the top button of his jeans, Michael held him close. He brushed Josh's erection, and Josh nearly came on the spot. *Fuck.*

At last, the button popped, and Michael's fingers immediately skirted across the head of Josh's leaking cock and around to his arse, grabbing a cheek and pulling their two bodies tight. The position trapped Josh's hand, still wrapped around Michael's dick, between them in a fierce grind. Then those long slender fingers found their way to Josh's crease and the soft pucker of his entrance with surgical precision. They teased the delicate creases with slick fingertips, and Josh almost didn't recognise the needy moan that escaped his mouth. Josh was pretty sure that was a first.

As if he'd been waiting for that one sound, Michael immediately pushed his leg between Josh's, amplifying the friction, and just like that, Josh was right on the edge like a fucking teenager. He worked Michael's cock faster, his hand rubbing against his own erection as he did. And then Michael's fingertip slid home into Josh's arse, and the world tipped on its axis. Josh's breath hitched, and he pushed back, driving the intrusion deeper.

"Shit, I'm gonna—"

"Right with you," Michael husked, arching hard into Josh's hand.

Their lips stilled but remained pressed together. The sensations were too intense for Josh to focus on anything but what was happening farther south. His balls drew up, he felt Michael's urgent thrusts, and then he was gone, riding the exquisite wave of pleasure with a deep groan.

Seconds later Michael's pulsing release filled Josh's hand, and they braced, leaning into each other, until the rush eased. Then Michael reclaimed Josh's mouth in a deep kiss and flipped their positions, pinning him against the wall. He withdrew his hand from Josh's jeans and kicked Josh's feet apart, bringing them to eye level. Then for the first time since they'd touched, he pulled his mouth away from Josh's and pressed their foreheads together.

"Damn, you turn my shit on," he huffed against Josh's cheek. "Christ, I haven't come in my pants since I was twelve."

Josh snorted, his hand still trapped in Michael's scrubs. He gave Michael's dick a rough squeeze just because he could. "Likewise."

Michael flinched and gave a soft chuckle. "Well, fuck me, Josh. You took your damn time." He leaned in and sucked Josh's lower lip into his mouth, biting, then soothing it with a lick and pressing a trail of kisses along his jaw, ending at his ear. His tongue flicked in and nibbled Josh's lobe.

"You are so fucking hot, wolf-man," he whispered against Josh's ear. "But we're both wearing way too many clothes—if you're up for another round, that is?"

Josh turned his head and bit down on Michael's neck. The idea of marking Michael was hot as hell. "You're not so bad yourself."

"Black eye and all?" Michael nuzzled into his neck.

Shit. He pulled back and ran his eye over Michael. "You okay? If I hurt you—"

"Shut up." Michael took his lips in a hard kiss. "I loved every damn second. I'm quite capable of looking after myself."

Josh relaxed and leaned into Michael, carefully wondering if he should be regretting what they'd just done, but he couldn't find a fuck to give anywhere. He angled his neck to give Michael better access, and they stayed that way for a minute, Michael nipping and licking a path around his neck, Josh trying not to embarrass himself by whimpering too loudly.

Then he remembered. "Wolf-man? Really?"

"Just go with it," Michael mumbled against his skin, then pulled back and considered Josh with a serious expression. "So, just out of curiosity, what the fuck are we doing here, officer? Not that I'm unappreciative, but two minutes ago, you couldn't stand the sight of me and now here you are with your fingers still wrapped around my limp dick." He glanced down pointedly to where Josh's hand was, as mentioned, still buried in Michael's scrubs.

The heat of a blush crept up Josh's neck and he cocked an eyebrow. "You want I should let go?"

"I'm thinking what we both want is crystal clear." Michael glanced at the clock on the oven. "But I'm guessing it's not going to happen today."

Josh released him and reluctantly removed his hand from Michael's scrubs. "Commando?"

Michael shrugged. "Wasn't exactly expecting visitors."

Josh raised his hand slowly and held Michael's gaze as he licked his fingers clean.

Michael's pupils blew up into deep dark holes. "Damn," he hissed, pulling Josh in for a soft kiss and slipping his tongue inside for a taste.

Josh bunched his fists in Michael's scrubs. He was in danger of getting lost. Michael was gorgeous, no doubt. Gorgeous and damned hazardous to Josh's heart. *Fuck*. He wasn't sure what, if anything, he should want from him and so he stepped away. "We need to talk."

Michael's head dropped like a stone. "Fuck me, I knew it."

"I just think we should clear the air. Put stuff on the table."

Michael raised his brows. "Really? We shared a crazy good hand job and grind. It wasn't a fucking marriage proposal."

Josh rolled his eyes as he sat down. "I didn't intend for *anything* to happen."

Michael pulled a chair up and sat down, his expression equal parts frustrated and wary.

Josh guessed he deserved that. "I just think it would be helpful to clarify where we stand."

"Where we stand, huh?" Michael nodded his head and pursed his lips. His gaze slid off Josh with a sigh and Josh heard the slam of those walls shutter back into place.

"Look, we had a seriously hot grind against the wall," he said. "Unexpected, but hey, I'm wearing a smile. How about you?"

Josh felt his stomach twist. Well, he'd asked for it.

Michael continued, "Having said that, I'd like to think we could take it further. A bed would be nice. Maybe even explore removing some clothing, there's a novel idea. A little doctor/patient role play perhaps. I'm open to suggestions." He eyed Josh through long batting lashes.

Josh didn't mind being made fun of, but he was beginning to think he should've kept his fucking hands to himself. For just a second in there, he thought he'd felt something more on Michael's side when they'd kissed. He'd been wrong. He scraped his chair back and stood.

"Well, I'd say that makes things pretty clear," he said. "Best we nip this in the bud, then. I'll drop you at the hospital when you're ready."

Michael stood to block Josh's exit. "Whoa, slow down there, asshole. You started this. You kissed me, remember? I'm not looking to analyse this too seriously, and I am sure as shit not looking for a relationship. I had fun. It felt like you did too. And yes, I'd fuck you in a minute since you're seriously hot, but you already know that. And although I'm assured by nameless sources that you're a nice guy and all, I'm not looking for more. But there was some hot sexual chemistry going on back there, in case you hadn't noticed. Be a shame not to explore that." He stared at Josh, waiting.

Josh felt the burn from Michael's gaze go straight to his dick. There was no denying that last bit. He wanted this man like none before, even Jase. They'd been good in bed, sure, but nothing as sizzling as the electricity he felt with Michael. And they hadn't even taken their clothes off yet.

It might not be wise, but fuck, Josh suddenly realised he needed this, needed something to kick-start his life again. Getting epically laid a few times by a hot guy with no strings was starting to sound like a good beginning. He just needed to be careful. Keep his emotions in check. Nothing serious. But short-term fuck buddies? Yeah, he thought he could do that, this once. He swallowed hard.

"Okay." Josh eyeballed Michael. "Sure, I could be up for an extended session or two." He ran his tongue over his bottom lip, and Michael tracked it with hungry eyes. "No strings, no expectations. And we keep it quiet. I might not be directly involved in the investigation or listed as a formal witness anymore, but you are. It would be smarter if we didn't do this, but..."

Michael stepped in and pressed his lips to Josh's, dipping inside for a quick taste, and just like that, Josh was rock-hard again.

"I'm not known for smarter..." he said. "And no strings sounds perfect." He stepped back and held Josh's gaze with those sapphire eyes. "How about tonight?"

Holy shit. Josh was really doing this. "I'm on shift at four," he said.

Michael frowned. "How about before?" Pushy.

Josh found himself nodding. "I'll bring you back after your check-up."

"Done." Michael winked. "Bring a packed lunch. There'll be no intermission." Michael turned and headed for his bedroom, talking over his shoulder. "I'll be ready in a second. Cam will tear me or you a new one if I'm late, and that could seriously screw with our plans."

Josh released the breath he didn't know he'd been holding, and a shiver ran through him. Why did he feel he'd just grabbed a snake by the tail? Already his pulse was flipping at the thought of getting the damn man in bed. *Fuck.* He was in trouble.

CHAPTER FIVE

MICHAEL RODE THE ENTIRE TRIP TO THE HOSPITAL WITH A SEMI from the sexual tension clogging up the inside of Josh's truck. In some ways he was thankful, since behind the arousal sat a bunch of jiggling nerves at the thought of being outside for the first time since the attack, and no matter what he did, he couldn't stop his eyes darting from side to side, checking out who was in the vehicles close by. Josh must have noticed, as halfway through the trip, he rested a hot hand on Michael's thigh and left it there, squeezing softly every now and then, reassuring him. The nerves didn't vanish but they muted under the rush of Josh's touch.

But it was also unnerving in its own way. Michael couldn't remember feeling this kind of intensity with another guy in a long time, if ever. That kiss had been unexpected and fucking brilliant. He loved kissing, although he never permitted it with hookups—the implied intimacy just complicating shit. And that was another thing. Michael liked to be the one to initiate and control how things went. Simon had been a happy bottom, more than willing to follow Michael's lead, and that's just how Michael usually liked it.

On occasion they'd switched things up. Simon had topped but it was more to satisfy Simon's rare need in that arena. Michael didn't really enjoy bottoming and usually managed to top from the bottom anyway. But when Josh had him caged against that wall, devouring his mouth, Michael had only fought it for a few seconds. His body was embarrassingly all over it, responding to Josh's dominance with a whiny need that hadn't been pretty or welcome.

Who'd have guessed Josh had it in him? It was always the quiet ones, and to say Michael couldn't wait to see what Josh was like in the sack unrestrained, that was the understatement of the century. *Damn.*

The ER was quiet, and it took less than an hour for Michael to be cleared by the resident neurologist. Josh went to grab a coffee in the cafeteria in the interim and Michael suspected he needed a little distance. To be honest, he was grateful. Every time their eyes met, he saw his own lust reflected back, and it was doing a number on him.

They were like horny kids; it was beyond ridiculous. Cam had spent the first few minutes casting veiled glances between them. So much for being subtle. Now, with the two of them alone, the charge nurse perched on the hand basin while Michael dressed in some fresh scrubs. Josh had thankfully offered to scoot by Michael's apartment so he could grab some of his gear on their way back.

"So, how long have you two been fucking?" Cam asked casually.

Michael froze. The nurse was sporting red eyeliner today, a rainbow gauge in his earlobe, and a matching leather wrist strap. "We're not fucking. Now would you turn around and give me some privacy?"

Cam slid off the basin and turned his back, giving his cute butt a wiggle.

Michael chuckled. "Really? As nice as that ass is, I'm not telling you anything."

"I don't know what you're talking about," Cam huffed and shook his butt a second time. "My back's tired, that's all. You think it's nice, huh?"

"Delectable."

"You better believe it." Cam straightened and faced him again, ignoring Michael's exasperated sigh. "Well, if you're not fucking him, you damn well should be. The air between the two of you is as thick as a porn star's dick. I needed a shower just being five minutes with you two."

"We're not fucking. Not yet, anyway. And you can't say anything. I might have to be a witness, yet."

"No kidding. Well, you better practice your poker face because your current one sucks big time."

"Point taken."

Cam arched an eyebrow. "Besides, I thought you hated our young civil servant and vice versa."

"Well, to be more accurate, he hated me."

Cam grinned, handing Michael his shoes. "Well, it appears he's had a change of heart."

Michael pinned Cam with a smirk. "He kissed me—well, he fronted me—and I was fully on board."

Cam's jaw hit the floor. It wasn't often you could shock Cameron Wano.

"As in, he made the first move?"

Michael nodded.

"Well, fuck me. Word in our little community is that our sexy handler is pretty standoffish. No one in the hospital has snagged a date with him, not for the want of trying. I did hear he had a partner for a while—no one I knew, though."

A partner? Huh. "Yeah, well, this isn't a date. This is just fucking. And it's yet to be even that."

"I'll take that bet and raise you."

Michael laughed. "You're incorrigible. And how do you get away with all this shit?" He waved a hand over Cam's makeup and jewellery.

The charge nurse struck a pose. "Because I'm so fucking good at my job, that's how." He turned on his heels and left, Michael grinning from ear to ear.

. . .

As promised, Josh went by Michael's apartment so Michael could change, gather some clothes and toiletries, and pick up his car. He grabbed a frozen pizza while he was at it.

"Sustenance," he explained, holding it up as he returned to the apartment parking lot where Josh waited. Josh rolled his eyes.

Back at Katie's, Josh parked behind Michael in the driveway but seemed reluctant to get out of his car. Michael sighed. *What now?* Had Josh changed his mind? Michael really fucking hoped not.

Michael bent alongside Josh's open window. "You coming inside, officer?" *Please.* He wasn't going to say it, though. If Josh left him with a case of blue balls, there'd be hell to pay. He was already fit to bust in his jeans from the anticipation alone. Twice in one day, and he'd have to hand his man card in.

Josh's face clouded in concern. "Are you sure you're up for it?"

Michael spread his arms. "Fully cleared, bar the bruising, and I'll let you know play-by-play if I have a problem. Cam gave me a dose of the stronger stuff, so I'm actually not feeling too bad at the moment. You sure it's me you're worried about?" He arched an eyebrow pointedly.

Josh's gaze flickered away. He checked his watch, and Michael wondered what the hell was going through that pretty little head, its honey-blond hair all stuck in unruly tufts like he'd just rolled out of bed. And those perfect features, all schooled and serious. There wasn't a hint of the fierce man who'd pinned Michael to the wall and kissed him senseless less than three hours before. He was just fucking adorable. *Adorable?*

He sighed. "Come on, Josh. Let's play a little. You're the hottest damn thing I've seen in forever, and in case you're worried, I'm told I'm no slouch in the sack."

Josh turned and met his gaze, a soft blush stealing over his cheeks and the hint of a smirk under those chocolate-brown eyes. "Believe it or not, doctor, that particular concern never once crossed my mind."

And just like that, the toppy man was back. The sizzling man Michael had encountered that morning. *Hell yeah.* Michael couldn't help himself. He leaned through the open window and took Josh's full lips in a gentle kiss, his tongue running the seam, the brief taste sending his dick rocketing skyward. He pulled back and let himself stare. "Damn, you're beautiful. Get your ass inside."

Josh broke into a huge smile, and although Michael had seen him smile before, it had never been aimed in Michael's direction quite like that. It fairly sucked the breath from his chest, and something fluttered in his stomach that he did his best to ignore. A part of him wanted to be the one responsible for all those smiles. *Shit.* He'd known Josh for, like, two minutes and already he was trouble.

They moved inside and Josh locked Paris in Katie's backyard, throwing the shepherd a few treats to keep him occupied. Michael smiled. He liked the animal more than he'd expected, and it appeared the feeling was mutual. Paris had found a soft place in his animal-neutral heart, but Michael wasn't fooling himself. He knew he'd be dog fodder without a second thought if Paris had to choose between them.

With his back to Michael, Josh stood watching the shepherd through the glass, and Michael again wondered if Josh was going to back out. One thing was sure, though—Michael wasn't going to be the one to push this. The ball was firmly in Josh's court. He wanted no doubt about that down the road.

He was about to suggest a drink to get things rolling when Josh abruptly threw his jacket on the chair and kicked his shoes underneath. *Well, alrighty then.*

Josh turned a smouldering gaze on Michael, his expression one of pure predatory lust. *Holy hell.* Michael's breath caught in his chest and his semi-hard dick sprang to full attention. An unexpected flight of nerves shimmied across his belly as he bore the full impact of the attention, and the most ridiculous thought skittered through his mind. *Am I up to this?*

Then Josh moved and Michael, expecting a replay of the morning, braced for impact, for the hard kiss and the clash of bodies. He was therefore somewhat surprised when Josh brushed past instead, trailing a hand lightly over Michael's groin as he did, sending a jolt of scorching desire straight through him. *God in heaven.*

"Are we doing this or not?" Josh teased over his shoulder, sauntering toward Michael's bedroom, hauling his T-shirt over his head as he went. Dropping it on the floor outside the bedroom door, Josh exposed a hard, muscled back with a generous smattering of blond hair and a trim waist. Michael was transfixed in place. Josh unbuttoned his jeans and stepped out of both them and his boxers, flashing a beautiful cock and more tufts of blond hair over a delicious ass. Then he disappeared into the bedroom.

Goddamn. Michael's mouth hung open, and he suspected he was drooling. Yep, confirmed. No one ever led him by the dick like that, and damn, if said dick didn't absolutely freaking love it.

Josh banged on the wall. "Get the fuck in here."

Michael obeyed instantly to his own mortification, stepping over the discarded clothing to join Josh as fast as humanly possible. Through the door, he was instantly gripped by his shirt and pulled in for a lengthy kiss. And when Josh's tongue pressed for entry, Michael opened without a second thought, his arms wrapping around Josh's waist, pushing hard against his naked body. They delved deeply into each other's mouths—tasting, sucking, probing, exploring.

Muscles ached and protested, and skin burned over the bruising that circled his waist, but Michael ignored every damn thing except the overwhelming sensation of Josh's touch. A surge of need pulsed through his body as Josh nibbled his lower lip, then soothed it with a lick and a kiss. This was followed by more kisses trailing along his jaw to his ear.

Michael tilted his head to give Josh better access, inviting another line of kisses from his jaw to his shoulder before Josh took possession of his mouth once again, his hands angling Michael's head to exactly where he wanted it. Michael was apparently just along for the ride. Who the hell was this confident, aggressive lover? And where was the uptight, prudish man he'd replaced? *God*, Michael was flying in the twilight zone.

Leaving one hand wrapped around Michael's neck, Josh moved his other under Michael's tee, lightly skimming his tender abs and up over the sprinkling of hair on his chest. Fingertips glided over one nipple, then the other—catching lightly on Michael's barbell piercings—and Josh hummed in appreciation with every moan Michael fed into his open mouth. He was turned on beyond imagination, and when Josh finally pulled back, Michael couldn't hold back the whimpering protest. Colour him mortified.

Josh looked down on Michael, his expression serious. "I meant it. I don't want to hurt you."

Michael nodded impatiently. "Yes, yes, fine. Whatever. Just get those lips of yours back on me right this second, you hear?"

Josh smirked. "Understood."

And with that, he sealed his mouth over Michael's once again and all bets were off. There was a single moment of unnerving recognition that this wasn't going quite as Michael had planned, before he simply gave in and decided to ride the wave.

A quick and dirty hard fuck had been his agenda, but Josh seemed in no mood to rush and Michael was surprisingly comfortable letting Josh lead. Not to mention his dick seemed to be loving every minute of it. In the back of Michael's head, however, a slightly panicked voice urged him to take control and get his head back in the game. But Michael's body wasn't getting the memo, apparently.

The hand under his T-shirt tracked down his stomach to the waistband of his jeans as Josh continued the onslaught of kisses that kept Michael breathless and on the edge. He shivered as wicked fingers teased over his jeans to cup his balls before gliding along the rigid length of his erection. *Ugh*. He was so damn close, and he was still fully dressed.

Thank God, the hand withdrew and cupped his face instead, Josh's tongue flicking lightly along Michael's lips. In all this time, he'd been pinned to the spot, a plaything for Josh to do what he wanted with. Michael hadn't even focused enough brainpower to touch Josh in return.

"Mmm. You have altogether too many clothes on, Dr Oliver," Josh whispered against his mouth. "Get rid of them." He stepped away and simply waited.

Michael had a snarky rebuttal poised to fall from his lips but found himself reaching for the button on his jeans instead. Before removing them, he reached into the pocket and threw a few packets of condoms and lube he'd grabbed from his apartment onto the bed.

Josh's mouth quirked up in appreciation.

Michael shrugged. "Seemed the right thing to do."

Then, under Josh's lustful gaze, Michael continued to slowly discard his clothes into a pile on the floor. He did his best to put on a bit of a show even though the state of his body was a little less than stellar. But for all the bruising Michael knew he sported, Josh's admiring gaze never faltered, Josh stroking himself slowly as he watched. It was a fuckton of sexy.

Naked at last, Michael stepped aside and simply waited. He was surprisingly enjoying this freaky dominant/submissive thing they had going on, and he wanted to see where Josh went with it. Handing control over was new to him, like shiny fresh-out-of-the-oven new, and it felt simultaneously liberating and terrifying. But for whatever reason, he trusted Josh enough to take the risk.

He stood still as Josh charted his body top to toe, his expression mesmerising. The lust, the concern when his eyes tracked all the bruising, the need, and the hypnotic intensity were the sexiest damn thing Michael thought he'd ever seen. Not because of who Josh was, but because of how he made Michael feel, like Michael was a work of art to be savoured, the centre of his universe. It was intoxicating.

Josh's gaze lingered over Michael's erection, his lower lip caught between his teeth, his hand continuing its slow stroke. Now Michael would never be accused of being shy—he was confident in his body— but having that appreciative eye and obvious arousal focused so acutely on him, well, it cranked Michael's juices no end, and he'd never been harder.

Josh's gaze lifted to the startling run of bruising that wrapped around Michael's waist and chest, and his fingers trailed along the edges. Michael held back a reflexive flinch, not wanting to worry Josh. He wasn't letting a few bruises deny him this.

"You let me worry about that, wolf-man," he said. "I'll let you know."

"Make sure you do. Your ink's hot, by the way." Josh ran a finger over the stylised kiwi. "New?"

"Wanted a reminder." Michael was done with the hands-off and stepped into Josh's space.

"No, you don't." Josh held him in place. "I want a good long look."

Michael's dick shot farther north at the instruction. May as well bury his pathetic ass now. His brain might want to quit with the damn tease and get on with the fucking, but his body clearly wasn't bothered. So he said not a word, did as he was told, and let his gaze wander Josh's hard flesh in return.

Josh had been blessed with a body to equal his beautiful face. Tattoo-free, smooth and hard but not overly muscled. Michael wanted to run his tongue and teeth over every inch, the sooner the better. He wasn't sure his own body matched up, to be honest, but he wasn't about to let that faze him. Josh had a dense covering of silky soft blond hair over the length of his well-cut torso. Certainly more than Michael usually preferred—he liked his men well-groomed typically. He might, however, have to review that after today.

His gaze tracked down, and as if reading his mind, Josh dropped the hand stroking his erection, letting it fall aside to reveal an ample cock, flushed and leaking precum from its thick head. Michael responded by gripping his own, giving it a few rough strokes, convinced if he didn't get a taste of this man soon, he'd explode.

"You done with the tire kick?" Michael quipped. "I'd kind of like to get on with the test drive, if it's all the same to you." He stepped right up into Josh's face and pressed his lips to Josh's. Next thing he knew, he was sitting on the bed with Josh looming over him, a wicked grin on his face. *Huh. Whatever.* Michael was past caring. Josh could do whatever the hell he liked as long as things started moving along pronto. The fact he was now eye to cock meant things were definitely looking up.

Michael loved giving head, although he didn't advertise that to his one-night stands, but Simon had always appreciated it. And with fuck-all gag reflex, he knew he was a pretty good experience. Wrapping both hands around Josh's butt, he pulled him close, leaned in, and ran his tongue from Josh's hefty balls up his cock and across the head, dipping into his slit as he passed.

A low moan rumbled from somewhere above him, and Michael dropped his head to take Josh's balls one by one into his mouth. He pulled at them gently, rolling them and adding a hum to send a quiver of sensation through them. Josh's fingers bunched in Michael's hair, holding him still, but Michael pulled free and rose slightly to get a better angle. He then took Josh whole in one swallow.

"F-fuck," Josh stammered, reasserting his grip in Michael's hair.

He tasted amazing, salty and herbal, with a hint of coconut from the body wash he used. Michael's eyes lifted, content to find a glazed look of pleasure on Josh's face, and with Josh's cock lodged deep in his throat, Michael continued to work Josh in a slow rhythm. He moved one hand to wrap around the base, holding Josh steady, while the other worked his balls in a leisurely roll. He then eased behind to tease Josh's entrance.

"Mmm," Josh rocked slowly, adding a slide in and out of Michael's mouth.

Michael lifted two fingers to Josh's lips, and he sucked them in, slicking them up. Michael figured it was as good a permission as any. He pulled his fingers free and slipped them to Josh's hole, sliding first one, then two inside, finger-fucking as he continued to suck relentlessly. Josh pushed back, encouraging them deeper. Then he arched with a groan and gripped Michael's hair tight, and Michael knew he'd hit the spot.

He let his jaw slacken and held still as Josh began a gentle thrust that grew more forceful, grabbing breaths when he could. He continued to work Josh's ass with his fingers but let Josh set the pace. It was rough and dirty, and exactly what Michael loved. Simon had always been too scared of hurting him to truly let go, but Michael trusted Josh; he seemed to be opting for depth rather than speed, keeping it manageable.

It wasn't long before he sensed Josh edging close, and when Josh pulled out of his mouth, Michael immediately withdrew his fingers and squeezed the base of Josh's cock to bring him back down. There were some things he wasn't prepared to leave to Josh's control. He sure as fuck wasn't coming before Michael was ready for him. Getting to his feet, he met those chocolate hooded eyes with a smirk.

"Fuck, you're good at that," Josh breathed, surprising Michael by pulling him into a soft embrace and placing a run of sweet kisses over his black eye. He pulled Michael's lower lip between his teeth and nibbled gently, teasing, licking, and kissing as if acknowledging Michael's efforts.

After a blowjob like the one Michael had just bestowed, Josh had to be fit to bust, and Michael had fully expected to be in the middle of a rough-and-ready fucking right about now. Instead it was this tender, heady display of affection. *Well, shit.* And it wasn't like Michael was gonna turn that down.

At length, Josh pulled away and pushed Michael to his back on the bed, falling on top and crawling up his body in slow motion. His gaze was intent as he paused to kiss the end of Michael's nose, and a shiver of anticipation slid over Michael's skin.

"I believe it's my turn," Josh whispered, looking for all the world like he was two seconds from eating Michael alive.

Bring it on. Michael gripped his chin in his hand and smiled up at him. "How long since you've fucked, did you say?"

Josh sucked Michael's thumb into his mouth, rolling it around his tongue a few times before letting go. "I didn't." He grinned. "But yeah, it's been a while."

"Figured as much. Well, just make sure you leave my bits up and running when you're done, okay?"

Josh grinned. "No promises."

"Fuck me." Michael threw his head back on the bed.

"You got it." He gripped both of Michael's wrists and pinned them above his head.

Holy shit. That hadn't been in the fine print. "Ah, Joshua?" Michael bucked and squirmed for release, admittedly not too desperately since his fucking traitorous cock was leaking like a goddamn faucet. Josh merely increased his hold and sat astride him, locking eyes.

"You gonna trust me?" Josh leaned down to press a kiss to Michael's lips.

No. Yes. Maybe. They stared each other down for a few seconds. *Fuck it. Yes.* Michael nodded. This wasn't a scene he ever allowed or was in any way comfortable with, but yeah, okay, he was prepared to see where it went. He made a mental note to be less cocky in his assumptions about quiet men. Although Josh was taller and bigger built, Michael had taken Josh for a bottom or an occasional switch at most. Wrong, he mused, nervously. Right now, there was nothing but bossy top written all over the guy. That was a minor concern as that was pretty much the role Michael played without exception and had no intention of relinquishing. This was going to be interesting.

"Do I need a safeword?" He arched a brow.

"How about 'stop'?" Josh deadpanned.

Michael laughed and immediately relaxed.

And with that, Josh began a top to toe exploration of Michael's body, trailing kisses and licks as he went, pausing to suck and nibble on each of Michael's nipples, rolling the piercings over his tongue and causing him to arch and groan at the sensation overload shooting straight to his dick. He traced the lines of each tattoo with interest, and every time he hit a hot spot, he lingered, nipping, licking, and teasing until Michael squirmed in frustration, cursing and swearing blue murder for Josh to get the fuck on with it or face the dire consequences.

"You're killing me here," Michael hissed. "My cock will be past its use-by date if you don't get a move on." Josh released his hands with an order to "stay put," and Michael snorted in disbelief. Why the hell would he move when paradise was right here? Every taste, every caress, every kiss and nibble grew Michael's desire and frustration equally. He was at best two licks away from self-combustion, and he couldn't give a flying fuck. Holding out until he got his dick inside Josh was all but a Hail Mary at this point.

Speaking of dicks, Josh's tongue skirted Michael's, much to his burning frustration, but did come to rest over his balls, paying some welcome attention there before continuing south. Tongue, teeth, and lips tracked down the inside of Michael's thighs to the tip of his toes, where he licked and sucked each one into his mouth before journeying back.

Christ on a cracker. Michael was busting out of his skin with need and ready to commit bodily assault when Josh suddenly took his cock deep in his mouth in one swallow.

"Thank God for that," he cried, bucking into Josh's mouth and eliciting what he could only assume was a muffled snort of laughter from the bastard. He pulled off, then took Michael down again, swallowing when Michael's cock hit the back of his throat, damn near dragging an orgasm from him on the spot. The warning tingle in the base of his spine forced him to grab Josh's head and pull him off.

"Too c-close," he huffed.

Josh slid to his knees, grabbed Michael's hips, and flipped him like a pancake but significantly slower, before gently lifting him up onto all fours. Michael still winced. "Ow and ow."

"Shit, sorry." Josh kissed the back of his neck. "You wanna stop?"

"Don't you fucking dare. It's okay." Michael hissed, holding his breath against the flash of pain. "It's fine." It wasn't yet, but it would be. *And anyway, what the hell?* Michael couldn't remember having ever been hauled around in bed before. *Christ.* He was going to need therapy if he survived the afternoon. *Still, in for a penny and all that.* So far this had been the best damn sex ever, but fun as it was, it really *was* time for Michael to clarify how things needed to go from here on in.

He swung an arm and latched on to Josh's shoulder. "Hey. Um, I don't bottom well... or at all, actually," he stated. "Not my style, sorry. Should've said, but I just thought... well I was wrong about you, or so it seems." Behind him, Josh had frozen in place, and Michael really, really hoped this wasn't about to ruin things. Seconds later a kiss was pressed on the inside of his wrist. *Huh.*

"Noted." Josh followed up with a second kiss, this one to Michael's butt. "I'll be sure to take it nice and slow, then." A further kiss to his other cheek and one to the base of his spine. "You're so goddamn beautiful, I can't fucking wait to get inside you."

Wait. What? Michael slapped Josh's shoulder and received a slap on his butt in reply. *Fucker.* "Didn't you hear me?" he demanded.

Josh licked a trail down his crease and across his hole, and it was all Michael could do not to dissolve into the bed and tell Josh to do whatever the fuck he liked, and Michael would simply be grateful.

"Yep, heard every word, but—" Josh's hand reached around and tugged at Michael's impossibly hard dick, which was currently drooling all over the sheet. "—this tells another story, Doctor Oliver. I think you want to be fucked badly, but you're running scared."

Yes. No! "Don't be ridiculous."

"Still not hearing that safeword."

Say it. Say it. "Ugh. Whatever." *No, that wasn't it.* "So, you just gonna sit there or are we gonna do this, wolf-man?"

Josh bit his ass, and Michael yelped. *Fucking embarrassing.* And... *shit, shit, shit.* Michael was about to bottom. So not in the plan, not in the plan at all. Even with Simon, he'd only offered a few times, the last over two years ago. He should just stop this nonsense now. He braced his hands to throw Josh off, but before he could, Josh's languid tongue slid between his butt cheeks and pressed slick and taut into his hole, obliterating all intention.

"Goddamn," he muttered, face-planting the mattress and biting the sheets, melting into the luscious sensations. *I am so totally fucking screwed. And yeah, literally.*

Josh's treacherous tongue slid over and against Michael's entrance, dipping in now and then to taste and tease, and Michael relished the soft burn of those whiskers, sure he'd have a rash to remember them by.

Rimming was another thing Michael hadn't allowed himself to enjoy in too long. Way too intimate for a casual fuck. It needed trust, for a start. And it was like Josh had a road map to Michael's happy place, intent on ticking all the boxes en route—any thought of throwing him off dissolving into a boneless pool of delight. And when Josh speared his tongue and pushed in hard, fucking Michael in quick darting prods, Michael sank farther into the mattress, grinding his teeth in needy frustration. *And yeah, dammit.* Hell, if he didn't want that tongue out and Josh's cock in its place in short order. Not that he was going to tell him that.

"Patience," the fucker replied, as though Michael had voiced the thought aloud. *Shit, maybe he had.* Then Josh added a finger to the mix, and then two, the combination damn near pushing Michael over for the umpteenth time. Sensing that, Josh pulled up and flipped Michael onto his back once again, a little more carefully this time, settling between his legs.

"Will you quit doing that?" Michael scowled, receiving a wicked grin in reply before Josh's lips pressed against his once again. *God, the man could kiss.*

Helpless against the onslaught and desperate for release, he slid his arms around Josh, gripped his butt, and jammed their bodies together, wrapping his legs around Josh's waist. Could he be more fucking obvious? Josh really needed to get on with it before Michael chickened out or his dick went incandescent.

Josh reached for the foils and lube thrown on the bed earlier. He handed a packet to Michael, whose hands remarkably found a will of their own, since his brain was on sabbatical, allowing him to roll the condom in place. He added a couple of light tugs to that ample cock in the process to spur Josh on. *God, was he really gonna do this?* Josh squirted some lube onto the head of both their dicks and slicked them up.

Michael batted Josh's hand away. "Enough already. If you don't damn well fuck me soon, I'm going to blow and there'll be no more fun for you," he said irritably.

Josh placed a kiss on the head of Michael's dick. "Or you," he answered. But he'd gotten the message, lifting Michael's legs to rest on his shoulders.

Shit. "Missionary? Really?" Michael tried to make light of it, but the whole idea of being face-to-face with this man freaked him out.

Josh studied him. "Yes, really. I wanna see that gorgeous face every fucking minute. Don't wanna miss a thing."

Oh. "Um, okay."

Michael couldn't believe he was doing this. He felt so damn exposed. In his entire life, he'd only trusted a couple of men enough to bottom for them, and he knew virtually nothing about Josh other than he'd apparently hated Michael on sight. Could he be more stupid? And yet, he did trust him. There was nothing surer.

Josh was poised above Michael, watching intently. Balanced on one hand while the other rubbed his full cock up and down Michael's crease, he waited. It was clear he was offering Michael a last opportunity to back out, and that was all Michael needed to know.

He nodded. "Just fucking do it already," he grumbled, failing to sound anything but desperate for it.

Josh grinned and pressed in, breaching Michael's tight outer ring with the flush head of his cock in a single slow push before pausing inside. Dusting off his CliffsNotes to Anal Sex 101, Michael bore down a little to make the entry easier, screwing his eyes shut for the few seconds it took the sting of the stretch to ease. It had been a long, long time, and he was tight as hell.

The bite of pain dissolved quickly, and Michael opened his eyes to find Josh watching him steadily. He gave him a tiny nod and locked on to his lips. They shared a deep kiss as Josh gave another gentle push, sliding in until Michael could tell he was buried to the hilt.

"Fuck, you're so goddamn tight," Josh said thickly. He was holding still, allowing Michael time to adjust. "So fucking hot."

Michael wriggled a little beneath him, feeling full and weird, and yeah, fucking amazing. "I'm pleased for you. Now move, you bastard, before you put down roots."

Josh snorted and began to thrust, starting slow and building up speed. He changed the angle a couple of times until he pegged Michael's prostate. The electric thrill fired through Michael, swallowing him in waves of heated pleasure that grew by the second. The glorious sensation of being filled and held, watched and attended to, every part of his body claimed in the process. *God.* He'd always wondered what guys saw in bottoming. How it could ever compare to what he felt as a top. *What an idiot.*

The intensity of the experience and the powerful sensations blew his mind. Not less or more than topping but blazingly different, and he knew, without doubt, it was down to Josh. He was being properly topped for the first time. Simon had never been fully comfortable in that role. A flicker of concern passed through his mind. Had he been a good top to his own partners over the years? The thought was there and gone before he could worry too much about it.

"Fuck. Me," he mumbled, balling the sheet in his hand to hold on as Josh thrust relentlessly into him, taking him closer to the edge.

"Yep, getting right on that," Josh hissed, his gaze locked on the sight of his dick moving in and out of Michael's arse. "Wish you could see this."

"Um... kinda... busy," Michael gasped, snaking a hand between them to work his own dick to the same rhythm. He winced a little as he grazed over his sore ribs but ignored it. This was not stopping.

Josh wrapped his hand around Michael's. "Come for me." He bent down to take Michael's mouth once again, and Michael gripped his head with his free hand, holding him tight against his lips. Josh kissed like a machine, and he wasn't sure what was driving him closer to the edge, Josh's cock in his arse or his tongue fucking his mouth.

"I'm close," Josh mumbled against his lips, straightening and batting Michael's hand away from his dick so he could take over, pumping swiftly. Josh's head fell back, and the look of pleasure on his face as he was about to come undone had Michael's balls drawing up and his cock erupting ribbons of cum between them. Chasing the waves of pleasure, Michael squeezed his ass to increase the sensation for Josh, knowing how good that felt from the other side. Josh groaned, shuddered, and spilled himself into Michael's ass. *Yes.* They both stilled as they came down, gazes locked on each other until Josh finally collapsed onto Michael's chest, breathing heavily.

"Ow, shit." Michael pushed Josh off his battered torso and onto his side. He flung his arms out wide, his entire body boneless, and waited for his brain to return to his head sometime next century.

"Sorry." Josh nestled alongside, tying the condom off and throwing it to the floor. Then he propped himself up on one elbow, leaned across, and cleaned Michael's dick and stomach with long sensual licks.

Michael summoned the strength to raise his head and watch open-mouthed. "Hot damn," he whispered, curling his fingers in Josh's blond spikes, stroking gently. He was generally all about the fuck and a quick wipe afterwards to get rid of the "ick" factor, not this. This was intimate. But hell if he wasn't enjoying every minute of it.

He just didn't get Josh. Damn reluctant to get in the bed, but once there, a freaking dominating sex machine with all the optional extras turned on. Michael couldn't remember the last time he'd had the full-service option, if ever.

When Josh was finished, he pressed a kiss to Michael's lips, flicking his tongue inside to share his taste before stretching out like a cat alongside. He draped an arm over Michael's chest, careful to avoid his bruises, and snuggled in. *Huh.* No leaping from the bed to keep things casual. No checking whether Michael was cool about the intimacy. No awkward "do I, don't I?", "is this okay?" shit. No. Basically Josh just owned the skin on skin and demanded a cuddle as if they did it every day of their freaking lives.

So, yes. Michael Oliver was officially snuggling, damn sure it contravened every fuck buddy commandment he was aware of. And yes, there went his hand to hold Josh's arm firmly in place. Michael shook his head. He was clearly suffering some kind of shock. Probably due to experiencing the best sex of his freaking life as a freaking bottom.

"Well, fuck me, wolf-man," he sighed, stroking Josh's arm, enjoying the hard muscle twitching beneath.

Josh buried his face against Michael's chest and inhaled deeply. "Mmm. You smell really good, but I think I might need a few more minutes." His tongue flicked over Michael's nipple.

Michael twitched and swatted him. "Quit that." He wrapped his other arm around Josh, enveloping him and burying his fingers in those blond spikes.

In response, Josh purred. "I could go to sleep." And Michael resisted the urge to tuck him up to do just that.

They were silent a minute or so, and Josh wriggled closer, if that were even possible. How such a tall man managed to cuddle in and around Michael like a soft ball of muscle was baffling. Gone was bossy, toppy Josh, and in his place, this soft, pliant pussycat. Michael couldn't have said which he preferred, more than happy to welcome both.

"So," Josh mumbled against his skin. "What's the verdict, Mr 'I don't bottom well'?"

Michael grinned to himself. "It was... fine."

Josh snorted. "Fine?" He bit Michael's nipple, hard.

"Ow. Cut it out. Okay, so I may have understated it a bit." Michael pulled Josh up until they were eye to eye. "I'm thinking... good. That's better than fine, right? Yeah, let's go with good."

Josh growled and reached down to grab Michael's soft dick in his hand. He gave a few gentle tugs, and damn if the thing didn't imme-diately perk right up. He certainly had a way with that part of Michael's anatomy.

Lifting himself on an elbow, Josh eyeballed Michael. "Seems you need a little more convincing. Up for another round?" His hand slid behind Michael's balls to lightly tap his hole. "Seeing as how you're so nice and relaxed."

Michael's ass was, in point of fact, throbbing in protest at the mere thought. His traitorous dick on the other hand had failed to get the memo and was standing ever hopeful at half-mast. Josh was a cock whisperer.

Josh glanced down. "Someone agrees with me."

Michael lifted Josh's chin with his fingers and placed a soft kiss on his lips. "He's thinking it's his turn next, that's why," he whispered against Josh's mouth. "'Cause there's no way that monster of yours is getting anywhere near my battered ass again for the foreseeable future."

Josh grinned. "Monster, huh? As for the other, well, I'm all for equal opportunity." He returned the kiss, then patted Michael's chest. "But unfortunately, not today." He drew slow circles around Michael's nipple with a finger. "I need a shower, food, and time to get Paris ready for our shift."

Josh swung his legs over the side of the bed, the loss of warmth a shock to Michael's system. He resisted the urge to pull Josh back under the covers and kiss him into surrender, settling for delaying his departure with a hand on his arm.

"In answer to your earlier question," Michael said quietly, "the true verdict? It was fucking awesome. I may not graduate to true nelly-bottom, card-carrying, believer status," he teased, "but I'm defi-nitely willing to attend the refresher classes."

A grin of pure delight settled on Josh's face, and a surge of warmth shot through Michael, hitting him with absolute clarity. He wanted to please this man. He wanted to see that smile. He wanted to be responsible for putting it there, and the realisation terrified him.

He needed to get whatever this was the fuck under control or finish it.

Josh planted a kiss on his forehead and headed for the shower. Left alone, Michael began pondering the risks Josh posed to his uncomplicated life. The shower turned on, and he briefly wondered if he should join Josh but dismissed the thought. A bit of distance was for the best right about now.

A head poked around the door. "You joining me?" Josh wore a grin from ear to ear.

Michael scrambled out of bed and followed without a second thought. That distance shit could start tomorrow.

CHAPTER SIX

JOSH COULDN'T REMEMBER FEELING SO BUZZED IN A LONG TIME. Mark had been right. He'd needed to get laid. Like really, really needed to get laid. And more than just a quick blow or anonymous hand job. Not that Michael was much more serious than that, but he wasn't quite a passing fuck either. Michael had some skills between the sheets, and there was no doubt they worked together in bed, possibly the best Josh had ever had.

Michael was gorgeous, true, but he also had a quick bantering humour Josh enjoyed, giving as good as he got. Josh loved sex, but he had little time for quick and dirty as a model. He preferred the slow-burn buildup almost as much as the bang at the end, and he'd been pleased to find Michael on board with the notion.

He grinned. Topping Michael had been a blast. Josh went either way and didn't usually force the issue, but there was something about Michael that had him cranked up. For all his posturing and self-importance, Josh had caught a glimpse of a softer, more vulnerable side to Michael Oliver, one that would normally be worth exploring. Having Michael accept his dick was damn near the most erotic thing Josh had ever experienced.

Michael was a puzzle. Even before they'd hit the bedroom, Josh had decided he'd push to top, especially when he learned Michael didn't usually bottom. The look on his face had been hilarious, and so he'd been more than a little surprised when Michael fell into line relatively easily. It had made Josh determined to look after him.

What Josh hadn't been prepared for was how relaxing it felt to be in Michael's arms after. Even the shared hand jobs in the shower afterwards had ended with them both on the shower floor, Michael wrapped in Josh's arms, talking back and forth about softball and rugby and eventually the assault. Josh sponged Michael's bruised and battered body, pressing kisses against his neck and shoulders as he talked. It was the decent thing to do, Josh reassured himself, nothing more.

The afternoon had only highlighted how much he missed Jase in his life and his bed. He didn't want the fucker back, but snuggling had been their thing, or at least Josh's thing. It was perhaps what he missed the most, and the biggest reason he didn't do the hookup scene. At least Michael hadn't kicked Josh out of his bed straight after. That was something, he supposed.

He thought of his upcoming coffee date with Brent and debated cancelling it. The guy was nice but nothing about him sparked Josh in the same way that Michael did. But Michael had been very clear that he didn't want a relationship. And after this afternoon, Josh knew that he at least was ready for just that. It was just a damn shame Michael wasn't on board with the same idea.

He scribbled a note for Katie, apologising for being such a dick that morning. Then, about to leave for his shift, he caught the message light flashing on his home phone. It was the principal of Sasha's school, wanting a word with Josh when he had time. *Shit.* He returned the call, and after the niceties had been covered, Erin got down to her concerns.

"I don't know if Sasha mentioned the family project her class is working on?" she checked.

When Josh made it clear she hadn't, the woman continued. "Okay, well, its focus is on grandparents."

Josh's stomach clenched. It didn't take a rocket scientist to guess where this was going. "Go on."

"We're asking the kids to interview their grandparents about their childhood experiences. To see how things are different for children today, better or worse. The object is to talk about change in generational understanding, nothing heavy or contentious."

"I sense a but," Josh ventured, and caught the sigh at the other end of the phone.

"*But*," Erin repeated, "Sasha is having some difficulties."

Josh was cautious not to jump to conclusions. "Because of me?"

"No," Erin leaped to dismiss the idea. "Well, not directly."

Josh tried to keep his temper locked down. "I'm sure she's not the only one with a *different* family situation, Erin," he commented dryly. "With divorce rates and custody issues and so on, having a gay dad can't be the only sensitive topic out there."

"Josh, please." Erin sighed. "It's got little to do with you being gay, as such. In fact, we told Sasha she didn't even need to mention it. After all, we don't expect other kids to talk about their parents' sexuality with their grandparents."

Thank God. Josh relaxed a little. The woman really did try. "Good. Then what's the problem?"

"Sasha doesn't want to involve your parents at all. She's happy to talk to Anna's parents but is adamant about not talking to yours. Along those lines, there was a bit of a scene in the classroom today, and she got very upset. Now, I know there have been difficulties there, and I'm quite prepared to make an exception for her if that's what you want, but I suspected she hadn't actually talked to you, hence the phone call. I just thought you should know."

Josh sighed. "You're right. I didn't know. I'll talk to her and get back to you. Thanks, Erin." *Damn.*

Josh wondered how to recover his good mood, the one that had just gone up in billowing furls of shitty smoke. For a ridiculous second, he actually considered talking to Michael. Right. Michael didn't even know Josh had a daughter. Josh checked his watch. They were due at Dog Base in forty-five minutes.

THE DEBRIEF on the joint exercise took about an hour. The remainder of Josh's shift was spent filing paperwork, running through training exercises with the dogs, and a two-hour call out to track and pursue a juvenile home invasion suspect in New Lynn. Another K9, Rage, had been the one to actually nail the boy in the back of a theatre car park. The kid was on his knees with exhaustion, barely able to speak let alone put up a struggle. Rage's handler, Colin Hardy, had the kid cuffed and jailed in no time. Josh and Paris were needed only as backup singers. Mark had been the detective on the scene, giving Josh an opportunity to check on progress in Michael's assault case.

"The doc's coming in tomorrow after the funeral, to finish going through the image file," Mark said. "The bottle threw up a partial, but not enough for a useful ID."

"Shit." Josh had hoped for better news.

"Yeah." Mark scratched Paris's ears, earning him a sloppy tonguing from the shepherd. "But we lucked out on the car used to pick them up."

Josh's ears pricked.

"A teenage boy supervising the family dog's evening piss caught the vehicle's rubber burning exit and got us a partial plate and a make —Subaru wagon, dark blue or black. That plus the partial threw up three possible hits but only one sent up flags. Great fucking red billowing flags."

Josh cocked an eyebrow. "No shit."

Though they weren't standing close, Mark pulled Josh farther from Hardy, who was busy writing up his notes in his vehicle. "An eighteen-year-old kid named Bradley Keenan," Mark elaborated. "Nothing but a few drunk and disorderly, threatening behaviour, and shoplifting arrests, but for the last year he's been hanging with members of the Hell Spinners. A wannabe, most like. And wouldn't you know it, by coincidence, there's word of a new/old face in town with deep ties to that pack of shitheads. Denton Cruz."

Cruz. Josh frowned. He'd recognised the last name straight off. "As in Sampson Cruz, head dickhead of the Hell Spinners?"

Mark nodded. "The one and only. His son."

Josh gave a low whistle. "Big fish, then."

"Well, Daddy is. Largest supplier of P north of Taupo. Mean motherfucker too. Word has it his son is keen to prove himself. Apparently, good old Dad has kidney disease and is looking to hand over some of his responsibilities. Denton's only twenty, more brawn than brain but nasty, just like his dad.

"Older brother Kane just got ten years for car theft and burglary, so he's out of the picture for a bit. Sampson has a lieutenant, though. A cousin who's got a decent brain and would've been the default choice but for Denton's sudden reappearance. He's apparently pissed as fuck about it. Denton meanwhile has been trying to prove his worth by running the street scene these last few months. He could well be our man at Downtown G and at your boyfriend's."

Josh frowned. "Yeah, that's not much of a stretch. And, not my boyfriend, dickhead."

Shit. It was just what Auckland didn't need. A fucking power struggle in its already volatile drug network controlled primarily by the gangs. P—crystal meth, ice, whatever you wanted to call it—was the number-one drug problem in New Zealand and accounted for a significant percentage of the profits of even half-decent suppliers.

The country had one of the worst per-capita meth problems in the world, second only, along with Australia, to Thailand. Three point four percent of the population used the damn drug. Social fallout was massive, especially in the lower-income suburbs of Auckland, and Josh had seen it all first-hand, taking Paris on countless P lab busts.

"So how come I've never heard of this kid?" he puzzled.

Mark shrugged. "Sampson stashed him with his ex in Wellington the last few years. Apparently, his new lady at that time didn't want any previous spawn around. Then Dad got sick and called the prodigal home."

Josh nodded. "So being jailed for killing Cory and stabbing Jackson would fair screw with his chance of taking over Daddy's empire. More than enough motivation to take a few risks to silence a witness."

Mark nodded. "More than enough." He waved a hand as another detective called his name. "Gotta go, sunshine. I'll keep you informed." He slid Josh a sly grin. "How's the witness doing, then?"

Josh felt his cheeks warm. *Fuck. There should be pills for that shit.* "Fine. Katie's got him staying as long as he wants."

Mark's eyes twinkled. "Has she now? Remind me to thank her. Should be entertaining if nothing else."

"Fucker."

Mark chuckled and left Josh stabbing the ground with his shoe.

AN HOUR later he'd managed to clock out on time for once and was sitting in his driveway. The house was in darkness other than the kitchen window, so there'd be no opportunity to talk to Sasha until morning. He checked his phone. Three texts from Michael in the past hour.

Michael: *Still feeling the burn. Need you to kiss it better.*

Josh snorted. The guy was an arse.

Michael: *Rematch tomorrow?*

Michael: *My turn.*

Josh's dick twitched. Of course it did. Damn thing had been starved of attention for a century. He glanced up the road toward Katie's house. A soft light glowed from her front bedroom. He typed a reply.

Josh: *I'll call you.*

He grinned. The standard "morning after" dismissal wouldn't go unnoticed.

The reply came back instantly.

Michael: *Fucking tease.*

Josh grinned and headed inside to get some sleep.

NEXT MORNING, Josh was up at seven. He intended to tackle Sasha about the family project shit before she left for school. Katie was already up, finishing breakfast at the table. She listened in silence as he caught her up.

"You knew this was coming, right?" she said pointedly. "Sasha's been getting more and more reluctant to see them. Last time you dropped her off with them, she called me every couple of hours while you were at work, begging to be picked up early."

Josh tipped his head back and closed his eyes. "Yeah, I know." He dropped his eyes to hers once more, knowing Katie struggled as much as he did with the whole parent-disaster thing. He added, "But when I try to talk with her, she just clams up. I don't know what else I can do. Does she talk to you?"

Katie shook her head. "Not really. But I think it's because she knows I'd tell you and she doesn't want to make things harder for you. I think she's protecting you."

"Just what I need," he grumbled. "My own daughter feeling sorry for me. What about them? Have they said anything?"

"Nah, just the usual bullshit, that they don't see enough of her and blame you and your 'lifestyle choices' and all that crap."

"So, nothing new there," Josh said, doing a poor job of keeping the bitterness out of his voice. "I'm gonna talk to Sasha this morning, but really, unless she opens up and gives me a good reason, I think she's just going to have to suck it up. They are her grandparents, and she is only coming up to twelve. She can decide for herself soon enough."

"I know." Katie placed her hand over his. "And for what it's worth, I think it's the right response. Sucks being a parent, huh?"

"Tell me about it." He fetched his toast and ruffled her hair on his return. She sat back and cast a critical eye over him.

He frowned. "What?"

She grabbed his chin and turned his face first one way, then the other. "Even with this Sasha thing going on you look... I don't know... different."

"Slept well for once," he answered, pulling away to spread jam on his toast. But when his sister said nothing more, he looked up.

"Nah," she said, grinning. "You got laid, didn't you?"

"You're being ridiculous." He tore his toast in half, chewing noisily. Katie had always been able to read him like a damn book.

She squealed. "Who was it? Mr Coffee Date?"

"Katie," he warned.

"Oh, come on. I've been waiting for you to get your freak on for two long years. Give me something, I'm dying here."

Josh cast a glance to the lounge and hallway beyond.

Katie tapped his hand. "She's in the shower."

"Ugh." The last thing he needed was his sister knowing about Michael, especially since it had gone down in her house for fuck's sake. Maybe not the best decision in hindsight. But it would just be his luck for Michael to spill the beans. It's probably what he'd do if their situations were reversed.

He sighed. "No, it wasn't the guy from training."

"Then who... oh." Katie's smile widened in understanding. "Michael." It wasn't even a question.

He scoffed. "You don't know everyone in my life."

"You just keep telling yourself that." She laughed. "Josh, you don't do one-night stands. It's taken you two years to get a damn coffee date with someone. So the only other new gay guy in your life is Michael. He's hot as Hades, by the way, and happens to be conveniently lodged just a few doors down in my house."

Her expression froze, and she punched him on the arm. "Ah,

goddammit. You did it in my house, didn't you, you piece of chicken shit."

Josh grinned. "Maybe. Still, you only have yourself to blame, you're the one who asked him to stay."

She scowled. "Just wash your own damn sheets and clean up any 'spills.'" She stabbed her spoon at him. "And keep off my new couch." She paused, looking sideways at him. "I assume it wasn't a one-time thing."

He shrugged. "It was... unexpected." He walked their plates to the sink, calling for Sasha to hurry up. The sooner his daughter arrived, the sooner this conversation would finish, and Josh was all for that.

Katie slid her arms around him from behind. "Okay, I'll shut up. But if you want my opinion, I think you should go for it."

Josh spun and grabbed his sister's shoulders. He stared down at her, his annoyance fading. Irritating and nosy she might be, but he loved her to bits. "It was just sex. Don't make it more than it is. I'm not going to date him."

"But what about Mr Coffee Date?"

Yeah, what about him? "We'll see. He's more... normal, if you get what I mean?"

Katie screwed up her nose like she'd eaten something nasty. "Normal, huh? As in reliable, comfortable, boring..."

Josh kicked the dishwasher door closed.

Katie threw her hands up. "Okay, message received. I'm outta here." She grabbed her handbag and scooted out the door, leaving Josh shaking his head. Sisters. Drove you nuts without even trying.

JOSH HAD Sasha's cereal and milk on the table before she appeared, her lunch ready to go on the bench.

"Hey, Dad." Sasha took her seat and began to tuck into her breakfast.

Josh kissed her head and sat opposite, scanning the newspaper headlines until she'd finished. Then he put a hand over hers when she made to leave the table.

He said, "We need to talk."

Sasha closed her eyes and slumped in her chair. "They told you, huh? About Mrs Leland getting mad at me."

He squeezed her hand. "More accurately they told me about you getting mad at her."

She sighed the dramatic sigh only an eleven-year-old girl could muster. "I don't see why I have to do it," she huffed, pushing her plate away and removing her hand from his. "You know what Gramma and Pop are like. It'll just become some big thing about how everything was better when they were growing up. How people had more respect, blah, blah, blah. Why can't I just talk to Nana and Pappy John?"

Josh took her hand again and linked their fingers. After a few seconds, she relaxed into the grip. "Is that the only reason?" he asked, watching her closely. "Seems that's something you'd be used to by now. There's nothing else going on?"

Her eyes skittered away, but the shake of her head was firm enough.

"Nothing," she answered.

He sighed. There wasn't much more he could do. "In that case I'm going to have to insist you include them in the project...."

Sasha groaned loudly. "But—"

"No, not this time. There are plenty of other kids who have to deal with that same kind of stuff from their grandparents as well. Older people are sometimes more rigid, that's all there is to it. Count yourself lucky your other set of grandparents aren't the same. At least you'll have a contrast, right?"

She rolled her eyes. "I guess. I just don't see why I have to do it if I really don't want to. They wouldn't even know. Can I at least just ask the questions over the phone?"

Josh raised his brows, saying nothing.

Sasha's expression reflected her disgust. "Okay, okay. But I'm not staying more than one night. You'll pick me up Sunday before lunch, right?"

Josh levelled his gaze at her. "I'll drop you off after netball tomorrow and pick you up after softball practice Sunday. There's no promise it will be before lunch, though."

She sighed. "I suppose." Then her eyes widened. "But the party's tomorrow. You said I could go."

Shit. He'd forgotten about the damn party. "I didn't say any such thing. And this is schoolwork, hun. The party has to come second, I'm sorry. There'll be other opportunities."

Her look of disappointment was epic, and he suspected it was about more than just a party.

He ran his thumb across her cheek. "If he likes you enough, he'll still like you on Monday, whether you go to his party or not."

Sasha stared at him in disbelief. "No, he won't! He'll think I'm just a kid."

Josh sighed. "Well, if he thinks that, then he's not worth it, right?"

She jerked her hand from his and stomped her way to the dishwasher, shaking her head in that "are you really such an idiot?" way. "You don't understand anything!" she shouted, escaping to her bedroom.

Josh remained at the table and forced down a mouthful of cold coffee. His daughter was a hundred percent correct. On the subject of preteen girls, Josh understood *nothing*.

Anxious nightmares and a sackload of aching muscles clouded Michael's sleep. He battled to ignore the craving for a shot or two from Katie's well-stocked bar to take the edge off. Instead he pondered how his well-ordered life had descended into such chaos over the course of one week. Of course, that included Josh. It baffled him how he became this pathetic, needy man whenever Josh was around. He didn't bottom, and he didn't do sweet and caring. Not anymore, not for a long time. End. Of. Story.

His body had fidgeted until close to 4:00 a.m., when he finally managed to sink into something resembling sleep. When he woke, the bruising was at its worst, fifty shades of green and blue. Every bone and joint in his body protested the attack, not to mention the physical workout Josh had put him through between the sheets. He fought a smile at the thought of Josh and lost.

His ass still flinched at the stretch a little, but Michael didn't mind that particular sting as much as he thought he should. Not that he'd admit that to Josh, and he had no intention of revisiting that particular scenario until they'd reversed roles. Josh had a fine ass, deserving of all kinds of closer inspection, and Michael was just the man to do it.

A text came in at eight thirty to say Josh would be at Katie's by nine but nothing more. Michael secretly hoped they'd be horizontal by nine fifteen and decided to opt on the side of caution. He showered and breakfasted in a record fifteen minutes, somewhat disturbed by his enthusiasm, but willing to ignore it for the sake of efficiency.

He intended to head to the hospital later that morning; he might not be fit for doctoring, but he could make a dent in the backlog of paperwork spilling across his desk. Then he was to meet Mark and finish looking through their photo files. He'd be lying to say he wasn't a little nervous about that, but he'd be damned if he'd be scared off.

Scratching at the back door quickly gave way to nails flailing on the hall tiles as Paris made his way into the house and launched himself at Michael. At least someone was pleased to see him. Michael dropped to the floor, ignoring his aching joints, to let the dog run circles around him.

"Hello to you too, gorgeous," he said, scruffing the shepherd's neck and planting a kiss on the mutt's forehead. "Yeah, I love you too."

He sensed the minute Josh entered the kitchen, his freshly showered citrus-and-spice cologne instantly messing with Michael's dick. He said nothing straight off, no need to appear too excited to see Josh after all, and instead bundled the shepherd into the backyard.

"There's a treat out there if you can find it," Michael told the animal, sliding the glass door shut and smiled as Paris planted his nose to the ground and took off. "Smart dog."

Warm breath fanned out across his neck, and arms slid tight around his waist. *Goddammit.* The guy had ninja skills.

"He can smell it a mile off." Josh hummed against his back. "You'll spoil him."

Michael leaned back into the contact. "I like to spoil my men." *Ugh. Where did that sap come from?*

A pair of lips pressed to his shoulder, nipping and nuzzling a line up to his jaw, and a hand slid under his shirt. Michael's cock was granite in an instant. *Christ.* He had no control around this guy.

He rocked back, relishing the unmistakable interest he felt in Josh's groin, and Josh locked his teeth on Michael's shoulder in reply. The sensation shot straight to Michael's dick. "Miss breakfast, did we?" he teased, angling his neck to give him better access.

Josh's fingers found a nipple while the other hand wrapped around Michael's dick and... *Fuck.* If he didn't get some breathing room soon, it was gonna be all over before the fat lady even got dressed, let alone sang.

He twisted to face Josh, hands on Josh's chest. "Whoa there, mister. I've got a reputation to uphold that doesn't include creaming myself in ten seconds flat. Arrogant asshole, remember?" He planted a firm kiss on Josh's lips.

Josh grinned. "I remember."

Michael stole another kiss, then another. "Yum. And good morning to you too."

Josh grabbed his hips and slammed their groins together, his tongue sliding through Michael's lips to claim his mouth. *Alrighty then.* He was clearly on a mission, and Michael had no problem with that.

"Mmm," he purred, somewhat embarrassed by the sound. Then he pushed Josh away just enough to put some air between their bodies while still resting their foreheads together. The blistering heat in Josh's gaze sent a shiver straight through him.

"Cold?" Josh smirked, arching his hips to rub up against Michael.

Michael was so close to shooting his load he had to count backwards from fifty, so he pushed Josh away, again, this time planting his hands on those broad shoulders to keep him in place.

"Time out," he blustered. "Or I'm going to embarrass myself, again."

Josh cocked an eyebrow, his gaze taking in Michael's tented sweats. "I could help with that. We're trained to serve, after all."

Fucking hell. All the lustful attention should've had Michael feeling right at home, should've had him messing with Josh's blatant desire, but for some reason he felt more vulnerable than he had in a long time.

He scooted into the kitchen, putting the breakfast bar between them for good measure. Josh grinned, wicked and delicious, and Michael groaned. *Oh, for fuck's sake.* He held up a hand.

"Believe me," he said, "I look forward to being 'served.' I really, really do. But perhaps we could discuss our plans for the rest of the day first?"

"Having trouble keeping up, are we?" Josh smirked.

Michael just rolled his eyes.

"Okay, message received." Josh was clearly trying to keep a straight face and losing. "Our plans, then." He leaned his elbows on the breakfast bar, his gaze slamming into Michael's with heated intent. "Well, *my* plan is to have your arse naked in under a minute and fucked senseless until you can't remember your name, shortly thereafter. You got a better one?"

Holy ever-living hell. Michael's jaw fell open and his brain packed its bags and headed south to visit its cousin. How the fuck did this man own Michael so easily without even breaking a sweat? They only had to share the same space for a few minutes, and Michael was cowering behind a damn breakfast bar with a raging hard-on. It was some evil, witch shit, for sure. Josh played havoc with Michael's equilibrium. Aware he was still staring, Michael slammed his gaping mouth shut and tried to thread a few thoughts together.

"Ah… yeah—" *Jesus, get a grip.* He cleared his throat and rolled out his best leer. "Well, since you put it that way… I'd of course be happy to take the advice of one of our 'boys in blue.' Or a version of his plan, at any rate."

Josh raised a brow. "A version?"

Michael answered with a smirk. "You heard me. A version. But I need to be at the hospital by ten thirty."

Josh frowned. "You sure going to work is a good idea? How's the bruising? Nice shiner, by the way."

Michael rolled his eyes. "Bruising is fine." He scowled and stabbed a finger at Josh. "Not that you seemed overly concerned about it yesterday. It appears I can be fucked senseless with no concern, but doing a bit of paperwork is a bad idea?"

Josh blushed, and oh my living Lord the man was delicious.

"Point taken," Josh said, and a flicker of guilt crossed his face.

"It was fine," Michael reassured him. "More than, as you well know. But I'm not gonna just sit here and twiddle my thumbs. I was going to go to the funeral, but I'm guessing you'd say that wouldn't be smart."

"Bang on," Josh agreed.

"Figured. Besides, there's paperwork I can do even if I can't cover the shift. And I'm meeting with Mark to go through those headshots."

Josh stiffened. "Well, I wouldn't expect the man himself, they're pretty busy." He sniffed. "He'll have organised some admin guy to hold your hand." He pushed off the breakfast bar and turned to check on Paris.

Huh. Michael smiled, sensing a subtle shift in the delicate balance of power between them. "Nah," he replied innocently. "He said to text when I got there, and we'd grab a coffee first, maybe a late lunch." Not actually what he'd said, but what the hell. This was proving fun. He watched as Josh chewed on his bottom lip, still pretending to look at his dog.

Michael added, "He's a nice guy. Kind of cute, actually."

Josh's gaze flicked back to Michael, his eyes dark. "Wouldn't have thought he was your type."

Michael kept a straight face. "Wouldn't have said you were either." *Liar.* "And yet here we are...." He never got to finish the sentence before Josh had him crowded up against the bench, caging him like prey.

"Enough talk." Josh's voice grew thick.

A thrill ran the length of Michael's body. Just being in kissing distance of Josh flipped every one of his switches. Josh was like a fucking tuning fork that Michael's body immediately aligned with.

He pressed his lips to Michael's, his tongue flicking along the crease. "So, are we doing this?" he breathed, nipping Michael's bottom lip. "Or are we just gonna fucking plan it all morning?"

Michael reached between them and cupped Josh's balls and Josh arched into the contact with a groan. "Well, you know what they say, officer," he purred, "failing to plan, is planning to fail." He undid the top button on Josh's jeans and slipped his hand inside to wrap around Josh's thick cock.

"Mmm," Josh hummed happily. "You know what else they say?" He breathed the question into Michael's mouth. "Overplanning kills the magic. So how about we just make some fucking magic, already." His tongue became more demanding, teeth nipping at Michael's lips, hands holding him exactly where Josh wanted him. He kissed down Michael's throat to the dip in the centre of its base where he paused a few seconds to nibble.

"Mmm," Michael groaned, inviting more, lots, lots more. "Not to labour the point," he murmured, "but ten thirty, remember?"

Josh nodded as he continued to nibble.

"And about your plan," Michael lifted Josh's chin with a wicked smile. "I have a slight amendment to make."

Josh's eyebrows twitched in amusement. "An amendment?"

Michael grinned. "Yes. I do believe, according to our contract, that it's my turn to fuck you senseless, officer."

Josh's pupils blew, and his eyes turned chocolate black. He captured Michael's lips and kissed him hard. "Then, need I remind you, doctor, you're on the clock." He stepped back and spread his hands. "Have at it."

Michael needed no further encouragement. He shoved Josh into the dining room and up against the table, pulling at his jeans. "Get them off, wolf-man. Now," he growled.

Josh was out of his jeans in a second, kicking them aside before hauling Michael closer, careful to avoid his injuries. He grabbed the hem of Michael's tee and had it off just as fast, running his hands over Michael's chest, grazing his nipples one at a time. Capturing each one in his mouth, he tugged gently while his other hand trailed south.

"Fuck," Michael hissed, throwing his head back. Somehow Josh was running this damn thing... again.

"You're way overdressed," Josh murmured, dragging Michael's sweats down to wrap a hand around his cock. "Damn." He ran a fingertip over Michael's flared crown. "Do you ever wear under-wear?" He held out the finger wet with precum, and Michael took it in his mouth, keeping his eyes locked on Josh as he sucked and tasted himself.

Josh's pupils went wide. "Fuck me."

Michael smirked. "That's the idea." He pushed Josh away and stepped out of his sweats before peeling Josh's shirt over his head.

They took a few seconds to appreciate each other before coming together again, Josh wrapping his arm around Michael's hips, spin-ning to reverse their positions and trap him against the table. Then he brought their dicks together in a rough-and-ready grind, fingers grazing Michael's ass, sliding into the crease. The man was a freaking octopus. Michael shifted his weight and spun them both back to where they started.

"What part of 'my turn' wasn't clear to you, wolf-man?" He sucked on Josh's lower lip before delivering a sharp nip.

Josh hissed in a breath. "Ow."

"Good. Now, pay attention." He sank to his knees, ignoring the brief stab of pain, and took Josh's cock in a single swallow, delivering it hard to the back of his throat.

"Ugh." Josh fisted his hair and thrust lightly into his mouth.

Nuh-uh, sunshine. Michael enjoyed being face-fucked by the right guy, but he wasn't about to cede his fragile grip on control just yet. He grabbed Josh by the hips and held him still as he slid his tongue up and down the length of his shaft and over the crown. Then he worked his balls, tugging gently and nuzzling deep into Josh's groin. He hummed as he worked, the sound vibrating through Josh's cock.

Unintelligible murmurings reassured him he was on track, and Josh squirmed under the barrage of sensation. His hands were now loose around Michael's head, tunnelling through his hair. Then one slid under Michael's chin, raising it until they locked eyes.

Josh grinned down at him. "Goddamn, what a glorious sight."

Michael pulled back a little so Josh got a better view, and Josh locked on every movement, apparently entranced. *Hell yeah.* Michael was damn pleased with himself. He needed inside this man so badly....

Shit. He pulled off, leaving Josh's cock bobbing. "Supplies," he breathed, struggling to his feet.

Josh gently pushed him down. "Jeans, back pocket, hotshot."

Michael's scowl morphed to a grin. "You good little boy, you."

Josh waggled his eyebrows. "There's even lube."

"Fucking brownie points on top," Michael said, chuckling. Retrieving both items, he found himself pulled up into Josh's arms for a further attack on his mouth. Josh sure loved to kiss. Michael preferred to keep his fuck buddies at arm's length, but he suspected any conversation with Josh to that end would have been a total waste of breath. Instead, he dropped his mouth to Josh's shoulder and bit hard, knowing he'd leave a solid mark.

"Fucker," Josh grumbled but made no attempt to pull away.

Michael kissed the spot. "Yeah, payback's a bitch, right?" He wrestled Josh around as best he could with his aching ribs and kicked his feet apart. "You need to shrink a couple inches," he complained.

"How about you grow?" Josh pressed his ass into Michael's groin.

"How about I give you something else to think about?" Michael pushed him over the table and pressed a hand to his back. "Don't move," he ordered, somewhat surprised when Josh actually complied. Wonders. He gloved and slicked up before dripping a little cool lube down Josh's crack.

Josh hissed and clenched his buttocks. "Arsehole."

Michael chuckled. "Give the man a prize." He ran his slick fingers over Josh's hole, then around to wrap around his solid cock, applying a few rough strokes before returning to his primary focus. By his own admission, Josh hadn't been fucked in a while, and Michael wanted him well prepped.

Josh's hand slid down to grab his erection, but Michael batted it away. "Nuh-uh," he warned. "That's mine."

"Well, get on with it, then. I'm good to go here."

Michael grinned, still working him open. He was tight as fuck. "Who says it's for you," he argued. "I love being up your ass." He pushed a little farther, curled his fingers and... there.

"Bastard." Josh twisted his hips and impaled himself on Michael's fingers.

Michael nearly came on the spot, the sensation and the visual was so freaking hot. Controlling Josh was like trying to herd those proverbial cats. He slapped his ass with his free hand and dropped to his knees, spreading Josh's cheeks.

"Push back again," he ordered, and when Josh obliged, Michael drove his tongue alongside his fingers.

"Jesus Christ. Fuck me already."

Michael pulled back and bit Josh's asscheek. "Ask nicely."

Josh growled.

Michael bit again, then stood and stepped between Josh's legs, one hand on his back, the other steadying his own dick at Josh's entrance. Josh's breath hitched and Michael knew he had him. "Yeah, babe, that's it." *Shit*. He let the slip go. Whatever. Not like Josh would remember.

From the other side of the glass slider, Paris watched the proceedings with an uncertain look in his eye. Thank God for the closed door. Michael nudged his cock against Josh again. "Come on, wolf-man. I've got you. Whaddya gonna say?"

Josh's shoulders relaxed, and the word came on a sigh, so quiet Michael almost missed it.

"Please?"

Thank Christ. "You got it." He kissed Josh's shoulder and pushed forward in one slow fluid motion. *Holy ever-loving crap*. He was tight and hot, relaxing and bearing down just right to take Michael up to the hilt on his first plunge. It was so smooth and snug it damn near pushed Michael over the edge. So much for Josh not having done it in a while.

Michael grabbed the base of his dick and breathed, counting marks on the table, trees in the lawn, any damn thing to stop himself being buried in embarrassment by blowing his load barely one second in. *Come on, wolf-man*. Josh clenched, then unclenched his hands as he adjusted to the fullness.

"You said it's been a while?" Michael breathed against Josh's back. "So, either you're gifted anatomically... or you've got some serious toy kinks we need to investigate further."

Josh huffed, and Michael thought he made out the word "gifted." *You got that right*. A reminder of yesterday, what it was like to bottom for Josh, sent a nervous shudder through Michael. He had some serious competition to live up to.

"Move already," Josh ordered.

So much for submission. Michael thrust slow and steady at first, adjusting the angle until he was sure by Josh's groans that he was hitting the right spot.

"Harder." Josh threw an arm back to grab Michael's thighs and pull him deeper.

Toppy bastard. Michael kicked things up and set about a

punishing rhythm, deep and fast, hauling Josh up against his chest as best he could, one arm slung over Josh's shoulder and one around his waist to keep him still. At the same time, he buried his teeth lightly in Josh's neck to anchor his ride.

"Touch yourself. This isn't gonna take long," he warned him.

Josh moaned, grabbing his dick. "I'm with you," he said on a breath. Then he pushed back hard, clenching his arse tight around Michael and sending him over, milking the orgasm out of him, forcing him to come first.

Michael unloaded into the condom, trembling as he rode the wave of pleasure, continuing to thrust until Josh began to tense in return. With that, he pulled out and spun Josh to face him, holding him lightly at his throat while he took over and jacked him hard.

"Wanna see you lose it, wolf-man."

Josh groaned. His head fell back, and Michael watched, riveted as Josh came undone before him. A myriad of emotions crossed his face as the intense sensations pumped through him. He was so damn expressive. Ribbons of cum flew to coat both their stomachs as he shuddered and collapsed against Michael, twitching as the last of the orgasm left his body.

"Fucking awesome," Michael mumbled against Josh's neck.

They held each other up a few more seconds, then slid to the floor as one, slick with sweat and cum. Josh stretched out on the cool tiles, arms above his head, breathing heavily. "Fuck me," he huffed.

Michael reached over and patted his chest. "Been there, done that. But, yeah, we really need to bag and tag that shit. We could make a fortune."

When he got no response, Michael rolled to his side and stared at Josh, poking his forehead with his finger. "I can hear the cogs grinding from here. Spill."

Josh snorted. "Say please? You really had to go there, huh?"

"Hey, I had to do something. You give new meaning to the term power bottom."

Josh's face flushed bright red. *Damn.* The guy was down and dirty and toppy as hell one minute, then cute as a button the next.

"So, yesterday." Josh was hesitant, a loose, sexed-out grin on his face. "It was great, don't get me wrong. But I kind of wondered if it was just me, you know, the fact that I was... well, not to put too fine a point on it... but I was kind of starved for it, I suppose. But today blew me away, all joking aside. Sex with you... it's pretty... intense, yeah? Then again, I have less to compare it with than you, I imagine."

Michael paused, wondering just how to respond. He knew what Josh meant, and yeah, he felt it too, but nothing felt remotely safe about owning that shit now. "Let's just say we're on a roll, wolf-man," he said jokingly. "And I'll try not to take offence at you calling me a slut."

"Shit, I didn't mean..."

Michael laughed. "It was a joke. Relax. Maybe it's the arrogant asshole twin thing we've got going on. That's some volatile shit right there."

"Maybe." Josh stared at the ceiling, his expression now more guarded.

Shit. Way to shut the conversation down, dickhead.

Josh sighed. "Or maybe the sexual chemistry is partly to do with the fact that we're *not* going any further with each other, just enjoying the ride. No expectations."

Michael tried to ignore the twinge of something like regret in his chest. "Yeah. Probably that."

THE SWITCH in Michael's mood was hard to miss, and it had Josh curious. He seemed almost... disappointed. But that couldn't be right. This was casual fucking, nothing more. Michael had been adamant about that, even more so than Josh.

They were crazy good in the sack, no question. Tinder-to-fucking-flame good, but that didn't change a damn thing about how opposite they sat on the stuff that was important to Josh like commitment, family, and oh yeah, monogamy. Josh had seen Michael in action. He'd be stupid to think Michael could want anything more serious. That would be a bad idea, a very bad idea.

They'd showered and were sharing a coffee at the table with Paris whining around their legs.

Josh snorted. "He can smell the sex."

Michael's eyes widened. "Really? That's... kind of gross, to be honest. He was watching us through the door when I was fucking you. Creeped me out for a few seconds."

"Just a few seconds, huh?"

"Well, I did have better things to focus on." Michael's sapphire eyes twinkled.

Josh groaned. Michael sat there in fresh jeans and a white button-down shirt, smelling of orange, spice, and coffee, and all Josh wanted to do was start at the top and lick his way down. He squirmed in his seat and adjusted himself.

Michael smirked.

Josh flipped him off. "Behave yourself." Paris lifted his head. "Not you, fella. He gets pretty protective."

"I noticed. I wouldn't want any of my bits dangling if he decided I was being a bit too rough with you for his liking."

Josh cracked up. "I'll bear that in mind." He glanced at the clock. Ten. "Thought you wanted to be at the hospital by ten thirty."

"Give or take." Michael sipped on his coffee, not seeming in any particular hurry, and they sat in comfortable silence for a bit.

It was almost too damn comfortable, that was the problem. Josh needed to draw this to a close. Instead he said, "You wanna come and watch my daughter play netball tomorrow?" *What the hell?*

Michael's cup froze halfway to his lips, a flash of panic lighting up his eyes. "Ah..."

Shit. "Forget about it," Josh sputtered. "Stupid idea. I shouldn't have asked. Not really part of our... um... thing... is it?" He fidgeted as Michael stared down at his coffee. But when Michael finally lifted his gaze, it was to flash Josh a smile, and then it was Josh's turn to panic.

"Yeah, why not?" he answered. "Though I don't have a clue about the game, to be honest."

He sounded wary, though, and Josh raised an eyebrow. "You sure? It's just a bunch of kids. You don't seem too certain."

Michael took a sip of coffee and studied Josh with a bemused expression. "It's just that you've never once mentioned having a daughter, that's all."

Because I never intended for you to meet her. Which only begged the obvious question, which Josh ignored. He took a gulp of his own coffee and steadied himself. "Oh, yeah, well—"

"A bit personal for fuck buddies, right?"

Heat bloomed in Josh's cheeks; he could feel it. "Maybe."

Michael gave a wide grin and held up his hands. "Hey, I get it. But then, why the invite now?"

Paris pushed his head into Josh's lap, and he slipped his hand around the shepherd's ears, grounding himself. "Just figured you had to be bored out of your mind holed up here," he lied. "But you don't have to...." He met Michael's eyes.

"No, you're right, I am. And I appreciate it." Michael reached to scruff Paris's ears himself. "So, how old is this daughter of yours, then?"

"Eleven. Sasha."

Michael glanced up. "Pretty name."

"Pretty girl, but definitely in the cranky preteen years. Not at all sure I'm equipped for what's to come, if you catch my drift."

Michael glanced into the yard, slowly spinning his empty coffee cup on the table. He spoke the next words softly. "That mean you were married? To a woman?"

Josh snorted. "Nah. Lived with one for a bit, though."

Michael frowned. "So, bi or just a late bloomer?"

Josh walked their coffee cups to the sink, taking time to decide how much he wanted to say. "Definitely not bi," he finally answered, taking his seat. "I knew I was gay from about fifteen. Went with a couple of girls, but then one time with a guy and it was a done deal. Awesome versus ho-hum." He grinned. "Didn't mean I was out, though. My parents are kind of a nightmare, and the police force was less gay friendly fifteen years back, ask Mark. He had it rough at the beginning. I'll always admire him for having the courage to be out with all the shit he took. I wasn't so brave." He stole a glance at Michael who simply nodded.

"But you have a daughter?"

"Yes, I do. Proof that once is enough. A disaster all round, but I love Sasha to bits. I was still closeted, and her mother, Anna, had the attention span of a flea, lacking a single mothering gene in her entire DNA. She took off in the first year, leaving us both to get on with it."

Michael's eyes grew wide. "Wow. Sorry."

"Don't be. I wouldn't change having Sasha in my life for anything. Grew me up quick, though. Made me into the boring, judgemental, vanilla, arrogant delight you see before you. Regardless of that, Sasha is the best thing that ever happened to me."

Michael raised his brows but remained quiet. Some gay men simply never felt the pull of children. Others saw the whole family/marriage thing as part of some heteronormative lifestyle they refused to buy into. Josh wondered where Michael sat on that continuum, not that it mattered. He wasn't sure he'd have gone the kid route himself if it hadn't been thrust upon him.

"Yeah, I can see that," Michael agreed in a quiet voice, though his tone sounded less convinced. "Did Anna keep in touch?"

Josh explained the recent contact and the mixed feelings he had about it.

"That has to be better for Sasha, though, right?" Michael commented.

"You'd think."

He cocked an eyebrow at Josh.

"Of course it is," Josh agreed. "I'm just still so fucking mad at her.

I mean who fucking does that? Who just walks out on their kid and throws them away like yesterday's trash?"

Tears pricked Josh's eyes, and Michael's hand immediately covered his. *Shit.* The last thing he needed was pity from Michael. He freed his hand and dropped it on his lap.

Michael frowned but made no comment. "Must have been tough," he said.

Josh sighed. "Yeah. Sasha doesn't talk much about it, but I always thought it was a blessing that she was only a baby when Anna took off. And I couldn't have done it without Katie. A surrogate mom, I guess."

There was a moment of silence, and then Michael cupped Josh's jaw, forcing him to meet Michael's eyes. "I meant *you*, actually. Tough on *you*. That was a pretty crap hand to be dealt. Still, I'd bet my life on you being a great dad." He pressed his lips gently to Josh's, then pulled back.

The kind words rattled Josh more than he was willing to admit. *Christ.* He'd thought he was so past this shit. He swallowed hard. "I'm not sure you know me well enough to be so sure, but thanks anyway."

Michael batted his arm playfully. "I know more than enough, wolf-man. What I see is a passionate, hard-working, honest guy with a big heart, plenty of friends, a sister who loves him, and an excellent bullshit detector for on-the-make queers like yours truly. Even if said guy is slightly too quick to judge same." Michael leaned in and brushed his lips across Josh's in a soft feather touch. "I know enough."

Well, fuck. Josh felt the flush grow on his cheeks. "Point taken, all of them... and thanks."

"You're welcome." Michael leaned back in his chair. "So, anyone since?"

"A few. One serious boyfriend. We lived together. Thought he was the one, until he wasn't." Josh wasn't willing to go further.

Michael didn't push. Instead he waggled his eyebrows wickedly.

"Well, I for one can absolutely see the whole power bottom thing morphing into one kick-ass dad."

Josh nearly choked on his coffee, having to lean over the table to stop the drips running down his shirt. "That sentence is never to cross your lips ever again," he warned, dabbing at his trousers.

"Or what?" Michael pressed. "Promise me there'll be consequences. Lots and lots of consequences." The heat in Josh's gaze ramped up.

"You have no idea," Josh answered, his cock replying with an interested twitch. "Be ready by nine thirty tomorrow. It's outdoors, so bring a jacket."

Michael's mouth quirked up. "Will I see you again before then?"

Josh snorted. "Maybe. I'll text." Michael's sexy grin sent a shiver through him. And when he leaned in and placed his lips alongside Josh's ear, Josh wanted to climb him like a tree.

"I'll be naked and waiting, then, just in case," Michael whispered.

Ugh. Josh couldn't stop the groan escaping his lips. "You do that," he said. "But remember, it's my turn."

Michael ran his hands down to cup Josh's balls and give them a gentle squeeze. "If you give me enough warning, I'll even wear my plug. Be good and ready for you." He sealed the deal with a searing kiss. "Now get out of here before I drag your naked ass into that bedroom and fuck you until you can't walk, and Paris has to carry you through your shift."

It was a thought that wildly pleased Josh, and one that would get him through Cory Bryant's funeral that afternoon.

CHAPTER SEVEN

BEST INTENTIONS ASIDE, A LAST-MINUTE ROBBERY OF A convenience store in the city centre after the funeral saw Josh's hopeful plans evaporate. He and Paris ended up tracking the idiot five kilometres through Symonds Street Cemetery and the Auckland Domain until one in the morning.

The funeral had been a gut-wrenching tearjerker, and Josh had looked forward to blowing off some steam. Seeing the twenty-three-year-old slain officer's young family fall apart at their loss had been one of the hardest things he'd ever witnessed. And although the man had been relatively new to the Auckland Station, his death brought home the reality of the job's risks in the worst possible way.

Manning a shift immediately after the funeral had been all kinds of hard, but when the robbery call first went out, Josh had reluctantly made the "no go" call to Michael and taken a minute to share the details of his crap day. Plus, he'd been keen to hear if Michael had been able to make an ID at the station. Answer, he hadn't. When later Josh had checked in with Mark, the detective told him that Michael had lingered over the image of Denton Cruz, a fact that got Mark all excited, but they'd only had a three-year-old photo to go by.

It was minus tatts, jewellery, and scars. Eventually, Michael had dismissed it.

It was bad news for any imminent arrest, but on the plus side, Mark had already passed news of the ID washout to their undercover guys, who'd make sure it got through to the gangs. By the next day, the threat on Michael should have eased, if not gotten him off their radar altogether. It made no sense for them to pursue him and risk getting caught in a police backlash if Michael couldn't ID them. It was a win as far as Josh was concerned, and it meant the doctor could head back to his place sooner than expected.

Michael had seemed equally disappointed at the cancelled booty call. "That sound you hear," he'd grumbled, "is the butt plug hitting the washbasin." And damn, if that image hadn't imbedded itself in Josh's mind for the remainder of the night. It ensured he spent the two-hour search sporting a semi.

It had been three before he'd crawled into bed. He'd been cold, wet, and without the buzz of a successful arrest to ease the bone-deep ache in his muscles. No surprise that the seven o'clock alarm came as a nasty shock. It was accompanied by thumping on the bedroom door.

"Dad, get up. We'll be late."

"There's no one by that name here." Josh groaned. "I'm pretty sure he died of an allergy to eleven-year-old girls."

"Dad! Get up or I'll let Paris in."

"Go away, demon spawn," he grumbled, dragging the bedclothes over his head. "Any real daughter of mine would never be so cruel."

The door flew open, and Paris landed on his bed, doubling Josh in half with a paw to his groin. "Shit... watch where you're landing, mutt."

"Swear jar, Dad," Sasha scolded with a grin, planting herself next to him. "Time to get up, pretty man. I've got a netball game to win."

Josh rolled to his side, enfolding his daughter in a fierce bear hug. "What did you call me?"

Sasha giggled. "Pretty man, pretty man, pretty man."

He tickled her sides until she squealed and squirmed like a jelly-fish, tears rolling down her face. When he finally let go, she collapsed beside him, grinning like a loon. A second later she reached up and brushed the hair out of his eyes. He didn't think he could love her any more in that moment.

"Pretty man, huh?" he said with a mock scowl.

Sasha cupped his face in her hands, turning it from side to side, inspecting it. "Janice's mom said you're a pretty guy in an Action Man package. She said that a lot of pretty guys are gay, but to get pretty and buff together was unusual, and it makes it harder to tell."

What the...? Josh nearly swallowed his tongue. "And she said this to you?"

Sasha laughed. "No, silly. She was talking to Holly's mom in the library. I just overheard. Anyway, I think it's kind of silly, 'cause Jase was gay, but he wasn't pretty."

Oh, he was pretty, all right. Try, pretty despicable. Josh kept his mouth shut.

She continued. "And he wasn't obviously gay."

Josh raised his brows.

Sasha blanched. "Not that there's anything wrong with being obviously gay," she flustered.

He grinned. "Go on."

She kept a wary eye on his face. "I just meant that if they didn't know you, no one would think it, right? Mom didn't pick you as gay straight off either... or not straight," she giggled.

Sweet Jesus. What rabbit hole had he fallen down this morning? Josh couldn't even think of a sensible response. "So, are you saying it's better not to be obviously gay?" Truth was, he was interested to know how she saw things, especially having a gay dad.

She frowned, clearly giving the question serious thought. "I know it shouldn't matter, but I think it's maybe easier when you're growing up. A lot of people are still dicks about it, like Gramma and Pop."

He winced inwardly. Out of the mouths of babes. Not the answer he'd wish for in an ideal world but truthful as she saw it, and at this stage he'd take that. *Oh God.* He was gonna have to revisit the whole sex talk thing again, wasn't he? Those conversations amounted to prodding a nest of vipers, point in case.

Josh tapped her chest with his finger. "Dicks? Not technically a swear word but not far off. Right, this conversation is done, missy. Vamoose."

He watched her go, wishing he could erase the last five minutes from his memory.

KATIE HAD left a note saying she'd opted for a sleep-in so not to wake her. Josh briefly wondered if she was seeing someone again, but it wasn't like her to be secretive about it. A little brotherly digging was clearly on the horizon. Payback was a bitch.

That left just the two of them when they called to pick Michael up for the game. His daughter hadn't even raised an eyebrow on hearing Michael would be joining them. "Cool," she'd said, barely lifting her eyes from her *Candy Crush* game.

Michael was waiting outside, freshly showered and looking lip-smacking delicious. The shiner added a certain bad boy element to the mix that was kind of hot. Wearing a pair of skinny light-wash jeans, black Vans, and a black woollen bomber open over a white tee, he gave Josh a huge smile followed by a wink that sent the blood straight to Josh's groin.

Michael greeted Sasha with a friendly enough "hey," which she returned. She made no mention of his bruised face, something Josh had forgotten to warn her about. And any concerns he might have had about the two of them hitting it off proved misplaced as they immediately embarked on a convoluted discussion about netball, Sasha's team, the merits of their opposition, and their relative chances of a win. Michael must have done some homework on the rules of the game, and the thought did funny things to Josh's stomach.

At the courts, Sasha pulled Josh down for a hug, whispering in his ear, "He's, like, totally cute, Dad." She punched his arm, then ran off to join her team. Standing up, he'd found Michael tight to his side, the smirk on Michael's face suggesting he'd caught the exchange.

"Nice kid." Michael clapped Josh on the shoulder. "Like, totally nice." He grinned and headed for the bleachers, leaving Josh no option but to follow. Yeah, right. Michael was totally cute, like a great white was cute.

Despite Josh's concerns, when the game got under way, Michael genuinely seemed to be having a good time. He asked lots of questions, cheered when Sasha's team was doing well, and grumbled at referee calls that went against them. The whole thing put Josh in a ridiculously good mood. Then Sasha's team scored a win in their first game, and Michael leapt to his feet, punched the air with a loud yes, and turned to high five Josh. Sasha heard and faced them from the court with a delighted grin. It was all Josh could do not to tackle him to the ground and kiss him senseless.

There was a thirty-minute break between games, and Josh spent the first part of that answering all of Michael's questions around rules and contact. Michael had picked up that, for a theoretically noncontact sport, there seemed to be an awful lot of fairly aggressive manoeuvring in the goal circle, where Sasha played defence. Michael listened attentively, one thigh pressed hard against Josh's, the heated contact doing funny things to Josh's insides.

The whole morning was going so well, Josh couldn't remember why he'd ever been worried it might not be a good idea. Then he was reminded like a bucket of cold water to the face. In the middle of explaining a rule about shooting, he glanced up and caught sight of Jase. The fucker was talking to Sasha at her team bench, and she was smiling up at the weasel, sucking on her water bottle and clearly lapping up whatever sappy shit he was throwing her way. Josh's good mood evaporated immediately.

"Shit."

. . .

MICHAEL CAUGHT the expletive and followed Josh's gaze. "Who's that?"

Josh sighed. "The ex. Jason."

"As in the lived together, partner ex?"

Josh nodded.

Huh. Michael studied Jason with interest. He was chatting to an animated Sasha with an ease that spoke of long periods of time spent together. It was a close familiarity that Michael may or may not have felt a slight prick of jealousy about. *Okay. That was unexpected.*

It had, after all, taken a fair bit for him not to run screaming at the first sight of Sasha. Comparisons with Marcia were unavoidable, especially the age, the cascading hair, and the olive skin. None of it bore up under closer examination, but the passing resemblance added up to a near-instant panic attack just the same. Michael had held it together fairly well, considering. And the more he studied Sasha, the more he saw the differences. It was enough to calm his heart and allow him to breathe.

He nudged Josh with his shoulder. "Problem?"

"What?" Josh replied, not lifting his eyes from his daughter.

Michael nodded to the ex. "Is *that* a problem?" he repeated.

Josh sighed, a deep frown etched on his forehead. "Nah. He's just a jerk. Hadn't expected to see him here today, that's all."

Michael continued to observe as Josh's daughter chatted to Jason, the two of them laughing over something. Then Sasha pointed their way, and he saw Jason's gaze laser focus on Josh before sliding sideways to Michael. The dick stared just this side of too long, then high-fived the girl and made his way toward the bleachers. This was going to be interesting.

Jason was a good-looking man and walked with the confidence of someone who knew he drew attention from both sexes, knew it and used it. In other words, full of himself—and Michael hated him on sight. There were physical similarities between himself and Jason, perhaps enough to confirm Josh had a type, and if this ex had done a number on Josh, as Michael's gut was telling him, then no wonder

Josh had given Michael the stink eye from the start. And if Josh ever learned about Michael's track record with Simon, it would only serve to cement that impression.

Without a word to Michael, Josh left his seat and headed down to meet his ex. Michael rolled his eyes. *Hey, no problem. Sure, I'll wait here.* He kicked himself for being childish and kept his eyes trained on the two men.

The ex saw Josh coming and flashed him a huge grin that had Michael's skin crawling. He pulled Josh into a close hug that Michael could tell was unwelcome, Josh giving new meaning to the word rigid. Glancing at Sasha, Michael saw she was watching the interaction intently, maybe even hopefully. *Crap.* Sasha might like the ex, but watching the two men together, it was easy to see that Josh couldn't stand the guy. Michael might not know Jason, or what had gone on between the two, but he tended to agree with Josh's sentiment. Not helped by the fact that Jason was way, way too handsy for Michael's liking, touching Josh's arms and back repeatedly as he talked.

Their discussion seemed friendly enough, with lots of shared glances at Sasha and the other team, clearly discussing the game. On one occasion, the ex indicated behind him to a young man leaning on a car in the car park, and Josh's hands fisted at his sides. Then in what was clearly a deliberate move to fuck with Josh, Jason blew the guy a kiss. *Bastard.*

Not that the young man seemed too thrilled about things either. He was hot, in that young, cool, aloof kind of way, hands in pockets, legs crossed, glaring. The latest boyfriend on parade, if Michael had to guess. So, this shithead liked playing games, did he? Michael couldn't help but wonder what the hell Josh had ever seen in him. Then he thought back to his own behaviour with Simon. *Yeah, pot, kettle.*

He had a panicked thought. What if Josh invited the dick to sit with them? He didn't think he could be civil to Jason for more than a few seconds, and he certainly couldn't just sit there and watch him paw his guy. *His guy? Jesus.* Since when had he started thinking of Josh as his?

And why the hell was Josh just standing there, letting it happen? The shithead ex was flirting in that patronising way that said "I know I'm hot and I'm pretty sure you haven't gotten over me," blah, blah, blah. *Shit.* Maybe Josh would feel obliged to leave Michael to go sit with that tool?

The mere thought had Michael's blood boiling, and seconds later when the ex reached out and tucked a lock of hair behind Josh's ear, Michael was suddenly done with this asshole. Josh tugged the hair forward again, but why he didn't just tell the jerk to keep his hands to himself, Michael had no idea. Then it hit him. Sasha. Josh was sucking it up because his daughter still liked Jason. *Well, fuck that.*

Michael shot to his feet, then paused. It wasn't like he could just bowl up and interrupt uninvited. If Josh had wanted them to meet, he'd have called Michael over. He needed an excuse, and just like that, Michael had one. A few minutes later he sidled up to the men with two coffees in hand.

"Here you go, hun." He held one out to Josh. "Just how you like it."

The shock on dickhead's face was worth a fucking photo. *Yeah, take that, asshole. He's too damn good for you. For me either, come to that. Now keep your fucking hands off him.*

Josh's brows peaked in surprise and his mouth quirked up, stifling a laugh. "Ah, thanks... babe." He accepted the coffee and allowed himself to be kissed on the cheek, even blushed.

Attaboy. Michael ran a hand down Josh's spine, settling it in the small of Josh's back, a territorial gesture that didn't go unnoticed by dickhead. But it was the way Josh leaned into the pressure that had Michael smiling. "Gonna introduce us, hun?" he asked innocently, as if Josh's ex hadn't even rated a mention between them prior to then.

Josh gave a soft snort. "Sure. Michael Oliver, this is my ex, Jason Clarke. Michael's an ER doctor."

"Oh." Jase offered his hand, somewhat reluctantly, Michael

thought. He accepted, making sure to add a good amount of pressure to his grip, then sipped his coffee, the ensuing silence growing somewhat awkward. He studied his cup.

"Not a bad brew," he commented. "Sorry, Jason, I would've brought you one had I known."

Josh sputtered, nearly choking on his own coffee.

Jason looked between them, sceptical to say the least. "Thanks, but, ah, we're not staying long."

"We?" Michael made a point of looking around.

"Yeah, my boyfriend." Jason waved toward the car park.

Michael glanced over. "Oh, well, you're both welcome to join us." *Ow.* Josh's hand closed around his in a bone-crushing squeeze. *Oops.*

Jason grimaced. "Maybe another time."

Yeah, right. He doubted the boyfriend could string more than a few adult words together. *I'd hide him too*, Michael thought. And Michael should know—he'd fucked more than enough just like the guy over the last couple of years.

"You're American, I take it?" There was a slight challenge in Jason's gaze.

Michael held up a hand. "Guilty as charged."

Jason's smile didn't quite reach his eyes. "On holiday, then?"

You wish. "No. Working here, actually. Auckland Med."

"Oh." Jason's gaze narrowed. "Enjoying your stay?"

"More so, recently." Michael glanced at Josh, pulling him closer.

"So, you're here for a while?" Jason's gaze slid to the courts.

Damn right I am, you shithead. He knew Jason was scoping out how serious things were between them. Michael was happy to put him on notice. "Yeah. Not going anywhere."

Jason raised a brow. "Get the shiner at work?"

Tricky little bastard. Michael grinned. "Disgruntled customer. Occupational hazard. Gets me plenty of sympathy, though." He placed another kiss on Josh's cheek, earning him a second death grip on his hand. A quick glance Sasha's direction caught the young girl staring their way. Mmm. He might have overstepped it.

The whistle blew, and the teams took to the courts once again. "Well, it was nice to meet you, Jason." Michael slipped an arm around Josh's shoulders. "Come on, babe, better get back to our seats."

Josh nodded to Jason. "Good of you to turn up, Jase. I'm sure Sasha appreciates it."

Jason placed a hand on Josh's arm, and it was all Michael could do not to deck him there and then. He settled for a low growl, not missed by the other two men. Josh bit his lip, clearly doing his level best not to break into laughter.

Jason's gaze slid to Michael, checking if Josh was on board with all his boyfriend's posturing.

Don't let me down here, wolf-man.

And just like that, Josh pulled his arm from Jason's hand and grabbed Michael's instead. *Good man.*

Jason let his arm fall to his side and continued with another ploy by saying, "I thought I might drop by next week to catch up with Sasha."

Fuck. For all Michael wanted to give Jason a piece of his mind, he had no choice but to let Josh handle this. As it was, Josh hesitated only a second before answering.

"You know Sasha's always happy to see you, Jase, but I'm gonna need some warning." He glanced Michael's way. "You know how it is."

Attaboy. Michael couldn't have been prouder, and the sour expression on Jason's face indicated he'd gotten the message loud and clear.

"Sure." Jason's tone was pissy, and for a second, Michael thought he was going to force Josh into another hug. *Not happening on my watch, douchebag.* Michael tugged Josh's hand, and he didn't bat an eye. He turned his back on Jason and followed Michael to their seats, holding his hand all the way.

Jason hung around the court another minute or so, then left with his boyfriend. *Mission fucking accomplished.* That said, Michael wasn't entirely sure how Josh was going to react to Michael's good intentions. He stole a glance sideways, but his expression gave nothing away. *Too late now.*

He gave himself over to watching the second game and tried to ignore the silence that had settled between them. It was ten minutes before he felt Josh's thigh press against his and settle there. He took that as a good sign, only then acknowledging just how worried he'd been.

"Hun? Really?" Josh chuckled softly. "You couldn't come up with something more manly?"

Michael blew out the breath he'd been holding since they'd left Jason. "Well, I had a hankering for stud muffin. Should I have gone with that?"

They laughed hard enough to garner a few nosy looks from the other parents.

Michael lowered his voice. "The coffee was a winner, though, don't you think? And speaking of names... babe? Never saw myself as a babe... just saying."

Josh fixed him with a smile full of affectionate warmth. "I beg to differ. You're absolutely a hundred percent, a babe."

Something skipped in Michael's chest and his cheeks warmed alarmingly. He. Did. Not. Blush. His gaze slid to Sasha on the court. He cleared his throat but couldn't seem to find any words.

Josh too went quiet, and they sat that way for a few minutes before Michael found his voice again. "So." He spoke softly, leaning closer. "You wanna fill me in a little? Maybe why you let that douchebag fuck with you like that?"

Josh stiffened and Michael thought too far, too soon. Then Josh relaxed.

"He's always been that way," Josh answered, looking around. "Come on, let's move." They found a more private place to sit, and Josh painted the picture about his relationship with Jase.

"Shit," Michael sympathised. "He'd been seeing other guys the whole time you two were living together?"

Josh winced. "Probably longer. We'd dated for nearly a year before he moved in. I just fucking trusted him, didn't ask the questions I should have. Stupid, huh? I was so fucking stupid." Josh stabbed his shoe repeatedly against the concrete seat in front.

Michael rested a hand on Josh's knee and squeezed gently. "Nah, you were just a man of faith, and you got taken for a ride by an asshole. Doesn't mean you should give up on the faith. Just means he didn't deserve a scrap of it."

Josh wouldn't meet Michael's eyes. "Maybe. But I should've noticed something. A fucking cop, and I got blindsided? That shit just fucks with your self-belief. I'm not sure I trust my own judgement anymore. Besides, it wasn't just me, it hurt Sasha too, and that shit's on me." He finally raised his gaze to Michael. "You ever had a guy do that? Cheat on you, betray your trust? Fucks with your head."

Don't ask that. Jesus fucking Christ. Don't ask that. Michael's tongue filled the back of his throat, and his thoughts fled to Simon. He'd never considered, not really, just how badly his actions might have affected Simon. At the time, he'd just wanted to be left alone and knew Simon was way better off without him. But Simon was in for the long haul. He was never gonna walk away, not without a fight. And Michael, barely keeping his head above the bottle, didn't have the strength for another fight. So he'd done the one, sure-fire thing he knew would end things between them with no drawn-out attempts on Simon's part to work things out.

He lifted his hand from Josh's knee, and returned it to his own. "Not like that. I was in a long-term relationship once, but it blew up, you might say. My fault. I'm not really good at that stuff, as you know. His name was Simon, a gastroenterologist at the hospital where I worked. He was one of the good guys, like you."

It wasn't altogether a lie. But how the hell did Michael tell Josh that he was the one who'd been unfaithful, who'd destroyed another man's trust and shat on his life? That would confirm every single one of Josh's fears and assumptions about him from the start? And it wasn't like they were looking long-term with this thing they had, anyway.

Josh looked surprised. "Yeah? I never pegged you as a relationship guy *at all*."

Michael shrugged. "Well, you were right. It was a one-time thing. Kind of why I haven't gone there again."

Josh nodded. "Well, lucky you. Getting one of the good guys, I mean. Nice to know they still exist."

"Hence your finely tuned asshole-player radar?"

Josh chuckled. "Hence. Guess it doesn't fail me all the time."

Ouch. Good call, Josh, good call. "Yeah, I can see that. And the fact Sasha liked Jason is why you let him screw with you now? Let him touch you, drop by whenever he wants, that kind of shit? You never told her about him, what really happened, right?"

Josh dipped his head. "I was protecting her, and I was so fucking embarrassed. I didn't want her to know what a huge mistake her dad had made. What an idiot I'd been. I thought she might not trust me to protect us. Might not trust the next guy. Jesus Christ, she'd already had her mother walk out on her." He scrubbed a hand over his face. "I just said we'd fallen out of love. That he'd hurt me, but we would still be friends, and she could still spend time with him. I try to make it look like we are friends, for her sake."

Michael sighed. "You know he still wants you, don't you? That if you asked, he'd be back in a heartbeat, although probably no more trustworthy."

Josh's head shot up, and he looked genuinely shocked. "What? No. He's just messing with my head. He made his choice."

"Not really his choice. You kicked him out."

"Yeah, but I was, am, never going to give him what he wants, an open relationship. He knows that. Besides, I could never trust him again."

"Do you still love him?"

The hesitation was short but noticeable, and Michael's heart dipped. But then Josh stiffened.

"No, I don't. I think I love the idea of what I thought we had, but not him, not anymore."

The relief Michael felt in those few words surprised the hell out of him. Then Josh continued.

"I think I'm just so damn scared. He betrayed my dream, you know? Mine and Sasha's. And I worry that maybe it's because it was an unattainable, stupid dream to start with."

Michael chuckled. "You're a romantic."

Josh blushed and shrugged. "I guess. I take it you're not."

It was said more as a statement than a question, and Michael felt the sting. He let it go. "You do realise," he ventured, "that by not telling Sasha the truth, she might well believe, or hope, you'll get back together."

Josh's eyes widened. "No. She doesn't, she can't possibly think that."

Michael gave a small shrug. "I was watching while you were talking with Jase. Her eyes never left the two of you. And Jase knows it, knows it, and is playing on it." Michael didn't know that for sure, but he wouldn't put it past the snake.

Josh's eyes widened. "Fuck. God, that would be a disaster."

"I only know what I saw," Michael said. "But I know for sure that Jase thinks he's still in with a chance. Is there a reason he might think that?" Michael suspected but wasn't sure of the answer he'd get, but the blush that flashed on Josh's cheeks removed all doubt. *Shit.* "You've slept with him, haven't you? Since the breakup?"

Josh's head fell back, eyes closed. "Ugh. Once. Once. It was a few months after the breakup. He'd called in to see Sasha, but she was out with Katie. I don't even know why I did it, but I offered him a drink. There was more than one, things got out of hand, and, well... I knew straight off it was a huge fucking mistake. Sasha never knew."

Michael was careful to keep his expression neutral, ignoring the urge to yank out great wadding clumps of his hair in frustration. "So," he said warily, "safe to say he harbours some legitimate hope, then, at least enough to fuck with you."

Josh's head snapped up, eyes blazing.

Michael lifted his hands. "Hey, I'm not judging. I'm just saying."

Josh deflated, his foot stabbing once again at the seat in front. "Yeah, maybe. But it's never going to happen again." He chewed his bottom lip, and all Michael wanted to do was kiss him senseless and ease the sting. Instead, he simply took his hand.

"Well, maybe he won't be so cocky after today," Michael said. "We gave him something to think about... hun." He squeezed Josh's hand.

Josh relaxed with a chuckle. "Yeah, thanks to you... babe. And I'll talk to Sasha. You know it felt damn good to see him squirm for a bit, even if it was a lie."

Maybe not so much of a lie. Michael's heart did that dippy thing.

SASHA WAS quiet on the drive to her grandparents', providing little more than one-word answers to anything Josh asked. He worried she'd noticed the face-off thing between Michael and Jason at the courts, but when he tried to ask her about it, she clammed up. It would keep. There was enough between them with the whole school-project thing without borrowing trouble.

At his parents' house, Michael waited in the car while Josh walked Sasha to the front door. Before he got a chance to go up the stairs, she pulled him down to eye level and patted his cheek. "You'll be back as soon as you can tomorrow, Dad, won't you?"

He nodded. "I promise. Now be nice and remember they're old and change is hard. They love you, and amazingly, I believe they love me, even if they can't accept me. Sometimes you have to take what you can get, and you don't need to fight my battles for me, princess."

"I know, Dad. It's just..." She blew out a sigh. "Nothing, it doesn't matter." She kissed his cheek, hesitating a moment before pulling back. "I saw him kiss you," she said softly.

Shit. Josh's throat tightened. He stared at his daughter, trying to read her expression, but it gave little away. "You mean Michael?"

She nodded. "He kissed you and held your hand."

Josh momentarily panicked, then pulled himself up and blew out a sigh. *Suck it up.* He ran a hand through his daughter's hair. "Yeah, he did. I didn't mean for you to see that, pumpkin. I'm sorry if it upset you."

She studied him, looking for something. Whatever it was, she seemed to find it and nodded. "It's okay, you know. It was just a surprise. I didn't know you two were—"

"We're not," he leapt in, taking her hands. "I've only just met him, sweetheart. I like him, but I'm not sure we're a good match. We're still getting to know each other. Right now, he's just a friend."

She frowned. "But he kissed you, and you always say only to kiss someone you really like."

Ugh. Does a fuck buddy qualify? God help him. Josh needed to get out of this conversation fast. "Sometimes it's a bit more complicated than that," he answered. "But I do like him."

She seemed to think about that. "Does that mean you and Jase...?" She didn't finish the question.

Damn. Michael had been right. He lifted her chin. "You understand that Jase and I aren't ever getting back together, right?"

Her gaze slid away.

Fuck. "You still miss him, huh?"

"Sometimes," she answered quietly. "He was crazy good at *The Sims*, and he got me all the cheats." She fiddled with the hem of her shirt. "But he did something bad, didn't he?"

Josh nodded carefully. "He did. He hurt me. But we're all good now." He pulled her tight to his chest.

Sasha lifted her eyes to his. "You don't mind he comes to see me?"

Yes, I fucking hate it. Josh would have preferred Jason to have taken his sorry cheating arse as far from his family as possible, but Sasha had loved Jason, and Josh wasn't about to screw her faith in yet another adult in her life. Besides, it had been two years, and surely Josh could hold a civilised conversation with Jason, at least for his daughter's sake.

"I don't mind as long as you're happy. But I won't love him again, okay?"

She nodded sagely. "Okay. But if Michael *was* your boyfriend, or someone else, I wouldn't mind, you know, as long as you tell me. I'm not a kid anymore, Dad. I want to know this stuff. You always say we're a team, right?"

"Right." Josh threw his arms around his daughter and held her tight. "Thanks, pumpkin. And I promise I'll tell you if things get serious between Michael and me. Cross my heart. But I'm not rushing anything. We do all right on our own, don't we?"

She nodded, returning the hug.

"But you promise?"

He kissed her cheek. "I promise."

"Okay." She released him and headed up the steps to the front door, with Josh hoping against hope that his parents would actually come through for him for once and not screw this weekend up.

HEADING BACK into the city, Josh was all too aware of the free evening he had looming. No daughter, no sister, an empty house, and a certain sexy doctor on tap. *Awesome.* He slid a hand to Michael's thigh and he immediately covered it with his own.

"Got plans tonight, Doc?" he asked. "Hot date, maybe?"

Michael turned to study him. "Maybe," he said with a smirk. "There's this guy, hot as hell but kind of difficult to pin down, if you know what I mean. Unreliable type."

Josh grinned. "I know exactly what you mean. Well, if he falls through and you need to ah... *plug* the gap, so to speak, I could be available."

Michael laughed, squeezing his hand. "*Plug* the gap, really? You had to go there, didn't you?"

Josh gave an innocent shrug. "I've no idea what you mean. I was just offering an alternative if you got well... shafted."

Michael snorted. "Jesus Christ, stop already or I won't be held responsible." His gaze raked the length of Josh's frame, damn near singeing the hairs on Josh's skin. "Are you asking me on a date, officer?"

"What? No." *Goddammit.* Josh felt his cheeks fire bright red.

Michael chuckled. "Relax. I was just joking. What time?"

"We could do pizza first, if you want?" *Still not a date.* They had to eat anyway. "And there's a rugby game on about four, so how about you come for that."

"Sure." Michael sounded pleased. "Build up our strength." He smirked.

Then it hit Josh. "Ah, shit." He slammed his open hand on the wheel.

Michael shot him a curious look.

Josh felt his cheeks begin to glow, again. *Damn it.* "I just remembered. Um, I'm supposed to meet someone, at three."

Michael went quiet.

"It's a guy... just for coffee. I shouldn't be long."

"No problem," Michael said, a little too casually for Josh's liking. "We can meet up another time. I need to check on my apartment anyway."

Josh wanted to kick himself. *He'd fucked up.* "It's just coffee."

"With a guy." Michael stated flatly.

Josh sighed. "Yeah. Brent."

"Brent." Michael rolled the name around his mouth like a bad taste and lifted his hand from Josh.

Josh flustered, "It's just a first-time thing, you know how it goes." *Oh God,* why did Josh feel like such a jerk? *You fucking know why.*

He kept his tone light. "It really is just coffee. I said yes before we, um... started... this. I'll be back by five... if you're still interested, that is?"

Michael said nothing. *Fuck.* Josh took the approaching off-ramp and tried to focus on the traffic as the whole conversation played in circles in his head. They weren't dating, they weren't boyfriends, so why did the whole thing feel so damn weird? But Josh wouldn't get upset if Michael told him he was going on a date, would he? *Fuck. Damn right he would.*

"Sure," Michael finally answered, though still not facing him. "I'll order the pizza."

Josh released the breath he didn't know he'd been holding. "Great."

Michael sighed. "Yeah, great."

CHAPTER EIGHT

Michael headed to Josh's house just before five, having spent most of the afternoon wondering why the fuck he was so damn hung up about Josh's stupid coffee "date." He'd barely been able to think about anything else since they'd parted company, pacing the rooms of Katie's house, downing too many coffees, and even casting a lustful eye over her liquor cupboard, a temporary lapse in focus that only served to highlight just exactly how strung out he was.

He'd found himself wanting to know just who this fucking guy was, where he'd suddenly appeared from, and what the hell were the two men doing right this very minute. By his own admission, Josh had been reluctant to date anyone, so what the fuck? Now, suddenly he was? And where did that leave Michael?

It was irrational, and it smelled sure as fuck like jealousy. Michael couldn't pretend otherwise and didn't even try. But no matter what he told himself about how he didn't have any claim on Josh, the not knowing ate at him. He'd even managed to piss off Cam, calling him while Cam was on shift, ostensibly to see how they were doing, but in reality, desperate for distraction. It was a point astutely noted by the ticked-off charge nurse who'd amply chewed his ear off for taking him away from his work and then promptly hung up. *Who needed fucking friends anyway?*

He was behaving like a prize idiot. After all, it had been Michael who'd pushed Josh into agreeing to a bit of no-strings fun in bed. He'd reassured Josh that he wasn't looking for anything more. Then again, he hadn't expected to actually like Josh. Maybe lust, drool over, and crave, sure. But actually *like* him? As in wanting to spend some time with him beyond the sheets, get to know him, his favourite foods, where he liked to vacation, watch what a great dad he was and wonder if Michael would ever be able to measure up to that? *Hell no.* That hadn't been on the cards. And yet here he was, mooning after a man who was currently out on a "date" with someone else. *Shit.*

It was all kinds of stupid. That kind of attachment had always freaked him the hell out, even with Simon. The need to consider someone else, their feelings, their wants, their hopes. No, he liked being on his own. And it had worked out just fine, hadn't it? After all, he'd dragged himself off that suicide road all on his own after Marcia had died, and now had a job he loved, was getting laid anytime he wanted, and was more than happy. He only hurt people who tried to get close. He'd proved that. Good people, like Simon.

Simon. That was a whole other bag of snakes, and Michael hadn't been able to get Josh's words out of his brain. About how Jason's screwing around had so deeply affected him. Now, Michael was no Jase, thank Christ. His treachery had been one guy, once, no more. And he'd done it to force Simon to leave him, to protect Simon. *Yeah, you tell yourself that.* But the truth was he'd let Simon believe there had been others. Just to slam the bullet home. *Yep.* Asshole didn't even begin to cover it.

He'd done that to a man who'd loved him. And Simon had loved him deeply. Enough to put up with all the shit that went down after Marcia died. All the crap Michael had thrown his way: the anger, the depression, the drinking. Michael had believed in his fucked-up way that he was setting Simon free. Of course, in the sober light of day and with a fuckton more perspective, he finally understood what a truly, cowardly, selfish prick he'd really been. He'd just wanted Simon to make the decision for him.

And now after listening to Josh... *Christ.* Had Michael's betrayal made Simon doubt himself, his judgement, and his self-worth in the same way? That had never been Michael's intent, and yet somewhere in his fucked-up brain, he had to admit he'd probably known that it would. He just hadn't cared enough at the time to stop. It wasn't like their relationship was a box of birds by then anyway. But now, the idea that Michael might have left long-term scars on his ex, well, that just sucked big time and he knew he'd need to fess up and actually talk to Simon.

And wasn't that just going to be fun?

Arriving at Josh's house, he noted his car out front, and some of the tension he'd been carrying slid away. At least Josh hadn't liked his "date" enough to be late. Of course, he was probably only being polite and doing what he'd said he would. Still, Michael wasn't about to let his own screwed up attitude mess with the evening.

Josh answered the door with Paris at his heels, the shepherd greeting Michael like a long-lost friend. Michael dropped to the floor and took a full-frontal assault, fur, tongue, and wet nose.

"Hey, behave," Josh scolded the shepherd. Then to Michael, "He's not supposed to do that. Bad habits."

Michael scuffed the shepherd's neck. "You hear that, my man?" He held the dog's head, looking deep into his eyes. "I'm giving you bad habits. What do you think of that?"

A long, wet tongue ran the length of Michael's face, and in turn he pressed a kiss to the animal's forehead. "My thoughts exactly. The world has altogether too many rules as it is." He fluttered his eye lashes at Josh who rolled his eyes.

"I give up," he said and headed off down the hall, leaving Michael to follow. "Between you and Sasha, that dog is more likely to check out the next bad guy for treats rather than rip his arm off. Remember that when you come to my funeral."

"Oops," Michael whispered loudly to the shepherd. "Come on,

boy, that man needs a beer." He caught Josh's chuckle as he followed him into the kitchen.

"The beer fridge is through there." Josh indicated a door to what turned out to be the laundry. "I'll get the dishwasher going so we have something clean to eat off. Make mine a Mac's Ale and help yourself to whatever."

"Thanks." Michael headed to the fridge. The kitchen was older in style and somewhat in need of a revamp, with its Formica counter-tops and dated avocado-green cupboards. But for all that, it was immaculate, tidy, and functional. The stainless-steel appliances were all new, he noted, guessing they'd been purchased with a different kitchen in mind, one that was yet to come to fruition. The fridge was large, modern, and in the laundry since it clearly wasn't going to fit in the tiny allocated slot in the kitchen.

"Got a Coke?" he asked.

"Should be Pepsi in there, if that's okay? Katie's at some barbecue thing, staying the night so it's just us."

"Pepsi's fine." Michael cracked a beer and handed it to Josh before opening his soda. "So, just us, then, huh?"

Josh took a long swallow and licked his lips with Michael tracking every movement. Josh caught his stare. *Busted.*

Josh grinned. "Gotta love focus in a man." He punched Michael playfully on the arm. "Grab a seat in the lounge. I'll be there in a sec."

Michael did as he was told, appreciating the functional but comfortable family-style furnishings decked out in kid-friendly dark blues and greens and arranged facing the huge-ass television on the opposite wall. Clearly a man after his own heart.

A sheepskin rug in front of the wide pillow-strewn sofa exhibited hairy evidence of long-standing dog appropriation, and the coffee table supported every game controller known to humanity and then some. In one corner a selection of board games was piled up, their corners soft and creased with frequent use. Two decks of cards sat alongside, and a selection of ring-marked coasters. The whole scene smacked of family, fun, and sickening domesticity. And Michael instantly loved it.

He detoured to check out the wealth of photos on the far wall. Most were of Josh, his daughter, and sometimes Katie. But there were also a couple featuring an attractive younger woman who Michael presumed to be Anna. Some of Josh in uniform with Paris at his side, and one or two of an older couple standing next to Josh and Katie, parents probably. Lastly, a few with Mark and even one with Jase, the two of them plus Sasha, laughing, arms wrapped around each other, and Josh smiling up at Jason like a man in love. He was still frowning at the latter when Josh sidled alongside, his coconut body wash doing Michael's head in, yet again.

"That was just after Jase moved in," Josh explained. "I was so damn happy." He reached out a hand and straightened the frame, then hesitated before removing it from the wall altogether. "Moving on, right?" he said. "Sasha can keep these in her room if she wants."

Michael held up his Pepsi. "To letting go," he said.

Josh raised his beer. "To letting go."

An awkward silence fell between them that Michael wasn't sure how to break. He made his way to the couch and claimed one end, toeing off his shoes and lifting his feet to rest on a bunch of newspapers on the coffee table. "This okay?" He indicated his feet.

Josh waved his concern aside. "Go for it."

Michael cleared his throat. It was stupid to ignore the elephant in the room. "So, how was the date?" He tried to keep his tone light and casual, but yeah... maybe not so much. "Worth a repeat?"

Josh sent him a curious look, then took a long pull on his beer before settling at the other end of the couch without answering.

Shit. "Sorry, just being nosy."

Josh's shoulders relaxed a mite. "It's fine. I, um, cancelled."

Michael's eyes blew wide. "Really?" *Fuck*, he sounded way too happy about it. He cleared his throat. "How come?"

Again Josh didn't answer for a second, just kept his gaze solid on Michael. Then he sighed heavily. "I don't really know how to answer that. It just felt... off. Not the right thing to do, to Brent or... you, I guess. Not while you and I... well... not while we're doing what we're doing, anyway."

Shit. Was Josh saying he'd cancelled... for Michael? Michael's chest grew tight, whether in pleasure or concern, it was a close fucking call. "I, um... you know, I don't want you to miss out on anything, or anyone, because of me. If you want to stop—"

"I don't... want to stop, that is. At least not right now." Josh sucked on his beer, his gaze skittering around the room.

Was he... nervous?

"So, yeah, I guess I don't do complicated, and it didn't seem fair, to anyone," Josh finished. "Now, can we just move on, do you think?"

Michael stared at him for a moment but could read nothing more from Josh's now carefully guarded expression. "Yeah, sure. And, um... thanks."

Josh smiled. "You're welcome. When the time is right for either of us to stop this, let's agree to just say so, right?" He raised his beer in a toast.

Michael responded with his Pepsi. "Agreed."

"I guess I'm just trying to do things differently this time around." Josh spoke quietly. "If there's one thing the whole fiasco with Jason taught me, it's that sometimes what you think you want isn't what's good for you, long-term."

Michael wondered if Josh was making a point about the two of them.

Josh went on. "It's hardly news that I like edgy, sexy guys who fuck like troopers but who have a commitment factor of zero." He sent Michael a half smile.

Ouch. And there it was.

"Plus I have Sasha to consider, and so stability is pretty important to me, to us, at this time. And if my dick isn't in it quite so whole-heartedly with a stable guy, well, maybe that's not the most important thing in a relationship, maybe not even in the top three. But right now, I'm not quite willing to give up the great sex we have going, not just yet."

What. The. Fuck. Michael didn't quite know how to respond to that. He took another swallow and thought a minute before answering. "You don't think you can get both?" he finally asked softly. "A guy who turns you on and who's steady as well? I get the whole 'avoid the players and assholes' rule, but settling for someone who doesn't fully do it for you seems just as... I don't know... risky? Not to mention boring."

Josh snorted. "Chance would be a fine thing. There's not exactly a wealth of guys who tick both those boxes hanging around waiting for someone like me, with an eleven-year-old and a job with crap hours."

Michael levelled his gaze Josh's way. "Are you fucking kidding me? Any guy would be lucky to have your gorgeous ass in their bed and their life. Don't you dare sell yourself short."

Josh held his gaze. "Yeah, well, know any guys like that who want to settle down?"

Michael felt the heat in his cheeks and dropped his eyes. "You'll find one."

THE CONVERSATION died a depressing death after that, and Josh realised he'd had enough angst for the day. Raking his gaze over Michael sprawled on his couch, he was done wasting time. Relationships be damned. Josh had a stunning guy sitting less than three feet away who thought Josh was pretty hot stuff, and Josh could sure work with that.

"So, Dr Oliver." Josh put his beer on the table and slid a little closer. "We have a house to ourselves and a whole night to fill. Whatever shall we do?"

Michael met his gaze with a heated one of his own. "I'm open to suggestions."

Josh's cock twitched.

Michael continued, "And I mean 'open' in the broadest possible meaning of the word." He spread his legs to make his point clear.

Fuck. Did that mean what Josh thought it did? He pushed Michael flat on the couch and crawled up his frame, loving the light whisker scruff and Michael's sharp jawline under his lips. "Mmm. Are you telling me you're packing, handsome?" he mumbled against Michael's throat.

Michael turned his face into Josh, claiming a kiss. "Maybe."

Josh's heart picked up, and his dick sprang to attention. "You're gonna be the death of me, you know that?"

Michael laughed, pulling back to eyeball him. "So, no pizza yet, I take it?"

"Fuck pizza," Josh growled, running his tongue over Michael's lower lip and nipping gently. "Or rather, fuck you, then pizza, if you're saying what I think you are." He covered Michael's body head to toe, doing his best to be gentle with the bruising he knew patchworked Michael's torso. They fit together so well.

"Now that would be telling," Michael said thickly.

Josh stared down at the sexy man laid out for his taking. "Fuck, you're beautiful," he whispered, surprised to see the faintest hint of red bloom on Michael's throat. *Adorable.* It was nigh impossible to reconcile this shy reaction with the arrogant player he'd first run into at the club. Michael Oliver was a mystery, one that currently had him salivating.

"Strip," he ordered.

Michael's eyes went dark and he obeyed instantly. Then he scooted back on the couch, took himself in hand, and began a languid stroke as he watched Josh doing his level best to get on with the whole naked idea himself, his feet caught in the bottom of his jeans. Finally free, he aimed a finger Michael's way.

"Do not move. Not a fucking inch." He sprinted to his bedroom and returned, throwing lube and condoms next to the couch.

Michael regarded him coyly. "Can I move now... sir?"

Josh didn't think his cock could get any harder. "No. And hands off," he rasped.

Michael did as he was told.

Goddamn. Josh was so turned on, he couldn't think straight. Didn't even know he had a leaning to that particular kink, but damn, if it didn't crank his shit like crazy, not least because it was so unexpected from the toppy arsehole. Michael caught his eye and winked like he'd read his mind.

"Spread 'em."

Michael pulled both his legs to his chest, exposing that delicious arse in all its glory, and, whoa, a stars-and-stripes butt plug planted in full view.

"Have at it, wolf-man. Tell me how you want me."

Holy shit. Holy, holy shit. Josh's legs buckled, and he nearly came on the spot. If he'd had any idea the doc was packing a plug, Michael wouldn't have made it two feet inside the front door before Josh nailed him against the wall. *Jesus Christ.* This sweet nut job was everything Josh had fantasised about in a lover, which only served to prove that the universe was unbelievably fucked-up at times.

So maybe Josh couldn't have it long-term with this particular man, but his body could damn well enjoy every second in the meantime, gift horses and all that. He claimed Michael's lips in a searing kiss while his hand travelled south, grazing his rigid cock before delving deep between Michael's thighs to grasp the plug. Getting a firm grip, he began a gentle slide in and out of that delicious arse.

A needy rumble vibrated deep in Michael's throat as Josh thrust his tongue in rhythm with his other efforts. Arms circled his shoulders and held him in place, letting him know Michael was as much into this as he was. Then he pulled back and grazed his lips in soft kisses along Michael's jaw, relishing the heady male scent.

"I fucking love the sounds you make," he breathed against Michael's neck, nipping and sucking at his throat and then lower, alternately laving and blowing cool air across each nipple, all the while maintaining the slow butt plug fuck he had going on below. He had to be pegging Michael's prostate, if the shivered jerks and arched back were any indication. "All in good time, babe," he murmured against Michael's taut belly. "I'm gonna enjoy every minute of this."

"Can't... wait." Michael hauled Josh up, dislodging his grip on the butt plug in the process. "Need you inside me, wolf-man," he growled face-to-face. "Unless you want this over sooner than expected." He tugged Josh's hips snug against his own, aligning their slick cocks and starting a sensual grind.

It was all Josh could do to hang on, his balls pulling up as he edged closer to losing his shit. It was so tempting to just finish like this, but that wasn't what he wanted for either of them. So, with gold-medal-winning determination, he yanked his mind from his dick and wriggled free, enough to straddle Michael and put some cool air between them.

Michael stared up at him from under a fringe of dark lashes, pupils blown and lips swollen. He looked totally fucking debauched, and the sexiest goddamn thing Josh had ever seen.

"Just... damn," Michael murmured, his tone dripping sex all over the place.

Josh swatted Michael's butt, causing him to jerk in surprise and release a rumbling groan of appreciation. *Huh.* He squirrelled that tasty titbit of information away for another time.

"Nice as that was, handsome," he growled softly, "this is my show." He added a slap to Michael's other butt cheek just because he could, and Michael's body shivered and stilled beneath him... waiting. *Damn.*

Michael grinned. "Yeah, I got the memo." He hung his head back, exposing a flushed throat and fluttering pulse. "So, are you gonna fuck me, wolf-man, or are you just gonna dick around all night?" He reached for Josh's cock, running his thumb over the slick head.

Josh replied by latching on to Michael's throat, imparting a solid bite before sucking and licking the sting away. When he pulled back to survey the deep red imprint of his handiwork, his chest fired hot. *Good luck hiding that, hotshot.*

Fuck. Was he really *that* guy now? He'd always dismissed marking as childish, refusing to indulge in it either way. But with Michael, yep, seemed like he was that man with fucking bells on.

Michael either didn't notice the bite or didn't care, wiggling to realign their cocks and forcing Josh's attention back where he wanted it. Giving him what he wanted, Josh scooted down Michael's body with a stripe of kisses ending at his cock, where he laved his tongue up and down its length a few times before taking the whole shaft down his throat in one swallow.

"Oh. My. Fucking. God," Michael hissed, throwing his head back and thrusting his hips up.

Josh pulled off.

Michael threaded his fingers through Josh's short hair in an attempt to steer him back where he wanted, but Josh resisted. "Keep your hands by your side."

"Asshole," Michael grumbled but complied immediately, and Josh went back to work.

The doc's dick was a beautiful thing, and Josh loved giving head almost as much as he loved fucking. He paid the organ some serious attention, enjoying Michael wriggling in pleasure and frustration beneath him. Then he let his fingers wander behind Michael's balls to tap the plug, and Michael bucked in response.

"Goddammit, if you don't fuck me now, Josh, I'm gonna blow my load in your sweet mouth, and it'll be all over."

Josh let Michael's cock slide from his lips. "I don't think so." He gave the butt plug a firm tug, dragging it over Michael's prostate, and watching his eyes fly wide. With his jaw clenched and his hands fisted around the couch cushion, he was clearly only just holding on, and Josh took a second just to drink in the sight.

He'd done that. He'd brought this sexy man to his knees, begging to be fucked. His chest swelled, and he dropped a kiss on Michael's groin. "Nah, you won't blow your load, because you want my dick deep in your arse right now, more than you want to breathe, right?"

Michael mumbled something unintelligible.

"Use your words."

"Maybe," Michael hissed through gritted teeth.

"Maybe what?"

Michael levelled Josh with a murderous glance. *"Maybe* I want your cock in my ass more than breathing, wolf-man. But I would remember whose turn it is next, mister. Payback and all that. Just saying."

He had a valid point. Josh slid the plug back, leaving it sitting just inside the rim as he ran his fingers over Michael's balls.

"Come on, I'm dying here," Michael groaned.

Josh sympathised. He was struggling not to just unload all over Michael that very minute himself. He took a shaky breath and positioned himself between Michael's legs, lifting both his knees. "Take 'em high," he said. "I want a front-row seat."

"Pervert," Michael grumbled but grabbed his thighs and pulled them up to his chest, exposing himself completely.

Jesus Christ and fucking hallelujah. Josh had to grab the base of his dick to stop himself flying over the edge at the mere sight. This sexy, smart-as-fuck man spread out like a damn candy store just for Josh's pleasure. And front and centre, one red-white-and-blue butt plug pulsing gently, half hanging out of that tight, sweet hole.

He rasped a breath and pulled the plug free.

Michael hissed. "Finally."

Josh grabbed the condom and lube, then slid two slicked-up fingers into that trembling hole, and watched them glide in and out.

Michael whined. "No more... fucking prep."

"Shh," Josh soothed. "It's not prep. I just love being in your arse. It's a goddamn furnace." He slid his fingers out, took Michael's legs around his waist, and breached him gently, summoning all his control to not blow his home run on the very first stroke.

Michael groaned. "Thank. Fucking. God." He ran his hand around Josh's neck and pulled him down for a blistering kiss as they both took a minute to adjust. "About fucking time." He then shoved

Josh away and gripped the couch cushions. "Now fuck me like you goddamn mean it."

My pleasure. Josh didn't need to be told twice. He hoisted Michael's legs up onto his shoulders, building quickly to a demanding tempo.

"Right. Fucking. There." Michael sputtered. "So... close..."

Thank God. Josh was barely hanging on by his fingernails himself. He secured Michael's hips with a punishing grip that was sure to leave bruises and let fly, stroking hard and fast into his tight heat. It wasn't long before his balls drew up and that familiar promising tingle spread from the base of his spine.

"Come on, babycakes, come for me," Josh encouraged, holding back, waiting for a sign of that telltale tension in Michael's body. That hitch that let him know Michael was about to explode. And... there it was.

With his head thrown back, mouth open, and eyes closed, he was a goddamn sight to behold as he fell apart in spectacular fashion. And with that, Josh let go, allowing his own orgasm to erupt in a wave of pleasure, keeping up a slow in-and-out glide until they'd ridden out the last of their tremors through to stillness. And for a few seconds, all was quiet.

"Fucking hell," Josh gasped, doing his best not to collapse on Michael's injuries, although Michael's man's current level of consciousness appeared up for debate. He lay motionless, eyes closed, quick shallow breaths offering the only sign of life. Josh released his legs but kept his softening cock tucked warmly inside Michael's arse as he licked the splashes of cum from his chest.

At length Michael lifted his head to watch, and Josh reached up to catch his lips with his own, sharing the taste. Michael's arms wrapped around him as the kiss lingered and became tender. His fingers traced soft lines along Josh's spine, adding twirls and delicate brushes. He seemed equally as unwilling to end the embrace, and Josh's chest tightened at the thought. It felt like so much more than just sex between them. But therein lay the hope of fools and far, far too much danger for Josh's heart.

The thought was enough to break the spell and have Josh lift his lips and a few walls as well. "Mmm," he nuzzled Michael's jaw. "I love the way you smell. You are one sexy-as-fuck man."

"Is that right?" Michael nipped Josh's earlobe. "Well, you're not too shabby yourself." He pulled back and glanced down meaningfully to where Josh lay still in residence in his ass.

"You thinking of signing a lease?"

Josh grinned widely. "Now there's an excellent idea." He withdrew and tied off the condom before dropping it to the floor. Then he shifted sideways and squished himself alongside Michael on the narrow couch, throwing his leg over Michael's thighs.

"I'm thinking of hanging a Home Sweet Home shingle on that sweet piece of real estate." He froze. *Fuck.* "Sorry, that sounded... I mean... I know we aren't..."

Michael put a finger to Josh's lips and wrapped his arm around his shoulders. "It's all good, wolf-man. We're just having fun, right?"

Josh hesitated just a second. "Exactly. Fun." Something flickered in his belly at the words.

Michael pulled him close. "I have to admit that was a sweet ride." He played with a curl of Josh's hair. "And a first for me."

Josh lifted his head and stared. "Exactly what *first* are we talking about here? The doing as you're told part, or the getting spanked part?"

A blush stole the edges of Michael's cheeks and drifted down across his throat, leaving Josh wanting nothing more than to track its path and bask in the unexpected innocence it betrayed.

"I think I'll plead the Fifth on that." Michael smiled softly. "Let's just say I don't like handing over the reins."

Josh gasped dramatically. "No, say it isn't so."

Michael punched his shoulder. "Yeah, yeah, laugh it up. Not like you don't have any control issues."

"True," Josh admitted. He took Michael's free hand and attended to each finger with a kiss, keenly aware of Michael watching his every move. "But you're okay with it, right?" He caught those sapphire eyes and held them.

Michael grinned. "If you call 'pretty fucking blown away' okay." The blush spread northwards.

Fucking adorable. Josh planted a kiss on Michael's chest, swiping his nipple with his tongue, enjoying the startled flinch it drew in response.

"I do have one bone to pick with you, however." Michael spun a swathe of Josh's hair into a tight ringlet and gave it a tug.

"Ow."

Michael narrowed his gaze. "What's with the whole cutesy name shit? I mean, babycakes? Really? I lost enough of my male mojo tonight, giving it up like I did, without needing the extra therapy hours, thank you very much."

Josh slid his arm around Michael's waist and hauled him closer. "It's a deal... sweet cheeks." He laughed all the way until his butt hit the floor, with Michael straddling his chest in reverse, diving straight for Josh's knees.

Josh threw himself back in defence. "No way, ah... stop... please... no... horse bites... stop," he begged, as Michael reduced him to a mess of squirming flesh. A few seconds of exquisite torture later, and Michael stopped, hands poised above Josh's knees.

"Give in?"

Josh lifted his head to run his tongue up Michael's butt crack.

"Hey." Michael's cheeks clenched.

Josh laughed. "Me give in? Not on your life, snookums."

"Bastard." Michael squeezed both knees, and Josh bucked, grabbing on to Michael's arms. "Okay, okay, okay. I give in. Jesus."

Michael looked down at him, eyes twinkling. "Say you're sorry."

Josh rolled his eyes. "You've got to be kidding me." He freed his arms and tried to pull Michael down for a kiss while attempting to grope that delicious arse still staring him right in the face.

"No cheating." Michael twisted in a feeble attempt to escape until Josh slipped a finger into that still-slick hole, and then a second, upon which Michael instantly froze. "Fuck." Michael's eyes rolled back. "Maybe just a little cheating." He pushed back, forcing Josh's fingers deeper.

"In that case," Josh murmured, quietly working his fingers in and out, "I'm more than happy to apologise." He pulled Michael around and took his lips. "How about we take this to the shower?"

Michael instantly nodded. "Lead on."

THEY ORDERED pizza an hour later, after a lengthy shower and a seemingly longer debate over toppings. The resolution involved ordering three completely different pizzas, only one of which could be shared.

Josh was an idiot, Michael determined very early in the heated discussion. There was no way in hell that mussels, and whatever the hell kumara was, should ever be allowed within a country mile of a New York pizza crust. Was the man insane? What the fuck was wrong with this country?

He was still musing on this abomination while wrapped in Josh's arms, watching the end of the rugby game that Josh had suspiciously had the foresight to record. He wriggled in close. Josh was a goddamn furnace, radiating heat against the skin of Michael's back, skin that he'd been forbidden to cover after their shower, making him also a pervert of the highest order.

Hidden from Josh's eyes, Michael was free to ignore the game and think. He'd reciprocated the clothing-optional demand onto Josh, so he really had no basis for complaint. Shifting in his seat, he rubbed deliciously against Josh's bare chest and all but purred. *Christ.* He barely recognised this version of himself, damn near drooling over a hunk of ass, albeit gorgeous ass. Okay so not just the ass—he wasn't stupid. Josh was a hell of a nice guy. But neither of them wanted more. *Yeah, right.* Did Michael really still believe that? He wanted to say yes, but he now knew that for the lie it was, at least on his side.

Not that the knowledge changed anything. He still doubted Josh would see him as ideal boyfriend material.

The chemistry between them had thrown Michael in a life-rear-ranging kind of way. He'd not just surrendered control but damn near thrown it at Josh, wrapped and tied up in a big red fucking bow. For a guy who bottomed rarely and begrudgingly, he'd allowed himself to be dominated and ordered around, and loved every mouthwatering, stupefying second of it. Best. Sex. Ever.

It scared the shit out of him. But while his mind screamed "what the fuck," his dick was on board with every damned order and slap. Oh, and by the way—the slaps—hot damn, who'd have guessed? Worst of all, as much as he'd waved the "my turn next" flag, all Michael really wanted to do was drop to his knees and beg for a repeat performance.

So much for being fuck buddies. He stole a backward glance, and Josh kissed his nose. The cuddly, touchy stuff, nose kisses included, that was just Josh, right? And even if, and that was a big if, Josh might be considering more with Michael, he didn't yet know all about Michael's dodgy fidelity past, or his drinking, or any of the rest of it, and Michael wasn't kidding himself that learning about all that would go down well. Cue someone like Brent, the "solid" option. *Well, fuck.*

When the pizza arrived, Michael sidestepped the offer of a beer in favour of a Pepsi with little more than a curious glance from Josh. They ate on the couch, then cleaned up the kitchen mostly in silence, moving around each other in a strangely comfortable domestic dance. Halfway through, Josh fielded a call from Sasha. Michael waved him away to talk and finished cleaning up. But a quick glance showed Josh's brows knit in concern, obviously less than pleased at whatever was being said. He then wandered into the living room out of earshot. Michael shrugged it off. It wasn't any of his business.

"Things okay?" he ventured when Josh returned.

Josh headed for the fridge and another beer, not meeting his eyes. "It was just Sasha."

Well, okay. Michael could take a hint with the best of them. But then Josh surprised him by walking across and brushing his lips across Michael's. "Grandparent problems. They, um, don't appreciate my 'lifestyle.' Nothing I want to think about right now."

It was an explanation he didn't need to give and had Michael rethinking once again if maybe Josh would consider something more between them. Maybe it was worth talking about at least. If Josh turned him down, so what? Michael was a big boy. He'd deal.

Josh took his hand and led him back to the couch, stepping over Paris to drop Michael into the cushions at one end while he took up position at the other. He looked like he had something to say, and Michael tensed, another ripple of nerves crossing his belly.

Paris spread his body over the newly arrived feet and cranked up a good snore. Michael scrunched his toes into the shepherd's fur, looking for a distraction, and Paris groaned in appreciation. If Josh wanted to talk, Michael would wait.

"He likes you," Josh commented.

Michael snorted. "You mean he sees me as a soft target."

Josh laughed. "That too. Still, police dogs are pretty standoffish with strangers as a rule, but from day one, he's been good with you."

"So, I should take it as a compliment?"

"Absolutely."

Michael dug his toes deeper into the shepherd's neck. There was something uncannily reassuring about that trusting warmth, so accepting of him, no questions, no judgement. He thought of Scout. Yeah, maybe it was time for an animal in his life. The dog rolled to his back, redirecting Michael's attention to his stomach. He laughed. "God, wish I had that effect on everyone."

Josh sent him a wink. "You only need it with those who count."

Okay, so maybe nothing bad, then. "And you'd be one of those, I take it?" he fished, so sue him.

Josh answered with a huge smile. "Yeah, I'd roll over and offer you my belly any day."

He crossed the space between them and pressed his lips to

Michael's. The kiss was tender, soft and lingering with just a brush of tongue. It stroked and whispered and fluttered with a hundred wished-for promises. And it filled every one of Michael's deeply empty spaces.

With all the sex they'd shared, why it was this one kiss that finally collapsed his walls, Michael didn't understand. But the why didn't matter. What did matter was that he could no longer deny that this "thing" between them had gone a million light years past just sex, at least for Michael. Yes, he wanted the sex. But he also wanted the cuddling, the talking, dates and movies and walks and fuck, fuck, fuck. This was so very, very not in his plans.

He jerked away and dropped his gaze, choosing to focus on Paris, anything to avoid Josh who was systematically and ruthlessly shredding Michael's defences. "Yeah, well I'm more an ass man myself." He refused to look up.

Josh laughed, kissed his neck, and returned to his end of the couch, seemingly oblivious to the devastation he'd just wreaked in Michael's heart.

"So," Josh said, "you know a fair bit about my coming out and my fucked-up life. How about evening the playing field?"

Nope. Not even a little bit. Michael sighed. He wanted to tell Josh everything, God how he wanted to, but what if he took it badly, what if it meant that this was it, the last time they saw each other? Did he risk it? Would it be better to just enjoy tonight, and then back off with some dignity before someone got hurt, namely Michael? *Fuck.*

Eventually he answered, "All right but go easy on me."

And with that they slid into an easy couple of hours talking, Michael sharing about his family and his teenage gay epiphany resulting from a little too much interest in a certain sexy member of the high school basketball team. The boy was straight as an arrow and never cottoned on, but the lengths Michael had gone to in his boy-lust haze to place himself at the same parties, classes, and lunch spaces had been enough to leave him in no doubt that he preferred dick.

His family was pretty accepting once the initial shock wore off, so all in all, he'd been pretty damn fortunate.

Josh managed to pin him down once about Simon, God knows how that happened. But Michael had managed to keep to the bare details, omitting the full ugly truth about his part in the breakup, alluding simply to the work pressure of two doctors trying to have a relationship. He volunteered a bit about his training—why he'd chosen it—because his dad was a doctor, and that he genuinely liked the adrenaline rush of the emergency room. But after that, conversation got tricky.

"So, I noticed you don't drink," Josh said out of nowhere.

Michael froze. "Oh, you did, did you?" he snipped.

Josh raised his palms. "Hey, it's okay. None of my business."

Michael sighed. Josh was a cop, for Christ's sake—of course he'd noticed. "You're right," he said. "It *is* none of your business." He pinned Josh with a glare that softened. "But yeah, I don't drink. There's a fuckload of stress in ER medicine and a lot of that shit follows you home. Let's just say I learned from experience that using alcohol to deal with it was less than smart, so I stopped altogether." It flew close enough to the truth to pass, and Josh simply gave a brief nod, and the conversation moved on.

Michael released the breath he'd been holding. It was the most he'd said to anyone about his brief train wreck with alcohol other than those who had to know. But this was Josh, and somehow that fucker just drew this shit out of Michael like pus from a wound. Still, it had gone better than he'd expected, so maybe Michael *could* risk telling him the whole story. Maybe. Tomorrow, if he felt the same, he would.

Josh studied the range of emotions that played out on Michael's face as he spoke about the risks of drinking as an ER doctor and knew he wasn't getting the whole story, but he didn't blame Michael one bit. They weren't boyfriends—hell, he wasn't sure if they were even good friends, not really, although he hoped things were heading that direction. They were just... well shit, he had no idea what the fuck they were anymore.

It sure felt like something had changed, though. And the odd looks Michael had been sending his way made it seem like he was equally puzzled about what was happening between them. Josh couldn't be in the same space as Michael without touching him and not just for sex—for comfort, for connection, for warmth, as well. But Michael was also a painful reminder of all the things Josh missed about having a partner, so maybe it wasn't really about Michael himself and more about what Josh ached for. All he knew was that he was more and more confused about what they were doing and what he wanted anymore.

He tried to focus on the story Michael was busy recounting— something about treating a famous musician who'd been admitted to the ER after falling naked from the Hollywood sign—but his mind had gone walkabout. All he saw was the movement of Michael's lips, the tip of his tongue, the way his eyes crinkled in the corners when he smiled, and the blue light that shone from them with every laugh. Michael barely had to glance Josh's way, and Josh was fighting the urge to spread his legs and hand Michael a fuck ton of lube.

And yet Michael had been so clear about not wanting to settle down, something Josh was desperately looking for—to make a family, the whole white-picket-fence bit. What was it Katie always said? Date the slut but marry the nerd. Maybe there was some truth in that. Michael was seriously hot but also seriously commitment-phobic. And yet he held Josh's attention like a fucking neon sign.

And what about the idea of monogamy? That was a deal-breaker for Josh and he wasn't sure what Michael thought about it. Michael seemed genuinely pissed at what Jase had done to Josh, and yet he also seemed uninterested in any relationship himself. He'd be a huge gamble, and every time Josh found himself wondering what it would be like to actually date Michael, he got a headache from the megaton of warning bells that went off in his head. On his own he'd take the risk... maybe. But Sasha had to come first, and that risk seemed just too big to put his daughter in the middle, again.

One thing was for sure—Josh was getting sick and tired of the what-ifs and maybes. They needed to talk. Josh needed to know where Michael's head was at, and he could take it from there. If talking meant this whole thing crashed now, better sooner than later. Josh had walked past fuck buddy a while back. Too late to stop himself being hurt now. Tomorrow. He'd force a conversation tomorrow.

"You'll stay the night, please?" Josh interrupted the end of Michael's story, and Michael's eyes widened in surprise. *Shit. That sounded too needy.* He dropped a hand to scratch Paris's head. "Just that it's pretty late and... well, I'd hate you to miss your turn." He glanced over coyly.

Michael didn't answer immediately, which panicked Josh just a little. "It was only a thought," he said. "Forget it."

"No. I mean, yeah," Michael answered softly. "Yeah, I could do that. You don't think it will... complicate things?"

Abso-fucking-lutely it will. But Josh needed Michael beside him tonight. And he needed to talk tomorrow. "Don't see that it has to. We're adults, right?"

Michael nodded. "On a good day."

CHAPTER NINE

"Goddammit, no!" Michael shouted. Why was no one paying attention? He reached for the gurney, his arms moving like concrete piles through crusted mud. His fingers stretched for the pale, flaccid hand only to wrap around air instead. "Help her." But no one was moving. Why was no one moving? They just stood, staring at him, eyes flat and lips in a tight line. She breathed, but the sound carried no hope, and he was drawn to her gaze, soft, young, pleading. Unable to look away, he caught the last flicker of life in those beautiful brown eyes, watched it drain and dull to a flat nothing. He sank to his knees on a floor slick with blood, and a pair of warm arms folded around him.

Michael fought the hold, his face slick with tears. "Let me go." But the arms pulled tight.

"Shh, it's okay," a soothing voice hummed in his ear. "I've got you. Shh."

His eyes flew open. The voice was familiar, safe. Josh. His body began to relax. A soft kiss was pressed against his neck, his hair, and his shoulder, each notching down Michael's panic a step or two. And with the last kiss, the arms around him loosened just a little. Enough to finally breathe.

"You're okay, babe. I've got you," Josh whispered.

Michael leaned back against Josh's warm chest and let his heart settle from its sickening gallop. The memories returned. He was in Josh's house, his bed, his arms, and he was okay. He needed to get a grip. *Don't lose it completely in front of the nice man, idiot.* It was just a short dip in the crazy pool. Just a reminder, but... *fuck. Why tonight?*

Josh's fingers trailed across Michael's belly and hips, releasing the knots of panic. He sucked in some deep breaths and found himself held and rocked, comforted like a child, swaddled as light kisses were pressed on the nape of his neck. God almighty, it felt good. So he let himself drift, happy in the moment to never leave that cocoon of flesh where everything felt right.

After a time, Josh slowed the rocking and they lay quiet. Michael twisted in his arms to face him, kissing him lightly on the lips. Memories drifted through his head of the evening before, the lazy blowjobs in bed before Michael had curled up against Josh, the little spoon for once.

"Thanks," he whispered against Josh's mouth, the word failing to convey anywhere near the gratitude he felt for Josh's silent acceptance of Michael's crazy.

"Nightmare?" Josh raised a brow.

"Yeah."

"You get them often?"

"Now and then." Michael felt the sting of embarrassment flush his cheeks. This wasn't a conversation he wanted, not now, not yet. And especially with this man who slipped so easily under and around every wall Michael had worked so damned hard to hammer in place.

"Wanna talk?" Josh pressed gently. "I have it on good authority that shit can actually help."

Michael grinned despite himself, but he'd avoided opening up to

Simon for eighteen months, and he wasn't about to cough up that easily to a guy he hardly knew. *But wasn't that exactly what he'd been planning to do, tomorrow?*

"No, not really," he answered, ready for an argument but getting none, nothing but concern in Josh's expression. *Damn.*

And so he gave him something. "The work I do, the shit I see, it leaves scars, that's all. Not too different from your job, I imagine. We don't get to save everyone, and sometimes the 'almost but not quite' comes back to bite me on the ass." He nuzzled against Josh's neck. "I'm sorry I woke you. I'll grab a glass of water and crash in the lounge for a bit, so you can get back to sleep. No need for us both to be red-eyed and cranky in the morning."

He went to push the covers off, but Josh's grip held him in place. "I have a better suggestion," he murmured, cupping Michael's chin and turning him for a kiss, his tongue warm and soft against the seam of Michael's lips. Michael opened, and Josh slid in gently, a sensual slow move that had Michael's dick rock-hard in seconds, thinking it was entirely possible he could come from kissing alone.

Hands trailed over his back, leaving searing swirls of heat and want in their wake. Michael could barely breathe, let alone move, his mind a puddle of adrenaline, fatigue, and sensitivity. He had no choice but to surrender and let this amazing man own his body once again, this time in the most tender, erotic path to arousal.

He had no idea how long they kissed, Josh's hands drifting over Michael's body with murmured moans and hums, betraying his own arousal as he delicately tasted every square inch of Michael's skin. The slow seduction elicited erogenous zones Michael didn't even know he had: elbows, the underside of his biceps, the lower run of his ribs—who knew? At some point he figured he should play his part, but Josh simply brushed his hand away.

"Shh," he soothed, pushing Michael back into place, which was apparently wherever Josh wanted him to be. "Let's see if I can bring the sleep bunnies back."

Michael snorted. "Sleep bunnies?" He licked up Josh's neck just because he could and the fact it required about as much energy as he could currently muster. "Your dirty talk could do with a little work, wolf-man."

Josh manhandled him onto his other side and spooned Michael from behind. "Oh ye of little faith," he whispered into Michael's ear, sliding a very erect, very demanding cock against his crack. "Now relax and let me chase the bad dreams away."

Okay, then. Okay. And with that, Michael gave in and surrendered to an act of soul-touching sex like nothing he'd ever known. Josh's mouth owned his skin anyway he wanted it. Touch, kiss, lick, suck, nibble, stroke, all soft and languid, silk on cotton wool. Michael's mind circled lazily around the question of how he could be so relaxed and yet so insanely aroused. It was a mystery he eventually put aside to ponder when he wasn't a hair's breadth away from self-combusting and taking most of the known universe with him.

Kisses blurred into gentle nips and soothing hums, as slick fingers found his secret switches and the not-so-secret ones. Balls rolled gently, dick drawn and coaxed in slow mesmerising strokes, his body burning ever hotter. And finally, wicked, slick fingers behind his balls, grazing his hole, dipping inside, gliding in and out while lips caressed his spine. His top thigh lifted and pushed forward, opening him up, two fingers, swirling, probing.

On and on it went until Michael was convinced his bones had dissolved into the very fibre of the sheets along with his brain. Then lips and fingers retreated, and blazing, solid flesh pressed up against him from shoulder to thigh. Josh threw an arm around his chest, slid in behind and breached him slowly, slowly, slowly slipping home in one tantalising slide. Then he sighed, warm and moist against Michael's neck, and breathed shakily.

"This isn't going to take long, sorry."

Michael groaned and pushed back, whimpering with need. "Not. A. Problem."

"Fuck," Josh moaned. "Give me a second, yeah."

From some distant planet, Michael heard Josh take a few deep breaths and then felt the first gentle thrusts. And just like the seduction, the fuck was slow and sizzling. Long strokes by that thick cock sliding against his prostate time and time again, pushing him ever closer to the blistering edge of orgasm.

It should have been frustrating, this slow maddening glide. But instead it was all-encompassing. Delicious and lavish, like the flow of melted chocolate, and Michael could do nothing but give himself over to its hypnotic promise, trusting Josh would get him there. And then, almost too soon, he felt the surge of pleasure begin.

"Close," he hissed, surprising himself with the ability to even form the word.

"Me too." Josh slid a hand over Michael's cock.

He groaned and arched into the grip.

"That's it, sweetheart," Josh murmured. "Give it up. I've got you."

And that was all it took for Michael to plummet over the edge riding an exquisite crest, vaguely aware of Josh's body stuttering at his back, the swell and release of Josh's cock in his ass. *Hot damn.*

Neither moved for what felt like minutes, lost in the simple need to breathe and hang on to each other. Then finally Josh's soft cock slid reluctantly from Michael's ass, bringing him back from wherever his brain had migrated to recover.

"Jesus Christ, wolf-man," Michael murmured, lowering his leg to relieve a cramp while sliding up against Josh's furnace of a chest. "Where the hell did you learn that?"

"If I told you, I'd have to kill you." Josh nipped the nape of his neck, then returned for a decent bite.

"Ow," Michael yelped, a little too highly pitched for his liking. "What was that?"

"Because you taste so damn good. Now go to sleep."

Michael wanted to protest, wanted to pin Josh down and make him yield to something... anything to not feel so, so grateful, but he didn't. Instead he lay in Josh's arms, the fucking little spoon again, cocooned in Josh's tenderness as if Michael were something precious to be treasured, and then, well, then he cried—big, fat, silent, ugly tears into his pillow. He kept himself still as it happened, as silent as he could manage, praying Josh wouldn't notice.

No one had witnessed one of his full-blown, middle-of-the-night freak-outs, bar one. Simon. After that, Michael had moved out of his and Simon's bed and buried the nightmares in alcohol and isolation, and no one had ever seen him that way again, until tonight and Josh. Sweet, determined, Josh. He hadn't asked anything of Michael, had just taken him somewhere safe and held him there. And hadn't that been a fucking miracle?

Josh's arm pulled against Michael. He was still awake. *Shit.*

"You okay?"

Yes. No. Fuck. Ah, goddammit. "Her name was Marcia." The words were out before Michael even realised it.

Josh stilled but said nothing.

Crap. Was he really going to do this? *I guess so.*

And he did. "She came into my ER nearly two years ago," he began and then continued to tell Josh the whole sorry mess, the biggest fuck-up of his career, while Josh simply held him close and listened without a single interruption. The only sign Josh was even still awake was the gentle in and out of his breathing in Michael's ear and the tight grip he kept around his chest.

It was easier not having to face those eyes as he spoke—he didn't have to hide his shame or see the inevitable pity or judgement when Josh finally understood what a fuck-up Michael truly was. He'd be glad he'd kept Michael at arm's length, then. Josh deserved better.

When he was finally done, they lay quiet for a bit, and Michael felt an odd sense of peace. Then Josh pulled at his shoulders, twisting him so they faced each other. He cupped Michael's chin and pressed their lips together in a sweet kiss, no heat, just comfort and acceptance. Then he pulled back and kissed the tip of Michael's nose and each eyelid in turn. He couldn't have missed the tang of Michael's tears but said nothing about them.

"Hence the alcohol issue," he stated, no judgement.

Michael sighed. "Hence the alcohol issue. Usual dumb-fuck story there. An escape that works, until it doesn't. Damn near cost me my job. Took a stint in rehab and then down the track this opportunity for a hiatus in New Zealand to take a breather."

Josh ran his fingers through Michael's hair, and Michael leaned into the caress. "But wait, there's more," he said sardonically.

Josh waited, his fingers continuing to channel through Michael's hair, creating their own slice of peace in his mind.

"That thing about me not doing relationships," Michael ventured, hearing the screaming hesitation in his own voice.

Josh's fingers stilled momentarily, then continued in their mission.

Michael sighed. "I was with Simon when all that shit went down, and not to bore you with the details, but the whole thing crashed and burned as a direct result. Not his fault," Michael was quick to point out. These days he felt pretty protective of Simon's efforts to save them—though that feeling had been a long time coming, too long.

"No. The blame for that whole shit-sucking fiasco lies solidly with yours truly. Simon's a good guy, a great guy actually, and he tried to help, but I was a proverbial asshole in return, and the drink didn't help. Let's just say he made the absolute right decision to cut my ass loose when he did."

Josh eyed me sideways, his gaze narrowing. "You mean he gave up—"

"No," Michael interrupted. *Okay, here goes. Been nice knowing you.* "That was all on me. It got to the point where I couldn't deal with all his 'trying so hard' kindness. I was too busy wallowing in self-pity. So when he took me to a bar for our two-year 'living together' anniversary, I, ah, I got drunk and deliberately fucked some random twink in the back room. I knew Simon would likely follow to check up on me. He did. So, now you know."

Josh froze, and his eyebrows flew to his hairline, but to his credit, he held fire on any immediate comment. Not able to hold his stunned gaze for long, Michael buried his head on Josh's chest instead. "So, you were pretty much right on the mark the first time you met me. I'm an asshole. It was a total dick move," he said. *And the rest.*

The silence continued for a few moments, and then Michael felt the press of Josh's lips on his head. "Then why?"

Michael snorted. "Because I'm a total bastard, jackass, prick."

Josh dipped his head to catch Michael's eye. "Yeah, I'm not buying it."

"That's because you're under the erroneous impression that there's a nice guy somewhere buried deep underneath all this shit," Michael scoffed. "And that just makes you naive, not right." He dropped his head to the pillow and his gaze to the network of soft hair covering Josh's chest. He raised his hand and ran his fingers idly through it.

"I was too much of a coward to break up with him, so I made him do it for me. I put him in an impossible position and hurt him so badly, but I just kept telling myself he was better off without me." He took a deep breath and risked a peek. Josh's expression held nothing but concern and affection. *Ugh.*

"It was a crap excuse," he went on. "Just how crap only hit home when you were talking about how Jase's cheating affected you. I hadn't even considered Simon's side, not really. Hadn't thought he'd feel much more than 'good riddance.' And that's why I don't do relationships. I'm the definition of damaged goods. Casual is my limit. Maybe someday that will change, but for now I'm just trying to keep my head straight and get back on track. Most days I can even believe I'm getting there. Admittedly you've thrown a small wrench in that thinking." *And there it was.*

Michael paused and waited for Josh to pull away, but instead he tugged Michael hard against his chest and started up that whole rocking thing again. *Goddammit.* Josh was the definition of a sweetheart and probably wanted to save Michael from himself, just like Simon. But fuck if it didn't just feel so insanely good, and with that he buried his face in Josh's neck instead and let his pain drift.

"You're a good man, Michael Oliver," Josh breathed the words softly into his ear. "None of us get it perfect or even get close ninety-nine percent of the time. Do I think you were an arsehole to Simon? Probably, yes. Do I understand why you did it? I think so. You were hurting bad and swimming in the crazy pool, trying to deal. There wasn't much chance you were going to get anything right from there."

Michael gave the barest of nods. Josh was taking things way too easy on him. Michael appreciated it but knew the truth was much harsher.

"So, yeah, you fucked up," Josh continued. "But it shouldn't define you. I wish you could see what I see. A strong, sexy, crazy-smart, and talented guy who wears snark like fucking armour to hide something special on the inside."

Yep, another would-be saviour. Josh was certifiably insane if that's what he saw. "Well, I'll trust you to keep those misguided insights a secret," he joked weakly. "Wouldn't do to have my manwhore rep dented in any way, yeah?"

Josh chuckled. "Okay, pretty boy. You got it. But don't think I didn't hear that bit about me being a wrench in your thinking."

Michael buried his face in Josh's shoulder. "Oh God. I'm sorry. I shouldn't have said anything. I just... well, right now I'm a bit confused... about us... but I guess you got that bit, huh? I, um... I just don't know what I feel about you anymore, just that this thing between us, it's getting to be—"

"More than just fuck buddies?" Josh pulled Michael's head back and looked deeply into his eyes. "Damn right it's confusing. I get it, Michael. I'm right there too. I just... don't know quite what we should do about it. Not to mention you don't technically even live in New Zealand. What happens when your time's up?"

Michael breathed a sigh of relief. "Me neither. So, it's not just me, then?"

Josh kissed the tip of his nose. "No. It's not just you. But... can we take it one day at a time? I have Sasha to think about and... I don't want to leap into anything heavier until I'm—*we're* sure."

Michael pressed a soft kiss to Josh's lips. "You read my mind.

Knowing we're both flailing around but on the same page is enough for now."

MICHAEL WOKE a few degrees short of self-combustion from the inferno of flesh glued to his back along with a serious hard-on pressed tight to his ass. He glanced at the clock: 7:00 a.m. Five hours' sleep. Not too bad considering a nightmare usually put paid to any further rest, period. Josh had indeed summoned those elusive sleep bunnies as promised.

He smiled to himself. Josh was an idiot in the best possible way. Zen sex. Who knew? And Michael had every intention of copyrighting it, play by play. Fucking breathtaking. Best part? Zero urge for a glass of Jack to deal with the nightmare.

Josh shuffled behind him, nudging Michael's crease once again with that gorgeous thick cock, although the drone of soft snores pointed to him being far from awake. Michael wondered what was going through that pretty, sleeping head, hopefully the same thing that currently had Michael's cock twitching, half-hard against his thigh.

Josh's bedroom had come as somewhat of a surprise. It was nicely decorated in a shabby chic beach theme. Soft blue and brown furnishings, driftwood-framed family photos, a soft cream linen duvet, and enough distressed wood to keep the feel masculine. Paperbacks were stacked in crooked piles on the whitewashed bedside tables, and floor-to-ceiling wardrobe mirror doors stole miles of light from the outside, keeping the interior bright and fresh. The whole room felt fresh and inviting, as if its occupant wasn't enough of a dynamite draw all on his own.

It had been a crazy-ass twenty-four hours, including some downright freaky and inexplicable oversharing on his part. *Jesus Christ.* And yet, after everything, Josh apparently still wanted Michael in his bed. Michael shouldn't feel so dopey happy about that, but that train had already left the station. God, had he only known Josh a couple of weeks? It was insane.

Not to mention Michael wasn't entirely sure what they were anymore. Not just fuck buddies, apparently. But not quite boyfriends either. Taking it slow. That part he got. Michael had a bagload of fuck-up potential left, and no right to lay it at Josh and Sasha's door. Even he knew he was a piss-poor bet. Taking it slow was the only way to go. If he were Josh's friend, he'd be advising him to make it glacial pace. There were no guarantees, and Michael still wasn't sure exactly how much more he wanted with Josh, only that he did want... more. But then there was Sasha to consider. He couldn't afford to play around with anyone's feelings here.

Michael reminded himself that he'd enjoyed his life before Josh. Hadn't he? He'd savoured the excitement of casual sex, the chase, the high, the walk away? No strings, no deep chats, no responsibility. Pump and dump had a lot going for it. If things fell through with Josh, going back to that wouldn't be so bad, would it?

Josh's lashes fluttered against Michael's shoulder and a set of lips pressed against his neck. "Morning, gorgeous."

Michael shivered despite himself, his cock leaping to attention. *Yeah, right. Not in a million years.*

Josh glanced at the clock over Michael's shoulder: 7:20. He was kind of surprised to find Michael still in his arms, expecting him to have hotfooted it out of there before dawn after those middle-of-the-night confessions. Not Michael's usual MO, and Josh felt some pride that Michael had trusted him enough to let him in on what must have been a really shitty, low point in his life.

It explained a great deal about the confusing man. The girl's death was one of those crappy, fucked-up life shitfests that you couldn't plan for or predict your reaction to. There was nothing Michael had to blame himself for as far as Josh could see, but that often meant crap in reality, and Josh knew that first-hand.

He pulled Michael hard against his chest, resting his chin on his shoulder. The wriggle back on his groin confirmed Michael was awake and interested. Josh smiled but that wasn't what this was about, yet.

"About a year ago we had a meth house to clear, a P factory on the North Shore," he began. Michael turned his head slightly to indicate he was listening. "A couple of dog teams were tasked to help, we were one. The wife of one of the two cooks turned them in, pissed about her husband cheating on her. It was a good bust, a huge production. Slowed the market a fair bit, for a while.

"Anyway, when we landed, the other team caught one of the cooks making a break and set about chasing the runner down. It wasn't the husband of the informant, even though his car was parked in the driveway. So while the other team was off, Paris and I swept the place, three times, top to bottom. We found no trace of the second cook, the husband, the one who owned the car. In the end we called it a miss and settled for what we had.

"Later that evening the missing cook/husband paid a visit to his wife and shot her and her two-year-old daughter as they watched television. The kid wasn't his. We finally caught him attempting to high-tail it to Australia. He told us he'd been in the house the day we searched, in a ceiling cutout above the kitchen. I'd missed him, and two people died because of it."

Michael twisted in his arms and kissed him gently on the lips.

"Shit, wolf-man. Sometimes the universe is just such a fucking bitch, isn't it? I'd say you're mad to let something like that get to you because you did your best, but I'm no poster boy for that advice, as you know. Which I'm guessing is why you told me."

Michael snuggled in, and Josh buried his lips in his hair. He smelled of cologne, last night's pizza, and sex. Josh grinned. Hell, he could've smelled of old tractor tyres and Josh wouldn't have given a shit.

"You okay, about last night?" he asked softly. "What we talked about?"

Michael nodded. "Yeah. You?"

"Fine."

Michael shifted and blazed a smouldering look Josh's way. "So, awkward conversation done with, I'd offer to take that sweet hard-on of yours currently banging away on my thigh and show it a place to call home," he teased, "but three times in twelve hours might be pushing it a bit if I intend to walk sometime in the next year."

Josh laughed. "Jesus, I'm glad you said it. I thought I'd have to lie back and think of England to avoid losing my man card. I'm sure as hell not twenty any longer."

Michael rolled his eyes. "Tell me about it. So, how about I race you to the shower instead. Winner gets to top next time round."

"You're on." Josh leapt out of bed and they fought their way to the en suite, elbows juggling.

KATIE RETURNED during breakfast cleanup, making no attempt to hide her surprise at finding Michael looking very much at home in Josh's kitchen. Josh knew she'd be fair chomping at the bit for details once they were alone. As it was, she spent a few seconds running her narrowed gaze back and forth between the two men before planting herself at the table.

"So, you two, here together," she said.

Michael smiled, gesturing for Josh to take point. Josh sent him a glare. "Yep."

Silence.

"That's all?" she pressed.

"Let me think. Ah, yes, yes, it is." He sent her a cheeky grin. "How was your night, sis? Been a while since you did the walk of shame."

The deep red blush that flew from Katie's neck to her forehead surprised the hell out of him. *Oh, well... damn.* He'd really only said it as a joke. Katie hadn't had a serious guy in a while and his sister was no one-night stand.

"Stop that," she warned. "I know what you're doing. Two can play at that game."

"Have at it, sis."

"It'll keep," she answered with a wicked smile and then added, "You're an evil son of a bitch, Joshua Dudley Rawlins."

A snort of laughter broke from the other side of the kitchen, followed by choking coughs.

Josh scowled at Katie. "Bitch."

Her eyes went all wide and innocent. "Oh, sorry. You hadn't mentioned your middle name?"

Michael appeared beside him, a Cheshire grin plastered across his face. "Dudley, huh?"

Katie burst out laughing, and Michael kept up with that maddening grin.

Josh drilled him with a glare. "It's a family name, and Michael, I swear, if you ever call me that, I will personally see to it that your balls are fed to the sharks, still attached."

Michael pouted and leaned in to place a peck on Josh's cheek. "As if I would do something like that."

Josh rolled his eyes but couldn't keep his lips from quirking up. "As if."

Michael held his gaze and bit his lower lip, something that never failed to do funny things to Josh's insides, and then he turned to Katie. "Hey, lovely lady," he said. "Thanks for letting me stay at your house, but I won't be putting you out any longer. Mark's given me the all-clear to head back to my apartment, so I'll just grab my stuff and be out of your hair."

Josh frowned. "You talked to Mark?"

"He called while you were out back with Paris. Seemed to think it's safe enough. The new locks and security system are in place and apparently word of the ID washout has spread well enough for the heat to be off me. Makes no sense for them to risk another attack for nothing. He just told me to be careful. I told him it was my middle name."

Josh rolled his eyes.

Michael ruffled Katie's hair. "I'll throw those pesky sheets in the washing machine for you before I go."

She slapped his butt. "Make sure you do. I don't want any of those gay-boy cooties hanging around."

"God, no!" He saluted her and headed to the back door, nudging Josh as he passed. "I'll see you in an hour, at practice." He ghosted his lips across Josh's and headed out, leaving Josh craving more.

Katie punched Josh on the arm as she made her way to the refrigerator. "We're so gonna have that talk."

He sighed. *Shit.*

JOSH FOUND time to corner Mark at softball practice and check the detective's take on Michael returning to his apartment, not that he didn't trust Michael, but he suspected he might be a bit of a maverick.

Mark reassured him. "Our informant got close to that kid, Bradley Kennan, the driver of the car. Kid's a slim spit away from taking an all-expenses-paid trip to Paremoremo Prison. A nice-looking, skinny little fucker like that wouldn't last half a day in there before being farmed out to some high-ranking gangbanger. Didn't take much pressure to get him to spread the word, and it seems the heat is off your man, for now at least."

"He's not my man."

Mark stared at him. "Yeah, right. And I don't wish Tom Daley was in my apartment getting naked for me."

Josh's brows peaked in disbelief. "You have a thing for Tom Daley?"

Mark shrugged. "Doesn't everyone?"

"Ah, no?"

Mark rolled his eyes. "Pfft. And you call yourself gay."

Josh shook his head. "You are so full of shit."

The detective hauled Josh onto the field and dumped him at first base. "Come on," he muttered. "You gotta admit, the guy's freaking cute."

Josh couldn't contain his laughter any longer, earning himself Mark's middle finger. He stayed afterwards for a beer with the team, careful to keep a bit of distance between Michael and himself. Wouldn't do to be chubbing up randomly every time he so much looked his way. Not that Michael was helping any. Every time Josh caught his eye, Michael sent enough heat his way to power a small Alaskan town.

After one beer, he headed out to collect Sasha from her grandparents, and that's when Josh's day went to shit.

THE PHONE call Josh had received the previous evening had been from a very upset Sasha. So when Josh arrived to pick his daughter up, he sent her ahead to the car so he could have a little chat with his parents, alone. The issue prompting Sasha's call had concerned a comment from Josh's parents about him dating, not that Josh was. But it had stemmed from the family background interview and Sasha mentioning she wanted Josh to fall in love and get married like everyone else.

His parents had immediately scoffed at the idea, no surprise there. The words "unnatural" and "gay nonsense" had then entered the conversation, goddammit, and of course, his daughter wasn't about to let that one go. Half of him swelled with pride at her ballsy defence of him, but the other, exhausted half just wished she'd let it go. He'd calmed her down during the call, but it wasn't something he could ignore, hence the chat. Just what he needed.

What had been said was inexcusable and wasn't up for discussion as far as Josh was concerned, and in as many words, he told them so. They either stopped with the derogatory gay comments or they wouldn't see Sasha at all, unless he was present. It went down as expected, like a fucking lead balloon.

They argued the right of any grandparent to "correct" any shortcomings in the parenting of their grandchildren, including, in their view, the ridiculous notion of homosexuality being in any way "normal." It was a lifestyle choice, no different than if being a "hippie or druggie." The conversation went downhill from there.

The comparison was so irrational and bizarre that it left Josh momentarily speechless and only served to highlight just how far his parents were from any real progress on the issue. He rallied for a bit, trading blow for hurtful blow, but then came to his senses. There really was nothing more he could do other than make good on his threat.

His parents seemed to sense they'd maybe gone too far and attempted to mollify him toward the end, agreeing to avoid any future discussions with Sasha on the "gay issue," as they called it. Not that their acquiescence implied any approval, they were quick to add. *Whatever*.

Josh was just happy the whole thing could be shelved for another day, although noting his daughter's rigid posture and barely contained fury on the drive home, he knew Sasha's patience with his parents' bigotry had worn transparently thin. And who could blame her?

When Michael called in as promised later that afternoon, Josh had been glad for the distraction. Sasha had beaten him to the door, greeting Michael like a long-lost friend before dragging him into her bedroom for a whirlwind indoctrination into an eleven-year-old girl's terrifying world of books, toys, reality shows, and netball. Josh didn't even try to intervene. The doc was on his own, sink or swim.

Thirty minutes later, the poor man reappeared holding Sasha's hand and wearing a somewhat bemused expression. The two of them commandeered the couch, chatted loudly and animatedly about the latest *Star Trek* movie, the merits of buttered popcorn over salted or, good God, sugared, and whether the Sony PlayStation was better than Xbox. Observing them from the kitchen, Josh couldn't help the tug at his heart. It was reminiscent of the banter Sasha used to have with Jase, something she must have missed when Jase left.

They'd shared toasted sandwiches for dinner, followed by a rowdy game of Monopoly, won by his daughter in what Josh deemed to be blatant disregard of the spirit of the game. She and Michael had teamed up in a successful partnership to bankrupt him and stop him from winning.

Still, the doctor learned a valuable lesson regarding the preteen female mind in the process. Namely, that they were cunning as a fox with the charm of a siren and the determination of a badger. They could smell blood in the water at a distance of light years and had an uncanny ability to home in on any weakness in their opponents with ruthless precision.

Having scalped her father, Sasha had shown no compunction in turning on her partner in crime next, taking out the good doctor in short order. Josh had watched with poorly concealed delight. Michael's expression had morphed from shock into grudging respect as he readily acknowledged Sasha's superiority on the board.

He left soon after, and even though they'd barely brushed shoulders the entire evening, Josh felt lighthearted and content. Later that night, as he lay thinking in the dark of his bedroom, there also came a reluctant acceptance that the kind of blissful peace the doctor so effortlessly induced in him wasn't easily found.

In that vein, just to further fuck with him, his phone had buzzed on the bedside table. Brent, asking if Josh would reconsider and meet him for coffee. Josh sighed and decided he'd leave that bag of snakes to answer until tomorrow. He rolled on his side and let sleep take him.

CHAPTER TEN

THREE WEEKS LATER.

MICHAEL SAT in the break room and kept a wary eye on Lucinda who was busy on her phone. Glancing down at his own, he saw the text message sent by Josh staring back unanswered. It was a happy face with a tongue stuck out and a few pointed words.

Josh: *One tongue in excellent condition seeks residence. Must be centrally heated with good plumbing. Willing to work for rent.*

Michael snorted loudly. Lucinda glanced over, scowled, picked up her coffee, and left. *Good riddance.* He stared at his phone. The previous three weeks had passed in a flash. His bruising was practically gone, he was back home, no muggers had reappeared. And, when their times off coincided, he and Josh spent nearly every damn minute together. Yeah, they'd thrown that whole casual fuck buddy thing to the wind. Not that they'd firmed up what was happening in its place, however. *Hell no.* That would make too much sense, right?

If their time off together fell between nine and three on a weekday, they met up early and fucked like bunnies on steroids, and then

Josh would bundle them off to introduce Michael to one of his favourite sights or things to do in Auckland. He was on a serious mission to share his love of the city, and Michael had bought into the package, hook, line, and sinker. Though that may have had something to do with who was selling it.

Michael loved his home country, he really did, but there was something intoxicating about New Zealand. That combination of laid-back, can-do attitude that punched well above its weight internationally, the amazing pristine environment, and the scarcity of people clogging the whole damn thing up.

So far, in Michael's NZ education, they'd covered the official "Josh Rawlins Tour of the Museum," which amounted to all Josh's favourite childhood exhibitions. This had a sidebar including all the dark places Josh had sucked and been sucked off as a randy teenager when he'd had a brief crush on a gay high school senior who happened to work Saturdays at the museum.

That had been followed by a ferry ride to the charming bohemian locale of Waiheke Island with lunch at a gorgeous winery. And just yesterday, they'd gone sailing with a detective friend on his catamaran in and around Auckland Harbour. The weather had been spectacular, and for the first time, Michael found himself seriously considering the idea of staying in the country long-term. Trouble was, he wasn't sure if that was simply down to Josh, and what would happen if that all came to an end?

If their mutual time off happened to fall on evenings or weekends, Michael hit Josh and Sasha's for dinner, followed by a board game or an hour spent playing *The Sims* with Sasha. She schooled him on how to create his own family and was currently busy trying to marry off one of her avatars to one of his. Michael was playing coy with that one. She'd taken to calling him Mickey, and though he grumbled endlessly to anyone who would listen that the girly nickname was screwing with his cool factor and rendering him undateable, Michael secretly loved it.

When she went to bed, he and Josh would curl up on the couch and make out, slowly and deliciously though always fully clothed and falling short of any actual sex. Michael was surprisingly okay with that. He knew Josh wouldn't want to go there with Sasha in the house. Aside from that one kiss she'd witnessed at the netball courts, they'd been careful not to show any further affection in front of her, keeping the "just good friends" label she seemed to accept easily enough.

Michael got it, he really did, and he worried endlessly about disappointing Sasha. He loved his time with the feisty young girl. She was smart, sassy, and quick as a wink. Messing up with her dad would hurt her too, no two ways about it.

Added to that, he still worried about whether he had it in him to really be what Josh needed. Josh wanted a partner. He wanted the picket fence, the forever thing, and Michael still squirmed at the thought, though less and less. There was no denying the chemistry between them, the sex was off the charts, and they got on really well, but a long-term, you-and-no-other, settle-down-and-grow-vegetables kind of thing? *Well, shit.* That wasn't something Michael had seen in his future ever, even when he was with Simon. And the fact he was considering it now with Josh, and Josh's *daughter?* Well that was just plain terrifying.

He grinned and punched a reply to Josh's text.

Michael: *One residence with two floors available. Luxury fittings, spectacular scenery and plumbing guaranteed. Top floor taken. Only bottom floor available.*

He hit Send and took a long pull on his Coke. Two seconds later his phone buzzed with a reply.

Josh: *Have heard owner of top floor is open to a swap. Heard he prefers the view from the bottom.*

Cheeky bastard, but yeah, spot on. Michael had in fact topped in a couple of their more recent sessions, but even he had to admit it had been more about keeping up appearances. There was just something about bottoming for that gorgeous man that cranked his shit hard. A fucking surprise for all concerned.

. . .

Paris damn near had to drag Josh to the police van, Josh was that knackered. The young thief had led them on a merry dance through a couple of the more well-to-do suburbs on the North Shore, having ripped off the takings from a local burger joint. About seventeen, the kid was fit and fast, and without Paris, Josh wouldn't have stood a chance of running him down. The shepherd took point and eventually herded the idiot into a small church car park where Colin and Rage lay in wait to nail him. He'd run like a dog possessed, and Josh fully intended to reward those efforts with Paris's favourite beef heart for dinner. When he told the shepherd just that, Josh could have sworn the dog wore a fucking smirk.

"If that's your way of commenting on my age, chum," he griped at the animal, "I'll start buying those cheap dog biscuits you hate so much." He scuffed the shepherd's neck and stood back to let him drink.

Colin appeared at his side, his red hair plastered to his head, freckles dancing on his nose. He slapped Josh's back. "Bang-up job by your mate there," he commented. "Jeez, he's fast. You, meh, not so much."

Josh snorted. "Maybe 'cause some of us ran while others had nothing more to do than stand and wait for the shithead to fall into their lap. Just saying."

Colin sniggered, and they watched Paris drink in silence for a minute.

"So, I heard Brent asked you out after the exercise last month," he asked with a smile.

For a second Josh had to think who he was referring to. Then it hit him. "Ah, yeah, I cancelled, though. Too, um, busy at the moment."

Brent. The guy was... pleasant, and their conversation had flowed easily enough during the exercise. They'd liked a lot of the same stuff, movies, bands, but compared to Michael? *Fucking hell.* There *was* no comparison and Josh was glad he'd never followed through on that coffee. Michael eclipsed anything Brent offered. The end.

Having Michael around pushed everyone else to the fringes. The two of them shouldn't work, but they did. And yet Josh was still struggling to raise a conversation with him about naming what they had—moving it up to the boyfriend label. And he didn't understand why. Sasha and Michael got on like a house on fire. Hell, Josh was pretty sure she loved Michael. So, what was it? He really needed to just get over himself and take the plunge before Michael got sick and tired and looked elsewhere. Not that he would. That was another thing. Josh trusted Michael, apparently. And wasn't that just a fucking miracle?

HOME BY five thirty, Josh walked into a house that smelled of... *hell yeah... Spaghetti bolognese.* He headed for the kitchen and found Katie at the stove, stirring distractedly. She didn't look up.

"Earth to Katie." He planted a kiss on her cheek. "Get your mind out of the poor guy's pants, sis. The amount of time you've spent together, he has to be rubbed raw as it is."

"You have a filthy mind, brother," she answered, holding up a spoon for Josh to taste. "Needs more garlic, right?"

He ran his tongue up the spoon. "Just a smidge," he agreed. "Dirty but bang on, I'm guessing."

She smirked. "Maybe."

The guy in question was one Kevin Hodder, Katie's latest and apparently mesmerising date/boyfriend; Josh hadn't been able to pry the correct descriptor from her yet. The two had practically lived in each other's pockets these last weeks, not unlike he and Michael. Yeah, the irony hadn't escaped him. Josh had even met the guy once. He'd run out of dog kibble and dropped in on Katie to pick up some spare he left there. Kevin had answered the door in a pair of bright red Calvin Klein briefs and nothing else.

Kevin had a hot body, it had to be said, not that Josh was looking.

But when his sister peeked around said hot body wearing nothing but a towel and a blush, he'd damn near choked on his tongue. He'd clearly interrupted something. *Well, shit.* There were some things a big brother ought to know about only in theory.

A day later after some subtle prompting and not so subtle bribery, in the form of a couple of slabs of Whittaker's chocolate, he'd gotten the CliffsNotes version. In Katie's words, Kevin was: hot—Josh already knew that; respectful—yet to be decided, considering the guy was banging Josh's little sister after less than two weeks, and okay, there was maybe a little double standard in play there; a thirty-five-year-old lawyer—Josh could live with that; and finally, he really seemed to like Katie. The latter was super convenient because Katie was clearly president of the guy's freaking fan club.

Josh was proud of himself for having swallowed the warnings about to roll off his tongue regarding taking it slow, not getting your hopes up, blah blah blah. Truth was he hadn't seen his sister this excited about a guy in years, and he was really happy for her. At the same time, he wondered if this was going to change things for him and Sasha. The short answer to that would be, of course it would. If Katie and Kevin became a long-term thing, he couldn't expect her to be available in the same way she was now. *Shit.*

Katie carried the larger pot to the sink and tipped the pasta into a colander. "Sasha tells me she's going to Mum and Dad's tomorrow, again." She gave him the stink eye.

Josh checked behind him.

"It's okay. She's in her bedroom with her music on." Katie poured a tiny bit of oil through the pasta to keep it separated, since it had to sit for a bit. "She's not too happy about it, in case she hadn't said."

He sighed and slumped into a chair at the table. "Like she was going to keep that a secret. I thought the whole sulky, moody, teenage-witch thing didn't hit for another couple of years."

Katie snorted. "Whatever gave you that idea? Strap in, sunshine, your parenting life is about to go to shit from now on, with an occasional ray of gobsmacking amazingness thrown in just to keep you hanging in there."

Josh let his head fall back. "Fuck, thanks for that." He pressed his palms into his tired eyes. "Anyway, there was no choice. She has to finish this damn family assignment."

Katie cocked her head. "There's always choices, Josh. They were right dicks to her last time, and you well know it."

He sighed. "I know, I know. Just... ugh. Don't give me a hard time about it, please. It's bad enough living with my eleven-year-old's disapproval. How young do they teach you girls that cold shoulder shit anyway?"

Katie sat beside him and reached for his hand. "There's something else. When I picked her up today, her teacher mentioned she's been playing up a bit in class."

"Ah, shit," he groaned and dropped his head to the table, banging it twice for good measure. "What the fuck, Katie? She's not *that* kid. She's never been *that* kid."

"I know. And it's nothing too bad," she explained. "Apparently, she's just not listening, distracting other kids, and her last two math results haven't been the best. Her teacher said that in any other kid they wouldn't be worried, but as you said, Katie's never been *that* kid. Something's going on with her, sweetie, and you're gonna have to talk with her."

Josh sighed. "Just what I need. It's this shit with Mum and Dad, isn't it?"

She levelled a look his way. "Give the man a prize."

"Fuck, fuck, fuck. Well, I'm not talking about it before Sunday. I don't want to make going to our parents' any harder than it is. And maybe I can sweeten tomorrow for her by agreeing to take a break from the grandparents altogether for a while. Guess it's time."

She squeezed his hand. "That's a good idea."

He leaned forward on his elbows and put his head in his hands. "Christ, this is gonna open a fucking hornet's nest. Still, maybe they'll appreciate what they have a bit more if they don't see her as regularly. Learn to keep their bigoted comments to themselves."

Katie planted a kiss on his cheek. "One can only hope. Now set the table and let's eat, I'm meeting Kevin in an hour."

NEXT MORNING, Josh dropped Sasha at his parents', and the sour look she sent him along with no kiss goodbye said exactly how she felt about it. He let it go, opting to hold his tongue until this last damned sleepover was done. If his parents could manage to keep their bigotry to themselves for a night, Josh might just have a chance at salvaging something.

With nothing on until he picked Sasha up at noon the next day, Josh finally relaxed. He glanced at his watch and realised he had just enough time to grab a coffee before collecting Michael for their date. Date. *Huh. My how times change.*

The early summer weather, a balmy twenty-one degrees, had decided today's destination. Piha Beach, on the west coast north of Auckland, was a popular stretch of black sand, dramatic rocky terrain, and big surf. Josh had organised for them to take a surfing lesson, but Michael knew nothing about that part.

"WE'RE DOING what?" Michael spun in his seat, slack-jawed when Josh broke the news.

"Mm-hmm. You know the thing, wetsuit, board, stand up, ride a wave, have fun."

Michael rolled his eyes so hard he risked whiplash. "You do realise that's the beach in that reality show of yours, the one where everyone. Always. Needs. Rescuing," he whined. "As in big, fucking, dumping surf, holes and—what are they called again? Oh yeah, rips... and surf and holes and shit... and rips... and shit."

"That's the one," Josh deadpanned, enjoying Michael's freak-out.

"Oh, come on, you're from California. You can't tell me you're scared of a few waves. Surfing's your birthright, isn't it?"

Michael glared. "I'll have you know I was born in Montana, a long way from the ocean. Mountains and skiing are my birthright, not freaking surfing and especially not drowning."

Josh laughed. "Don't be a baby. I checked with the learn-to-surf guy we're going with, and he said the waves are pretty small today. You can swim, right?"

Michael rolled his eyes. "Yes, Mom, I can swim. Can you surf?"

"No. But I can swim, pretty damn well actually. I was a Clubbie as a kid."

"A what? Is that some Kiwi gay teenager kinky shit?"

Josh snorted. "No, you idiot. A clubbie is someone who belongs to a surf lifesaving club. It's pretty big in New Zealand and Australia. Kids train and compete all over in rescue-related stuff."

"Huh, like *Baywatch*?"

Josh grinned. "Something like that. It was awesome as a gay teen. Lots of fit flesh and impressive dick on display in those tiny Speedos, and, man, when they pulled the backs of those things up and exposed those plump cheeks to get a better grip on the IRB seats—inflatable rescue boats—well let's just say I nearly creamed my own gear on more than one occasion."

Michael cracked up. "So, less Pamela Anderson and more—"

"The Hoff." They laughed in unison.

"Yeah, working out my sexuality was kind of a no-brainer after that," Josh admitted dryly. "With masses of flesh on display from both genders and you only have eyes for dick, it doesn't leave much room for debate."

"Not to mention the difficulty of hiding all those teenage stiffies," Michael quipped.

"Pretty much. Also explains why I gave it up around sixteen. I had a crush on this older kid in the same IRB team. The guy sat smack bang in front of me and, holy shit, did he have a fabulous arse.

I spent more time in the toilet whacking off than in training that year."

Michael howled with laughter. "So, surfing, huh?"

"Yes, you chook, surfing. So, get your big-boy pants on and let's do it."

"Oh, for Christ's sake, whatever," Michael finally gave in. "But I want it on record that you owe me big time for the loss of dignity that's about to take place. And I know exactly how you're gonna make it up to me."

Josh laid a hand on Michael's thigh. "And that's a punishment how exactly?"

Michael laid his hand over Josh's. "Shut up and drive, wolf-man."

JOSH WRAPPED himself around Michael, his dick still buried balls-deep in Michael's arse, trembling from another amazing round of sex. He loved this coming-down time, replete, nerves tingling, mind empty of all but the intense high, and still surrounded by Michael's inner heat. This odd quirk of Josh's seemed to amuse Michael no end, yet he never complained, happy enough to indulge him.

Between them, Josh topped almost exclusively now, though he always offered it up to Michael just in case. Once or twice he'd taken Josh up on it but mostly he seemed happy to bottom. It was a dramatic turnaround, but one Josh didn't dare mention. Not that Michael was a passive partner, hell no, but he did seem to enjoy a little manhandling, and Josh was more than happy to oblige. He'd do almost anything to see that blissed-out expression on Michael's face when he came undone at his hand.

Josh's softening dick finally slid out of Michael, a perfect ending to a great day. The surf lessons had been fun, and Michael had done better than expected, though not as well as Josh who'd had some board experience under his belt. They'd laughed themselves into tears more than once, grabbed meat pies and eaten them picnic style for lunch on a blanket on the sand, and then gotten caught in traffic on the way home. They'd filled in time trading amusing stories about their families and growing up.

They'd made it home by six for pizza and a movie, although the movie hadn't made it further than the opening credits and the pizza lay half-eaten on the lounge floor along with most of their clothes. Round two had at least gotten them into the bedroom, where they'd remained.

Michael hummed contentedly, dragging Josh's arm over his chest. "You finally done with the sleepover down there?" He chuckled.

Josh nuzzled Michael's neck. "You mind? I guess I never really checked out what you think about me... ah, taking my time, I guess."

He turned in Josh's arms and kissed his nose. "It's nice. It's... well, it's you. And it's kind of a compliment. Makes me feel too good to leave. Better than hightailing it, right?"

Josh felt his cheeks burn, thankful they'd left the lights off for once. "Maybe you are," he said softly, "too good to leave, I mean." Michael went still in his arms and Josh didn't follow up.

But Michael quickly relaxed and brushed warm lips over his in a tender pass. Josh opened instinctively. He loved kissing this man; it was damn near his most favourite thing to do. This thing between them had moved so far beyond "just sex" that Josh couldn't even remember passing the sign. They were making love, time and again, day after day, and he could no longer pretend otherwise. He wouldn't have it any other way.

Michael caught Josh's soft cry in his mouth and tugged him closer, pressing gentle kisses along his jawline as he filled Josh's head with cruel wishes and hope.

"Mmm," he hummed contentedly against Josh's throat. "Whatever am I going to do with you, Joshua Rawlins?"

Josh thought, *anything, everything*. But more importantly, he thought, *what the fuck would he ever do without Michael?* He couldn't begin to imagine. But even if they moved to the boyfriend label, they still hadn't solved the whole "but he lives in the US" issue. *Ugh.*

. . .

Josh woke up pretty much as he'd gone to sleep: wrapped around Michael, who lay sprawled on his stomach, sheet discarded, exposing a rather enticing rear end. He trailed his fingers lightly over Michael's hip and across his crease, aware of his morning wood morphing into something a little more demanding of attention. He was such a goner for this guy.

He slid a finger between Michael's cheeks, gently brushed his hole, and Michael twitched. *Yeah, that's it, sweetheart. Wakey-wakey.* Keeping an eye on Michael's still-closed eyes, Josh reached for the lube under his pillow and slicked his fingers before delving back to Michael's crease. This earned him a definitely interested hum. Risking the full enchilada, he dipped his finger in to the first knuckle and Michael pushed back, sliding it home.

Josh leaned over and kissed his ear. "Morning, sunshine." He gently added a second finger and began a slow fuck.

Michael wriggled and lifted his arse in the air. "You gonna play preschool games back there or you gonna bring out the big guns?"

Josh nipped his ear. "Don't wanna hurt you."

Michael squirmed, his arse clenching around Josh's fingers. "Well, considering you've earned yourself a frequent flyer card down there over the last month, by now you pretty much only need to look at me sideways and my ass seems to throw open the door all on its own."

Josh laughed. "So I take it you're ready, then?"

"Give the man a balloon. Now fuck me, wolf-man. And make it hard, so I can't get up for breakfast. I'll need pancakes, by the way... in bed... in case you missed that part."

Josh snorted. Nope, Michael could never be described as passive. But then Josh could take instruction with the best of them.

. . .

THEY'D CLEANED up and were curled in bed, facing each other, Josh laughing at Michael's pitiful assessment of his fitness to walk, a sad ploy to get that breakfast in bed that Josh was still holding out on, when the front door flew open and a distressed shout shattered their postcoital calm.

"Dad!" Sasha.

"Joshua."

Fuck. His mother. And that hackle-raising tone that heralded she was on the warpath.

Josh leaped to the edge of the bed, dragging the sheet from Michael as he scrambled for his boxers. But it all proved too slow to head off his daughter, who burst into the room and immediately stopped short, eyes wide. *Shit. Fuck. Shit.* Behind him, Michael swore and hauled the duvet across to cover himself.

"Dad? Mickey?" Sasha sputtered, her expression drawing down into an angry frown and no small amount of betrayal and hurt.

Goddammit.

"But, Dad, you promised—"

He caught the hitch in her voice. *Oh God. Oh God.* "Sasha, I..."

Marie Rawlins stormed into the room and nearly ran into the back of her granddaughter. Catching sight of Josh and Michael in bed, she froze, slack-jawed. Josh might even have found it funny if it weren't so damn mortifying.

"What the hell is going on here?" the woman hissed, her gaze flitting between Josh and Michael, who was making a first-rate attempt to crawl under the covers and disappear. His mother gripped Sasha's arm. "Get out of here, child, now."

But Sasha just kept staring.

Pat Rawlins appeared at his wife's shoulder, took one look, and fled to the safety of the hallway. To be honest, Josh couldn't blame him. There were altogether too many people in his bedroom as it was. And that's when it hit him. It was his fucking bedroom not theirs. And barring not being upfront with Sasha about Michael, he had *nothing* to be ashamed of.

He took a breath and steeled his nerve. "Mum, enough—"

"Shut up," his mother snarled, shooting daggers at Michael while pushing Sasha roughly toward the door.

"Mum, let her go. I'll handle this." He held his daughter's angry glare.

Marie Rawlins turned bright red. "No, Joshua. Enough is enough. I will not allow my grandchild to see her father and some, some... filthy—"

Sasha whirled on her grandmother. "Don't you dare talk to him like that."

"You be quiet," his mother snapped.

And that was it.

"*Enough!*" Josh barked. His mother's mouth opened to argue further, so he threw out a hand. "I mean it, Mum. One more word and you and Dad are out of here." He watched her struggle to swallow whatever venom she was about to unleash, fairly vibrating in self-righteous fury. *Well, too bad.* "The two of you can wait in the lounge. I'll be out after I've spoken to my daughter."

His mother locked eyes with him, her disgust and disbelief written in every clenched, disapproving line on her face. But Josh held fast and stared her down until she spun on her heels and huffed out, whereon he crossed immediately to Sasha and dropped to his knees. He pulled her into a hug.

"I'm so sorry I didn't tell you," he said, stroking her hair. "Michael and I, well... I didn't lie, Sasha, we aren't boyfriends, yet, not really. It isn't serious like that. That's why I didn't tell you." He winced at the half-truth and glanced over at Michael, shaken to see the obvious hurt in his expression. *Damn it all to hell.* There was no way Josh could protect Michael's feelings, not with Sasha in the room, not in a million years. But he couldn't be worried about that right then.

He turned his attention back to his daughter, whose anger had dissolved into soft sobs. "I just didn't want to say anything too soon. I didn't want you to be disappointed down the road if you didn't see him anymore, so we kept it quiet," he explained.

Sasha pulled back to look at him. "But why wouldn't I see him? He likes us, doesn't he?"

Josh sent an imploring look Michael's way, and to Michael's credit and Josh's eternal gratitude, Michael joined them on the floor.

"Of course I like you," Michael said softly. "And I'm having a really good time doing stuff with both of you. I like your father a lot, but I don't live in New Zealand, you know that, right?" He glanced at Josh to check if he was handling it right. Josh nodded.

Sasha nodded too. "You live in California."

Michael squeezed her hand. "That's right, and I have to go home sometime. I can't stay here. So, it's complicated. Your dad was only trying to protect you from getting hurt."

Sasha looked between the two of them. "But you're not leaving yet?"

Michael turned to Josh, who took up the reins.

"No, sweetheart," he answered. "Not yet, but things between us might change before then. This is new between us."

She stared at him, and Josh caught the first glimmer of ease in her expression. Her shoulders dropped, and she sighed. "I guess. I like him, though."

"I know, sweetie, I do too. Enough to want to be more than friends with him for a while and that's why he stayed the night, but it's still not the same as a boyfriend." *Only because you haven't asked him yet, dickhead.*

Beside him, Michael leaned close to Sasha. "The most important relationship is the one between you and your dad. That one always comes first."

He felt Sasha finally relax at those perfect words, and Josh could have kissed Michael.

"Okay," she finally said, then eyeballed her father. "But we're gonna have a talk."

Josh sighed. "Absolutely." Then he stood. *One down, two to go.* Give him strength. He kissed his daughter's cheek. "Now, how about you go out with your grandparents and let us get dressed. I'm not talking to them in my underwear."

Sasha frowned and shot a glare into the hallway. "I hate them." As if that explained everything.

Josh sighed. "I'm getting the picture. Now scat, and we'll be out in a minute." She did as she was asked, and Josh turned to Michael, who was slumped on the floor, leaning against the bed.

"Hey." Josh reached for Michael but he pulled away. "I'm sorry I said..."

Michael raised his palms. "You don't have to be. I get it, what you said, I get it. Sasha needed to hear that you hadn't let her down. You don't owe me any explanations."

"But—"

"Right now, you need to go sort out whatever's happened between your parents and Sasha. Just tell me how I can help."

Josh pulled him into a hug, grateful for Michael's understanding, but Michael didn't return the embrace, a million miles from the intimacy they'd shared not fifteen minutes earlier. Josh's gut churned. *Fuck, fuck, fuck.* But it wasn't something he could smooth over now.

"Could you maybe take Sasha outside while I deal with *them?*" he asked.

Michael nodded. "Of course."

They got dressed hastily and in silence, and when Josh entered the lounge, his parents turned as one, glaring at both of them. He nodded to Michael, who placed a hand on Sasha's shoulder.

"Get your filthy hands off my granddaughter," Josh's mother hissed, moving to where Sasha was slowly backing herself against the wall.

Josh stepped between them and eyeballed his mother. "If you can't hold your tongue, you can leave now, but you better take a good look at your granddaughter because it's the last you'll see of her for a long time. And that man there," he indicated Michael, "is more welcome in my home right now than either of you, so I wouldn't push it."

Marie Rawlins clenched her jaw but said nothing.

Michael dropped to his knees in front of Sasha and took her hands. "Come on, sweetness. Let's get Paris fed and play some ball."

Sasha looked between Josh and her grandparents, clearly unsure about leaving them alone, but Michael rested their foreheads together and Josh's throat tightened at the sight.

"Let's go," the doctor repeated. "Your dad will talk to you after."

She took another look at the three, then nodded. "Okay."

Michael took her hand and led her out the back door, closing it firmly behind them.

Josh sighed and turned back to his parents. "So help me God, this had better be good," he warned them.

MICHAEL DID his best to distract Sasha, chatting and throwing the ball between them while Paris tried desperately to intercept, but the young girl's gaze returned to the house every minute or so, her frown deepening. She'd said not a word about what had happened with her grandparents other than repeating how much she hated them, and Michael hadn't asked. It wasn't his place, though he couldn't ignore how his heart ached for her.

Truth was, he was still reeling, trying to come to grips with how much had changed between him and Josh in the span of a half hour. How such a great night and start to the morning had turned into such a mammoth shitfest in a matter of seconds. Just when Michael had finally convinced himself that he and Josh could do this, try being together in the long-term, Sasha had arrived home, and as quick as that, it became clear as a fucking bell that Josh was still keeping Michael in the maybe basket. He may have apologised, but Michael could read the writing on the wall. And maybe that was simply karma, after how he'd thrown away everything Simon had offered him like a piece of trash?

It was a much-needed wake-up call. As he'd listened to Josh explain what they were or rather weren't to each other, things became crystal clear. Josh needed to put Sasha first—hell, Michael would do exactly the same. And when he'd seen the confusion on the little girl's face at finding Michael in her father's bed, it had wrenched at something deep in his chest. He'd been a selfish prick putting her and her father's relationship at risk like that. Nothing new there.

Josh was a good man with responsibilities, with a daughter to protect, with a decent life. He'd already been fucked over once and had bigoted parent issues that screamed for his attention. The last thing he needed was someone like Michael, a man with a sackload of his own issues, and not even living permanently in the country, to add to Josh's worries. No, Josh needed a steady, stable partner worthy of him, and that sure as shit wasn't Michael. It was about time he stepped up and put his own needs second for once, God knows it had been a long time coming. He needed to salvage what he could of his dignity and get the job done.

When the front screen door slammed and a car headed up the road, Michael caught Sasha's eye. "Come on." He took her hand. "Let's see if that father of yours is still alive."

He was, slouched in a living room chair, his face pale, eyes closed, looking totally fucking exhausted, and Michael's heart physically pained at the sight of him. Josh stirred when they entered, and opened his arms to his daughter. Sasha launched herself at him and burst into tears. Michael found himself wanting desperately to do the same.

Father and daughter rocked and hugged for what seemed the longest time, while Michael looked on, a pang of grief stabbing at his chest for the impending loss of something he'd never thought he wanted. Watching the two of them, he recalled being rocked in those same arms himself. *Jesus Christ, could this day get any worse?*

Josh caught his eye over Sasha's shoulder and held it, the thank-you unspoken but clear as day, those liquid chocolate pools burrowing into Michael's heart, a heart Josh already owned. Knowing what he needed to do, Michael winced. *Yeah. The day could definitely get worse.*

"I should go," he said. "Leave you two to talk."

Josh frowned but then sighed. "I suppose we need a bit of time. Thanks. But, ah... we'll talk soon, right?" Josh looked done in but also... troubled.

Fuck. Michael nodded, then collected his stuff from Josh's bedroom. On his return, Sasha was running her fingers through her dad's hair, the worry stamped on her face. It almost broke Michael's heart. Josh's gaze locked on his, but Michael couldn't hold it and glanced away.

"Right, I'm off," he said.

Josh scooted his daughter to the side and stood. "Go empty your backpack, sweetie, while I walk Michael out."

Sasha ran up to Michael for a hug, and he obliged, wondering if this was the last time he'd have the opportunity. His eyes pricked.

She pulled back and eyeballed him. "I wasn't really mad this morning," she said. "I do really like you, Mickey."

She kissed his cheek and ran off, leaving Michael's throat tight and tears threatening to spill. He got to his feet, shaky at best, and ran his hands across his face in an effort to hide the emotion. He sensed Josh's gaze burning deep.

"So," he said, amazed at how fucking calm he sounded when his heart was ripping in two, "the parent thing. Redeemable or not?"

Josh put a finger to his lips and waved him to the back porch. Michael followed with his bag. Paris raced up to snatch his owner's attention, and Josh obliged with a half-hearted scruff around the ears. He remained standing a few feet away from Michael, hands shoved deep in his pockets. The body language couldn't be clearer, the atmosphere between them awkward as hell.

"My parents had friends around last night," Josh began, barely above a whisper, "and although Sasha was supposed to be in bed, she overheard a conversation about me being gay. Now I've only heard their side, of course, so it's likely to be watered down. Sasha will no doubt have a different take. But let's just say what they were more than happy to admit to saying was totally unacceptable, bigoted, and hateful. It was all the usual stuff about my sexuality choices, and parenting screw-ups, and so on. But this time there were a few charming additional insults thrown into the mix that included my lifestyle being disgusting and irresponsible, and that Sasha shouldn't be exposed to that vulgarity, and that I was brainwashing her with all my fag friends."

Michaels jaw dropped. "What the fuck, Josh?"

"Yeah, pretty much. They, of course, blame her for eavesdropping."

I rolled my eyes. "Jesus Christ. They actually called you that? A fag? To their friends?"

"Yeah. That's not all, though. Their friends answered that Sasha would be better off being raised by her grandparents."

"Holy shit. Unbelievable."

"If only it was. Anyhow, Sasha stormed in at that point, and you can guess the rest. They obviously knew she would dob them in, so they had no choice about owning up to some of it at least. Not that they believe there was anything wrong with what was said."

Michael snorted. "What fucking planet are they on? I can't believe they copped to that shit."

Josh sighed. "It's nothing I haven't heard from them before. But it's the fact that they discussed it in a semipublic conversation with their friends while Sasha was in the house, that boils my blood. It can't go on. I've had it with them. I haven't decided exactly what I'm going to do other than tell them they've seen the last of her for a while until I'm good and ready. And not to hold their breath about when that will be."

"Jesus." Michael whistled long and low.

"Yeah, and just think, I haven't even heard Sasha's version yet."

Silence fell between them, and with it an awkwardness Michael hadn't felt since they'd first met.

"So, about what I said back there..." Josh began uneasily.

Shit. Here it comes. Michael raised a hand to interrupt. "Look," he said, his voice far shakier than he'd have liked, "while you were inside with the hounds of hell..." He made a stab at a grin that fell dismally flat. "I had some time to think, about us—"

"Michael, don't..." Josh took a step toward him.

Michael stepped back and raised his hand, again. "Let me finish," he begged.

Josh froze, a deep frown nestling in his brow.

Michael continued, "We both know you've got a whole lot going on. Your parents, Sasha, they need your attention, and I don't want to mess with that. They have to be your first priority, not us, not—" He waved his hand between them. "—not whatever this is. We agreed at the start, right? And we agreed to take this slow when things changed, see if it had legs first. It's just like you told Sasha this morning—we aren't boyfriends, not yet. And maybe we need to stop at that now. You have to put Sasha first."

"Michael, I didn't mean—"

"No, it's okay." Michael sighed. "I totally agree. We probably let it go too far. I have to leave after this contract, we knew that."

"You agree?" For a second Josh looked confused, and Michael felt a surge of hope. But then Josh's lips set in a thin line and he just looked... disappointed. Disappointed and pissed. *Fuck.*

Michael went on. "But it's been fun, right? I really like you Josh, and I wish it could've been different." Hurt flared in Josh's eyes. "But it's what I said to Sasha. Your relationship with her is more important than anything, certainly more important than us, than me. And maybe we crossed some kind of line that we shouldn't have.

"Sasha's hurt. And sure, you might not have told her about us, but the reasons were the right ones. And that's okay, it really is. I don't want to mess her around, she deserves so much more than that, and so do you. Perhaps you had me pegged from the start. I'm not that guy, Josh. And with everything that's happened, I think it's better if we maybe leave it at that."

Josh shook his head. "Don't do this, Michael."

A range of emotions played across Josh's face. Sadness, hurt, anger, but also maybe relief. *You know I'm right, babe.*

"Dad," Sasha called from somewhere inside.

Josh's gaze tracked to the door. "I... ah, shit, Michael. Jesus, there's no need for this. Can we just wait and talk about it?"

But Michael had caught the crack in Josh's voice and knew he had to end this before he couldn't. The urge to wrap him in his arms and never let Josh go nearly overwhelmed him. Instead he shoved both hands in his pockets and looked away. "Go," he said. "Your daughter needs you. I'll tell the team you won't be at practice this morning."

"But—"

"Dad," Sasha yelled again.

"Go," Michael repeated, eyes glued to Paris, knowing if he dared look at Josh he'd be undone.

Josh hesitated only a second, then grabbed Michael by his jacket and kissed him hard, then disappeared into the house. Michael rocked on his feet, the warm touch of Josh's lips sliding too quickly into memory, stinging his eyes, shattering his heart. He grabbed his bag and strode to his car, desperate to hold himself together and get home before he lost his shit completely. He didn't make it. Half a kilometre down the road, he pulled over and broke apart.

CHAPTER ELEVEN

Two weeks later.

Michael glared at the pager going nuts in his hand and promptly threw it on the break-room sofa. "Jesus Christ, give me a fucking break," he grumbled. "I'm trying to finish my fucking lunch here."

Cam's head popped through the door. "You got a problem, sexy?"

Michael threw a cushion at his head. "Fuck off. I'm hungry, and I'm exhausted. I should've been off at eight, and yet here I still am at noon." He'd volunteered for a run of nights the last two weeks. It was better than not sleeping.

"Yes, you're a saint," Cam agreed, altogether too readily for Michael's taste. "Which reminds me," the charge nurse continued, "why *are* you here at noon?" He slipped inside the room and closed the door.

Before Michael could answer, his pager started up with its infernal squawk yet again. He went to pick it up, but Cam got there first.

"Hold it, hotshot. Everyone deserves a break." The nurse picked up the wall phone and punched in some numbers. "Mary Anne? Is Steve around? Oh, is he now? Well, tell him that his boss is on a much-needed break after sixteen hours on the trot and I don't care if the woman in five is sex on a stick, he's to get his butt out of that room and call—" He glanced at Michael's pager. "—the blood bank on behalf of Michael. That is unless he wants a rotation through the colonoscopy clinic next week. Got it?"

He hung up and sat his ass on the chair opposite Michael, arms folded across his chest. Michael swept an eye across his pretty features and found himself with the closest thing to a smile on his face in two weeks. The colour of the day was obviously green, and Cam's eyelids fairly glittered with it.

"So, Dr Oliver," he drawled. "You going to tell me what's been stuck up your arse lately, and I don't mean in a good way?"

Michael raised a brow. "Is this an intervention?"

"Does it need to be?" Cam leaned back on his chair, legs stretched before him.

Michael slapped Cam's leg. "Do you know how insanely annoying you are?"

Cam smirked. "Yes. Now stop distracting me. What's up? You've been chewing out my staff left, right, and centre for the last week. I wouldn't care if you kept your foul temper to the medical staff, mostly they deserve it, and it saves me the bother, but when you start leaking it all over my nurses, I'm gonna have your balls in a bag before you can say cocksucker."

Michael winced. "Jeanne said something, huh?" Michael had torn a strip off the night charge nurse over something petty, something he'd normally have laughed off. She hadn't deserved it, and he knew it.

"I was holding back saying anything, hoping you'd grow a pair and offer her an apology," the nurse chided. "It's not like we don't already know you can be a dick."

"Gee, thanks." Michael rolled his eyes.

"You're welcome. But usually incidents of your dickishness are justified in some way. A big trauma case, life-and-death shit, and such like. But throwing your weight around over stupid piss shit stuff like that isn't you. So, I'll ask you again, what's up?"

Michael's gaze slid away. "You're gonna give me hell, huh?"

"I'm gonna burn your ass into next week is what I'm gonna do if you don't spit it out."

Michael sighed. "Okay, but it's really nothing. It's just... well, that thing I had with that cop," he said softly. "It's... well, it's not a thing anymore. I ended it." He shook his head. "Happy now?" he snapped.

Cam leaned forward, golden eyes blazing. "Say again? I could swear you just said that you're all twisted up and nasty because you broke it off with Mister Tall, Blond, and Sexy, but that can't be right. Because that would mean you really liked the guy. And that would make it something like a relationship, and Michael Oliver doesn't do relationships, and he especially doesn't do attachment."

Michael rolled his eyes. "Fuck off, Cam. You heard me the first time. And it was me who broke it off, so I guess I still don't do relationships, or attachment."

Cam went deathly quiet for a moment. "Can I ask why you broke it off?" he finally asked.

Michael clasped his hands behind his head and leaned back with a sigh. "It was getting messy. He's got this kid, a gorgeous girl, eleven years old. And there is all sorts of complicated shit going down with his bigot-assed parents, and I was just getting in the way, making things harder. We were fuck buddies, nothing more. So it made sense to let it go, let him sort his shit out and find someone that wants what he wants, house, family, and all that shit. I'm not that guy, Cam. You of all people know that. I'm not the picket-fence, weekend-brunch type. We were getting too close."

Cam cocked a brow. "We?"

"Fuck. No. Not we, me. I was getting too close. And I'm nowhere near ready for something like that. I'd fuck it up, and it's not just him. Sasha would get hurt too."

Cam slid him a sympathetic grin. "Oh how the mighty have fallen."

"Asshole."

Cam kept his gaze level on Michael. "You really liked him?"

Michael stood and leaned against the break-room bench. "Maybe. Makes no difference. It was headed nowhere."

Cam shook his head. "You don't know that."

Michael eyeballed him. "Yes. I. Do. He didn't need me complicating things for him."

"Did you ask?"

"No, I didn't ask. There was no need. It was crystal clear."

Cam winced. "Ouch."

"Yeah. Whatever. Anyway, he told his daughter in front of me that we weren't serious." *You know damn well why he did that.* "And even if he was interested in more, I realised I'm still a million miles away from being ready for that, especially with a kid involved. I'd just screw it up."

"So you keep on saying, over and over again. And yet you seem to have fallen for this guy, so just maybe think about that. You might be more ready than you want to believe. Maybe it's not that you aren't ready, but that you're just plain fucking terrified."

"I don't want to think about anything. We're done, end of story. I'm sorry for being such a prickly bastard, and I promise to do better. And I'll apologise to Jeanne. Happy?"

Cam rolled his eyes. "Over the fucking moon."

"Then this conversation is over." Michael strode to the door, but before he got there, Cam placed a hand on his arm.

"You do know that going out and simply screwing more guys isn't going to get you what you want, right?" the nurse said.

Michael held Cam's gaze. "I'm not an idiot. It might not solve anything, but it's a damn good way to pass the time."

"Whatever. But if you're serious about not trying to mend things with Josh, then you need to get over it and move on, before I'm forced to drown you head first in the sluice room sink. Because if I have to watch you waxing pathetic any longer, I swear I'll lose the will to live. You're clogging up my ER with your damn self-pity, and the sooner we get the old, irritating Michael Oliver back, the better for all concerned. Best chance of that happening is getting you back in the saddle. So, and I cannot believe I'm about to do this, a few of us are heading to Downtown G tonight. Join us."

Michael waggled his eyebrows. "You asking me out on a date, Mister Charge Nurse?"

"Oh, for fuck's sake." Cam pushed past Michael and through the door.

Michael kept his smile in place until the nurse was out of sight before collapsing against the wall. The last thing he felt like was cruising, but maybe Cam had a point. Maybe it *would* get him out of his funk—nothing else was working. Two weeks hiding out in his apartment, running from the nightmares, trying not to give in and fill the hole in his chest the size of Chicago with booze, sure as hell hadn't helped. He hadn't been able to stomach the thought of other men, just the one, the one he couldn't have. And if a cute girl with blond hair sometimes also crossed his mind, well, that was under-standable—he'd liked the squirt well enough.

No. Cam had it right. Michael was better than this. He didn't do needy, and he sure as hell didn't do sentimental. With the bruising gone, his face was marketable again. A hot and heavy romp with a stunning piece of ass was likely just what he needed. The fact that his cock adamantly refused to perk up at the thought was a moot point, and one Michael did his best to ignore.

"For fuck's sake, Josh," Mark muttered as he landed a boot to Josh's shin. "If your bottom lip sinks any lower, you can suck the damn beer spill off the table and save the server the trouble. Though that would be a crying shame because those looks he's been sending me, well, let's just say there's a good chance that sweet arse is mine by the end of the night. Ergo, I'll be real pissed if you screw it up for me."

Josh sat up straight and plastered a fake smile on his face. "Better?"

Mark winced. "God, no. Now you'll really scare him away."

Josh sighed. "Sorry, man. I told you I wasn't up for this."

"Rubbish. You've been moping around that damn house of yours for too long. You needed to get your gay on."

Josh snorted. Mark had appeared at his house, having organised Katie to babysit, and simply dragged Josh to the G.

The detective's expression hardened. "Don't push me, Joshua Dudley Rawlins. Sometimes you make it damn near impossible to be your friend."

And wasn't that the truth. Josh had been avoiding everyone, including his best friend, who'd just full named him to underscore his level of pissedoffedness. "Sorry. I know I've been a wanker."

"A cocksucking wanker," Mark corrected. "Now drink up. If you aren't going to get laid, you can at least get drunk. Make me feel like I've done my job."

Josh took a half-hearted swallow and surveyed the bar. On Fridays, Downtown G was generally hopping, and tonight was no different. With pounding bass, lots of hot skin on display, and a dance floor jammed full of men, some of whom hadn't been shy in sliding Josh a few blatantly interested looks, and still his cock hadn't mustered any interest whatsoever.

And why is that, Josh? Yeah. Try as he might, Josh couldn't get the damn doctor out of his head. He'd missed Michael way more than he'd expected, and it shocked him. They'd had fun, lots of fun, in and outside the bedroom. And yeah, he was pissed as hell Michael had just walked away from, well, from whatever it was they hadn't named, because for sure they were boyfriends, even if neither of them had used the damn word.

But maybe Josh shouldn't have expected anything more. Michael had made no bones of how commitment-phobic he was at the start, and he didn't make a move to fight for what they had when the chips were down—he just ran. What the hell had Josh been thinking even starting something with him?

Mark was still eyeing up the blond server, now busy at the next table. The twink was fit, tanned, and yeah, pretty damn cute. Josh caught the two exchanging a look and booted his friend under the table. "Too young and cute for you, old man."

Mark gave him a wide grin. "Watch and learn."

The blond approached their booth, and the detective sat a bit straighter. "Anything you need?" he asked, keeping his gaze firmly locked on Mark.

Close up, Josh could fully appreciate the young man's looks, and watching Mark's reaction was amusing in its own right. The detective was clearly smitten and appeared... well, flustered. *Huh.* Mark had been a one-and-done guy for a long while now. This reaction was... new.

"Another two of the same, sweetheart," the detective answered, holding the server's gaze.

The guy blushed to his roots. "Coming right up." He rocketed off as if his life depended on it.

Josh snorted.

Mark scowled. "What?"

"Not your type, I'd have thought."

Mark shrugged. "What is my type, smart-arse?"

"Tall, hot, heavy on the muscle, light in the head, fuckable but not dateable, and usually totally wrong for you."

Mark winked. "But they do as they're told and go home after the job's done."

"That's because most of them can't even read." Josh laughed.

Mark flipped him off. "Fuck you. Anyway, this guy—" he nodded in the direction of the server. "—Josh, honey, he's everyone's type."

Josh laughed and shook his head. "You're incorrigible."

"That's way too big a word for this number of drinks," Mark quipped. "So, how are the parents from hell?"

Josh blew out a sigh. "Nice change of subject, arsehole."

Mark saluted him with his bottle. "I'll raise two bigoted weasels to your one arsehole." he grinned.

"And the rest," Josh grumbled. Mark knew his parents well. "The short answer is I haven't called them, and they haven't tried to contact me, which is probably for the best. I'm still fucking furious with them. Not sure what I'd even have to say at this point."

"No kidding. And Sasha?"

Josh shrugged. "She's okay, I guess. Her teacher says things have settled at school, so that's something, right?"

"You don't sound convinced."

The server returned and set two new beers on the table.

Mark tapped the guy's wrist. "What time you done, gorgeous?"

The guy smiled. "An hour, maybe less."

Josh shook his head. "What a shame. We have to leave, right, Mark?"

The detective fired him a sizzling glare and nudged his boot into Josh's shin, again.

"Ow." He stifled a laugh. "Just saying."

Mark glared. "Button it, *friend*."

Josh made a zip motion across his lips and took a slug of beer.

"Fancy a dance after?" Mark asked the server.

The guy hesitated, then nodded. "Yeah, okay." He stuck out his hand. "Bryce."

Mark shook it. "Mark. So, Bryce, how about you come find me when you're done, and we'll have that dance?"

The blond flashed the detective a stellar smile. "Looking forward to it."

He left, and Mark craned his neck to watch the guy's arse every step of the way.

"Wow." Josh chuckled. "Look at you, all smitten kitten, detective."

Mark scowled. "Shut up. He seems a nice guy, a gorgeous, nice, available guy with a very fuckable arse. Back to Sasha."

Josh closed his eyes and sighed. "She seems fine. She does all her usual stuff, finishes her chores, plays her games but... she just seems... flat, if you know what I mean. And she won't talk to me."

"Can't be great hearing your dad trash-talked by your grandparents."

Josh pulled a face. "I guess. It's just so damn frustrating, and I hate that she's pulling away, at least that's what it feels like." He sensed Mark's hesitation. "Go on, spit it out."

Mark placed a hand over Josh's and squeezed gently before letting go. "You think she's missing him. Michael, I mean?"

Josh had already thought of that. "Maybe. She won't talk about it, so I don't know for sure, but the fact that she won't talk about it..."

"Yeah," Mark agreed.

Josh twirled his bottle in his hand. "She's mad at me, and I get it. She thinks I lied about Michael, and she's right, in a way. I probably should have told her he was a bit more than a friend, but I didn't want to confuse her. Bad enough her dad's gay—"

"Hey! There's nothing about being gay that makes you any less of a great dad."

"Maybe not, but it doesn't exactly make it any easier for her growing up and wanting to fit in, does it?"

Mark pursed his lips. "Maybe not, but fitting in can be highly overrated."

Josh snorted. "Not when you're an eleven-year-old girl."

"Okay." Mark threw up his hands. "Look, I don't pretend to understand the difficulties of being a gay dad, with a teenager. But did you consider maybe her mood's nothing to do with her being pissed about you guys sleeping together and just that she misses him, kind of like *you* obviously miss him?"

The detective's look was pointed, to say the least.

"I don't miss *him*," he argued. "At least not like you're implying." *Liar.* "The sex, maybe the company."

Mark nodded sagely. "Yeah, right. Because we all know you're such a shallow manwhore."

"Whatever." Josh shifted his gaze to the dance floor. "My point is, this is exactly what I was afraid would happen, why I shouldn't have ever started anything with him."

Mark ignored him. "You realise this whole thing has screwed up our fast-pitch team. He's pulled out, you know that, right?"

Josh frowned. *No, he hadn't. Fuck.*

Mark barely broke breath. "And, hello, you're a grown man. You're allowed to have a life. You don't have to be a monk until she's eighteen."

"I know, believe me I know. But I do need to keep it real, for Sasha's sake. No more *inappropriate* relationships, none of this 'friends with benefits' shit, or guys who don't even live in the damn country. I have to set a responsible example. Sasha understands dating, but she's too young to be exposed to... other things."

Mark rolled his eyes and tapped his coaster on the table irritably. "Oh right, responsible dating, as in the 'hamster'—what's his name?—from the exercise. I'd heard he called you."

Josh bristled. "His name's Brent. And I *didn't* go out with him. But so what if I had? There was nothing wrong with him. He just wasn't..."

"Michael. That's who he wasn't. And no, there's nothing wrong with the guy. He just makes grey look an interesting colour, that's all."

Josh glared. The comment was way out of line.

Mark winced. "Sorry. He's a nice guy."

"Damn right."

"He's just not right... for you. Come on, Josh, even you have to admit, the guy's boring as a paperclip."

"He's not. He's just... quiet. Not everyone has to fuck a new guy every week to be fun, you know?"

Mark flinched. "Ouch. Touché."

But Josh was on a roll. "At least chances are he wouldn't run like a fucking rabbit at the first hint of trouble. There's a lot to be said for a bit of damn staying power." *Shit.*

"I thought you didn't care about the sexy doc in that way." Mark eyed him pointedly.

Josh closed his eyes for a second to calm his heartbeat.

"Does he know that you... maybe way more than just like him?" Mark asked quietly.

Josh pinned his friend with a defiant stare. "No. But Jesus Christ. I've only known him a month, and at the first sign of any relationship shit, he flew the coop. *Ugh.*" He dropped his head, took a few deep breaths, then sat back.

Mark covered Josh's hand with his own. "You deserve the best, Josh. I just want you to be happy. You're the most passionate, deserving guy I know, a wonderful dad, and you'd make a great partner."

Josh sneered. "Yeah, right. I'm so *everything* that my last serious partner, who I was about to ask to marry me by the way..." He caught Mark's shocked expression. "Yeah, didn't know that part, did you? Had the ring and everything. Well, anyway, that guy cheated on me the entire time we were together because clearly I wasn't *everything* enough for *him,* more specifically, in bed."

This time Mark stood, almost taking both their beers with him in the process. "That's it. I'm done with this bullshit. Get up."

Josh startled. "What?"

"I said get up. We're dancing."

Josh slouched lower in his seat and shook his head. "Nope. I don't wanna dance. I did warn you I wasn't in the mood."

Mark glared at him. "I don't fucking care what you want, Josh. You're coming on that dance floor with me right this minute, so guys can hit on you and grind thick hard cocks into you, so you can see what a hot piece of shit you really are. I didn't pry you out of those sorry-arse daddy pants and pour you into that pair of tight fuck-me jeans for nothing. Now dance with your best friend." He stood there with his hand out to Josh. "Please."

Josh hesitated, then sighed. As much as he didn't feel in the mood, Mark was only trying to help. He took the offered hand and let himself be pulled up. "Fucking bossy bastard," he grumbled.

Mark grinned widely. "Damn right. Now get moving."

The dance floor was heaving, but his friend pushed his way through the grinding throng to the middle, dragging Josh behind. Finding a few inches to move in, he spun Josh around, plastered Josh's back to his front, and started swaying. After a minute or two, Josh found himself relaxing to the rhythm and even, damn it, enjoying it. The sensory overload churning up from the dance floor left little room in his head for those endless conversations he'd been having with himself. He turned his head to yell in Mark's ear. "If that dick of yours slides any farther up my butt I'm gonna arrest you for sexual assault."

Mark laughed. "I wish I could say it was standing to attention for you, but truth is, Bryce is eyeing me from the bar. Told you. I'm in there, sugar."

Josh chuckled. "Whatever. In the meantime, just watch yourself back there, mister, or it could be the end of a beautiful friendship."

Mark answered with a brief kiss to Josh's neck and kept them moving. Josh closed his eyes and left his body to Mark's guiding hands. It felt good, really good to just let loose and get lost in the rhythm and the sensual sway of bodies on the floor. He hadn't danced since Jason left, and Mark had been right, he'd needed this. Maybe he was right about Michael too. Maybe Josh should have told him how he felt. And just maybe it wasn't too late.

A few songs in and the cute server bounced excitedly alongside looking flushed and hopeful. Josh nodded to Mark. "Go for it. I'll get a taxi."

"You sure?" Mark looked a little guilty.

Josh grinned. "Absolutely." He watched them dance off to the side until a familiar face on the other side of the floor caught his attention. Michael Oliver, dancing hot and heavy with a gorgeous young man. The guy's hands were all over Michael, his tongue halfway down his fucking throat. Then, as Josh watched, the younger man grabbed Michael's hand and hauled him in the direction of the bathrooms.

Bile welled in the back of Josh's throat and his knees buckled. *Fuck.* So much for maybe taking a chance and telling the doctor how he felt. Michael fucking Oliver appeared to be a long way shy of missing Josh. *Goddammit.* Josh grabbed his jacket and sprinted for the door.

CHAPTER TWELVE

Cam jabbed a finger in Michael's chest, forcing him to step back. "Listen up, arsehole," Cam growled, sapphire liner flashing. "I'm having enough trouble keeping my own staff from nailing your ass to the wall without getting a complaint from radiology that you swore at their receptionist for not answering her damn phone quick enough, on a busy Saturday no less. As if I don't have enough legitimate crises needing my goddamn attention, I've got to add the indulgent hissy fit of one pouting doctor. Inviting you out to get laid last Friday was supposed to deal with this filthy mood of yours, and yet—here we are."

Cam had called Michael into his office and closed the door, so the dressing-down hadn't exactly come as a surprise. But his friend's overwhelming frustration with Michael had, not that Michael didn't deserve it.

His face heated. "Yeah, well, maybe that didn't quite go to plan." Michael pushed the charge nurse's hand away and slid his gaze from that too-clever scrutiny.

Cam's eyes popped. "Are you saying you tanked that night? Doctor Sexy drew a blank?"

Michael rolled his eyes but said nothing. He didn't care what Cam thought. He was still getting his head around having zero interest in pursuing anyone, but Josh. He'd allowed the young guy to lead him to the back of the club, to a quiet corner near the emergency exit. And there it was. *Fucking déjà vu.* Almost the exact spot he'd first laid eyes on Josh.

And yes, the young guy had been gorgeous, but Michael couldn't ignore the churning in his gut, and his barely interested cock, which had apparently decided anyone other than Josh wasn't worth the effort. He'd stopped everything in its tracks, apologised, and headed home. So yeah, he hadn't been laid in three weeks and counting, a fucking goddamn record.

Cam snorted. "Well, well. I'd seen you eyeing that blond at the bar and just figured..."

Michael's gaze flicked to the wall, the calendar seeming to require his immediate attention. That is until Cam stepped between, forcing them to lock eyes again. He stared at Michael with unwavering attention until a grin split his face.

"Well, fuck me," Cam said with a smile. "You're not joking, are you?"

"Asshole." Michael walked to the bookshelf on the other side of the office and started absently rifling through its contents.

Cam was hot on his heels. "Did you get *any* action?" he pushed. "And quit moving my stuff around." He slapped Michael's hands.

Michael snarled, "It's none of your goddamn business." He sidestepped Cam and headed for the door, pausing only when he heard Cam's low whistle. *Fuck.* He turned, and Cam walked straight up to him, cupping Michael's cheek with his hand.

"For what it's worth," he said softly. "I'm sorry, Michael."

And Michael was left to figure out if Cam was sorry about Josh, or sorry Michael hadn't got laid, or just sorry for interfering. Not that it mattered, as the lingering heat from his hand on Michael's cheek immediately sent his thoughts to Josh.

"Yeah," he replied to the empty room. "So am I."

. . .

Josh EDGED two chairs into the shade of the massive elm in a vain attempt to avoid the surprising heat of the new summer sun. It had been a long-arse Friday night, half of which he'd spent dragging his legs like lumps through tidal mud flats by spotlight, meaning most of Saturday morning had been spent washing said mud from Paris's coat.

So bite him if attending a kid's birthday party immediately after wasn't exactly hitting any high notes. And yes, he was sulking. And no, he wasn't being very discreet about it. But Sasha had begged, and he'd thought a little sucking up to his daughter wouldn't hurt seeing as how they were just getting back on track after the whole grandparent/Michael fiasco.

Michael fucking Oliver. A week after running into Michael in the club and it still didn't take more than his name to wind Josh up and get his stomach acid boiling. When he'd got home that Friday after watching Michael make out with some skinny piece of ass, he'd been fit to kill, cursing having ever been stupid enough to moon over the dickhead motherfucking manwhore. How much better he was to be free of him, blah fucking blah.

A couple of hours and five or six tequila shots later and he'd finally admitted that he was maybe, just maybe being a bit harsh. After all, he'd been open to a hookup himself that night, supposedly. And besides, he had no claim on the doctor, Michael was a free agent. But fuck if it hadn't nearly driven him insane seeing the two of them together like that.

His first thought had been to push the skinny dipstick aside and shove his own tongue down Michael's throat, remind him what he'd been missing. But seeing Michael so happily back at his old game had just reaffirmed all Josh's fears. He had to move on and let Michael do the same.

Hence the reason he'd invited Brent to tag along to this damn birthday party a week later. Brent had asked Josh out yet again for coffee, and this time Josh had caved, but swapped the suggestion for the birthday party instead—may as well find out how Brent handled kids. Brent had leapt at the invite, of course he had, and Josh couldn't decide whether he was pleased or disappointed. Brent was no Michael Oliver, as Mark had warned him, but he was a nice guy and deserved a chance.

He'd introduced Brent to Sasha as just a friend in the getting-to-know-each-other stage, part of Josh's agreement to keep things honest with his daughter. She'd been cool toward him at first but that had quickly eased to something more akin to indifference, and Josh was okay with that. And so far, Brent had seemed, if not actually to be enjoying himself, then at least to be relatively amused by the preteen dramas on display. Conversation flowed easily enough as they'd chatted about work, movies, and Sasha.

Brent had no children of his own and little experience but made a decent enough effort to engage Sasha in conversation, and in truth Josh was pleasantly surprised. If only he could garner more than a passing interest in dragging Brent to bed. He already knew it would be their first and only date. In that Michael had been right. Josh deserved the friend and the lover, and so did Brent.

A water gun landed at Josh's feet, breaking his train of thought. He lifted his gaze to find his daughter grinning at him like a loon.

"C'mon, Dad," she pleaded. "Toby grazed his knee and we're short a person. Jessica's dad is killing us here."

Josh raised an eyebrow Brent's direction and Brent laughed and said, "Go ahead. And play nice."

Josh grinned. Jessica's dad was a sniper in the Armed Offenders Squad and none too modest about it. It was a prime opportunity to take the sucker down. He nodded enthusiastically at his daughter. "Lead the way."

One hour and a soaked set of clothing later, the party came to an end, and Josh and Sasha were collapsed on the grass at Brent's feet. Jessica's dad had unfortunately held his own in the battle of water cannons, and they had eventually called a good-natured truce and

deemed the fight a draw. This was met by a series of boos and accusa-
tions of a police stitch-up by the kids. As far as raucous teen parties
went, it hadn't turned out too bad.

Josh ruffled Sasha's damp hair. "Grab your stuff, kid. We're out of
here."

She eyed him slyly. "Can we get pizza?"

Josh groaned. "You've just eaten a bakery weight of sugar in the
last three hours. I'm expecting Child Welfare to turn up any minute
and arrest me for neglect."

Sasha brought her best puppy eyes to the table and threw in some
eyelash batting for good measure. "Please, Daddy?"

Josh rolled his eyes. "Oh, for Pete's sake. I suppose so." He
glanced at Brent. "You mind if we stop on the way back?"

Brent grinned. "Are you kidding? I'm a huge fan of pizza, all the
food groups covered on a thin crust of deliciousness. What's there not
to love? No anchovies, though." He screwed up his nose.

Sasha stuck out her tongue. "Blech. I'm with you. Stinky little
fish don't belong anywhere near good pizza."

Josh shook his head. "Uneducated heathens. Go get your stuff
and don't forget Katie's plate, the one I brought the muffins on."

Sasha took off, and Josh turned to Brent. "I hope it wasn't too
boring for you. Kind of a weird date, I know. You've been a good
sport."

Brent reached over and tucked a few stray locks of hair behind
Josh's ear, brushing Josh's cheeks with the back of his fingers in the
process. Josh froze. The affectionate gesture had taken him
completely by surprise, and he felt strangely guilty, almost pulling
away at the contact. No one had touched him like that since...
Michael. *Goddammit.* He'd managed to avoid going there all day.
Idiot.

Brent held his gaze. "I had a really nice time but I get the feeling
that you're not—getting the feeling, that is." He took Josh's hand,
rubbing his thumb in circles over its back. "Sasha's a great kid, and

her dad's pretty cool as well. But after the pizza, I think I'll just head home and wish you well. Friends, maybe down the track?"

Josh's chest tightened. "I knew you were a good guy. Yes, friends, I'd like that... down the track. And sorry."

"Nothing to be sorry for." Brent smiled warmly. "It either works or it doesn't, right? Can't manufacture that chemistry shit."

Josh sighed. "No, you can't." He willed Sasha to appear and save him from any further awkwardness, and as if by magic, she did, plate and bag in hand, running full tilt across a deck strewn with party trash. *Shit.*

"Hey, slow down..." he called out, but it was too late. Sasha's foot had landed on a discarded water gun, twisted, and gave out, sending plate, bag, and daughter crashing to the deck.

CAM POKED his head into the doorway of Trauma One just as Michael was finishing the paperwork on a forty-year-old man with a known allergy to mussels who'd decided after a few beers at a family wedding to tempt fate and down a couple of paua fritters.

"You free?" Cam asked.

Michael closed the file and threw the notes on the man's bed.

"No more shellfish, period," he warned him. "Next time you might not be so lucky."

The man nodded guiltily. "Thanks."

Michael followed Cam out the door. "What's up?"

"Just a head's up." Cam's lips pursed, and a line formed between his perfectly coiffed brows. "Josh is in room five, he's here with his daughter."

Michael's heart lurched. "Is she okay?"

Cam nodded, those tawny eyes searching Michael's reaction. "She's fine. Went over on her ankle. Needs an X-ray to check it's not broken, but that's all."

A whoosh of relief left Michael's body. "And?"

"I've assigned her to Paul," the charge nurse said flatly, daring him to argue.

Fuck. Michael bit back his immediate protest. By rights Sasha should have gone to him. Paul was good, but he was still a junior. He raised his eyebrow at Cam.

"Don't look at me like that," Cam growled. "I've told him to run everything by me."

Michael sighed. "Fine. But I could've handled it, you know. I'm a grown man."

Cam put a hand on his shoulder. "I know you could have handled it. I just didn't think you needed to."

Okay, so he was being a dick, again. Michael's shoulders relaxed. "Thanks." Cam walked off, and Michael tried and failed to get a grip on his emotions. Josh, the man who filled most of his waking thoughts was sitting three doors away, and Michael's chest was so tight he could barely breathe with the proximity. The ER suddenly felt overwhelmingly claustrophobic.

He glanced at the clock—too early for his break. He could go talk to the ambulance crew, or see if he could be of help to another team, or head up to radiology, or... *Oh for Chrissake.* He mentally slapped himself. He was being an ass. He couldn't hide from Josh forever. The police were in and out of here all the time. He was acting like a child. Cam was only trying to protect him, but fuck if Michael was going to hide from anyone.

At the closed door to room five, he paused and sucked in a deep breath. To his right he was suddenly aware of Cam's gaze glued to him from the nurses' station. He raised his hand and nodded. He could do this. He cracked the door, poked his head inside, and damn near dropped to his knees.

Sasha was lying on the bed, covered by a blanket and clearly drowsy with pain relief. Josh sat in a chair alongside, his attention focused solely on his daughter, her hand tucked inside his, the lines of worry etched deep on his face.

But that wasn't what had nearly taken Michael's legs. No, that was down to the second man, the one seated next to Josh, one hand resting on Josh's shoulder in support. The whole concerned family portrait thing simply stole Michael's breath as everything he was so sure he didn't want stared him in the face and screamed "liar" at him. It was all he could do to not tell the guy to get his fucking hands off what was his, and by that Michael realised he meant not just Josh, but Sasha as well.

Josh turned wearily at the sound of the door opening and his eyes widened. "Michael?" He stood, and the other man's hand fell.

Awesome. Michael hated whoever the guy was on principle. He struggled to find his voice, still frozen in place. "Ah... hi. I, um... I heard Sasha had been brought in, and I just wanted to check... you know... how she was," he stammered clumsily.

Josh frowned. "Oh. Ah... sure. She fell at a birthday party. Running, not looking where she was going, you know the story." He squeezed his daughter's hand.

Michael gave an awkward half laugh. "Yeah. You've described half our clientele."

The second man stood, and his gaze flitted between Josh and Michael, curious.

Josh glanced behind as if taken by surprise that someone was actually there. "Oh, sorry," he apologised, his cheeks flushing pink as he turned back. "Brent, this is Michael. Michael is... a doctor here," Josh explained hesitantly. Then he turned to Michael. "Brent is... a friend."

Michael felt the emotional blow as a kick to the stomach. So this was Brent. *Well, shit.*

Michael offered his hand reluctantly, noting Josh's discomfort.

"Nice to meet you," he said, doing his best to be polite. It wasn't as if Brent had done anything wrong, after all. By the look of it, Brent didn't even know who Michael was. And didn't that just sting a little more.

"Likewise," Brent replied, eyeing Michael like he knew he was missing some vital piece of information.

Sasha stirred and opened her eyes. "Mickey!" she croaked, then pouted and stuck out her lower lip. "I hurt my stupid ankle." She tugged at the blanket to expose a very bruised and swollen foot. Then she opened her arms to him for a hug.

And fuck if that didn't feel good. He plastered on a smile and took the girl in his arms. "Hey there, missy." He kissed Sasha's cheek, then switched his attention to the offending ankle, turning it gently from side to side. Sasha winced but held still. "How's that pain?" he asked softly.

"Not too bad," she answered, covering her leg again.

"They gave her some morphine," Josh added.

Josh had moved alongside Michael, and Michael was acutely aware of his proximity. The familiar scent of Josh's cologne swept over him, and his cock twitched in recognition. So many memories flooded through his head and a ridiculous regret at the ones they would never make.

A warm pressure pushed against his hip as Josh's hand rested there, his fingers drawing small circles in place, raising every hair on Michael's goddamn body. Michael couldn't move, smiling at Sasha and stroking her hand like his world wasn't wholly focused on those six square inches of connection between himself and Josh. What the fuck was Josh up to? Michael kissed Sasha's nose and stepped aside, forcing Josh's hand to drop. He thought he caught the word "sorry" but wasn't sure.

He cleared his throat. "Well, Doctor Paul will take good care of you, and don't worry, I'll be keeping an eye on you as well."

Sasha's eyes flew wide. "But I thought you'd look after me?" Her bottom lip trembled.

Michael nearly broke in two. "I can't, sweetie. I have other patients, but you'll be okay, I swear. You're such a brave girl. I am so, so proud of you. You're going to be just fine, and I'm only down the corridor if you need me."

Sasha gave a weak smile. "Okay. But you'll come and see me when I get home, right?"

"I'll see," he answered, wondering how in the hell he was going to survive that. "But right now, you need to get better, so I'm going to let you rest, okay?"

Sasha's brow creased, and she looked less than happy. "Okay," she finally agreed. "For now."

Michael made for the door, willing his legs to hold out long enough to get him there. But before he could escape, Josh put a hand on his forearm, bringing him to a stop, and said, "Thanks."

Michael turned his head and found himself swimming helplessly in those chocolate eyes once again. His chest tightened, and he had to force himself to look away. "Just doing my job."

Josh snorted. "No, you weren't. But thanks anyway. Sasha needed that."

And what about you? Instead Michael said, "She's a great kid, and Brent seems... nice." And with that, Michael couldn't remain another second in the same room without either throwing a punch through the wall or kissing Josh senseless. Neither was what one might call a sensible option.

He pulled free of Josh's hand and headed for the nearest empty room to shut himself in. As he collapsed against the wall, his legs shook like jelly. He'd done it. It may not have been his best performance, but he'd managed it without looking like a complete idiot, so that was a win, right? The door cracked open, and Cam pushed through.

"There's a coffee in the break room with your name on it. I phoned an order to Milly's down the road. Figured you might need the real stuff."

Michael stared at the godsend that was Cameron Wano and realised for the first time just how much he'd undervalued Cam's friendship. That shit needed to change.

"I could kiss you right now," he said, then blushed, finding he probably even meant it, he was that desperate for a shoulder to lean on.

Cam snorted. "In your dreams, sunshine." His expression turned serious. "Can't have been easy. You done good."

Michael gave an appreciative nod.

Cam waved a hand at him. "Take twenty. We can hold the fort. I'll call if I need you."

It took some effort, but Michael kept his head in the game long enough to get two further patients written up and admitted without obsessing too much about who sat just down the hall. But when the orderly had arrived to take Sasha to X-ray, he found a sudden interest in the ambulance bay to avoid running into them. He wasn't sure he had the energy for another encounter. *Coward? Pretty much.*

But he couldn't ignore his promise to Sasha to keep an eye on her, so he called radiology to check on the results and was ridiculously relieved to hear there was no break, just bruising. When he saw them return, Josh walking alongside Sasha's bed, holding her hand, he yanked up his big-boy pants and strode to meet them. The delight evident in Sasha's expression was reward enough. As for Josh, he just looked plain exhausted, and it was all Michael could do not to haul him into his arms and hold him close.

"Good news," he said instead. "Nothing broken." The worry eased from Josh's expression, and he returned the first genuine smile Michael had seen that day. "A supportive bandage and a pair of crutches for a week should do it. Paul will sort you out with the details, but it could be an hour or more yet." He eyed Josh. "Have you eaten?"

Josh seemed to need to think for a minute. "No... I guess. We were headed for pizza when this happened."

Michael wondered if *we* included picket fence, but kept his expression neutral.

"Well, then, how about you grab something from the cafeteria and let Brent sit with Sasha. My shift's over, but I'll be around for a bit yet, if she needs anything."

Josh studied him with an odd expression. "I sent Brent home."

Oh. "Well, um, I could keep an eye on pipsqueak here, if you want?" Look at him, being all helpful and shit.

Josh's eyes widened. "You sure? You seemed pretty busy before."

The knowing look that accompanied those words wasn't lost on Michael. He returned Josh's stare. "I've got that sorted now. I can hang out for a bit, no problem. If I'm needed, someone on staff can sit with her."

Josh blinked slowly. "Well, okay, then... um... thanks. I need to call Katie and... ah, Brent too, but I'll try to be back in fifteen or twenty, tops."

Michael shrugged. "Whatever you need to do. We'll be fine."

Josh bent to give Sasha a kiss on her nose. "See you soon, kiddo."

"No vegetables, Dad." Sasha grinned up at her father. "I'm in pain here. I need to keep my sugar levels up if I'm going to cope."

Josh laughed. "There are two chances of that, gorgeous, slim and none."

Michael watched him leave, reeling in the memory of also being called "gorgeous" but in a very different tone.

Getting Sasha back to her room, he left the orderly to manoeuvre the bed through the door while he waited in the hall. Raised voices caught his attention a couple of rooms down, and he wandered over to check it out. Adele, a young ER nurse, was attempting to get an IV into a heavily tatted man's arm while the guy cursed her out from one end of the room to the other. Drunk, most like. Saturday nights sucked.

A second man leaned on the wall off to one side, his back to Michael, offering no help whatsoever in calming his drunken friend down.

"Hey," Michael said, catching the tatted man's attention. "Settle down and let her do her job or I'll call security."

"Who the fuck are you?" the man cursed, spittle flying from his lips. "This bitch is fucking useless. What kind of shit hospital you running here?"

The second man took that moment to turn, and Michael's legs nearly dropped from under him. Wavy, dark brown hair with a tattoo on the right side of his neck, a dragonfly, not a bird as Michael had first thought. His gaze darted to the guy's hands. The left sported two bandaged fingers and the right... a silver chain. *Fuck.* Michael's eyes flew back to his face in time to catch a thin smirk. Then the guy winked, he fucking winked.

Jesus Christ. Michael tried to keep his panic at bay. He breathed slow and steady, praying the wink meant the man was just fucking with him and not that he recognised Michael. That might at least give him a chance to leave and call Mark without drawing further attention. But first he had to get Adele out of harm's way. There was no way in hell he was leaving her with them.

He calmed his jangling nerves and schooled his voice. "Adele, how about you take a break for a few minutes before you have another go." The nurse looked at him strangely, a frown forming between her brows. Michael continued, "Try a different approach, maybe a smaller gauge needle."

The nurse hesitated a few seconds, clearly confused by the odd request, but Michael held her gaze with a straight face. *Come on, don't fight me on this.*

Finally, she pursed her lips and nodded. "Good idea," she said calmly, though her eyes told a different story. One of "what the fuck is going on here?" But she went along with him. *Thank God.*

"Yeah, go get your shit in order, bitch," the man on the bed spat. "And bring me a fucking sandwich or something, I'm starving here."

With her back to the man, Adele rolled her eyes in distaste. "Sure," she replied, easing past Michael to disappear down the hall. Michael was confident she'd raise some kind of concern at the nurses' station, even if it was only to ask what the hell had gotten Michael's crazy going.

The second man hadn't moved, continuing to simply stare at Michael with unwavering interest. Michael pushed himself off the doorjamb and calmly turned to leave. "I'll be back in a minute," he said over his shoulder and walked off, trying not to turn and check if the man was following. Five metres along the hall he grabbed his phone from his pocket and ducked into Sasha's room to quickly check on her before calling Mark and warning the staff.

"Hey, princess." He grabbed Sasha's hand and she pulled him down for a hug. "Listen, I have to duck out for—" The words dried in his mouth as the door clicked shut behind him. He spun to find the man from the other room wearing a vicious smile—the man he'd seen at the bar that night, the man with the knife.

"Aww," the guy said, and the smarmy tone raised goosebumps on Michael's skin. "How touching."

Michael placed himself between Sasha and the guy. "What do you want?"

"Your phone for a start." He held out his hand.

"Get out of here," Michael growled.

The man stepped closer. "I don't think so," he challenged. "Thought I didn't recognise you, Dr Michael Oliver. Now give me that phone."

"You're too late, I already—" Michael barely got the words out before his head snapped back with the force of the blow to his jaw. His vision went black and his head spun, but it was the steamroller punch to his stomach that doubled him over and sent him to his knees, gasping. His phone was snatched from his hand and the glint of a knife appeared to his side.

Sasha gasped. "Mickey!"

The man's free hand lashed out and backhanded her, slamming Sasha's head sideways against the wall with a sickening crack. And all Michael could manage was to lift his head and watch as she slid down the wall and collapsed on the bed, unmoving.

"You bastard," he shouted, lunging toward Sasha. But his balance was shot, and he crashed face first into the side of the bed instead. The man kicked his legs out from under him and dropped him to the floor. Then he sat on the bed, the knife twirling in his hand at Sasha's throat.

"I suggest you calm down, Doc, unless you want the girl hurt."

Michael instantly stilled.

The man grinned. "That's more like it. So, this is what's gonna happen. You're gonna leave with me so we can take this somewhere private and do a bit of business, yeah? You should've kept your head down, Doc. I said no IDs. Thought I made myself pretty clear. Lucky you came up a loser. But then, this." He held up his bandaged fingers. "Bad luck for both of us, I reckon. I could tell you knew who I was the minute you saw me." He shook his head. "Too bad. 'Cause based on your track record, I can guarantee you're not gonna do as you're told, and I've got too much on the line for you to screw it all up."

Michael's gaze flitted from the man to Sasha and back again. She appeared to be breathing but fuck if she wasn't frighteningly still, a trickle of blood running the length of her jaw from her ear. He couldn't tell how badly she'd been hurt, but the brain was a fragile thing. It didn't like being bounced around. All Michael knew was he had to get this guy away from her as soon as possible and get her help.

"I'll go with you. Anything you want, just leave her alone."

The man tapped the blade against Sasha's throat and grinned. "Good boy. Now get up and face the door."

Michael obeyed, taking a second to steady his legs. The man took a position behind him, the blade pressed somewhere close to Michael's right kidney.

"Now we're going to walk out of here nice and calmly. No talking, no running, no fucking even looking at anyone, understand?"

Michael nodded.

"Behave and maybe they'll even find your little friend in time."

Michael panicked. Josh was due back from the cafeteria but just when, Michael didn't know. He had to get this man out of Sasha's room and get her some help, now.

The guy followed Michael through the door and closed it behind them, keeping the knife tip pushed into Michael's side. He nudged Michael down the hall toward the waiting room, pausing at the other room to catch his injured friend's attention.

"Call Jeff to meet us outside," he ordered. "Engine running. We're done here."

"But..." The man waved his still unstitched hand.

"Now!"

The guy stood and started punching numbers into his cell.

It was only a few seconds, but Michael figured it might be his last chance. While the two men were focused on getting their ride out of there, he lunged sideways and dropped, twisting to free the man's hold on him. It worked, and he almost couldn't believe it, but once free he was able to reach up and punch the cardiac arrest alarm on the opposite wall. The ER was immediately lit up with a series of three-bell alarms. Voices rose, and feet hit the floor. *Yes!*

He sprang in the direction of the nurses' station, expecting the guy with the knife to head for the waiting room to escape, but the bastard didn't. That's where it all fell apart. To Michael's horror, he instead headed straight back into Sasha's room, reappearing seconds later with the girl slung over his shoulder, knife at her throat. "Stay put, arsehole." He threw Michael's cell at him, made a "call you" hand signal, then sprinted out the ambulance bay, followed closely by his mate.

Michael set off after them just in time to watch the guy throw Sasha into the back seat of a blue Toyota and then join her just before the car took off. *Fuck, fuck, fuck.* He flew back down the corridor, grabbed his phone from the floor, and called Mark. Then he pocketed his phone and ran to the nurses' station.

The place was in an uproar. Two crash carts filled the hallway, and staff were milling around Sasha's room wondering where the hell they were needed, confusion written all over their faces.

"Turn that damn alarm off," Michael shouted, and within seconds someone shut it down.

Cameron appeared at his side. "What the fuck's going on?"

"Michael?" Josh joined them from Sasha's room, his expression panicked. "Where's Sasha?"

Fuck. He turned a frantic eye to Cameron. "Your office, now."

Then to Josh. "Come with us." He grabbed Josh's arm.

Josh threw him off. "I'm not going anywhere. Where's my daughter, Michael?"

Michael took a deep breath. "Josh, please. Just come with us."

Cameron took Josh's elbow. "Come on."

Josh threw a furious look Michael's way but let himself be led.

Inside Cam's office, Michael handed Cam his phone and told him to dial the number last called and put it on speaker. He wasn't going to waste time telling the story more than once. Then he turned to Josh and grabbed his hands. Josh eyed him warily but didn't pull away.

When Mark came on the line, he was already on his way, so Michael repeated his earlier story to the detective but with a lot more detail. He was acutely aware of the stunned silence of Cam and Josh sitting alongside, listening in. At one point, Josh attempted to jerk his trembling hands free, but Michael held fast, watching Josh's face pale into shock and disbelief. When he finished and hung up, he locked eyes with Josh.

"I'm so fucking sorry," he blurted. "I didn't think he'd go back for her. I thought he'd take the chance to run or come after me. I just wanted to get him out of Sasha's room, so I could get her help. If I'd just left with him like he wanted, she'd be safe now. But I was so fucking worried about Sasha. It was all I could think of." His voice cracked.

Josh sucked in a trembling breath and squeezed his hand. "You tried."

"No, I screwed up, Josh. And now he's got Sasha, and we don't know where she is, or how badly she's hurt. I'm sorry. I thought I was doing the right thing. I'm so, so sorry." Tears brimmed in his eyes.

Josh lifted a trembling hand and brushed his cheek. "I... I can't... do this right now... I just want her back, okay?"

Michael swallowed hard and nodded. "Of course." Like fuck it wasn't his fault. He'd fucked up again, and again a young girl's life was at stake. The urge for a drink roared in his head.

Josh pulled away and got shakily to his feet. "I need to let Katie know," he said as he pulled out his phone and left the room.

MARK ARRIVED ten minutes later with two other detectives in tow. He commandeered the break room and herded everyone he needed inside, demanding an update.

"And you're positive it was that guy you saw in the mug shot?" Mark eyed Michael.

Michael nodded. "I just needed another look. He's older than your photo of him, and with the tatts and stuff I just..." He swallowed. "I'm positive."

Mark turned to the other detectives. "It's Cruz."

Cameron and his team had used their time waiting for Mark to do a quick canvass of the ER for anyone who might have seen anything. A woman in the parking lot and a paramedic restocking his vehicle in the ambulance bay both saw the car with Sasha head out the north entrance and turn right onto Manukau Road. Both agreed the car was blue, and the paramedic added it was a Toyota, which meshed with Michael's account. More importantly, the paramedic's intuitive unease had him check the plate. He'd only caught the first three letters, KED, but it was a start.

When Katie burst into the break room, she immediately eyeballed Mark. "Don't even think about asking me to leave. Here." She pushed a plastic bag holding a T-shirt into his hand. "For the dogs. Josh said to bring something." She then turned to her brother. "He's in the car."

"Who?" Mark demanded.

Josh glared at Mark. "Paris. And I don't want to hear a fucking word about it."

The detective threw his pen on the table. "Damn it, Josh. You can't be involved."

"No dog knows Sasha's scent better than Paris," Josh argued, lifting his chin in defiance.

God, how Michael knew that look.

"Who would you want searching if it was you out there?"

"Come on, Mark," Michael agreed with Josh. "He's right and you know it." Josh sent him a grateful nod.

Mark's eyes narrowed to slits. "Okay, but you cannot be on the end of that harness, got it?"

Josh nodded. "Got it."

But Michael saw the lie in Josh's eyes. There was no way Josh was going to keep that promise, and Michael didn't blame him. Then his cell vibrated with an incoming call, ID unknown, and something cold slithered through Michael's chest as he raised the phone to his ear.

"You like to make things difficult, don't you, Doc?" a familiar voice mocked.

He recognised the kidnapper immediately, but something stopped Michael alerting the others. He scanned the room. No one seemed too curious except Josh, who was busy eyeballing him intently. *Shit.* Josh knew him too well.

"If you want the girl safe, keep your mouth shut and get somewhere you can talk. Do anything stupid and she's dead."

Josh raised a brow his way, but Michael shook his head and mouthed the word "work" before excusing himself from the room.

"Where is she?" he hissed into the phone.

"She's fine... for now. Still out like a light so she can't talk to you if that's what you're hoping. But it's not her I want, so she can stay safe as long as you agree to replace her."

"How do I know you'll let her go?"

"You don't. But you agree to keep your mouth shut and meet me where I say, and I'm telling you I'll let her go. Best offer you're gonna get, so I'd take it if you want her to ever see her family again."

Michael didn't hesitate. If he wanted a chance at redemption, this was it. He'd get Sasha back to Josh. No little girl was going to die this time.

"Tell me where."

. . .

Josh held tight to Katie's hand, keeping one eye on Mark and the other on the break-room door waiting for Michael to reappear. Mark was busy organising the helicopter search for the car, and Michael had left with his phone to his ear. What the fuck was so important that he'd needed to leave them now? And work? Michael was *at* fucking work.

He knew he had no real right to be angry. Sasha being taken wasn't Michael's fault, but Michael was here, and Sasha wasn't, and Josh was terrified. Still, he wouldn't have wanted Michael to be taken either.

And Brent? Josh knew Michael had jumped to the conclusion that Josh was *with* Brent. He'd seen the hurt flash in Michael's eyes and he'd let it stand uncorrected. Childish? Sure. But he'd wanted just for a minute for Michael to regret running away, to have him think the worst. He wanted to have him feel what Josh had felt seeing Michael in the club that night with that other guy. It was stupid and hurtful and... unnecessary, and Josh needed to right that mistake as soon as possible. He'd take Michael aside when he returned and tell him the truth.

Cameron appeared at the open door, frowning and out of breath. "Has something happened?" he demanded. "Adele said Michael left in a hurry about five minutes ago. Said he had his bag, car keys, and his phone to his ear. He ignored her hello and headed straight for the car park at a run."

Mark's head snapped up and the other two detectives put their phones aside as they all exchanged a look. *Fuck.* It didn't take a genius to guess what they were thinking.

Josh blurted, "He got a call, just before."

Mark spun to face him.

"He took it outside. Said it was work."

A suffocating silence filled the room.

Josh's hand hit the wall. "Fuck. I should've known. He looked...

off. Why didn't I follow him?"

Katie grabbed his arm. "What do you mean? What's going on? Josh?"

"It was never Sasha they wanted," Josh explained. "It was Michael, always Michael. Damn it to hell. Why didn't he say something?"

Mark sighed. "You know why. He thinks he can save her for you, Michael. And Cruz just wants him gone. Best way to do that? Persuade Michael to swap for Sasha."

Bile coursed up the back of Josh's throat. "Shit. He felt responsible for her being taken. Thought he should've just gone with the guy to start with."

Mark nodded. "I know. So let's just get them both back, yeah?" He clapped his hands for attention and started dishing out orders. "I want the number that called him, and I want a trace on both phones. Plus everything on Denton Cruz and where he's likely to hunker down. And what about the nurse who stitched him up?"

A young constable Josh didn't recognise popped his head around Cameron's shoulders. "They've got the Toyota," he said.

Josh leapt to his feet. "Where?"

The constable focused his answer on Mark. "The chopper spotted it in the Pohutukawa Drive car park in Cornwall Park, up One Tree Hill. They've put down close by and are trying to lock the place down. Armed Offenders Squad and dogs are on their way."

Mark pinched the bridge of his nose. "Jesus, that's less than a ten-minute drive. We haven't got much time."

"Sasha?" Josh begged the constable.

The young man glanced at Mark, who nodded. He turned to Josh. "Nothing yet. Car was empty," he answered.

Mark sighed. "Tell them to look for Michael's vehicle, that might get us closer to the meetup point." He turned to the others. "Bloody hell. Six hundred and seventy acres with loads of cover, and a ton of entrances and exits, especially on foot. Christ, they could just hop over any one of the low stone walls that surround the place. And you can forget about Denton returning to the Toyota. There'll be another car waiting to pick him up, or several if he needs options. And if he leaves that park with Michael or Sasha, we're screwed." He glanced at Josh with an unspoken apology.

Josh shook his head. Wasn't like he hadn't already known everything they were saying.

"Toyota was registered to a Jeff Brady," another detective said, looking up from his laptop. "And Michael's car is a no-show in the car park as yet, but he could've parked anywhere and made his way in. They're doing the rounds."

"Brady's not the name of the guy he came into ER with. That was Trent Miles," Cameron supplied from his notebook.

The young constable returned. "The nurse picked Cruz out from a photo. Called himself Anton Smith and this guy Brady who owns the Toyota, he's a gangbanger mate of Trent Miles. So, there were three of them. Chances are Brady drove them both here and was also the one who picked them up outside."

Mark slammed his fist on the desk. "At last. Now let's make damn sure we get them."

The team scrambled and headed out, and Katie threw Josh her keys. "I'll wait here," she said. "Call as soon as you know anything."

Mark laid a hand on Josh's arm. "Where the hell do you think you're going?"

Josh jerked away. "She's my daughter, Mark." He glared at the detective.

Mark dropped his hand. "I must have lost my fucking mind," he grumbled and left.

Josh signalled Cameron. "Give them something of Michael's, something the dogs can use." Cameron nodded and disappeared.

ARRIVING AT Cornwall Park, Josh saw the police still working on getting it cordoned off. *Good luck with that.* If Denton Cruz was still in the area, he'd be hard pressed to miss what was going on. Josh had to hope Michael hadn't gotten to the swap yet, as that would be the only reason for Cruz not to have hightailed it out of there already.

On the back seat, Paris whined, picking up on the tension and the police action around him. He leaped from one side of the car to the other, head butting the windows, excited as all hell.

Colin Hardy and Rage were all over a blue Toyota parked at the far end of the car park, clearly getting a scent range before heading out. He caught Josh's eye and gave him a thumbs-up and a sympathetic nod. Paris howled, keen to join his mate. The two dogs always worked well together. *Not today, boy.*

Next to him on the passenger seat, Paris's harness burned a hole in Josh's concentration. Sasha's pyjamas sat in a plastic bag underneath, and Josh blessed his sister's presence of mind in remembering the extra clothing. His mind drifted to Michael. The idiot was gambling with his life to save Sasha, and if they both made it out, Josh didn't know whether he wanted to punch him or kiss him. It was a debt he'd never be able to repay, regardless the outcome.

Mark jogged over, and Josh read the unspoken warning on his friend's face. "Since it's one of our own, the brass is here, just so you know." He flicked his head to where John Stable stood in earnest conversation with someone from the Armed Offenders Squad. "So you damn well better behave, Josh. I'm trusting you here."

"Guess I should feel grateful they're pulling out all the stops," Josh relented.

A constable ran across to Mark. "Michael's car's been spotted on the southern side, close to a walking track entry. Engine's still warm. A dog team is on its way."

Mark squeezed Josh's arm. "We'll get them," he promised. "Both of them." Then he headed off at a run.

Josh let him go. He wanted to trust Mark and the others, he really did. He didn't want to cause trouble or make things difficult, but he knew in his heart of hearts there was no one out there, dog or man, who was more likely to find Sasha than Paris. As far as the shepherd was concerned, Sasha was his kennel mate, and he knew her scent like no other. But Josh also knew there was no way he was getting official permission to be involved, so that left only one option. He'd wait for an opportunity, then slip away on his own.

It didn't take long. In half a minute, the car park had emptied of most of the police teams, allowing Josh to quietly harness Paris in the car and give him a long sniff of Sasha's pyjamas. He then slipped the shepherd out and disappeared over the brim of the hill in the opposite direction to the other teams. He'd circle back once he was clear.

"Find Sasha," he urged Paris in a low voice, and the shepherd took off. As a new team, Josh and Paris had trained like this for hours at home and in local parks, using his daughter as the lure. The dog knew exactly what he had to do. Josh kept him on a shortish lead until he was sure they were clear of the others, then gave the shepherd his head and kept pace. Paris tracked off in the general direction of the other teams and travelled that way for a few minutes before giving a sudden bark and swerving sharply to the right. Josh frowned. He could hear the other teams still hard to his left.

He pulled Paris up short. "What's up, boy?" He scuffed the shepherd's neck. "You got something?"

Paris whined and pulled at his harness. Josh didn't want to free the animal to track in case he joined up with the others. Mark might never speak to him again.

Fuck. It only took him a couple of seconds. If there was ever a time to trust the animal's instincts and skills, it was now. If Paris was wrong, the other team had it covered. Couldn't hurt to widen the search area. "Okay, boy. It's your show." He released the lead. Too late now.

Paris took off through a section of thick bush at the base of the hill, well below the car park. He ran, nose to the ground, delving left and right on occasion to check a scent but always returning to the central path and moving forward. They seemed to be circling a little more to the left than before, but still a fair distance away from the official teams. Josh tried to keep positive. He had little option but to trust his partner's nose when it came to finding Sasha.

Halfway around the back slope, Paris suddenly banked hard to the right, and Josh called him to a halt. He ran back and forth, intently focused on something just ahead, but there was nothing but dense manuka scrub and kahikatea, so thick it blocked the sun, moss covering the ground.

"You got something, boy?" Josh knelt alongside, fingers hooked in Paris's harness. Paris barked excitedly. Somewhere to his left, Rage bayed, nowhere near Paris but tuned in to his search mate's familiar sound. Any second now all hell would rain down on them. His only hope was that Paris was on the money. God, what he wouldn't give to see his daughter's face.

His heart hammered in his chest. They had so little time. For all he knew, Cruz could be long gone and Paris had simply latched on to Sasha's residual scent. She'd make a damn good insurance policy for the bastard, but Josh couldn't think that way. Not yet.

Paris launched himself out of Josh's hands, and this time his bark carried an entirely different tone. Josh's heart leapt. He'd found something.

"Sasha!" He surged ahead, following his partner through a tangled mass of manuka and blackberry, into a tiny clearing no more than a couple of square metres. There, Paris went quiet and lay down alongside what looked like a discarded pile of clothes. Josh's heart leapt to his throat. *No.* He knew that shirt. Sasha had worn it to the party. It was her favourite.

"Sasha!" He collapsed at her side and a soft moan rose from the bundle of clothes. *Oh, thank Christ.* "Sweetheart, can you hear me?" He shook her gently.

Sasha stirred. "Dad?"

He crushed her to his chest and held tight, tears washing over his cheeks. "Oh, honey. Are you okay? Are you hurt?"

Sasha cuddled against his chest. "My head hurts."

Josh pulled back a fraction and brushed the hair from her face, taking his first good look. Sasha was pale and shocked, her lips trembling, her eyes unfocused. A trail of dried blood ran from her ear down her jaw and throat. Her shirt was stained red from neckline to underarm. But it didn't look fresh.

Barking and voices closed in on Josh's left.

"Over here," he shouted, pulling Sasha against him to rock her in his arms.

"Paris?" Sasha buried a hand in the shepherd's hair.

"Yeah, he found you, pumpkin. You did real good, baby. I love you so much, you know that, right?" He didn't want to quiz her, but with his daughter safe, all Josh could think of now was Michael.

Paris surged to his feet, hackles pricked as Rage raced onto the scene. The other dog stopped, and the two shepherds eyed off, Paris placing himself between Rage and Sasha.

"It's okay, boy," Josh soothed the dog.

"Settle down," Colin Hardy instructed his shepherd from somewhere to the left, and Rage immediately dropped to the ground.

Hardy caught sight of Sasha and frowned. "She okay?"

Josh nodded. "Far as I can tell."

"Thank God," Hardy breathed in relief. "I'll get the medics."

WHILE THEY waited, Josh peppered Sasha's head with kisses as he asked what he needed to. Michael's life could very well rely on something she had seen.

"Do you remember anything, sweetheart?" he asked gently.

Sasha shook her head. "My head hurts. I was trying to find you."

"You did great, pumpkin."

She snuggled against him, sobbing. "I was scared."

"I know, sweetheart, I know." He wrapped her tight in his arms.

Colin Hardy placed a hand on Josh's shoulder. "They're on their way."

"Mickey was there," Sasha murmured.

Oh God. Josh's heart lurched. "Was he... was he okay, honey?"

She shrugged. "The man said Michael had to stay."

Josh's throat closed over. Cruz had taken Michael after all. He brushed a stray lock of hair from Sasha's eyes. "He saved you, sweetheart."

She gave a small smile, and it was so damn good to see.

Colin tapped Josh's hip with the toe of his boot. "A word of warning. Mark's on the warpath, not to mention what the chief's gonna say about your shenanigans. What the hell did you think you were doing?"

Josh had the grace to blush. "I know, I know. I'm sorry, but I couldn't just sit there, man. Could you?"

Colin sighed. "Probably not. But that's not gonna save your ass, you realise that?"

Whatever. He'd do exactly the same again.

Colin's radio crackled, and he moved away to answer, stabbing the ground with his boot as he talked. When he returned, Josh caught something in Colin's expression that gave him hope. "Michael?"

Colin nodded. "Not that I should tell your interfering ass a damn thing, but yeah, they found him. He's okay."

The air rushed out of Josh's chest, and it was just as well he was already on the ground. *Thank God, thank fucking God.* His heart settled, and warmth swelled in his chest. Relief and something more, something he couldn't put words to yet, wasn't sure he wanted to. He buried his face in Sasha's hair to hide his damp cheeks. Fuck, he'd come so close.

Colin patted his back. "He's a bit banged up. Took a few hits by the look of it, but they got him just as Cruz was trying to bundle him into a car on the northern side. He's damn lucky. If you're going to be the chief's main course over this fuck-up, that man's a shoe-in for dessert."

Josh wiped his face on his sleeping daughter's clothes and raised his head. "The chief will have to get in line. That idiot's mine."

When the paramedics arrived, Josh reluctantly handed his daughter over while staying as close as possible. As desperate as he was to see Michael, Sasha needed him. Michael was okay and that had to be enough, for now.

CHAPTER THIRTEEN

NINE DAYS LATER.

SASHA HEADED to her classroom with Josh watching her every step. It was her first day back since the kidnapping, and it was all he could do not to gather her in his arms and lock her in a padded cell for the foreseeable future. It was ridiculous, of course, but after the kidnapping, he'd been left feeling helpless to protect her, and he hated it. Not that she felt the same way. Hell, she'd refused to even let him walk her in, the little minx.

He'd wanted her home another week at least but she'd insisted, citing his mother hen routine was driving her crazy. He'd give her that. She said she needed some "kid normal" time, as she called it, but Josh wasn't sure anything about her world or his would ever be normal again.

To her credit she stuck to her guns, and after some epic preteen pouting on her part, he'd finally caved and agreed to let her return. None of that helped this morning, however, and it had taken all his will not to slap a tracker on her and chain her to the bed. Katie, who'd barely left Josh's house since that fateful Saturday, was right there with him in his worry, bless her heart.

Somehow, they'd bitten their tongues, plastered their happy faces on, and followed through on his promise. Katie left for work, her eyes loaded with concern and a few tears, and Josh had done the school run. He was still on personal leave, though he suspected John Stables regarded it more in the line of a suspension over the whole Paris tracking thing. *Fuck them.* At least he still had a job.

The hospital had kept Sasha only a couple of nights due to her concussion, then released her. But the following week at home with his daughter had played holy hell with Josh's head and his heart. Coming so close to losing his daughter had triggered huge anxiety that he had no clue how to deal with. It swamped his thinking, making it damn near impossible to come to any decision about anything. And he couldn't bear to have Sasha out of his sight for more than a few minutes at a time.

In the end it had been Sasha herself, storming to her bedroom on the fourth day home, screaming at him to get out of her hair, that had pushed him to seek help. Two sessions with the police psychologist had improved things, but he'd need a few more yet. He also needed the damn woman's clearance to return to work, and she didn't seem ready to give it just yet. He was quietly relieved.

Sasha had completed three sessions with a child psychologist, the first three of many, Josh understood. She didn't talk much about what went on during those sessions, but she seemed calmer afterwards, so he guessed that was something. The concussion thankfully meant she didn't remember much about the kidnapping itself, which Josh was eternally thankful for. But she did remember getting backhanded by that bastard and then wandering confused and alone in the park.

Both of those things had tipped her world of trust on its axis, and although she reassured him she was okay, she suffered nightmares most nights and the fear would take a long while to leave her eyes. In those early days, Josh had caught her checking for him constantly when she thought he wasn't looking. In returning to school, she was showing huge courage, and he guessed he needed to as well. His job was to be there, hold her, let her make decisions and talk things out and be the reliable, dependable dad... and to keep going to his own sessions.

The last couple of days had shown a lot of progress, and leaving for school today, Sasha had been happy enough to have him only a cell phone away, and the teachers all understood she was to have the freedom to call him at any time, class or no class. They'd take it day by day.

Offers of help had been endless, and although Josh appreciated all the concern, the food that kept turning up on his front door had filled his freezer and was now making its way to the local women's refuge. Just that morning he'd put a note on his Facebook along the lines of "thanks but enough."

Jason had called in to see Sasha, and Josh had kept the visit short and sweet. He wanted less and less to do with the dipshit. Still, he'd been civil and held his tongue. It was all about his daughter's needs not his own right now.

Brent had kept in contact to be supportive, and Josh was increasingly hopeful about the whole friendship idea between them. Brent had even been out on a coffee date with another handler, a much better match all around. However screwed up Josh's relationship with Michael had been, Josh wanted the kind of passion they'd shared with whoever he committed to. Life was too damn short.

On the plus side of the whole fucked-up kidnapping mess, Josh's parents had turned out to be unexpectedly helpful. Nearly losing their granddaughter had galvanised something. They made a point of visiting each day and keeping their homophobic bullshit to themselves. Sasha's coolness toward her grandparents had mellowed somewhat as they'd shamelessly plied her with books, computer games, and her favourite snacks. They'd even asked for their thanks to be passed on to Michael for his role in Sasha's release. *Fuck me.* Josh had nearly fallen over backwards checking the sky for flying swine.

Another plus had been Anna. Sasha's mother had kept up an

admirable run of contact with her daughter, one that boded well for a future relationship. She'd even promised to visit after her baby was born.

Mark had popped in and out, keeping Josh up with the case and generally just checking up on them. Denton Cruz was screwed every which way till Sunday: murder, kidnap, assault, the works. He was going away for too many years to count, and Josh couldn't feel happier about it. Not that he hadn't caught himself wishing on a number of occasions that the motherfucker had given the Armed Offenders reason enough to shoot him.

Through Mark, Josh learned that Michael was doing okay, a bit of bruising from the assault but nothing that wouldn't heal quickly. He'd given all his statements and was on temporary leave from the ER to recover. Josh had tried calling and texting to thank Michael too many times to count, but his attempts had gone from continual voicemail pickup to "this number no longer exists," and the hospital was being gnarly about handing out Michael's new contact information.

Josh finally decided to simply drop by Michael's apartment, but even that hadn't elicited a response to his knocking. It was clear Michael was avoiding Josh, and Josh was beyond pissed about it. He had enough to deal with keeping Sasha on the mend and stopping his own pyramid of fears and anxiety from toppling over without Michael playing coy. Josh had things that needed saying and Michael needed to damn well listen.

To make matters worse, when he'd asked Mark about it, he'd been unusually cagey, saying only that Michael had requested to keep his new number private, and Mark had to respect that. *Like fuck.* Josh wanted to slap his friend six ways till Sunday for suddenly finding some squirrely ethics. Mark did, however, promise to pass on Josh's request that he call him.

That had been two days ago and still nothing. Well, that bullshit stopped today. After dropping Sasha at school, Josh headed to the ER, and he wasn't planning to leave without some way to contact Michael.

He found Cam in his office, brooding over staff rosters. The charge nurse looked up as he entered and immediately pushed his chair back.

"Hey there, you." Cam pulled Josh into a quick hug.

Initially stiff in his arms, Josh quickly relaxed. It wasn't that he was uncomfortable, just caught unawares. Cam was ordinarily a cool customer, quick with a flirt, but other than that, professional to a fault. He couldn't remember ever seeing Cam hug another person on duty. As if on cue, Cam pulled away with a sheepish grin.

Josh held his gaze. "Thanks."

Cam nodded. "Yeah, well, I've been thinking about you guys." He indicated for Josh to take a seat. "So, how's our girl?"

Josh took a second to scour the nurses' station through Cam's window, looking for any sign of Michael. He wasn't even trying to pretend. The need to see Michael had grown frantic over the last forty-eight hours. With his obsessive worry about his daughter finally abating, just a little, Josh was now consumed with the need to catch up with Michael.

He wanted to thank him, to apologise, to... *well shit*, to kiss him, taste him, and a whole lot of other stuff that went along with that. The difference being that he was now beyond trying to justify or deny it. He wanted to try again with Michael, potential disaster or not, and he intended to tell him precisely that as soon as possible.

"She's doing better," he answered sounding far steadier than he felt. "She actually went to school today. Said I was drowning her in sap and cotton wool. Her words, by the way."

Cam snorted. "Gotta love kids. Good news, though, if she's feeling that feisty. You must be relieved as hell."

He blew out a sigh. "Pretty much."

Silence fell between them and Cam shifted awkwardly under Josh's scrutiny. "I'd take a bet you're here about Michael," he said.

Josh nodded. "He's dropped off the face of the freaking earth, apparently, at least as far as I'm concerned. Changed his phone, won't answer his door, won't let Mark give me his number. It doesn't make sense. He sent a really great letter to Sasha, three pages long. She pinned it up behind her bed, the only one allowed to go there. But as far as me... zip. I haven't even been able to fucking thank him. And it's not just that, I want to... ah, shit."

Cam picked up his pen and twirled it through his fingers. He studied Josh with sadness and what looked like apology. "He's gone."

Josh frowned. "Gone? What do you mean, gone? Gone for the day? Gone from the hospital, taken time off?" But even as he said it, there was this sinking feeling in the pit of Josh's stomach about the real meaning of the nurse's words.

Cam shook his head. "Gone, as in left New Zealand. He flew back to the States, yesterday as it happens."

Josh felt his eyes burn as a surge of fury spiked in his chest. *No! Michael wouldn't do that, not just leave without a fucking word.* Not without seeing Sasha or Josh. Something gave way and caught in Josh's throat and it took two attempts for him to draw more than a hitched breath. He tried to focus and calm the fuck down. "But his contract?"

Cam hissed. "Jesus Christ. He's such a fucking coward. I thought he'd at least let you know." He took a deep breath and appeared to steady himself. "Look," he said apologetically. "With everything that happened, the hospital wasn't going to stand in the way of Michael breaking his contract. It was understandable he'd want to get home where his support was."

"Where his supp—ah, shit. So he just left without a word? What the fuck?" Anger replaced rejection in Josh's heart and snowballed fast. "Who does something like that after what happened? Sasha wants to see him. And what about the police case?" Mark was gonna have his balls burned the next time Josh laid eyes on him.

"They gave him the green light. As long as he comes back for the trial, they'll sort anything else through phone calls and lawyers in California. I take it no one told you?"

Josh thought of Mark and glared. "Not a fucking word."

Cam nodded as if that came as no surprise. "Anyway, he resigned and was gone within a day. And..." Cam blew out a weary sigh. "Shit. Look, when he called in to collect his gear, he'd been drinking. I could smell it on him. He was a mess, and he wasn't about to listen to anyone."

Drinking? Josh's eyes snapped open. "You spoke with him?"

"Of course. I had to sign off on all the paperwork the fucker created." The charge nurse's mouth quirked up. "I think he knew you'd come because he mentioned a few things without placing a gag order on me. I assume that's because he wants you to know."

Oh God. "Tell me," Josh ordered.

Cam sighed. "Understand this is my take on what he said, okay? There was nothing direct."

Josh nodded.

"I think Michael really fell for you but, and I'm reading between the lines here, he either didn't think it was mutual or he didn't think he could offer what you wanted. And I thought you'd moved on, with that guy who was here, when Sasha hurt her ankle?"

Josh sighed. "He was just a friend."

Cam hesitated. "Michael didn't seem to think so."

"That's because I was being an idiot. I let him think I..." Josh shook his head. "It doesn't matter. It was just... complicated."

Cam nodded. "Okay. None of my business. But Michael really loved your kid, you do know that, right? I don't imagine it ever occurred to him not to take her place that day."

"That was never in question."

"Good. I take it you know what happened in his old hospital?"

Again, Josh nodded.

"Well I don't think he ever really got over that. Maybe he just needs more time."

"But the drinking?"

Cam shrugged. "You got me there. Not a good omen, huh? Still, that's his shit to work out. Not sure you could help with that."

Josh sat in silence, trying to find a glimmer of hope in anything he'd been told. His anger drifted, replaced by a mounting deadness in his chest.

It was Cam who broke the quiet. "I saw you at the club a couple of weeks ago. We'd taken Michael. He'd been wandering around the ER snarling at anyone who looked at him sideways and generally being a right dick. I told him he needed to get laid." He fired Josh an apologetic look. "I didn't know at the time how serious you guys were."

Josh replied with a weak grin. "Seems he took your advice. He was pretty cosy with some guy when I saw him."

"Yeah, about that. I don't know what difference it makes, but according to Michael nothing happened with any guy that night. He took off not long after you."

Josh didn't know what to do with that.

Cam stood and rested a hand on his shoulder. "I've gotta go, sorry, but don't be a stranger. Bring that girl of yours back for a visit when you think she can cope. Let me know and I'll have ice cream waiting."

This time Josh hauled Cam into a quick hug. "Will do and thanks, for everything."

Cam nodded. "Stay as long as you like."

Left alone, Josh took a few minutes to think. Michael had left, without a word, an email, nothing. Fucking unbelievable. And he was apparently drinking again. *Goddammit.* And yet Josh ached for him. What was Michael thinking beating himself up like that? He'd saved Sasha. In Josh's eyes he was a fucking hero. He had to be in a bad place, and yes, Josh felt some responsibility for that. He'd left Michael erroneously thinking Josh was with Brent, thinking he couldn't go to him. Josh had fucked up. He could've been there for Michael if he hadn't been lost up his own arsehole. *Shit.* What the hell was he going to tell Sasha?

He grabbed his coat and headed home. He needed to find Michael but he wasn't sure how. No one was giving him what he needed and Michael didn't want to be found, he'd made that clear.

For all that, Josh wasn't giving up, no fucking way, but he needed to get Sasha in a better place first. And maybe give Michael time to get his head together about the drinking—that was something Josh couldn't save him from. What to do about his battered, fucked-up heart, and the troubled gorgeous man responsible for it would just have to wait a little longer.

Four months later.

MICHAEL STEPPED out of the shower and wrapped the "soft as a duck's butt" towel around his waist. Not usually a linen snob, thick soft towels had apparently become a "thing" of his now. That Josh stocked the same towels had nothing to do with it, of course. The scent of coffee brewing wafted from downstairs and something that smelled encouragingly like pancakes. His stomach rumbled.

On his morning run he'd taken the longer route to clear his head and let the shit up there settle. His sleep had been broken by a nightmare that left him feeling less than chipper and with a few cobwebs that needed seeing to. He'd succeeded, mostly. He'd even managed to straighten the duvet and fluff his pillows so at least it didn't look as if he'd played host to half the club they'd all danced at the night before. *If only.*

He could count on the fingers of one hand the number of times he'd been clubbing since he'd arrived back in LA, and most of them at the behest of friends who were worried about him. He welcomed their concern, but if they thought they were doing him a favour trying to get him laid, they were sorely disappointed. That ship hadn't sailed in quite a while. His thoughts drifted to a certain dog handler. *Nope, he wasn't going there either.*

He threw on some clothes and sorted a pile of laundry. It had taken everything Michael had not to go completely fucking off the rails after Sasha's kidnapping. The relief he'd felt at securing her release had been short-lived, overwhelmed by the terror of facing his own death and the swarm of emotions that went along with that confronting thought.

For the first time, he'd faced the reality of the emptiness of his own life, and it wasn't pretty. So he'd sought that same brainless relief he'd found before in a bottle, not every night and not to the point of being stupid drunk, but more times than was healthy. He knew exactly what he was doing, and the fact he couldn't seem to talk himself out of it had scared him shitless.

He'd needed to get out, to leave. If he hadn't, he would've lost himself completely, and there was no way in hell he was going down that road again. And though they'd probably never know, it simply wasn't in Michael to disappoint Josh and Sasha any further. They'd believed in him, at least for a while. He might be a fuck-up, but he finally believed he had it in him to change.

To that end he caught the first flight he could and headed back to LA. That he'd left without talking to Josh and Sasha was his one regret. At the time, though, he just didn't know how he'd survive seeing Josh again and saying goodbye. At some point he'd face that particular demon, but he hadn't quite found the courage yet.

On arrival, the first thing Michael did was quit drinking and find a therapist. It didn't take a genius to figure out he couldn't do it on his own. Tried that one already. The most important thing he'd discovered from the whole debacle with Josh was what he wanted in life. And surprise, surprise, it was a life with a guy he loved and maybe even a family—a fucking picket fence. More importantly, he was beginning to believe he was actually capable of having that life, maybe even deserved it. His therapist, he had to give the woman props, was pushing hard on that particular point.

In LA, Michael was welcomed back into his old hospital a month after landing. A step down from his old job, but he didn't care, not really. His new/old boss knew about his recent brief slip in sobriety, and after a few sideways looks and an exchange of calls with Michael's therapist, he'd agreed to a two-month probation including random testing, in return for a future full contract. Three months on, and it felt damn good to be back at work, a distraction from the grief that welled up periodically when Michael's thoughts turned to Josh.

He'd spoken to Mark a few times who'd reassured Michael that Josh and Sasha were doing well after a rocky first couple of weeks. Mark had gone so far as to tell Michael that Brent wasn't in the picture with Josh, or at least as far as Mark knew. He'd sounded surprised that Michael had thought he was. And he tried damned hard to get Michael to call Josh or to at least let Mark give Josh his contact details, but Michael had said no. The same when Cam pushed. Michael just wasn't ready. Brent or no Brent, he had shit he needed to sort out: the drinking, his life, and what he wanted out of it. He wanted more than just stability. He wanted to feel he was moving forward again. But if what Mark had said was true, maybe he'd give Josh a ring sooner than he'd planned.

He grabbed the pile of washing and threw it in the laundry before making his way to the kitchen to see what was cooking. Lorde was playing at damn near full volume, of course she was, just another unwelcome reminder of New Zealand.

Michael paused in the doorway, taking a minute to study the handsome man cooking at his stove, bopping away to the music, wearing an apron and waving a spatula over his head. He was an intoxicating blend of lean muscle and sensuality. Michael reached to turn the volume down a bit on the speaker dock on the counter.

"Too damn cute." He chuckled.

The other man startled and spun, a searing blush racing across his cheeks. Then he narrowed his gaze and sashayed that cute butt right over to Michael.

"Hiya, good-looking." He planted a kiss on Michael's cheek. "Thought you were never going to get out of that shower." He sashayed back to the stove, giving Michael a booty shake for good measure, a born tease.

Michael grinned. "With pancakes and bacon in the air? You've got to be joking."

The man rolled his eyes. "Ugh. Cupboard love, I knew it. Men only want me for my skills at beating and making sweet things rise." He grinned lasciviously.

Michael snorted.

"Pancakes better be the only thing rising in here," a voice warned seconds before its owner joined them. Cliff Stewart was a tall, rangy man with golden locks that cascaded to his shoulders and a pair of wicked blue eyes packed full of mischief.

Michael hugged the newcomer. "Hey there, you." Simon had done well for himself with Cliff, and Michael couldn't be happier for them both.

The ease between the three men had been hard-won, and three months ago, Michael wouldn't have taken a bet that they'd even be able to inhabit the same room together. Simon had been more than a little leery of the contact Michael had initiated on his return. Cliff even more so. But Michael had meant it when he'd committed to apologising to Simon for how he'd ended things between them.

Still, it had taken a fair few long discussions, with Michael doing most of the talking to clear the air, and Cliff had been present at them all. He was a far better match for Simon than Michael had ever been. Michael even opened up about Josh and Sasha and how he'd fucked up that relationship as well. Eventually they all decided to bury the flogged horse once and for all and move on. And in an unexpected move, Simon suggested trying to build a friendship between all three of them, and even more surprisingly, Cliff had backed the suggestion. Michael was incredibly humbled and grateful.

From there they'd fallen into a routine of a shared brunch together most Sundays, sometimes with friends, more often at a café but occasionally at one of their homes, like today. And just last week they'd celebrated Simon and Cliff's engagement. Their unusual friendship worked. It shouldn't, but it did, and watching Simon working in his kitchen as if it were his own, Michael was just so damned thankful for it.

He leaned over the bacon on the stove and inhaled deeply. "God, that smells good." He grabbed a cup and angled for the coffee machine, but before he got there, Simon pulled him in for a dance.

"Oh, for Christ's sake," Cliff grumbled from the doorway. "We have got to get you a boyfriend of your own, Michael, so you stop damn well borrowing mine."

Michael threw up his hands. "He threw himself at me. Can't help that I'm irresistible."

Simon whacked his ass with the spatula. "In your dreams. That ship sailed a long time ago." He launched himself into his fiancé's arms in a full-frontal lip attack.

Michael grinned. "Don't you dare burn the bacon." He poured his coffee and leaned back against the bench as his ex and his new fiancé made out less than two feet away. *Yep, parallel universe material.*

The chime of the doorbell broke up the lip-fest and Michael put his coffee down to answer it.

Cliff stayed him. "I'll get it. Drink your coffee."

Simon put the last of the pancakes to cool on the rack and turned off the stove. Then he removed his apron and pulled Michael into a fierce hug.

Michael tentatively returned the embrace, wondering what the fuck was going on. "What am I missing here?" he asked over Simon's shoulders.

"Just remember we love you," Simon said, not releasing the hug.

"Ah, guys?" Cliff's voice carried from the hall. "You might want to break up the love-fest, yeah?"

Michael turned, and his mouth ran to dust, his chest tightened, and every scrap of grief and longing he'd felt over the last four, no five months, rose and filled his throat full enough to choke him. Silence crowded the room as he struggled to find his voice. *Shit.* Finding his legs would be a start.

In the end all he could manage was, "Josh?"

In the dining room, Josh appeared tense, red-cheeked, and seemingly desperate to be anywhere else. And so, so fucking beautiful that Michael wanted to haul him into his arms and kiss him senseless.

"Ah... maybe this... um... maybe it wasn't such a good idea," Josh stammered, taking a step back. "I, ah... I shouldn't have come. Sorry." He spun to leave, but Cliff held him in place.

"It's not what it looks like," the tall man reassured him.

Still in shock, Michael couldn't have spoken a word to save himself, his brain having slid sideways out of reach. Simon had dropped his arms from Michael's waist, now busy regarding Josh with open interest. *Yeah, welcome to the twilight zone for exes*, Michael thought.

Cliff regarded the two of them and simply shook his head. "That handsy idiot next to Michael is Simon, my fiancé and Michael's ex," he explained, picking up the slack, and Michael thanked Christ someone had his brain screwed into the right socket. "Though he may not be for long if he doesn't pick his tongue up off the floor," Cliff added with a grin.

Simon blushed and rolled his eyes at his fiancé. "I'm engaged, not brain-dead," he huffed. "And the guy's freaking gorgeous, in case you hadn't noticed."

Cliff grinned widely. "Not saying I hadn't noticed, sweetheart. I'm just not offering to have his children, unlike some."

Simon snorted. "As if. There's only one man in the running for that job, babe."

Cliff blushed a deep crimson and his eyes lit up.

Michael narrowed his gaze at his ex. "You knew about this?"

Simon shrugged. "Knew, invited, plotted, planned... splitting hairs really."

Michael glared in response, and Simon beat a hasty retreat from the kitchen, grabbed his coat, and threw Cliff's to him. Then he stuck out a hand for Josh to shake. "Pleased to finally meet you," he said. "Love to stay and chat, but we have to run... like right now." He tugged at Cliff's shirt. "As in now, baby."

Cliff startled. "Oh, right. Yep, we've gotta go. Got... um... some friends to meet. Yeah. At um... a café?" He glanced at Simon, who rolled his eyes.

"Yeah, babe, at a café." Simon stroked his fiancé's cheek affectionately, then pulled him to the front door. "Have fun, you two," he threw over his shoulder before disappearing in a cloud of devious haste.

That left Michael and Josh staring at one another.

IT WAS Josh who broke first, a slightly hysterical laugh erupting from his throat. *Christ almighty.* After a twelve-hour flight, an endless cab ride, and the shock of finally seeing Michael, but in someone else's arms, Josh was finally face-to-face with the subject of every thought and fantasy that had occupied his mind over the last four months.

He hadn't given up on Michael but Sasha had taken a while to truly settle and Josh had been reluctant to rock that boat, to give her any hope before he thought she could handle it if it didn't pan out. She'd asked about Michael constantly, and through a dropped hint from Mark, Josh had finally nailed the hospital where Michael now worked and had a contact number to try. He was about to make his move when out of the blue, Mark passed on a request from Simon, Michael's ex, to get in contact. Simon had even emailed the Auckland Police Department to make sure the note got to the right man.

But it had thrown Josh. Were Michael and Simon back together? Was he being warned off? In the end, the opposite had proved to be the case.

Simon *wanted* Josh to visit Michael, convinced they might have a future. That Michael talked about him all the time. That Simon had heard from Michael that Josh was perhaps still single. That threw Josh as well. He knew the lie Josh had allowed.

Simon reassured Josh that Michael was sober, in therapy, and had been from the minute he'd set foot back in the country. Josh's relief and the surge of hope had been immediate and overwhelming. The fact that Michael had moved to heal his relationship with his ex was also a welcome surprise. Everything boded well, but nothing was guaranteed. Michael still might not want anything Josh had to offer. But he was going to try.

And so this reunion Josh had so much hope for, one he'd imagined fraught with apologies, explanations, and please God, hope, now appeared well on the way to derailment. Jet-lagged and seemingly unable to extricate himself from the stream of crazy flowing from his mouth, all Josh could do was flop against the wall and close his eyes in an effort to summon his sanity. The last thing he saw was Michael regarding him warily as Josh had lost his freaking mind. *Maybe he had.*

Maybe he also should've talked to Michael first, before arriving. But Simon had thought it would be best if Josh just fronted up. And so he'd done just that. But had Simon been wrong? Did Michael not want him here? Had Josh fucked up well and truly? He needed to open his eyes, but, honestly, he didn't want to. He was too terrified of what he'd find in Michael's gaze.

A shadow fell across Josh's face and his skin tingled. Warmth cloaked the front of his body, close but not touching, that familiar scent of orange and spice with that ridiculous back note of antiseptic flooding his senses.

He opened his eyes and locked gazes with Michael, standing so close he could almost taste him on his tongue. Michael cupped his face, studied him hard. And Josh's knees damn near caved at the feel of those hands on him once again, like he could finally breathe for the first time in months. Then Michael smiled, and warmth exploded in Josh's chest.

"I'm gonna kill both of them," Michael grumbled, still smiling but a bit too thinly now for Josh's liking. His eyes went quiet for what felt like a lifetime, as he seemed to drink Josh in, searching for... something.

Josh remained quiet, content to have Michael find whatever truth he could in Josh's expression, hoping it was something Michael understood and also wanted. He was past hiding, and he knew his face radiated all the anger, hurt, love, and concern he'd struggled with over the months. It wasn't pretty, but it was real, and if they were to have any chance at something more between them, they needed to be honest with each other.

But Josh was also looking. He'd waited too long to see Michael, and the sight didn't disappoint—he still took Josh's breath away. He sported a light stubble, Josh's favourite look. His dark hair was shower damp, soft curls at the nape begging Josh to swipe his tongue and catch the drips clinging to their ends. And all of that deliciousness poured into a faded pair of thin-as-crap jeans stretched across that tight arse and a worn Roxy Music T-shirt that highlighted his barbells. *Christ almighty.*

Josh inhaled every last detail and tried to keep the shiver from his skin. He ached to reach out to touch, but he knew there were no guarantees yet. For all he knew this might be as close as he'd get. It could even be the last time he saw Michael.

Michael dropped his hands from Josh's face, took a step back, and frowned, as Josh tried to keep his expression steady. This wasn't his show to run, not yet, but at least Michael wasn't pushing him away.

Michael's gaze burned the length of Josh to the floor and back, and he couldn't help but glance down, surprised to find his clothes not burned to a crisp. It was all he could do not to pat his hair in place and tuck his shirt in. Then they locked gazes, and Josh was instantly pinned by a heated stare.

"Brent?" Michael queried.

The question needed nothing added, and Josh kept his gaze steady as he answered. "Brent and I never were, not in the way you're thinking... the way I let you think. He came with Sasha and me to that party, and yes, I invited him, as a friend, just to see. But we both knew it wasn't going to go any further. We'd already agreed to just friendship... before you even saw us at the hospital."

"But you—"

"I know. I'm sorry. I was hurt and angry with you. I'd seen you at the club... with a guy, the night Cam took you out, and so I let you think—"

"Nothing happened that night—"

"I know, now. And as I said, it was a dick move on my part and I'm sorry. I was going to tell you after you took that call but... you had to go be a hero." He smiled weakly. "I've regretted it ever since, wondered if you might not have left if I hadn't—"

"Stop." Michael hesitated. "I don't know if it would have made a difference or not. I had a lot of stuff I needed to sort through, about us, about all of it. I'm not sure I would have done that if I'd stayed."

Okay, then. Josh waited.

"So, tell me, why nothing with Brent, then? You said he's a nice guy. Seems like he'd be more your style—"

Josh put a finger to Michael's lips. "He's not you, Michael. And it's *you* I want."

Michael grunted, and Josh saw the corner of his mouth twitch. He leaned in and brushed a stray lock of Josh's hair into place behind his ear, and it was all Josh could do not to mewl in hope and press his cheek into Michael's hand. "There's been no one else."

Michael's gaze flickered with something. Happiness?

He ran a finger down Michael's cheek. "Look, I didn't just expect you to be waiting. What I'm trying to say is I understand, if you've moved on, that is."

Michael put a hand up to silence him. "There's been no one else for me either. I'm not sure there's ever been. Not like you."

Well, shit. Josh bathed in the pleasure and relief those words brought, and a blush heated his cheeks. "Yeah, that too... for me, I mean." He took a breath. "But before we get into anything heavy, can I just say one thing?" He waited.

A frown creased Michael's brow. "Okay?"

Josh smiled. "Thank you, you fucking idiot, sweetheart of a man. You put your life at risk to save Sasha, and we... I... am so fucking grateful to you for that." His eyes brimmed. "Damn it, I swore I wasn't going to cry."

Michael ran his thumb across Josh's lips, leaving a searing-hot trail in its wake. "Jesus, wolf-man." He rested his forehead against Josh's. "I don't know why you're here or how this... whatever it is... is about to pan out, so it's my turn to do one thing first, before we talk more, before anything. Just so I can fucking breathe again."

He brushed a soft kiss across Josh's lips, lingering at the corner of his mouth, hovering, tasting, breathing him in like Josh answered his most important questions. As if without Josh, Michael's world made no sense. And Josh revelled in it, whimpering at the contact. Melted against Michael. Closing his eyes so the delicate sensations had full rein to roll through him. The in and out of Michael's breath against his lips, the soft caress of his fingers on Josh's cheeks and through his hair, his delicious scent layering over Josh's skin like a promise.

And as always, his body reacted instantaneously to Michael, blood draining south at the first touch of Michael's skin, the first hint of desire in Michael's eyes or his breath on Josh's lips. The fire in Josh's belly reignited in a raging desire for this singular man he was so sure he'd lost. But he held still, his mind adrift in the soft kiss and the gentle puff of breath on his skin, floating in the tender fragility of the moment. Somehow everything seemed possible in that one brush of lips. *If only*, he prayed.

At length Michael pulled away and dropped his hands again, and the inevitable unanswered questions between them loomed large. He looked wary. And Josh offered the only response he felt mattered in the moment. Yes, they needed to talk more, but Josh knew they needed to connect first, they needed... this. He reached behind Michael's neck and drew Michael back to his lips, inviting him to taste and take what he wanted.

"Please?" he whispered the word into Michael's mouth.

Within seconds, he was flattened against the wall, Michael's body hard against his, shoulder to hip, cocks aligned and... *oh shit...* it was so good... it was so fucking good. Something twisted in Josh's chest and locked into place, and *dear God*, how had he survived without this? And with Michael's tongue halfway down his throat, and a pair of liquid hot hands roaming under his shirt, Josh was sure of at least one thing. Michael wanted him, and Josh intended to be in on that action like a rat up a drainpipe.

His hands found the hem of Michael's shirt and tugged at it, breaking their kiss for a second as he hauled the offending item over Michael's head. Then he took a minute to cast a long look over the man. *God, where to start?* He leaned in for a taste of Michael's skin, licking a swathe over the kiwi covering his heart toward the left nipple, but before he could suck the nub into his mouth, Michael pulled back and eyeballed him.

"Last chance, wolf-man," he said softly.

Josh shivered at the nickname. "Last chance to what?"

Michael held his gaze and smiled. "To talk more... before we do this. Because once I get my hands on you, I'm not stopping. I need you inside me like I fucking need to breathe. So if you want to talk, say so now."

Josh's cock strained at the zip of his jeans, damn near breaking into a happy dance. He pressed his lips against Michael's in a fierce kiss. "Bed, now." He figured it counted as an answer, grabbing Michael's hand and heading... well, somewhere... *shit.*

Michael chuckled and redirected them to the stairs.

They made it up, though not all their clothes fared the same fate, and by the time they landed on the bed, they were naked. It was a fact that made Josh's heart ridiculously happy. "Lie back for me." He pushed Michael onto his back. "It's been too damn long. I need to see every inch of you."

Michael obliged, and Josh straddled his thighs, their cocks brushing as his gaze travelled Michael's length. It was the body Josh had so loved and missed, now spread across this bed, Josh's for the taking. Running his fingers over Michael's tattoos, he traced each one.

"Josh... please?" Michael's breath hitched at his touch. His muscles quivered, and Josh loved that he could still reduce this sexy man to a trembling bundle of need.

"Shh," he soothed, dropping his mouth to suckle first one nipple, then the other, rolling the bars around in his mouth, eliciting soft whimpers from Michael as he arched and clenched the sheets in his fists, eyes fixed on Josh. The need to bury himself deep inside Michael was overwhelming, but Josh had waited too long to rush things.

"You're killing me here," Michael groaned.

Josh kissed his nose. "Not gonna kill you, babe. Just gonna love you." Josh froze as the words split the air between them. *Shit.* Too soon? *Ah, fuck it.* He didn't imagine it came as any surprise to Michael. You don't fly six and a half thousand miles for fucking coffee and a catch-up.

He risked glancing up to find Michael smiling down at him, and sighed, half-embarrassed, half-relieved. "Yeah, about that." He crawled up Michael's body to nibble on his lower lip. "I was hoping —" Nibble. "—that... well, that we could maybe—" Nibble. "—or at least that I was feeling a lot more for you... than..."

Michael grabbed his chin and stared deep into Josh's eyes with those blue ocean eyes of his. "Less talk, wolf-man," he whispered, brushing his lips across Josh's, "and more of that loving me shit. So, I can set about returning the favour... of loving you, that is." Another kiss, this one full of promise.

A huge grin split Josh's face, and he couldn't stop the delighted laugh that bubbled from his throat. Nor apparently the moisture that gathered in his eyes. "Yeah? Is that so?" was all he could muster.

Michael nodded. "Yeah. That's so. Although that might change if my ass doesn't see some serious action in the next few minutes."

Josh planted a firm kiss on Michael's lips, sure he was still grinning like a loon. "I'll get right on that," he said, and shimmied down to dip his tongue into Michael's belly button. Then he followed the run of soft hair down Michael's treasure trail to his dick standing at full attention.

Steadying it at the base, he licked the shaft bottom to top, keeping his eyes fixed on Michael. A wealth of emotions passed between them in that one look. But for the first time, Josh believed there would be time for it all to be said, every last bit of it. In the meantime, he had a mouthwatering body fanned out beneath him waiting to be worshipped, and Josh was just the man for the job.

MICHAEL CLOSED his eyes and fell back on the pillow, letting Josh's mouth wrap around him like a searing velvet heaven. It was as close to coming home as he'd ever felt. How he thought he could simply walk away from Josh, he'd never understand. *And holy shit.* They'd just said they loved each other. That had happened. It was a thing. He could scarcely believe it. Then all thought was lost in the wet heaven of Josh's mouth as he took Michael deep, and Michael fought the urge to slam into Josh's throat.

Josh pulled off to stretch Michael's hands above his head and leaned in to take his lips. "Keep them there, gorgeous," he growled.

Hell yeah. Michael loved when bossy Josh came out to play. He rocked his hips, desperate for friction to ease the mounting ache in his groin.

"Behave." Josh slapped his butt, and the sensation travelled straight to Michael's balls, sending a warm flush through his body. "Let me play a bit. I'll get you there."

And when Josh took Michael's cock deep into his throat once more, Michael damn near lost his mind. He was past trying to understand how or why Josh lit this particular fire in him, this willingness to be cared for. All he knew, all he needed to know was in doing so he became the centre of Josh's world, the focus of his entire attention. And in those moments, Michael didn't want to be anywhere else. Josh created a soft space solely for him where Michael's only job was to receive pleasure. He fired Michael's body and grounded him in his own. No one had ever cared for him like that.

Josh stretched a hand to the side as he worked, and Michael dragged enough brain cells together to slap a bottle of lube and a condom into them. The lid snipped, and seconds later Michael felt the cool slick slide down his cock, over his balls and finally, finally teasing at his hole.

"Yeah," he groaned loudly. "About time."

Josh chuckled and blew cool air across Michael's sac, causing him to arch up on the bed. "Have I told you how much I fucking love your arse?" Josh said, blowing another swathe of air along Michael's shaft. "I've missed you so goddamn much."

Fucking hell. "Then shut up and get on with it," Michael whined. "Or this particular sweet ass is walking."

"Like hell." Josh growled as he breached Michael's hole with a slick finger straight up and over his prostate.

Holy hell. Michael arched his back, and the hungry whine he released should have mortified him, but he was beyond caring. Stubble brushed his taint as Josh's tongue joined his fingers in their exploration. *Christ.* This man would be the death of him.

"More," Michael gasped.

Josh's fingers withdrew, and he crawled up Michael's body to press a firm kiss to Michael's lips. "Hey, you," he murmured, his breath hot against Michael's mouth. "Fuck if you're not the sexiest damn thing I've ever seen." He sucked Michael's lower lip into his mouth and nipped at it gently. "And I love every sound that comes out of your throat. I'm so damned turned on, I don't know how I'm gonna last."

Michael gripped Josh's hair, pulling him in for another kiss. "Don't sweat it." He rubbed noses with Josh. "If I last more than a few seconds, it'll be a fucking miracle."

Josh grinned and sat up, spreading Michael's thighs. "Nice and high, babe."

Michael gripped his thighs and gave Josh what he asked for. It still shocked him that he could spread himself like a fucking buffet for Josh without a second thought. If Josh wanted to hang Michael in a swing covered in cream, hands cuffed above his head, he'd do it in a heartbeat. *Damn.* Josh's thick cock slid through his crease and all thought evaporated. Michael was home. *Yes.*

. . .

MICHAEL'S COMPLETE willingness to hand himself over to Josh still astonished Josh. That this complicated man wanted to come undone under his hands was a gift Josh had no way to repay. He could come from the visual memory alone and had, more than once over the last few months.

He pressed into Michael, feeling the tight heat of his lover engulf him as Michael writhed beneath him, soft nonsense spilling from his lips. Then fully seated, Josh paused, bending low to take Michael's mouth in a lingering kiss that was rewarded with a soft purr of approval against his lips.

"Move, wolf-man," Michael ordered, clenching his ass around Josh's cock for emphasis.

Josh needed no further encouragement and set up a solid rhythm that had Michael gripping the sheets, eyes rolled back, dark lashes fluttering. He changed the angle slightly until Michael electrified, arching up against him.

"Ah... right there."

Josh kept up the pace, laser focused on Michael's responses. Michael's pleasure was his pleasure, and when he saw Michael reach for his cock, he batted his hand away and replaced it with his own, stroking long and hard in time with his thrusts. His control was running on a knife-edge and keeping his own orgasm at bay was becoming increasingly difficult.

"Close," Michael groaned.

Thank Christ. Josh wasn't sure he could hang on any longer. "Come for me," he growled, biting down on Michael's shoulder.

With that, Michael tensed and a deep groan of pleasure escaped his mouth. Josh raised himself to watch him peak, Michael's face lifted up, his body arched, but his eyes fixed on Josh as his cock emptied into Josh's fist seconds before Josh's own orgasm hit in equally wordless and spectacular fashion.

Neither looked away as Josh pumped them slowly through the

last shivers, with Michael milking every drop from Josh until they both became too sensitive. Then Josh collapsed atop Michael, their bodies slick between them, and Michael's arms wrapped tight around him.

Every bone had fled Josh's body, and he wasn't sure he was capable of thought, let alone movement, happy to simply listen to Michael's heart tick down to something resembling normal. His softening cock remained content inside Michael's heat, and he saw no reason to change that anytime soon. A pair of lips ran soft kisses the length of his jaw, coming to rest nestled against his shoulder.

"You bit me," Michael hummed softly against his skin. "That'll cost you extra."

Josh turned to press a kiss into Michael's hair, damp with sweat. "Take it out of my tip." He chuckled.

"Mmm and what tip would that be? The one that's still buried in me, if it ever packs its bags and moves out, that is."

Josh laughed. "I wouldn't count on that happening anytime soon. It seems to like the neighbourhood. It's all snuggly."

Michael snorted. "Snuggly? I'm worried about this kink of yours." He nuzzled Josh's neck. "I'm starting to feel like Siamese twins joined at the ass. It's gonna be hell on our wardrobe."

"*Our* wardrobe, huh?" Josh stared down at Michael, warming at the faint blush that crossed Michael's cheeks. "I could get used to the sound of that. I'm a bit gone for you, in case you hadn't noticed."

"Likewise, wolf-man." Michael opened to Josh's kiss, and their tongues did a slow dance, happy to simply taste and enjoy each other. Then when Josh pulled back, Michael chased his mouth to steal a few more kisses before letting him go. Josh tied off the condom, then slid back alongside.

"So," Michael murmured, those deadly fingers brushing over Josh's soft cock before coming to rest on his hip. "Here we are."

Michael's soft eyes pooled the colour of liquid sky, and Josh saw himself reflected in their depths. And with Michael's mouth almost in reach, Josh stretched to close the gap.

"Nuh-uh." Michael laid a finger on Josh's lips, holding him at bay.

Josh's tongue swept out to chase the touch and was rewarded with a flare of heat in Michael's eyes.

"God, you're killing me," Michael sighed. "But I'm thinking it's time to finish that talk."

Josh sandwiched Michael's finger between their two sets of lips.

"I'm thinking you're right." He breathed the words into Michael's mouth. "Finally."

EPILOGUE

Eight months later.

"Sasha, if your butt isn't in that car in five minutes, there'll be consequences, young lady."

"Okay, Dad," Sasha yelled, staring at the mound of clothes still strewn across her bed. She sighed to herself. "Jeez, don't give yourself a brain explosion."

"I dare you to repeat that, pipsqueak, but loud enough for him to actually hear this time."

Sasha startled and spun to face him. "Sheesh, Mickey! Don't scare me like that. Between the two of you sneaky snakes, it's not looking good for me making it past adolescence at this rate."

"Make that three sneaky snakes." Katie strolled past behind Michael. "And I think *jeez* counts as a swear word, miss."

Sasha pouted, fixing Michael with a beseeching gaze. He rolled his eyes and put a finger to his lips. He was such a sucker for this girl. "Our secret, sweetheart. Just get in the car and we'll sort what you're going to take camping when we get back. Did you feed Paris?"

She nodded and reached up on tiptoes to kiss his cheek. "Meat and kibble, easy on the kibble."

Michael grinned. "Good girl. I'll lock him up while you get in the car before your dad pops a blood vessel." Every month or so, Josh's family, including his parents, and Katie's boyfriend, Kevin, met for dinner at a buffet restaurant in the city. Neutral territory. Tonight was such a night.

Sasha's face scrunched up in a scowl. "Do I have to go? They always make me sit next to them and answer stupid questions about school."

Michael sighed. "They love you, honey. Be thankful. Me? I'm lucky to get 'hello.' Goodbye's easier 'cause they're so damn pleased to get my gay butt out of their sight." He grinned and nudged her shoulder. "But it's better than before, right?"

"Yeah, lucky me," Sasha deadpanned and went to slip by him.

"Not so fast." He grabbed her midstride and swung her in for a hug. "Love you, sweetheart." And Michael did, more than he'd ever thought possible.

She kissed his cheek. "I know. I love you too, Mickey."

He watched her go with a sigh. Although Josh's parents had softened significantly in their stance toward Michael and the whole "gay son" routine, they still struggled to keep the disapproval from their faces, especially in response to anything remotely physical between the two of them, even holding hands. To that end, Josh seemed to have made it his mission to grab Michael's hand or plaster a kiss on his cheek as often as possible in the presence of his parents. *Bastard.*

Michael cast an eye over the clothes piled on Sasha's bed and shook his head. How many clothes could one twelve-year-old girl possibly need for a two-night camping trip? He'd make sure he was the one to help her sort it. Josh had way less patience than Michael. Go figure.

Sparing a glance toward their bedroom opposite, his heart filled. *Their* bedroom, his and Josh's. Most days Michael could still hardly believe it. Sharing a life with this amazing man, a life he'd never thought he wanted. A house, a boyfriend he loved the shit out of, a family, the whole white picket fence, nine yards, full enchilada. Not that it had come easy, but nothing worth it ever did.

They'd taken it slow, principally for Sasha's sake, building a family together. Building trust, love, and Michael's sobriety. He'd spent three weeks in New Zealand, and Josh and Sasha spent three in the US, including a trip to Disneyland and all the iconic tourist shit.

Getting long-term residency in New Zealand hadn't proved as difficult as they'd expected due to a shortage of doctors, and Auckland Med had been more than happy to take Michael back. After three months, Michael finally packed up and made the move back to Auckland accompanied by Simon and Cliff. The newly married pair wanted to eyeball Michael's new life before heading off as tourists for two weeks.

Michael slid his hand into his jeans pocket and grinned as he headed out the back door. He was more in love with Josh than he'd believed possible. With everyone already in the car, he made his way across to join them, Paris loping amiably alongside.

From the driver's seat, Josh frowned and leaned through the open window. "Michael? Paris needs to be locked in his kennel."

Michael ignored the instruction. "Everyone out," he ordered.

Josh rolled his eyes. "Michael, we're late."

Michael silenced him with a kiss. "Shut up for once and get out of the car, wolf-man."

A brief spark of annoyance flared in Josh's eyes, and then he sighed and slid out of the car, grumbling all the while. He stood alongside Katie, Sasha, and Kevin, tapping his leg impatiently.

"Paris, get over here." Michael pushed the shepherd alongside Josh, who automatically dropped his hand to scuff the dog's neck.

Josh's gaze rolled over Michael with a mix of curiosity and suspicion. "So, what's this about, baby?"

Michael held his breath, his mouth suddenly dry as dust, a bevy of cats turning somersaults in his stomach. *Here goes.* He locked eyes with Josh, so full of love for this man, and so incredibly nervous.

"It's about us," he answered, hearing the break in his voice.

Josh's frown deepened, chocolate eyes darkening to almost black. "Us?"

Michael looked to Sasha. "All of us." The girl's eyes suddenly widened in understanding. *Smart kid.*

Michael dropped to his knee in front of Josh and retrieved a small black box from his jeans pocket. Inside lay two simple platinum bands. He reached out and took Josh's hand.

Sasha gasped and reached for Katie, who latched on to her niece with a soft cry.

"Dad!" Sasha squealed. "Say yes, say yes."

Michael chuckled. "I haven't asked him yet." With eyes still firmly locked on Josh, he saw shock and disbelief register in Josh's expression. *Yeah, you didn't see this one coming, did you, sweetheart?*

"I love you, Josh," he said, "with all my heart and with every fibre of my body, and I love Sasha as my own. I can't imagine life without you, and I never intend to. From one arrogant asshole to another, will you marry me?"

For a few seconds there was total silence, and Michael's fear skyrocketed. Then Josh's mouth quirked up at the corners and those fucking chocolate eyes lit up like fireworks. He dragged Michael to his feet and into his arms. Then, with his face buried in Michael's neck, he gave his answer.

"Fuck, yeah, gorgeous. I'll marry your sorry arse any day. Forever isn't gonna be long enough." He covered Michael's mouth with his own and set their tongues dancing.

Paris leapt up at their embrace, picking up on the whirlwind of emotions, and ran his claws down Michael's back. Katie pulled him off as she and Sasha cheered, and Kevin looked on, smiling.

When their lips parted, Sasha jumped into their arms and wrapped her arms around both of them. "It's about time," she said. "And don't think I didn't hear that answer, Dad. That's a double fine for the swear jar. I'm scarred for life. And you—" She turned to Michael with a stern eye. "—you're gonna have to deal with being called Pops, cause I'm not calling anyone Daddy."

She grinned and planted a huge kiss on Michael's cheek. "And you better adopt me as well, just saying."

Holy hell. Michael glanced at Josh and caught the glisten in his fiancé's eyes. He hugged Sasha tight. "It'll be my absolute privilege, kiddo."

"Okay, team." Josh gathered their attention. "Let's get these rings on and go horrify the grandparents. I can't wait to tell them their embarrassing gay son's getting married."

He grabbed Michael's hand, slid one of the rings on his finger, and pulled him nose to nose. "You and me, gorgeous," he whispered. "I can't fucking wait."

Michael returned the favour before answering. "For you," he said softly, "I've waited my whole life."

THE END

ALSO BY JAY HOGAN

(Written as part of Sarina Bowen's
True North— Vino & Veritas Series and published by Heart Eyes Press)

Digging Deep
(2020 Lambda Literary Finalist)

ABOUT THE AUTHOR

Jay is a 2020 Lambda Literary Award Finalist.

She is a New Zealand author writing in MM romance and romantic suspense primarily set in New Zealand. She loves writing character driven romances with lots of humour, a good dose of reality and a splash of angst. She's travelled extensively, lived in many countries, and in a past life she was a critical care nurse and counsellor. Jay is owned by a huge Maine Coon cat and a gorgeous Cocker Spaniel.

Join Jay's reader's group Hogan's Hangout for updates, promotions, her current writing projects and special releases.

Sign up to her newsletter HERE.

Or visit her website HERE.

Milton Keynes UK
Ingram Content Group UK Ltd.
UKHW021307091123
432266UK00027B/1286